REV

PIONEER TOWER

BURNING THE APOSTLE

Also by Bill Granger
in Thorndike Large Print ®

There Are No Spies
Henry McGee Is Not Dead
Drover and the Zebras

This Large Print Book carries the
Seal of Approval of N.A.V.H.

BURNING
THE
APOSTLE

BILL GRANGER

Thorndike Press • Thorndike, Maine

Library of Congress Cataloging in Publication Data:

Granger, Bill.
   Burning the Apostle / Bill Granger.
      p.   cm.
      ISBN 1-56054-692-1 (alk. paper : lg. print)
      1. Devereaux (Fictitious character)—Fiction.   2. Spies
—United States—Fiction. 3. Large type books. I. Title.
[PS3557.R256B8   1993b]   93-21869
813'.54—dc20   CIP

Thorndike Large Print® Basic Series edition published in
1993 by arrangement with Warner Books, Inc.

Cover design by James Murray.

The tree indicium is a trademark of Thorndike Press.

This book is printed on acid-free, high opacity paper. ∞

For the Chicago girl I met in
Washington one afternoon —
Who stayed for all these adventures.
Lori.

"Go, set the world on fire."
— Ignatius of Loyola

One

It was another bad morning in the Pentagon. A sudden power surge in the electrical sub-basement had shut down every computer in this part of the building, which was a series of wood-paneled corridors leading off C ring. It had rained hard during the night and the roof had leaked again and a storeroom full of computer printouts that contained analysis of the Mediterranean terrorist threat for the coming fiscal year was ruined when the ceiling collapsed.

At least G2 hadn't screwed up. There was that.

Brig. Gen. Robert E. Lee was very angry as usual, and if G2 had not sent down the videotape cartridge when it did, he would have gone up there and chewed ass, and it would not have been about the videotape but the problem of trying to direct an intelligence operation in a building that should have been condemned thirty years ago.

General Lee wore no insignia of rank on

his black pullover sweater. The empty satin epaulets attested to his power. He didn't have to prove a damned thing.

He carried the surveillance videocassette in a manila envelope under his left arm as he swung down the empty corridor to the nest of offices used by this division of the Defense Intelligence Agency. People watched the way Bobby Lee walked — ambling sometimes, striding like now — and judged the advisability of being in the same corridor with him.

He turned into the bright anteroom that led to the other offices and stopped in front of the desk where S. Sgt. Lonnie E. Davis acted as gatekeeper.

Like all sergeants, Lonnie Davis was not afraid of generals. He gazed at General Lee for a full three seconds before pressing the security buzzer that admitted the general to the carpeted side of the room.

General Lee glanced at the computer screens, all blinking malfunction. With the computers down there was nothing to do.

"We got coffee?" the general said to the sergeant.

"We got coffee, machine in the next room, we hooked it up to the temporary line."

"Goddamned wiring. Trying to run an op with this wiring would make a Russian weep."

"At least the coffee machine works," Sergeant Davis said. "You'll like it. New coffee maker came in from purchasing, I don't know why we got it but we took it. Makes two pots at once, we can have regular and decaf," Sergeant Davis said. His voice rambled as much as his words.

General Lee strode into the second room, glanced once at a terrified specialist four sitting doing nothing in front of his blank computer screen, and grabbed a ceramic mug. He stared at the machine for a moment. It was a beautiful fancy machine. Probably set DoD back five hundred bucks a copy. Bobby Lee poured regular coffee into the mug. The world was just too damned decaffeinated to suit Bobby E. Lee's taste.

He followed a gray-walled corridor farther back into his realm until he came to the last office. He opened the door. Sp7c. Mae Teller, his private secretary, had arranged everything the way he liked it — six number-two pencils lined up like soldiers on the green felt paper pad in the exact center of his mahogany desk. There were two phones. The red phone on the right was very private, and the gray phone with six lines listed was not. He closed the door and locked it and opened the manila envelope. He inserted the black cartridge in the black VCR above the black-faced Japanese television monitor on the far wall.

He sat down behind his desk, opened a drawer, and took out the remote. He pointed it at the television set and VCR and pressed a button.

The black-and-white picture on the screen jiggled for a moment and then focused. The camera revealed the Red Line Metro underground platform beneath Union Station.

The Red Line was the most prestigious of the four Metro subway lines that snake across the District and probe into the near suburbs. It bisected the northwest quadrant of the District and reached into the posh suburb of Bethesda.

In the upper right-hand corner of the monitor, a digital clock ran in minutes and seconds, marking the real time of the recording and the actual time of day depicted on the screen. G2 had worked long hours overnight to edit out the garbage; this was what was left, what Bobby Lee would want to see.

0003:51, 0003:52, 0003:53.

The camera fixed on the sole passenger waiting on the platform. The focus was directed by a heat-seeking device, similar to that used in missiles. The heat of the man's body directed the robot camera.

General Lee sipped his coffee in the semi-darkness of the windowless room and watched the screen.

Above the hum of the videotape came the sudden sounds of steps down the escalator stairs. The escalator had been deactivated for the surveillance because it made too much noise on the soundtrack. This was a visual and audio surveillance.

General Lee put down his cup.

He stared at the waiting man who had turned to look at the escalator stairs. It was a familiar face.

It was Devereaux. Every night of the surveillance, Devereaux had come to this platform and waited until the last train. They thought he might have been waiting for someone to arrive by train, but each night, he stepped into a car of the last train without meeting anyone. They had followed him on the last scheduled train each night to his stop above Georgetown and a surveillance car had followed him to his apartment, and for ten mornings, G2* had given Bobby Lee the videotape and it hadn't been worth spit.

"Come on, Devereaux, you son of a bitch," Bobby Lee said to the monitor. He might have been cheering at a football game.

Devereaux was senior adviser for operations inside R Section. He was a little too senior to

*Officially, Deputy Chief of Staff for Intelligence (DCSINT).

11

be messing around with secret meetings and letter drops and all the other stuff you do in the field. Too damned senior to suit Bobby Lee.

The robot camera fixed in a false stone above the escalator well jiggled, momentarily confused by the presence of a second heat source.

Bobby Lee saw the second man's back. At last. There was going to be a meet.

The second man walked across the concrete platform.

The camera refocused, compromising on the two focal points. The picture was grainy and harsh.

The second man spoke.

The hiss on the videotape soundtrack overrode the speech.

"Damn," Bobby Lee said. He punched the stop button on the remote. He pushed rewind and started again.

The second man walked backward toward the camera. Stop. Play.

Bobby Lee turned up the sound.

The hiss was louder.

". . . something is going . . ."

Something something then "something is going" then something.

The second man turned in profile.

Bobby Lee stopped the tape. He knew the

face, anyone in certain circles would have known the face. Carroll Claymore. Carroll Claymore. What the hell was this about?

Bobby Lee just stared at the screen, his mouth open as though trying to catch the words by inhaling them. Carroll Claymore was the pal, protégé, and confidant of Clair Dodsworth, who was one of the six or seven permanently important men in Washington. Clair Dodsworth had more money than God and sat on a lot more boards of directors.

And here was his protégé meeting at midnight on a Red Line platform with an intelligence officer for R Section.

Bobby Lee got up from his desk, still staring at the monitor. What the hell would this have to do with Clair Dodsworth?

He hit the play button on the remote control. He stood behind his desk with the control in his hand.

"I told you," Devereaux said. "There's not —"

Not *not*. *Nothing*. "There's nothing" something something. "To worry about"? "I told you there's nothing to worry about." That's it.

Bobby Lee filled in the words, watched the way Devereaux's mouth moved, figured it out like doing a crossword puzzle in sound.

Carroll Claymore turned all the way around,

13

looking back at the camera, looking at the silenced escalator he had just walked down. His face was ashen.

"Scared," Bobby Lee said in the silence.

"Nobody's coming," Devereaux said. The firm voice. When you've got a scared source, you milk him, you mother him, you tell him fairy stories. Bobby Lee knew how to do it, it was part of the profession. Bobby Lee had seen Devereaux do it when their paths had crossed during the hot war in the middle of the cold war, back in 'Nam, back in the old days, when he was running an op for DIA and Devereaux was running for R Section and they knew about each other.

"Just lie to him," Bobby Lee said to the videotaped Devereaux.

Good. Good.

Devereaux touched Carroll Claymore on the shoulder, brought him back to the moment.

Carroll Claymore said something. Bobby Lee frowned, stopped the action, rewound, played it again and again, but couldn't make it out. Damned G2, damned cheap-shit equipment, how you gonna run an op, you got a building where the computers go down every other day, the goddamned roof leaks, you got Mickey Mouse surveillance junk? Christ, if the Russians had only known how fucked up we were, they would never have backed off.

Damn. Bobby Lee hit the stop button. He picked up the gray phone and dialed an internal number. Waited. Tapped the top of the desk, made the pencils jiggle in line.

"This is General Lee, I want Lieutenant Rumsfield." Waited. "Lieutenant, I am watching this piece of garbage you people were supposed to edit down overnight and I can't pick up a goddamned word, what kind of Mickey Mouse outfit —"

Waited, his face bright and hard.

"Yes, Lieutenant, I'm sure you can cover your ass with all that techno bullshit, but I am trying to run an op and I see a face on the screen and I can't make out a goddamned word of what these people are talking —"

Waited, waited. Oddly, as he listened to the lieutenant's explanation, he calmed down. What was the point of it? You chew out this candy-ass, and he covers himself with garbage about audio-enhanced electronic ironing and stuff nobody even heard of twenty-seven years ago when Bobby Lee was a bushtailed second loo trying to learn the ropes. What was the point of it, except to vent a little frustration? After ten days they filmed the meet and now they couldn't hear what it was about.

He said, "Next time you send down a tape, Lieutenant, you don't send garbage, I can't use garbage, am I making myself clear, Lieutenant?" Waited a moment, listened to the apology that was just another way of covering your ass, and then slammed the gray phone back on the receiver.

What was he going to do then? Like everything else, you improvise. The computers go down because of some outage in the basement, you hook up a temporary generator to keep the coffee pot boiling. Damned army was falling apart. But even as he thought this, Bobby Lee was smart enough to realize he had always thought this and somehow the army was still around, snafus and all.

He pressed the play button again. Carroll Claymore said something unintelligible and then pulled something out of his overcoat pocket.

Bobby Lee stared. Envelope, he had an envelope to give Devereaux, and suddenly his voice was as clear as the picture on the screen: "This is the last of it, I don't want to do this anymore, this is what you wanted. Copy of the transfer from Lebanon. Into the account you wanted at District. This is the last of it."

Devereaux: "Not the last. This is good and the next thing will be good. I'll tell you when it's the last of it."

"Do you realize how powerful Clair is, if he suspected —"

"Don't be afraid of Clair. Be afraid of me, Carroll —"

"But Clair —"

"The train's coming. I've got to catch the train, it's the last train of the night," Devereaux said. "I'll be here every night, Carroll, I want you to know that."

There was more, but the sound track was filled with the rumble of the approaching subway train.

". . . please," Carroll Claymore said. His face was in profile to the camera again.

The right side of the picture was filled with the train sliding into the station.

Devereaux turned from Carroll.

The doors opened.

Devereaux waited, looked left and right.

"Our man's on the train, Devereaux. We aren't that stupid," Bobby Lee said.

But then again, maybe Devereaux knew. Sometimes you could feel a thing when you were good enough, just feel it. But why would he know?

Devereaux stepped into the waiting car. He turned in the doorway and stared at Carroll Claymore on the platform.

The doors slid shut.

The train began to pull out of the station.

Carroll stared at the train rushing past.

The platform was empty except for the man

17

in the overcoat. Devereaux would get off at the same stop as the other ten nights, walk down the same streets to his apartment building, and he would be followed all the way and it wouldn't matter because he had something now.

And Bobby Lee had something now. Had a name and face and something something about money going into an account at District. What was District?

He thought of it then. He read the *New York Times, Wall Street Journal,* and both Washington papers every day for the sake of filling up anew the hard disk of his memory. Something stuck out now. Clair Dodsworth on the board of District Savings Bank. That was it. District Savings Bank. Money from Lebanon going to a local bank. What the hell was this, was Devereaux shaking someone down after all those years of honorable service for R Section? Or was it something else?

Please.

Carroll Claymore was being squeezed and he was pleading with Devereaux to stop squeezing him.

"Devereaux," Bobby Lee said aloud in the empty room. Devereaux had been messing into the affairs of DIA, and Bobby Lee had resented it and then become intrigued by it. He had set up the surveillance of Devereaux and followed him because Devereaux had started it, messing with DIA's Mediterranean terrorist counterop for six months, probing this and that, and now there was money from Lebanon going into an account at District Savings Bank. Bobby Lee was supposed to find out all about Devereaux. Find out what R Section was up to.

And now this.

Bobby Lee stared at the dark monitor in the semidark room.

This was going right to Clair Dodsworth, the dog with the biggest balls in Washington.

"What are we getting into, Devereaux?" he asked the darkened screen.

Brig. Gen. Robert E. Lee humbly believed he was not afraid of anyone or anything after twenty-seven years of seeing everything and doing everything in every place in the world.

But he was uncomfortable just now.

Damned uncomfortable.

Two

"I don't want to go to the Round Robin. You see the same people in the Round Robin. Besides, everyone we know went to the play tonight and everyone we know is going to the Round Robin and we're going to have to talk about the damned play again and I didn't want to see the damned play in the first place," Michael Horan said.

Britta Andrews smiled at him. They were in the car, in the big Lincoln limousine — because a Lincoln went over better with the public than a Caddy. That was something Horan would say and really believe when he said it.

Michael Horan was the junior senator from Pennsylvania. He had knocked off the Republican exactly nine years earlier. It had surprised everyone from Pittsburgh to Philadelphia all the way to the White House and the GOP National Committee. Right up to Michael Horan's ex-wife and, truth be told, Michael Horan himself.

"They won't talk about the play," Britta said. "They'll all come over to fawn around you and touch me to see if I'm wearing underwear."

Senator Horan smiled at that and ran his own large hand across her lap and down her left thigh.

"You like being touched."

"Women like to be touched when they invite being touched, but you wouldn't understand that because you're in the Senate and you think every woman is made to be touched."

He shook his head then and removed his hand. "You see this one fag play and now you're going to give me the lecture. I hate the lecture. I like women, I'm pro choice — and you don't know the kind of heat I get for that from everyone from the pope on down to my father-in-law — and I support the EEOC and everything from Lesbian Awareness Week to gay motherhood, but I endured the play as well as I could for your sake and I don't need that lecture." He said this in a flat voice and every word counted for as much as every other word. It meant he was angry and he knew how to control it. Britta knew that. They realized they were talking too much.

So she kissed him. Haley, the driver, had

heard it all, of course, but when people keep servants, they endure them by living their lives as though servants did not count. Haley watched the kiss in the rearview mirror. He saw the senator slide his hand along the stockinged thigh under the blue dress, and he thought about that, about what it would feel like. Haley was very loyal. He was more of a friend than a servant because he had been Michael Horan's driver, and the driver of a politician hustling votes in hostile precincts is closer to the politician than even a chief of staff. He had been with Michael Horan back when they were in a Ford and they were living on Big Macs going up and down the endless valleys of Pennsylvania, talking to church groups and women's clubs and the American Legion smokers and every damned thing and it had all looked so hopeless. Haley saw her push against him a little, not too hard, and the kiss was finished and the senator's hand stayed right there on the stockinged thigh, and that little quarrel was over until next time.

"If we don't go to the Round Robin, where do you want to go then?" Britta Andrews said.

"Sam and Harry's. You'll like Sam and Harry's. It's got a hetero crowd and everyone won't have been at the play and we won't have to talk about it — we won't have to talk to anyone — and we can get a sandwich,"

Michael Horan said.

"I ate today." She was a size four by nature and still worked at it. In some shops, in some lines, she could even be a size two but she wasn't a social X ray, she wasn't small enough. She had blond hair and it was her real color. A blonde with blond hair, angelic features, blue eyes, great body, long legs, just a living, breathing doll, and she hated it sometimes and yet she didn't hate it. She could quote Lenin and get it right; she would have preferred to be big and black and a man and she would have led the goddamned Symbionese Liberation Army. . . . Yet she was beautiful and that was useful too and she took pleasure in being beautiful. There was always this conflict about beauty and brains and will and desire. Like Michael's hand between her legs right now. She looked straight at the rearview mirror and saw Haley's eyes. She wanted to empathize with Haley because she really did care about ordinary people and what they thought, but the only way to treat Haley right now was to deny his existence. Let him look.

"I ate today but I have to eat again," Michael Horan said.

"And have a drink."

"No one ever has one. Never lie to yourself. A man who says he's going to have just one is halfway to being an alcoholic."

She liked that and gave him a quick peck of a kiss. She liked a lot of things about Michael Horan. He didn't lie to himself or to her or to his ex-wife back in Pennsylvania, who pretended they were still married. "If you don't lie to yourself, you make it easier." Michael said that once. Michael had brains and guts. When you walk into an empty hall because your advance man screwed up and your handlers are embarrassed and one little old lady shows up and you make the best of it, you try to sell that one little old lady, then you know you have the guts. It's what people who have never run for office can't understand, all those columnists and thumb-suckers and pundits who were never elected to anything, they couldn't begin to understand guts, but Britta could. She had guts herself, but she knew her courage was a different kind, much colder, much more reasoned.

Haley paid attention to traffic. Washington traffic dazzles at night because the streets and parkways and malls are so dark that the lights of the limousines stand out and form necklaces of light. Haley brought the car through the after-theater traffic, past the Willard Hotel and back north, then around N Street to a tow-away zone on Nineteenth Street facing south. Sam and Harry's was an expensive bar-and-grill set back from the curb some thirty-five feet, a place with bright lights and noise and the manufactured common touch that is not cheap to obtain. Another kind of senator would have taken Britta to the kind of bar that John Towers used to drink in when he was the big man, dark and down and no questions asked, where a pretty girl can be groped in a booth without anyone seeing or telling, but Michael Horan didn't lie. Not about Britta, not about anything that was important. He would lie about raising taxes, but that was something else.

Britta didn't lie either. She had so much money that she never had to lie to anyone for anything. But she loved being with Michael because Michael had the other thing, the power that doesn't come from inherited money but comes from grabbing people by the throat and getting them to vote for you. There is such beautiful poetry in that kind of power that Britta could be in love with the idea of it, even if she wasn't half in love with Michael Horan.

Haley opened the rear door for them, and she stepped out first, the blue dress riding high on her thigh. Haley was looking at her and pretending not to look at her. She didn't mind that, how could she mind being beautiful? Maybe Haley thought she was the senator's bimbo. She couldn't figure out what

Haley thought, but then, she didn't spend a lot of time thinking anything about Haley.

Michael came behind her. He took her arm. Part of not lying. The *Philadelphia Daily News* had caught him escorting some redheaded socialite to a Washington ball and manufactured it into a scandal, and then Michael Horan had faced a tough primary and won it by 60 percent. The papers back in PA had taken the hint: the public didn't really give a damn about who Horan was screwing as long as it wasn't a little boy and as long as he voted to put a surtax on incomes above eighty thousand a year.

Sam and Harry's was one of the places that the important little people went to, along with the Monocle over by the Hill and that Mexican place in Northeast and three or four others. The important little people were congressional aides with their own domains and powers, as well as spooks from Langley and newsmen and newswomen from National Public Radio and the *Washington Post* and the *Washington Times* and people who put spin on stories for the sake of senators at $76,400 a year and others, all little, all envious of the wealthy and very powerful. These mandarins of the bureaucracy, the Congress, and the press were very small and mean and petty, and they counted because they were always there. Michael Horan and Britta Andrews had begun their relationship after they realized that they both, in their separate ways, despised the mandarins created to serve them.

So let them look, fawn, and feed their greedy envy. The important little people would tell the other important little people that Senator Horan was at it again: this time it was a blonde, a rich society type from a screwball family, and the man was so brazen that he took her right into Sam and Harry's as if she was a trophy attesting to another good hunt.

The bar was long, wooden, and functional. The place was filling up. The rich wood colors were polished by bar lights that gave a false sense of friendliness and made wan faces glow warm.

Everyone in Washington had gone to the National Theater to see Robert Morse's one-man show, *Tru,* based on the life and remarks of Truman Capote. The capital had almost no live theater, and each road show offering sent down from Broadway was attended as a religious exercise. It was the way peasants of another time gathered in their villages to hear a famous London preacher making a tour of the provinces.

The fawners, their envy contained in green eyes, pressed toward the senator and the senator's "friend" and yet parted for them as they presented themselves and moved with majestic calm through the throng, plunging into the interior of the bar.

Michael Horan gave an easy grin. It said that he was famous and powerful but he was just like them, a regular guy trying to have a night on the town with the real people and not the phony baloneys in the Round Robin at the Willard Hotel. Britta turned to him, caught the profile of the grin, matched it. Hers was a little harder. Her smile had money, distance, and yet a keen political eye behind it. Her smile said she knew the names of the principals of all the European Green parties, had visited them, dined with them, gave them money, been respected by them . . . but was still willing to be a woman, a beautiful woman, endlessly desirable. It was a complicated smile, and the women among the little people studied it and knew it for what it was.

"Fanueil Hall without fish," Michael Horan said under his breath and under his smile. He pushed her by the elbow.

"SoHo," she said. "East Village. Maybe Little Italy on Saturdays in summer."

"South Philly," he said. "Thirtieth Street Station at night."

"Newark," she said. "Airport to downtown."

"Cleveland," he said.

"Gary, Indiana," she said.

He thought about it. "Detroit."

"Gary wins," she said.

"Pierre, South Dakota," he said.

"Have you ever seen Gary?" she said.

"You win," he said.

One of the owners gave them a good corner table where they could share the illusion of privacy. The waiter was young and good-looking the way Irish boys are before they really discover beer and potatoes. He was staring at the front of her dress, guessing and wondering at the same time, and he did not have the skills yet to hide it. The frank gaze warmed her because he was good-looking, not like the grizzled Haley, and if she had been shopping for an ornament, she might have put him on her wrist.

Michael Horan notched up the grin. "Hiya."

"I'm Michael, can I get you a cocktail?" Soft voice, very nice, and Michael the senator said he was a Michael too and the Michael who was a server said he knew and Michael Powerful asked where he was from and young Michael told him. It was all over in less than ten seconds, like working the crowd behind the rope at the airport before going on to Altoona and the next event of the day. Britta had grown used to it, but she was not comfortable with it. Elections, electioneering, precincts, polls . . . it fascinated her because there was power there that could be used, but the details were so boring and stupid. Cut through the details and just grab the power and hold it. She touched his hand on the table.

The waiter brought his Black Label rocks in a short rounded glass. He armed Britta with a chardonnay. She rarely drank and the white wine glass was a device, the way Robert Dole arms himself with a perpetually held pen in his crippled right hand. It invites people to keep their distance.

"Up the Irish," Michael Horan said to her.

"Up the rebels," she said. "Up the ANC."

"Not too loud."

"Loud enough," she said. She made a pretense of tasting the chardonnay.

Michael Horan made no pretense. He took the drink with real thirst. The whiskey numbed and then burned. The whiskey spread across his wide, Irish face and gave it a false color of health. Michael Horan functioned with whiskey. He made whiskey the glue of his life. Whiskey was comfort and aid and oblivion when he needed oblivion. When he really needed total oblivion, he would tell Haley he was going to be alone and Haley would bring a bottle of Black Label, a bucket of ice, and a glass to the cubicle he used in the old Senate Office Building, a clothes-closet of a room, totally unmarked, totally secret. And Haley would leave the bottle and the man, and the man would drink until he was drunk and then would fall asleep in the soft, red leather chair and ottoman and snore and awake without a memory of the bad thing that had chased him.

Michael Horan said, "I talked to Clair Dodsworth today. He was telling me I should change the portfolio again, that money was back in petrochemicals and —"

"I really don't want to hear about stocks and especially oil company stocks," Britta Andrews said. "I wish all the oil in the world would dry up tomorrow."

"You don't mind riding in my Lincoln," he said.

"I'd rather ride in a rickshaw."

"You'd rather be carried through the streets by slaves."

"Like that waiter. Four who looked like him," she said. She stared into Michael's eyes and saw them glitter, and she felt she was up to a fight now if that was what he wanted. If he wanted a fight instead of being nice and going home with her, he could get a fight and end up drinking himself drunk alone in one of those nasty dark bars they use around Dupont Circle, she didn't need him.

Michael was still smiling, but it was just the way his lips were arranged, it wasn't in his eyes. "And Clair said he had a little meeting with you yesterday and I said I didn't know that you knew Clair and Clair said that Clair had known your grandfather and I said I didn't know that and Clair said he had a most charming lunch with you. Now, what have you got to do with Clair Dodsworth?" The voice was even, the smile was still there, but there was something else.

Britta said, "We're having an affair."

Michael just kept smiling. He picked up his scotch and tasted it. He put the drink down on the white tablecloth. He had Irish eyes and they were not smiling.

"I go to his office once a week and massage his balls until he comes, and then I wipe him off with a towel. He feels my tits," Britta said.

"Britta."

Her blue eyes were the color of an arctic sea on a clear summer's day.

"Fuck you, Michael. What I do with Clair Dodsworth is nothing to do with you," Britta said. "You told me in the beginning that my ideas were too radical for your constituents. I said Fine and we left it at that. We talk, but what I do, who I give money to, my ideas are my business." She was very angry and

32

they both knew it.

"I was just asking about Clair. You know he's managed my portfolio for years, going back to my father. I was just asking about him."

"I knew about Clair and he knew about me and we talked. Clair is on the board of District Savings Bank and we were talking about money."

"Clair Dodsworth is on the board of every top corporation in the country," Michael said. "He doesn't handle your portfolio, does he?"

"Clair Dodsworth is arranging some matters for me," she said. She was still cold in tone, still holding her glass of wine like a sword.

"Is this about your work?"

"Do you want to know, Michael, or do you not want to know? The way we've kept it, you don't know and what you don't know can't hurt you."

He let the smile go. There was no sense in it. They were alone, at a corner table in a large, crowded bright room. The fawners and seekers and wannabes and the other apparatchiks were stealing little glances at them, wondering about the Important People in the corner, wanting to be them for just one day, just for fifteen minutes of one day, to escape their fabricated existences for one touch of real wealth and power. And she was making everything hard edged, she wanted to fight, it didn't make sense.

"What can't hurt me?"

He wanted to know. For the first time he really wanted to know. Not in an idle way but in a way that would involve him. She had been leading him to this for a long time. She could have scared him if she had told him from the beginning, but she was very good at not scaring people if she didn't want that to be the effect.

"I talked to him again about the institute."

"The Institute for World Development."

"The Institute for World Development," she repeated.

"A lot of 'save the whales' stuff." He turned to his drink; he was losing interest. The Institute for World Development was one of those "Green" political ideas that existed on paper and in discussion at Green party meetings here and in Europe. Save the earth by going back to a simpler life. Stop oil, stop gas, stop coal, and most of all, stop nuclear power.

"You can have contempt for the environment because that's what Pennsylvania wants to hear, they want Pittsburgh to be smoky, they want —"

"Pittsburgh," Michael said. "You've never been in Pittsburgh in your life. Pittsburgh is beautiful."

"Coal mines, dirty mine shafts full of danger, people with black lung disease, emphysema —" She had a vision of Pittsburgh fixed in the 1950s, when steel mills clogged what was now the Golden Triangle area. It was an image passed down from her father to her. She had legacy, loads of it.

"Cut it out, Britta. I don't want to fight with you about something you don't know anything about."

"I know a lot of things," Britta Andrews said. She even tasted her wine, she was so angry. And annoyed. That's what she was, annoyed.

"Is he going to arrange financing for the institute?"

He was quiet, trying to stop the fight building between them.

"He's been doing that for some time. Arranging for things," she said. "For the institute. For things."

Britta did not frighten him just then. That would come later, when he thought about it. Her voice was so calm, and it colored all her secrets the same shade of gray. He knew she was dangerous for him when they first went to bed together. He needed women the way he needed scotch on the rocks, as a refuge from the reality of things. He didn't lie to himself about it. He didn't even lie about being afraid of things in real life. He used women like a narcotic. They had understood that. She had loved his body, his power, and his wit. He had left his wife in Pennsylvania more than a few years ago, and if his wife wanted to stay married to him in her mind, that was her problem.

"What kind of things?"

"Do you want to know, Michael?"

"I guess I want to know."

"Guess isn't good enough. You want to know, Michael?"

"Will it hurt me?"

"Nothing is going to hurt you."

"Knowing you hurts me, but I wanted to know you so badly that I could stand the hurt."

"You don't know me. Not really. Not the way you could if you really wanted it."

"I really want it."

She waited. She was very good at waiting, as most women were; yet it had been her grandfather who taught her to wait. When her father spent part of the fortune on the Black Panthers and the Weather Underground and on other things, she had loved him for his courage and deplored his inability to wait. The revolution in the things that mattered — the true revolution when everyone would be equal, have equal wants and needs fulfilled — well, it was coming, but slowly. Her grandfather had been very good at waiting, and he had passed it on to her, skipping her father's generation. And then Dad had blown himself up in that stupid bomb factory he had financed, it was all so stupid, what was he going to do with a few sticks of dynamite anyway, burn down the world? That wasn't the way things really got done.

"I want to know you. Know Clair."

"You know Clair."

"I couldn't have imagined in my wildest dreams he knew you."

"I told you. I have sex with him once a week."

"Jesus, Britta." He made a face then because he was out of scotch; it was just ice in a glass and a little water. He looked around for the other Michael.

Part of waiting was hurting the person you were waiting for. Grandfather hadn't said that in words but in the way he had done things. Britta had watched him hurt people. She had appreciated the skill of it.

Michael the server came up and took his empty glass. Then Michael the server brought back a new drink and a bowl of cashew nuts.

"Would you like menus?" he said.

"I've seen menus," Horan said. When he started drinking, he stopped eating. There was going to be some real drinking tonight because Britta was different now, she had something secret in her that was beginning to haunt everything they said.

"Nothing," she said.

They were staring at each other. The waiter went back to the bar.

"I do what I do and I do what I want," Britta said in a very soft voice.

Michael Horan picked up his drink. "OK. You do what you want. I do what I want."

No. That wasn't the direction she wanted at all. "Michael," she said. She touched his wrist. It was a very feminine thing to do. She leaned forward, attending to him. She stared into his eyes with her beautiful face full of attention.

He sensed the change in balance. He finished a long sip of his ice-cold drink. Took his time. Put the drink down on the damp spot on the tablecloth.

"Do you want to know everything?"

Michael said, "If you want to tell me."

"Clair is part of . . . a necessary part . . . of arranging a financial scheme for the group."

"What group? The Institute for World Development?"

"The Dove."

"Dove? The Dove Group? What the hell is the Dove Group?"

"Let's just say it's Dove. You know. An acronym."

"For what?"

"Another time." She didn't want to frighten him. Not at first. One step at a time. Her grandfather had owned five senators in his day. Owned them and their wives and the futures of their children, their mistresses, their fortunes, their very freedom not to be in prison where they certainly could have gone.

"What are you talking about?" He was walking carefully across a dark, strange field. There was moonlight but not enough. The field had unexpected pits in it. It was a beautiful, dark night where he walked, looking for her and her secrets. He was utterly absorbed in it. The noisy and bright room had receded, all the fawners and wannabes were no more than background noise on a television set that no one was watching.

"The Institute for World Development was set up by a coalition of Green parties here and in Europe and Canada to find environmental energy solutions —"

He said, "I know about that. I already

knew about that. But what about Clair?"

"He introduced the institute to a source . . . of funding. A means of making the institute work for itself without me propping it up all the time. I made that clear to them: I'm not my father, I'm not throwing my fortune down a rathole just because someone tells me the current rathole is a good cause. I know what a good cause is. I'm committed, but I'm not a fool."

"You're not a fool but you say someone is willing to be."

She smiled at that. Michael was very bright and she liked bright people. It almost was sexual. She kept his wrist in the palm of her hand. "Let's say someone has money and someone wants to support the institute —"

"The Institute for World Development is a lot of crap, Britta. You and your environmental pals meet and talk and dine on wine and cheese and change the world in your dreams. No one is going to stop driving cars for you and your pals or stop heating their homes in winter."

"Maybe not," she said. She smiled. "But it's a lot of money for nothing, then. A lot of money."

"A lot of money," Michael said. Money was endlessly interesting to him, as it is to all politicians. Money is always needed, you can never have enough, you are always offered it, you seek it as you seek votes and the power to rule men.

"For a start."

"Clair's arranged credit."

"His directorship on District Savings is useful. Money comes from one place and is made available."

Michael said, "Is it legal, Brit? You want to watch yourself. Clair has the best reputation in the city, one of the best in politics, so I wouldn't trust him very much."

"No. I don't think so."

She might have been disputing Clair Dodsworth's reputation. Or she might have been answering his question.

"You don't need it, then," Michael said. He knew it was the question she had answered.

"Of course, I'm not a lawyer. Clair Dodsworth is a lawyer. I trust his advice."

"Why is he involved? I mean, with this thing for you? For your institute? Or this Dove, whatever Dove is?"

"Why do you think Clair does anything?" Britta said.

"Are you having an affair with him then really?"

"Is that any business of yours?"

"Britta, I'm jealous."

She considered how she would tell him. She said, "I want you to make love to me tonight. I thought about it while we were watching the play. Imagine, watching a play about Truman Capote and I was thinking about you in bed, about you naked. I really want that."

Her eyes were beautiful now. The arctic-sea blue had shifted to a Caribbean blue, tinged with darker green, and her mouth was wet and he hadn't even noticed it until now.

He said, "Let's get out of here."

"I want to tell you," she said.

"We can get out of here and go to your condo and —"

"Five million dollars in a line of credit. It was arranged five days ago and Clair did it. He knows the source, but I don't — I just present the opportunity."

"Five million? In credit? From someone you don't even know?"

"Clair puts everything in compartments, and that way one compartment never knows about another. He mentioned it to you, that we had had lunch, he mentioned it because I told him to make a point of telling you."

"Why, Brit?"

"Because I want you to know."

42

She had said it softly so that the menace in the words was covered in velvet. It was cold now and dangerous and he understood that, but he was also understanding himself, that he had to know all the secrets. The moon was hidden in clouds. The field did not have an end. He stepped so carefully now.

"Clair was my father's friend and is my friend," Michael said.

"He has a lot of friends. Now I'm one of his friends. Friends help each other." She paused. "Are we friends, Michael?"

He said, "We're more than that."

"But we can't be less. We've been less and I want to change that."

He understood then.

He saw her in the reflected lights from the bar, saw the depth of her blue eyes and the perfectly coiffed hair, the golden beauty of her shining in those eyes. And now this, this deep mysterious knowledge that she insisted he share with her. Even if it led to hell, he would have to share it with her.

It was a moment that thrilled him, to understand something this important.

"Tell me," Michael said.

"The Institute for World Development is positive. A positive thing. It develops papers, writes op-ed pieces. The piece last week in the *Times* on destruction of Amazonian rain forests. You saw it. But you can't just talk, talk never gets anyplace. You've got to translate the ideas and positions into action. Someone has to do the dirty work."

"What dirty work, Britta?" He was holding his drink very tightly and his fingers were becoming numb with cold.

She was smiling, eyes glittering in the light. "Take Chernobyl, Michael. A bad thing but with a good result. The questioning now of all nuclear power plants, how safe they are, whether more should be built. The government is backpedaling just to stay in place on nuclear power. The greatest danger on earth is nuclear power plants."

"But you can't win that fight, not without coming up with an alternative —"

"They're unsafe, Michael. Even you agree with that."

He stared at her, tried to see where it was going.

"Nuclear power should destroy itself," Britta said.

Silence between them, noise all around.

"What way could it show its true colors? To show it could not be trusted?"

"Where is this leading, Britta?"

She shook her head. "Not terrorism. The world is tired of terrorism. The real terror always comes from inside yourself. Let it

44

come from the nuclear power plants themselves."

"Is that what Dove is for?"

"Dove. Dove is to do things that have to
be done, Michael. What we all know has to
be done," Britta said. She held his wrist and
stared at him, and he looked away because
he could not return the stare. She held his
wrist and he did not move it.

Three

Carroll Claymore had been very afraid for two months, the amount of time he had been working for Devereaux. Devereaux had made it clear to him from the beginning that there was no recourse in this matter and that the only way he would escape from the job was to finish it.

The blackmail was simple. It involved children and it was complete enough to destroy Carroll Claymore and even to send him to prison. Even a man as rich as Carroll Claymore might have been locked up. The blackmail was cruel and they had both known it, but Devereaux used the blackmail the way he had once used a knife or a gun or a garrote.

The job assigned to Carroll Claymore involved spying on the affairs of his friend and mentor Clair Dodsworth. They had been friends for seventeen years, and Clair had made him a partner in his law firm and opened up all the doors for him. To spy on a friend was difficult enough. But to spy upon a powerful friend was worse.

Carroll Claymore suffered from dreadful nightmares in those two months, and he was afraid of everything Clair Dodsworth said to him, for fear that Clair knew or Clair was suspicious of him. He habitually worked late at night in the offices they shared on L Street, so there was no problem in spying on Clair by going through the office papers, but everything made him nervous.

He was afraid of Devereaux and he was afraid of Clair Dodsworth. He lost fifteen pounds in those two months and he stopped jogging in Rock Creek Park on Sunday afternoons. Clair said he should go to a doctor, he looked so tired all the time. That had made him feel guilty. A man he was spying on, his friend, his concerned friend, giving him advice about his health when he was really losing weight because he was afraid and under pressure. It is easy to betray trust once but not to do it over and over again.

Then there were those dreadful visits set up for the Union Station stop of the Red Line Metro.

The only thing that Carroll Claymore did not fear was that he was going to die for anything he did. This wasn't about death. This was about transactions in the international credit division of the District Savings Bank.

Devereaux wanted to know about every transaction, especially the transactions from the Middle East. And he wanted to know who really owned the District Savings Bank.

The last question was so absurd. It was easy. It was owned by, it was owned by . . .

Carroll Claymore became more nervous as he realized it was impossible to determine the ownership of the bank, that all the papers filed with the Securities and Exchange Commission and the federal banking regulators were purposely complex and fragmented, and he did not understand what Devereaux really wanted him to do.

And then, three nights after his last meeting with Devereaux on the Metro, the job ended.

There were two men who did not speak English very well, and they took him to Potomac Park near the Jefferson Memorial. Carroll had dined late and decided to walk home in the safe precincts of upper Georgetown, which is very far from the much meaner streets of the rest of the District. The two men approached him brazenly on a well-lit street and shoved him into the back of a car. They tied his hands with wire and put a tape gag across his mouth. Not that he would have cried out. They had guns, both of them.

"You like the Jefferson Memorial?" one of them said in the park. The night was very dark, it was very late. "It's a good place for you." He did not understand that at all.

They were beneath the cherry trees that ring the Tidal Basin. The gleaming memorial building was the only bright spot in the deserted park. It was about three in the morning, Carroll guessed, and they had been riding around in the limousine with the darkened windows for about two hours. They had gone over everything with him. It had taken him nearly the entire two hours to realize they were going to kill him.

It was wrong to be killed over something like this, over something he knew so little about, over a small act of betrayal he had been forced into by a bloodless intelligence agent. When he started to tell them this, when he started to cry, they taped his mouth shut again, and one of them humiliated him deeply by raping him. They just pulled down his trousers and his underwear and raped him. He was still wearing his suitcoat and tie. He cried, the tears staining the leather seat they had thrown him across.

Why were they doing this horrible thing? Who were these men?

When that was done, they were in the park and they marched him out under the cherry trees. His trousers were still around his ankles, and he realized they intended to leave him this way. His thighs were wet and he thought he was bleeding and he was afraid he might faint from the pain. He could smell the dew on the brown grass, and the trees shivered damply in the thin moonlight. It had rained and cleaned the sky.

Carroll said a prayer, a thing he had not thought to do since childhood. He prayed fervently, and they threw him facedown on the grass and made some remark to each other in a foreign language he did not understand.

The one with the garroting wire took his time, but he was very thorough and he made sure that Carroll was dead when it was over. Then they pulled the duct tape from his lips, and the other one pulled out the tongue of the dead man and cut it off and threw it into the Tidal Basin. They went back to the car, and the driver took them out to the airport. It was around three in the morning, and they would have to wait for the morning flight to London.

Four

Devereaux lived with Rita Macklin in a condominium on Thirty-ninth Street Northwest, just west of the National Cathedral, at the top end of Georgetown. They could hear the bells of the cathedral from their balcony on Sunday mornings. The apartment was not large, but it was in a fine neighborhood and the building was very polished and quiet. The rent was two thousand dollars a month and they afforded it. The owner of the apartment had been transferred to Kuwait for three years to help build new oil wells, and he did not want to sell the place because the prices of things kept rising in Washington. Devereaux and Rita Macklin felt out of place in this expensive world, but they had wanted to live in the heart of the city for a little while.

The car from R Section came for Devereaux at seven this morning and he was already on the curb, waiting for it. The day was cold and clear for a Washington autumn, which is usually languid, with pretty leaves stuck on the trees until deep December. This morning had a harsh wind.

Devereaux opened the passenger door of the gray Dodge sedan and climbed in next to the driver. The driver was Hacker, the man who called him at five-thirty.

Hacker was now a jack-of-all-trades in Section, but he had been in the field once, like Devereaux.

Hacker grunted at him as a greeting. He wore a black overcoat. His thick black and gray hair was cut short, and his eyebrows, which were black, nearly joined above his large nose. There was no soft edge to the look of him. He had the hands of a coal miner, and the steering wheel seemed small in them.

Devereaux knew that Hacker had lost part of one leg. It had been shattered beneath the knee on a stupid mission in Albania that had gone bad. Devereaux had read about Hacker in the files and felt a sympathy for him and for all the people who had been lost on all the stupid missions of the long cold war that began in 1946 and killed everything in its path for nearly half a century. Devereaux had been a soldier in that war and had sympathy for all the other soldiers, even the ones on the wrong side.

Hanley, who was director of operations for Section, had kept Hacker on but given him little to do. Hacker had stayed on because he had a wooden leg now and there was no point in looking for another job. Devereaux had thought of Hacker's loss and then thought of Mona.

That was months ago. Now, in the gray car cutting through the cold, crisp morning, he thought of Mona again.

Mona had gone to Lebanon in the spring and disappeared. Mona. He thought about Mona all the time and he had asked Hanley to let him use Hacker in this Mona matter, and Hanley had agreed because he never had enough for Hacker to do and because he wanted to wash his hands of Devereaux and this Mona business.

Hacker and Devereaux understood they were not friends and would never be friends. When Devereaux had told Hacker a little about it — about Mona — Hacker had understood what had to be done. There would be no job waiting for Mona back at R Section because Mona had to be dead, and if she wasn't dead, she would wish she was dead. Hacker had no qualms about going after the people who had killed Mona and the others who had disappeared. It was revenge. Hacker and Devereaux had agreed on that.

The gray Dodge sedan flowed in the light traffic of early morning south and east down

Massachusetts Avenue, leaving behind the cathedral hill, where the street converged with Wisconsin Avenue.

Devereaux stared out the side window at the joggers on the walks. There was no point in asking Hacker what Hanley wanted him for. It must be about Mona, about this business that had consumed six months of his life and had led him to midnight meetings on Metro platforms and the sense that someone was on his trail as much as he was on another's trail.

"You ever gamble?" Hacker said.

His voice was unexpectedly gentle. The breaking of the silence was unexpected as well.

"No," Devereaux said.

"I gamble. Redskins Sunday, take the over. I mean, if you gamble. It's thirty-seven and I don't know why it's so low but take the over."

"I wouldn't know what it was."

"You got to have a bookie. I could get it booked for you. I could do that."

Devereaux glanced into the side mirror. Was the green car the same green car that had been parked at the end of the block when Hacker picked him up? He stared at the green car until it made a right turn.

"You should get involved in sports. It gives you something to talk about."

Devereaux wondered what this was about. Then he realized that Hacker knew why Hanley had ordered him in early and that Hacker was softening Devereaux for something. Something bad.

Hanley had no subtlety and that suited Devereaux. Hanley was a man of flinty clichés and he was a bureaucrat, but he was utterly ruthless when he had to be and that suited Devereaux. Hanley was the last of the old breed left in intelligence. Angleton and Dulles were dead. Helms and Colby were still around, but they were retired. Turner didn't count because Langley thought Turner had gutted them at the bidding of that damned Carter. And Bush had gone on back into politics. No, there was no one left really except Hanley. Someone had wanted to give Hanley a medal once for years in service, and Hanley had quashed that because there was no point in reminding anyone how long you had been around. Hacker knew what this was about and he was trying to prepare Devereaux for the bad news.

Devereaux realized he was holding his breath. He let it go slowly.

Embassies stood like palaces in soldierly ranks along Massachusetts. Hacker and Devereaux passed in review in the dim morning light. It began with Cape Verde and Norway above the Naval Observatory, and then, below the circle, Great Britain stood with South Africa on the same side of the street. The gray car went down past Bolivia and Brazil into the tighter cluster huddled beneath Belmont Road: Japan, Venezuela, Ivory Coast, Tunisia, Paraguay, Korea, Oman, Bukina Faso, Haiti, and Pakistan, the Johnny-come-latelies who had not staked out loftier neighborhoods.

He closed his eyes a moment. He was tired. He had waited on the platform for the last Red Line train and the train had come and Carroll Claymore had not been there. He had taken the train, and when he walked the last few blocks home, he thought someone had been following him.

Rita had waited for him last night as she usually did. He had told her not to wait for him at that late hour, but Rita had smiled and told him that women like waiting for certain men. She had arranged a late cold supper, which she shared with him. There was pâté with peppers and French bread and a plate of onions and tomatoes and herring and a cold bottle of California merlot. They had listened to the Mozart she had put on the stereo.

Devereaux opened his eyes to dispel the image of the night before because she was a sacred thought and this was a profane morning.

Hacker twisted the wheel in the vise of his hands. Tires squealed around Dupont Circle and then they continued down to Scott Circle, where Rhode Island Avenue, grander than its namesake, strides in a broad ribbon of road northeast to the rest of the city that the tight northwest part of the District ignores. Hacker did not follow Rhode Island Avenue. Hacker turned due south on Fourteenth Street from Thomas Circle toward the federal heart of the District.

There were linden and maples that shimmered with autumn leaves. The slight morning haze made everything seem wet and fresh, the way it is in spring. But this was November, the dying season, and the wind was harsh. The colors made Devereaux feel sad because they were so abundant and languid. It is the way of autumns in Washington because the summer lingers too long to make autumn bracing, and the dying of the leaves goes on too long.

Hacker said, "You don't follow football do you? You don't follow the Redskins?"

"I was from Chicago," Devereaux said. It was a gesture. He felt sorry for Hacker because Hacker was sorry for him. The whole world could feel sorry for each other. Sorry for Mona, sorry for Hacker's missing leg. "Everyone has to be a Bears fan. It never leaves you."

"Sort of like an eczema," Hacker said.

Devereaux smiled at that. "It isn't catching."

"That's the thing about most skin diseases."

"You have the Skin disease," Devereaux said. The pun was so unexpected for both of them that they didn't say anything more. There was nothing to say anyway. Hacker had just known what was coming, and in the way people did, he had tried to prepare Devereaux for the blow.

Five

Devereaux looked at the photographs.

"When did they find him?"

"About three-thirty," Hanley said. Hacker was there as well. The room had no windows. It was Hanley's room in Section, bare and cold. A map of the world decorated with pins hung on one wall. The photographs of the dead man were in color.

"This is blood."

"He was bleeding from the rectum. You can't see it but they cut out his tongue."

"Did you find his tongue?"

"They must have thrown it into the Tidal Basin. Anyway, I got the call at oh four-thirty and we put a priority on it. For once, nobody screwed up. The policeman who found him radioed the District and District checked their stop list and his name was on it. So the police just know that we wanted to know and that's all they know. They'll send someone around to talk to me, and I'll pull rank on him and tell him it's top secret. But this will get back to Clair Dodsworth, our involvement with Claymore."

"Maybe Clair already knows," Devereaux said.

Devereaux stared at the photographs in his hand. He looked at them again, one by one, putting them facedown on the gray metal table when he was finished. He had large hands and the photographs looked small in them. "Middle East with garrote, the wires to bind the hands. Arabs like to choke you to death."

"Why did they do that to him?" Hacker said.

"I told him there wasn't anything to worry about. I wanted to follow the money from Lebanon through the International Credit Clearinghouse. Get some proof of who owns District Savings Bank. The last person I was worried about was Clair Dodsworth," Devereaux said. "Poor guy."

"Well, it wasn't anyone's fault."

Devereaux knew that wasn't true. He had watched his own trail, he had sensed he was being followed, being watched, but he thought Carroll Claymore was just another amateur and was having anxiety attacks over nothing. Clair Dodsworth was seventy-nine years old, one of the most respected men in the country. He wasn't going to have anyone killed.

And maybe he didn't.

60

Maybe this went to something else.

Devereaux turned over the last photograph and then stared at the white backing of all the photographs.

"The Tidal Basin," Devereaux said. "Where exactly?"

Hanley looked at a piece of paper. "Fifty feet from the shore."

"But where?"

"Hundred feet east of the Jefferson Memorial."

"Jefferson."

Hanley nodded. "I thought of that."

Hacker said, "Thought of what?"

"*Jefferson* was the code word Mona was supposed to use when she wanted to split. She sent out 'Jefferson' and we arranged to pick her up in Syria but she never made it. None of them made it."

"Jefferson?"

"It was just a random word. They know the word so they did have Mona," Hanley said.

"She's dead," Devereaux said. "All six of them are dead. They went into Lebanon to get to the source, the middleman of International Credit Clearinghouse. Mona was close to it. She really was close to it and I told her to go ahead. I greened it. My first act as a senior adviser in operations. I greened Mona

61

and the others and I let them all get killed."

It had become his obsession. Hanley knew it and so did Hacker. They had backed away from Devereaux in the intervening months. Devereaux had worked once with the agent named Mona. They had been lovers once, it was said. Everyone believed they had been lovers once. You couldn't talk to Devereaux about that, of course. If they had been lovers once, it had been a long time ago. Sometimes agents are thrown together as Devereaux and the agent called Mona had been thrown together, and sometimes, because of anxiety and a shared sense of fear and isolation in the enemy camp, agents become lovers. It is the human element in intelligence operations. It is always lurking there but you don't talk about it.

Devereaux was going to finish it for Mona and the other dead ones. Find and kill the thing called International Credit Clearinghouse, the bank of criminal terror in the world that had tentacles in nearly forty countries. Devereaux said Mona was convinced that District Savings Bank in Washington was the United States link to ICC, but there was no proof of it and any examination was blocked by the reputation and power of the director, Clair Dodsworth, the adviser to presidents since the forties. So Devereaux had done a dirty blackmail on Carroll Claymore so that Carroll would do dirty things on his mentor and partner, Clair Dodsworth.

Mona and the other agents had disappeared inside Lebanon in spring. Mona had called out one word: "Jefferson." Coming out, finishing . . .

And they had raped Carroll and cut out his tongue and left him in the shadow of the Jefferson Memorial. Carroll had once had sex with children, and that poor, sick man had been set up by a crude blackmail and now he was dead.

Devereaux felt a cold anger that he could not describe if he had wanted to. The anger was frozen in his belly and it would not move from there and he could not dislodge it.

He shook his head then and thought of Mona the last time he had seen her, before she took the cab to Dulles International and caught the morning BA flight to London. Her hair was beginning to gray and it was cut short. Her eyes were the color of green olives. Her skin was dark. Mona had courage and spoke in a very soft way that always had its way. They had worked in East Germany in the cold war, and they had shared cold beans in a cold field and slept beneath a cold blanket. They had huddled against each other for warmth.

"Well, they're telling us, Devereaux,"

Hanley said. He said it as a final thing.

"They followed me. They followed me into the Metro when I met with Carroll. The last time was three nights ago."

"You didn't tell us that."

"I don't tell you a lot of things." Devereaux looked at Hacker. "Money was credited in an anonymous account. The account is at a bank in Liechtenstein that we know is controlled by International Credit Clearinghouse. What was the money to be used for? A line of credit for some other paper outfit called the Institute for World Development. It's a shell of some kind, nonprofit, organized by someone named Britta Andrews. We don't have her in the morgue."

The morgue was the files of everything uncovered by R Section in three decades of existence. It was the place for dead names and old secrets.

"I used Nexus then," Devereaux said. Nexus was a powerful news storage system that catalogued everything that appeared in dozens of newspapers and magazines. Everything. He had run her name through Nexus and found twenty-nine items.

"Britta Andrews dates Senator Horan from Pennsylvania. Apparently, he has an ex-wife who thinks she's still married to him. Britta is something of a radical. Very rich.

Inherited money. One reference to her father. He was killed in 1969 when he and four other radicals blew themselves up in a house in Queens where they were running a dynamite factory."

Hanley made a face. It was too damned domestic and R Section had no domestic intelligence charter. Not that it ever stopped them, but this was getting deep and names like Clair Dodsworth were surfacing.

"This sounds like something for the FBI now. We should just give this to the Sisters on Pennsylvania Avenue and let them do this thing the legal way," Hanley said.

Hacker stared at Devereaux.

Devereaux said, "The Sisters wouldn't care very much about Mona unless we told them all about her. And then we would get into trouble for pursuing something we should have given to the Sisters in the first place and they would have given to Langley, and we would have all the information but they wouldn't care. They wouldn't use what Mona had developed, the others had developed."

"Mona is dead now," Hanley said. He said it in his quiet voice. "So we have to cut this thing off, that's all. They killed Carroll and they did it in that Middle East way of making a warning and using the dead body to carry the message."

65

"I want to finish this. You owe it to the six we lost in Lebanon last spring. Sometimes you have to finish a thing," Devereaux said.

Hanley said, "You approved the Lebanon mission. It didn't work out. That happens. I've been sitting here a long time, and during the cold war things didn't always work out. You can't carry it home with you and you can't always finish it."

"Why was a five-million-dollar line of credit made available to a paper shell environmental outfit? What the hell does the Middle East — what does ICC and the Lebanon connection — have to do with the environment?"

"Let the FBI find out."

"The FBI doesn't care," Devereaux said. "The FBI will start on Clair Dodsworth and Clair Dodsworth will go to his good friend in the White House and the FBI will drop it yesterday."

"We're skirting the edge of our authority," Hanley said.

"We've gone over the edge," Devereaux said.

Hacker's surprisingly soft voice broke in now. "You have to take care of your own, Mr. Hanley. They're telling Section to back off, that the dead agents in Lebanon don't matter, and that if we don't back off, they'll do something worse. Worse than what? Go after me, Devereaux, you? Go after Mrs. Neumann? Kill our wives and friends? Make everyone their goddamned hostage?"

The soft voice and hard words surprised them to silence for a moment. But then Hanley frowned again.

"We play by rules, we broke the rules doing domestic . . . well . . . inquiry," Hanley said to Hacker.

"There are no rules," Devereaux said. "Not in this. We have to do the right thing in this. You know that as well as I do."

Hanley said, "We blackmailed Carroll Claymore with those pornography pictures. He used boys and we bought the pictures and used them to force him."

"We killed him," Devereaux agreed.

"We didn't cut out his tongue. We didn't rape him and strangle him," Hacker said.

The men were speaking separately, in monotone, their words forming a shared, single thought.

"Mona is really dead," Devereaux said.

"That's the message, part of it," Hanley said.

And the three men said nothing for a long time. They thought about what the right thing was and how they could get away with doing it.

Six

When Clair Dodsworth arrived at his office on L Street at the usual hour of 9:30 A.M., he saw the man standing in the doorway on the street. The look of the man struck him so, that he paused. The man stared at him. The man had gray eyes and a face chiseled from ice. There was nothing warm in the face or in the stance of the man. The eyes might have been the eyes of a killer. Yes, Clair Dodsworth had known killers in his years as a trial lawyer before coming to Washington, and he knew their eyes all looked alike, even if they denied they had killed anyone.

It was Devereaux, of course, but Clair Dodsworth did not know his name in that first moment.

When he arrived at his office, there were two police detectives waiting for him. He gave them his gracious smile but they were not returning it. They didn't want coffee or tea or anything. They went into his private office and Clair closed the door. He hung up his coat and they told him that Carroll Claymore had been found dead in the park by the Jefferson Memorial. They did not show him photographs, they just told him what had happened.

Clair Dodsworth took it calmly.

He was a cautious crocodile who watched where he stepped, and he went to his desk and sat down behind it so that the two officers were arrayed in front of him. He shook his head and there were tears in the old rheumy eyes. He said the name *Carroll* over and over again.

The detectives waited for the moment of grief to be eased and they asked him many questions. He ended up calling in the secretary, who went down through the list of appointments that Carroll had had in the previous days and the cases that he had been working on. The detectives said they appreciated the cooperation.

They asked him to identify the body of his partner because Carroll had been a bachelor and had no known relatives. The old man said he would. He stoically bundled himself in his overcoat and left the office with the two detectives at 11:15 A.M.

The gray-eyed man was waiting across the street. For a moment Clair thought to say something to the detectives, but as always, he allowed himself to hesitate prudently.

The business at the morgue was brief, cold, not pleasant. He signed a paper, and a policeman drove him back to the office. It was 12:15 P.M. Traffic was dense but mobile. When the policeman dropped him off, Clair looked around for the gray-eyed man but he was not there.

Clair went to lunch at 12:30 P.M.

He lunched at That Place On K Street, a bistro where the food was French and simple. It was a mauve-colored restaurant two steps up, very spare and quiet. Some of the old intelligence masters liked to eat there, though never with each other. Clair had developed many friends in intelligence over the years, at Langley and inside the FBI. He had never cultivated R Section because, frankly, R Section wasn't very important. Therefore, he had no reason to know Devereaux at all.

He spoke to the owner in French and the owner took him to his usual table in the front dining room with windows that look out onto the street at pedestrian level.

And then he saw the gray-eyed man again. The man was in the same dining room, already eating his lunch at a table opposite Clair's.

The same man.

It ruined his lunch. The gray-eyed man seemed to take no interest in him. He ate his salad last, in the French manner, and spoke French to the waiter. The man left the restaurant before Clair paid his bill.

"Do you know who that was?" he asked the owner in French.

The owner made a shrug. He went to look at the credit card receipt, but the man had paid the bill in cash. He had merely walked in around quarter to twelve and asked for a table in the front dining room. Was there anything wrong?

Clair Dodsworth said he was upset because his partner in the law firm had passed away. Those were the words he used because Clair Dodsworth and people like him do not use more vulgar words. The owner sympathized and offered to buy a *digestif* because a restaurateur greets every human experience as an excuse for ingesting something. Clair begged off. He left the restaurant at 2:10 P.M. That man, whoever that gray-eyed man was, had ruined his lunch and done more. He had intruded on Clair's careful and private world. It was rude and insulting.

And it frightened him.

He could not remember the last time he had been frightened about anything. His path to power had been smooth and with little effort and much grace. Born in Mount Vernon, Illinois, in the downstate province called Egypt because of the fertile delta there, where his powerful family made powerful friends, he had become a lawyer. After Pearl Harbor he sought a naval commission, reasoning that ships were nicer places than battlefields. On the other hand, he thought Washington might be an even better place than any ship.

His uncle had arranged a transfer to the staff of Adm. Horace Higginbotham in Washington, and when Clair got there, he looked around to find his opportunities. He had found them with a position as liaison to the Office of Strategic Services in 1944. After the war, the OSS turned into the Central Intelligence Agency and he had had a hand in drafting the charter of the document. He was always too modest to take too much credit but he was always able to put himself in all historic contexts in a favorable light.

He was very rich now, powerful in a quiet way, and he enjoyed his life.

He turned into L Street and saw the man again, the same man, and now he was very frightened and very angry. Was this some sort of fanatic who intended to assassinate him? That would be a very stupid way to end one's life, to be shot down by some lunatic who wanted to prove something to some movie star or something.

He wanted to cross the street and confront the man.

And he also wanted to retreat into his building, go to the fourth floor, close the office door, and call the police. No. Not so soon after Carroll's murder, the police.

He was white faced when he reached his office, and his secretary asked him if there was anything she could do. He was rude to her and he was a man who was never rude to women.

He forced himself into a routine. He made calls to his friends — his professional friends — to tell them about Carroll. The detectives said that it was likely that Carroll had been killed by drug dealers who were known to do all kinds of strange things, and it was true that Carroll had defended a drug dealer the previous year in a federal appeal, but, well, could there be any connection? He asked his friends this with all honesty. Clair thought his phone might be tapped, and if the police had tapped it or some other police agency, they would record the voice and the grieved tones of an honest man.

His routine was to leave each afternoon at three-thirty, to beat the rush-hour traffic back to his house above Rock Creek Park. He was a bachelor and thought he lived simply. He had a housekeeper who made him mild Mexican dishes and a chauffeur and handyman who did the shopping and drove the Cadillac.

The car was usually waiting for him across L Street at the same time each day.

He stood on the curb, looking right and left, deciding on a cab. He didn't even notice the heavy man with the limp until he was behind Clair.

"The car is coming around," Hacker said. He had his hand on Clair's bony elbow.

Clair said nothing. He thought he could not trust his voice. He felt old in that moment.

The car was a gray sedan, large and indistinguishable from other gray sedans.

Hacker opened the door on the driver's side and shoved Clair in. Devereaux was behind the wheel. Hacker climbed into the back seat and slammed the door. The car started up the street.

Devereaux began it in a monotone. Clair stared straight ahead.

"We want to know about the money that came into District Savings."

Clair said, "I haven't the faintest idea —"

"We want to know about Mona. We want to know why Carroll was killed."

Clair said, "I don't know why anyone killed Carroll."

"You see, we can watch you, we can snatch

you whenever we want."

"Who are you?"

"Friends of Mona. Friends of Carroll."

"I was his friend —"

"What about the money? What's the money for, Clair?"

"I don't know what you mean?"

"The money from Lebanon. Through Liechtenstein."

Clair realized his right hand was trembling and he willed it to stop. His right hand continued a life of its own.

"We want them. The Lebanon connection. We don't care about you, Clair, except now you have to tell us everything to make us go away."

"Do you have any idea who I am?"

"Do you know who we are?"

Silence. The car was heading along Connecticut toward Dupont Circle. The sidewalks were filled with shoppers and workers and men and women who carried their phones in briefcases. There were beggars with crude signs pleading poverty, and doormen in front of hotels to shoo them away. Clair stared at the gray cityscape and pondered the last question.

The car braked at Dupont Circle and Hacker got out of the back. He opened the passenger door and helped Clair out. "You can get a taxi here, sir," Hacker said in his gentle voice.

Clair stared at his large, impassive face. "Who are you?"

"Friends of Mona, friends of Carroll's," Hacker said. "Like the man told you."

Hacker got into the sedan next to Devereaux and they pulled away. Clair noted the Maryland license plate. A purple and white cab turned into the circle and he hailed it and took it home.

His chauffeur was in the kitchen, eating a sandwich with the cook. They were both Mexicans, and their green card privileges were hostage to Clair and his connections, all of which made them, in a technical sense, his slaves. He treated them kindly and they stole from him gently. When they had enough, they would not need the anglo anymore or his permission to live in the country.

Fernando said that Señor Dodsworth's secretary had called at one to say that Señor Dodsworth would not need the car that day. Fernando was perplexed by Señor Dodsworth's mood as the old man went into his ground-floor study and shut and locked the door.

Dodsworth thought about calling the Washington police. He turned the possibility over in his mind as carefully as any lawyer

76

contemplating the options presented by trial. He decided against it.

He called a secret number instead. The number was an 800 exchange and the computer voice answered, suggesting a number of options to the caller.

Clair chose option nine. He punched nine on the phone and heard a ringing.

The voice that answered was familiar to Clair. Clair began at the beginning of the day, with the police coming to question him, with the gray-eyed man waiting for him, down to the extraordinary kidnapping on L Street. He recited the number of the Maryland license plate.

"One question," said the slightly accented voice at the other end. "Did these men inquire about our friend? About the Dove?"

"No."

"Then it's all right. Rest easy, Mr. Dodsworth."

"I still have friends in Langley I'd like to know about this."

"You do as you will, Mr. Dodsworth, but consider everything carefully. Langley does not know about Mona —"

"I don't know about Mona. Who is Mona?"

"Ah. That's right. You don't know about Mona. Then don't inquire, Mr. Dodsworth. Good day." The voice broke the conversation with a tone of gentle regret that Clair knew was only convention.

He thought to call Britta Andrews then. But what was the good of that? If she became hesitant, she wouldn't use the line of credit arranged for her and her institute, and that was, in part, what Clair Dodsworth was paid for: to arrange transfers of loan monies through District Bank to be made available to various people he knew very little about. He was paid half a million dollars a year for his influence and for very little work, and the less he interfered with the business of District Savings — the less he interfered with the workings of International Credit Clearinghouse out of Lebanon — the better.

Why was Carroll killed? But he knew, didn't he? Carroll had spied on him.

The voice from Lebanon had told him this the week before with exquisite Middle Eastern regret. Carroll a spy. It had shocked Clair. The Arab must be mistaken, Clair had protested. But no, sadly, the Arab voice was not mistaken.

Poor Carroll, he never thought it would come to this, to Carroll's actual death, but that was not his matter, that was out of his hands entirely. Why had Carroll spied upon him?

When the Lebanese agent presented him

with the facts of it — photographs of Carroll in Clair's office late at night, faxing Clair's secret documents — Clair had been horrified and wanted to confront Carroll. But the Lebanese agent had told him it was none of his concern. The less he knew of certain things, the better his deniability. Clair had understood then that half a million dollars a year was intended to buy much more than mere influence.

Clair Dodsworth felt very tired then. He sat in the gathering gloom of his study and closed his eyes. He had not authorized anyone's death, certainly not poor Carroll's. What could he have done to save Carroll? How could he have known Carroll needed special pleading?

Clair opened his eyes and shook his head.

He could see the gray-eyed man in the shadows of the study, hear the low monotone of his voice.

Friends of Mona, friends of Carroll's.

Mona.

He sat for a long time alone in the silent darkness and thought of that name.

Seven

Britta Andrews chose the setting for the meeting as carefully as she chose her clothes. She wore a blue dress — it was her favorite color — with small gold buttons of the kind and quality that shoplifters steal. Her outfit spoke of money in an understated way. Money always spoke of power, even when it was inherited. She had chosen an intimate corner of the expensive dining room in the Mayflower Hotel. The room was not the best restaurant in Washington — far from it — but it might impress someone like the man she had come to meet. He was one of the important cogs at the moment, but he had to understand a cog does not drive the engine. She was impressing him.

He was ten minutes late when he arrived. She only had a verbal description of him because he had not allowed himself to be photographed when working for the Green movement on that business of sabotage in Denmark. But this was him, she had no doubt.

It was in the way he carried himself.

Max Escher wore a corduroy sports jacket, checked shirt, black knit tie, and chinos. His face was flushed, as though he had scrubbed it or shaved too close. His brown spiky hair was cut short and uneven. His face was square and he had a look in his eyes that gave him away. It was a look of mixed contempt and amusement, even now when he let the maître d' lead him to her table and he stood and gazed at her a moment before sitting down.

She started off establishing herself. "You're late. I don't like to be kept waiting."

"I'm never late, you must have been early." He tapped his watch. "Rolex, I wear it because it's the best watch in the world, not because I drive a BMW like some goddamned yuppie. I've got respect for time. You get that when you do what I do."

"And what do you do?" She might have been a personnel officer asking the job applicant to do tricks.

"Lady, if you don't know that by now, then we've got nothing to talk about."

"I'm interested in hiring someone who can give me a very clear idea of what he's capable of."

That made him grin. His grin was lopsided and there was a hint of malice in it. He didn't say a thing.

The waiter took their orders for drinks. He ordered something called Wild Turkey on the rocks. She had never heard of the bourbon. She ordered a glass of chardonnay.

"I guess I'm capable of anything," Max Escher said. "I guess you knew that. Depends on what you want." His voice was easy, soft, the voice of a man who did not have to impress anyone.

"I want something very large. Something larger than you arranged in Denmark."

"That wasn't much but I did it thoroughly. Clean fire, clean in and clean out."

"I'm curious about arson. Does it turn you on, Mr. Escher?"

"You call me Max and I'll call you Britta. Funny kind of name, Britta."

"Anyone with a name like Max isn't in a position to criticize," Britta said. She regretted the comeback because it had provoked another one of his damned smiles, as though she was a kid who had said something cute.

"Let's keep this formal, Mr. Escher."

He grinned at that as well. His grins were easy and often but the malice was always there, mated with the grin and the brown, mocking eyes and the slight tilt to his head as though he was looking at everything askance.

"You asked me about arson. No. Arson is just a piece of work like anything else. I'm not a firebug or a pyromaniac or whatever. They like to set fires and hang around and watch them. Those are the people who end up in the psycho wards, and for what? Half the time they don't even do it for money. Arson is just a skill like carpentry or plumbing. Or demolition."

"I want to burn something."

"No kiddin'." The drink came and he tasted it just the way Michael Horan tasted a drink. She didn't like that. Michael was on the verge of being a lush and he was weak at odd moments. People who drank were weak at odd moments. Her grandfather had never touched a drop. He was dry, flinty, and very mean. He had inspired her all her life.

"I have to make some judgment on you, Mr. Escher, to see if you're big enough for it."

"What do I have to do for you? You want me to burn down this hotel tonight? Well, I couldn't do it tonight anyway because I don't have my tools. I could set a nice fire but they got sprinklers and it wouldn't be much. You don't want to fool around with amateurs, Britta. I told you to call me Max."

"This is business, Mr. Escher."

"You look rich to me. I like that in a woman. Rich means you got the money to pay for whatever it is you want. The trouble with rich people is that they got rich by holding on to a buck, and I don't like that."

She ignored him. She sipped her chardonnay. She took another sip. He was rattling her. His speech pattern was hard to define. It rambled in a monotone, but there were little mocking turns to words as though he had everything under control and she might be some four-year-old dressed in mommy's dress.

"What brought you to your . . . profession?"

Grinned again. Damned grin.

"Uncle brought me, you might say. I was in Special Forces for a while in 'Nam and we learned how to use napalm to fry the slants, set up booby traps nearly as good as theirs. Then into EOD. That's Explosive Ordnance Disposal, you take apart bombs. That's in theory. In practice, you try to just blow the fucking things up while you keep your head down in a bunker as far away as possible. All kinds of technical information about it I won't bore you with — so many feet away per pound of explosive. . . . Well, sometimes it's a booby trap and the brass says you can't detonate it because there're civilians around or it's in the fucking embassy or something you don't have any choice but go in and take the cocksucker apart wire by wire. That will wilt a hard-on, I can tell you."

"I've lived in a man's world all my life and

I appreciate your crudities as a way of impressing me but it doesn't impress me at all," she said.

"I wasn't trying to impress you, Britta. I was trying to explain where I came by my talent for burning. I am a burning machine, but it started somewhere."

"What were you? In service?"

"I was a light colonel at the end but that was too light."

She looked puzzled.

"No slots open," he explained. "No clout. You don't move up in grade, they want you to move out. The end came six years too soon. I had twenty-four in, and now that we won the cold war, we want the soldiers to go home, so they induced me to go home. A little shit named General Bobby Lee. I was attached to his office over by the Pentagon, and he gave me an efficiency report that said 'Retire early' all over it. They don't need us anymore, Britta, I'm sure you've read the papers."

"I'm glad. I wish they'd close down the military-industrial complex tomorrow. I wish there was no army, no navy, no anything. Who are you supposed to fight?"

"Well, we kicked a little ass in Iraq." She had wounded him and he was frowning for the first time.

"You killed a hundred thousand people or

more to save a feudalist desert kingdom from a dictator. Terrific accomplishment. You managed to displace the Kurds, provoke civil war in eastern Turkey, pollute the world with half a thousand oil well fires. . . . Terrific, Mr. Escher, the army deserves our thanks."

"The army did what it was supposed to do. They told us to kill and we did it. The rest of it was the politicians. It's always the fucking politicians that fuck everything up. You radicals, you just don't get it. You think the world is supposed to be peace and love, baby, and —"

"If I was a believer in that crap, Mr. Escher, I wouldn't be thinking of hiring you."

That stopped the conversation. The waiter came over and took their orders and went away. The dining room murmured with dozens of subdued conversations.

"What do you want to hire me for?" Max Escher said.

"Something very large. Very, very large. Something bigger than you've ever done or anyone's ever done."

"They paid me fifty thousand in Denmark."

"They overpaid you."

"What do you want done?"

She saw it in his brown eyes glittering now in the dim dining-room light. He was interested. Really interested and it was beginning

86

to gnaw at him because he couldn't figure out what it was. And he wasn't showing any fear of the unknown, the way Michael had shown fear the other night when she had pulled back the edge of the secret she carried. Michael had been afraid to know.

"I want to set the world on fire," Britta said.

"You got enough money for it?"

"Can you do it? is more important."

"I told you. I can do anything."

"Prove it."

"All right," he said in an easy voice. "It just so happens that what I had in mind coincides with meeting you here."

"I called that number three weeks ago."

"I know but I was busy." Grinned. "I can prove it and then what will you do, honey? You'll get scared and back down and find a hundred reasons why right now is not a good time to go ahead with what you had in mind. I know you limousine radicals, you got the guts of spayed bitches when it comes down to it."

It wasn't the crudity of the language; it was the challenge. She said, "You're an asshole. You talk like one, you act like one. I don't deal with assholes. Why don't you just leave?"

"I could do that but I want to know about

you, Britta. Like, are you wearing a wire? You an agent for the G or something? You been blackmailed into talking to me?"

She sat still with her mouth partially opened.

"See, the way you people all work, you all know each other but you don't really check up on each other. Those Denmark terrorists might think you're a good guy but it's no sweat to them if you're not. See what I mean? Now, I can prove I can do what you want, whatever you want, but you've got to prove to me that you aren't some kind of government spy. I know, I know, but you are Senator Horan's Beltway wife, aren't you? He's a leftie but he isn't over the edge like you are, is he? Maybe the FBI forced him into forcing you into something."

"How do I prove I am who I say I am?"

"We can take a walk over to Lafayette Park. Weather's warmed up, it's a nice night —"

"And do what?"

"Oh, I'll just check you to see if you have a wire. When we get in the park."

"You won't touch me." She was angry. She was afraid now because he was still sitting there with a cockeyed look on his face and that grin had no warmth to it at all.

"Do it that way and we're friends and we can do business. Do it the other way . . ."

"The other way."

"Break your neck."

"We are sitting in the dining room of the Mayflower —"

"I once broke a slant's neck sitting in the lobby of the Hilton in Saigon and nobody knew he was dead until I was practically in Japan. You know, I like you radicals, you all hate the military and all that, but where would you get a few good men like me if it wasn't for the military? Like that guy got himself blown up in that bomb factory in New York a few years ago, maybe ten years ago —"

"That was my father." Ice cold.

That stopped him. He shook his head in silence for a moment. "I'm sorry, Brit, I didn't know that, didn't even remember his name. But what kind of Mickey Mouse was that, making dynamite in a house in Queens, for Christ's sake? What was he going to blow up besides himself? Fucking amateurs ruin it, draw too much attention to it."

"And what about you, Max?" She didn't even notice she was using his first name. "You can handle anything, right?"

"Just about. There. Now I've admitted everything and nobody has come storming in, so if you're wearing a wire, maybe it isn't working or maybe you're just taped or something. You want to show me?"

She wasn't afraid of him, she really wasn't afraid of anyone. And then she thought he really could break her neck.

She looked at his hands on the table. They weren't that large but they loomed large in her mind's eye. She was angry with him and she was afraid of him and the mix of emotions was very exciting in that moment.

"When do you want to take that walk?" she said.

"Well, you got some guts then, if you're bluffing."

"I never bluff."

"People who say 'never' are always lying."

"So are people who say 'always.'"

He nodded. "We could just take a little stroll now."

"You don't want dinner?"

"I've eaten here," he said.

"I might be hungry."

"Sure, suit yourself."

But they did leave, to the consternation of the maître d', who refused to present them a check, who wished Miss Andrews a good evening, and nodded to the ill-dressed man in the corduroy jacket.

It was a perfect night in Lafayette Park across the street from the White House lawn. Korean students on a hunger strike were bedded on mattresses, their signs calling on the U.S. to make Korea a nuclear-free zone. Britta paused and looked at them and read their signs.

Britta said, "No one wants nuclear weapons. No one ever wanted them."

He had her arm. He strolled in a swinging, big-gestured way, smiling at the protesters as well as the homeless woman with her shopping cart full of possessions, bedded down on a cot for the night. She had lived there for more than ten years.

"We should have dropped one on Hanoi and that would have ended the whole god-damned war. Just dropped a small one. They would have shit in their little black pajamas."

"Didn't we do enough once before?" she asked. Her voice was cold and full of contempt.

He turned to her. "Did it twice in fact. And ended the war with the Japs. There's a lot to be said for bombs. I wasn't one to make fun of the air boys, I even liaisoned with them once on TDY in England. Y'know, when we were pasting them with B-52 raids every day, I mean over Hanoi, they came close to quitting, but then that candy-ass Johnson stopped the raids because Jane Fonda didn't like them or some such reason. But years later, the Viets said that they were close to suing for peace because of those B-52 strikes, they were unnerving the population up there. Give peace a chance. Christ, I hate you people."

"But not our money."

"Not your money," Max Escher said. "Business is business."

"What are you going to do to prove you can do this thing I've got in mind?"

He stopped. They were on the grass. Traffic grumbled on Pennsylvania Avenue. He embraced her. She felt his hands on the silky back of her dress, tracing the outline of the back of the bra, dropping down her back to her waist. He grinned and she looked up at him.

"I hope you don't think I'm taking any personal pleasure in this."

"But you are," she said.

"Naw, it's just being careful. I can have women, I don't have to go 'round copping a feel. Besides, you're not my type, I like really big women."

She couldn't speak. His breath was on her and she could smell him, a strong, dark smell. He touched her breasts and traced the brassiere lines to the strap on her shoulders and then stopped and stepped back. "You're probably about a size two or four. I had a girl in Saigon was about that, she was very nice. But I like a woman about up to here, about one twenty, you know, someone's got some meat."

"You talk like a loser, Max, I can't take a chance with a loser. Are you through?"

"Do I? People of my class, is that it? Loser. I'll show you about five tomorrow morning who's a loser." It was a punk's stance and a punk's way of talking. He really was a punk.

"Five? Sunday?"

"I said oh five hundred hours Sunday, that's what I said little Miss Rich Bitch," Max Escher said. There was no ease to him now, he was sprung, his face was pure malice without the grin. Only the voice remained flat.

"What happens then? You set fire to those Korean demonstrators? Or you nuke them instead?"

"The Pentagon. I worked there my last assignment, I told you that if you were listening in the restaurant, worked for General Bobby Lee, little cocksucker."

"What are you going to do? Kill him?"

"I don't think so. He wouldn't be working that hour of Sunday morning. I don't know who I'm going to kill."

That got her for a moment. The word *kill* was uttered without concern, without emphasis.

"Kill? Doing what? What are you proving to me? I don't want a bomb expert."

"I know what you want, little Miss Rich Bitch, I was listening to you. Why wouldn't you do the courtesy of listening to me? Was I talking about bombing any fucking thing, was I? You should learn to listen."

"I'm listening, for God's sake, what do you think I'm doing in this fucking park ruining my fucking heels for?"

They were both agitated now, their eyes were locked on each other, breathing hard.

"Jesus." He held up his hand. "Take it easy. I just wanted to know if you were listening."

"I'm listening, Escher."

"Don't wear out my name. And don't wear it out with your boyfriend."

"He doesn't know your name and you talk like a punk."

"I know, I know, people like you only want people like me when they get themselves so fucked up that they need someone to bail them out," Escher said.

"I said I was listening. It's cold."

"You ought to've worn a coat."

"Say what you're going to say —"

"I told you if you listened. I said I was going to burn something and then I said I was working at the Pentagon. So what do you think I'm going to prove to you — that I can do the biggest job you got with no sweat? I mean, Britta, honey, what do you think I'm going to do to prove it to you — and get back at those cocksuckers for fucking up my life?"

She took a step back on her heels and nearly fell when one heel caught in a tuft of grass.

He grinned at her. She stared into that grin.

The Pentagon.

The biggest building in the world.

She saw it in the grin, in the breathless simplicity of his manner with her.

He was going to burn it.

Eight

The computers in intelligence all went down at 0400 hours Sunday. But that was not part of what happened an hour later, just the usual way machines failed in the frayed nerve center of the Department of Defense in the Pentagon building.

Brig. Gen. Robert E. Lee was notified by G2 at 0430 hours that the surveillance tape done overnight on Devereaux would not be edited in time for the morning briefing because the computer outage was a symptom of the power outage that had also affected the editing room. Bobby Lee cursed the world for a moment and then hung up the phone and went back to sleep in his rental apartment in northwest Washington.

The fires all began burning between 0500 and 0505 hours on Sunday. There were nineteen separate fires. Each fire began in a plastic-skinned automatic coffee maker rigged to become an incendiary device.

The coffee makers were all alike. In their

manufacture, each had been fitted with a heating element that was controlled by a rather simple fuse. If the element overheated, the fuse connector broke the connection exactly as a circuit breaker or screw-in fuse in a service box breaks an overload.

The coffee makers had been altered. The fuse had simply been bypassed by a wire connecting the two sides of the heating element. The wire connector was activated by a second and serial timing device apart from the automatic coffee maker's own timer. This enhanced timer was set in all the coffee machines fourteen days earlier. To the hour of 0500 Sunday, this last Sunday of November.

When the coffee makers all went on automatically in the darkest hour of this Sunday, the heating elements quickly melted down through the plastic storage handle and began to ignite the accelerant stored in the hollow of the handles.

The accelerant was a gooey mix of Styrofoam bits in a small mix of gasoline and a powdery white substance, which a civilian would call rocket fuel. This solid-state rocket propellant had a burn temperature of 3,500 degrees Fahrenheit. At that temperature, nothing on earth could be used to put the fire out until the rocket fuel consumed itself. The resulting fire could burn through any common substance. It could burn a hole into concrete and only gradually, as the rocket "soup" consumed itself and as the temperatures it created into fires began to lower in intensity, could common retardants like water be used to any effect. All of this would be noted in a voluminous final report on the fires issued a year later.

In all of this, there was not a single explosion. Only fires throughout the immense building on the Potomac River.

It was the deadest time of the week and the deadest hour of the day, even in a building that knows no sleep.

The electrical workers on duty were all in the subbasement, trying to find the power overload that had shut down all the computer screens in intelligence. If the overload had extended to the other levels, the coffee makers would not have fired off so precisely between 0500 and 0505 hours.

There were smoke detectors in several of the rooms containing the lethal coffee machines but several of these were out of order. General Services Administration later claimed it had maintained the detectors but that they were disconnected by military and civilian personnel annoyed by sudden false alarms. The first fire alarm was not sounded until 0521 hours, and by then flames had already melted through containers in a dozen rooms and were spreading poisonous clouds of toxic fumes. Most of the rooms were locked and shuttered for the weekend.

The fires broke out on three of five levels of the immense five-sided building on the Potomac River. Because there are so many fires so often in that huge building, the personnel aware of the presence of fire took a long time to realize the immensity of what was happening. They could not believe in sabotage, in arson, against this leviathan building that is the center of the military earth.

A twentieth fire began at 0515 hours in the Pentagon Metro underground station of the Yellow Line that connects the building on the west side of the river with the rest of the District on the east. Acrid black smoke billowed across the platform and raced up the escalator stairs to the upper platform that sweeps into the entry of the Pentagon.

In B ring on the second level inside the building, a specialist five in Communications named Oral Flemings opened the door of his section's radio room without feeling the door for heat. He had heard the fire alarms and he wanted information on them.

An immense backdraft blew him to eternity. The sudden rush of oxygen into the smoldering room blew the flames into a bomb-burst intensity, and Oral Flemings died of sudden suffocation while the napalm-like flames fried his skin crisp black.

Here and there, the separate fires detoured around asbestos ceilings and walls to find new bridges to feed their flames.

The electricians in the subbasement tried to get elevators up but the elevators shut down. Electrical surges up and down the lines now blacked out more computers in more levels.

All the sabotaged coffeepots had melted down totally and the rocket fuel was totally consumed.

By 0546, on the fourth floor, some of the interior walls began to collapse, and in some places the fires were burning hot enough to break down inflammable materials like steel and stone and melt and twist and pulverize them until they could not be trusted to bear the weight of the structure above. Survivors of the Sunday-morning fires said they had heard groans in the building during the ordeal and thought the groans had come from the building itself.

Navy Ymn2c. Clark S. Johnson, a specialist radio operator on the third level, died of smoke inhalation halfway up a stairwell. The fire extinguisher in his right hand eventually melted into the flesh and bone and fused with them. He won a posthumous medal for courage.

On the same floor Marine Gun. Sgt. Malcolm Lowe of the marine liaison office with the Defense Intelligence Agency tried to put out the fire that had melted the coffee maker. He burned his hands and then broke a window and jumped to the concrete walk at the north entrance of the building. He broke his right leg in two places and fractured both hands.

The Metro station fire spread very quickly to the corridor of the Pentagon's south entrance and punched out the glass doors at the top of the stairs. Glass splattered security personnel in the cubicle to the left of the entrance. Army Lt. Lorraine L. Sonderby was cut horribly all over her chest and face by flying shards of glass. She survived by crawling on her bloodied hands and knees toward the underground shopping kiosk west of the subway entrance.

The Pentagon's own fire brigade reacted more slowly than they later claimed. The water mains inside the Pentagon are old and underwhelming in their efficiency — one main burst fighting a small fire that nearly knocked out all communications in the Pentagon during the Iraqi invasion of Kuwait.

The overwhelmed brigade called for outside reinforcements at 0612 hours and alarms rang in company houses in Arlington, Alexandria, and in the District. From a dozen firehouses the empty morning streets were filled with sirens and flashing lights and the rumble of pumpers. The wails boomed across the solemn dead ground of Arlington National Cemetery above the Pentagon and down the Jefferson Davis parkway from Alexandria. It was dreadful to hear the sirens in the darkness of that Sunday morning.

The duty officer in intelligence finally reached Brig. Gen. Robert E. Lee at 0646. He was calling from a mobile radio truck set up in the south parking lot. Lieutenant Krause could still see the smoke and flames, and the ambulances were still carting away the injured, dead, and dying.

"The Pentagon's on fire," he shouted twice into the phone, and now Bobby Lee showed why he was a general. His tone of voice was very calm, very soothing, talking to the lieutenant, who seemed on the verge of hysteria.

"Nobody knows what happened, just fires all of a sudden all over the place," Lieutenant Krause shouted.

"Take it easy, Lieutenant, what about our section?"

"We caught it too. Sergeant Mowry is missing, we couldn't find him before we had to get out." He suddenly sobbed, a single and terrible sob.

"Take it easy, son," Bobby Lee said. "I'm coming right down. You want to send a signal to Major Hornsby, Major Scott, call up Colonel Jack Cavett, he was EOD liaison, maybe we can use that right now." He went down through the Rolodex of his memory, calmly issuing names and orders of instruction. It calmed down the lieutenant, it set out a course of things to do.

Bobby Lee was ready when his driver came around at 0719. The drive to the Pentagon took twenty-one minutes.

His eyes were bright in the darkness of the car, the battle-bright way.

The last casualty of the Sunday-morning fires was a specialist six in Ordnance from Aberdeen Proving Ground named Monica Daniels. She jumped from the fourth-floor window when the flames and smoke and heat pushed her, and she landed in the parking lot forty-six feet below. She broke her pelvis, three ribs, both legs, and her right arm. She lay in the parking lot for twenty-six minutes before an ambulance pulled up and two civilian paramedics jumped out and set up a stretcher beside her. They talked to her while injecting her with a stimulant, and they said she talked to them but none of them ever remembered what had been said. She lived.

Nine

Senator Michael Horan had wanted to have sex with Britta Andrews. It was dark in the bedroom, dark outside, and when he kissed her, she had nearly turned away from him. But then he had touched her between her naked thighs and she had felt some urge that was her own, that would make it possible.

They had sex, and then he fell away from her and began to snore, and she was dissatisfied and very awake. She had risen from the wrinkled wide bedsheets and gone to the bathroom and taken a shower. She had put on her red satin robe and knotted the belt and gone to the kitchen. She had selected a piece of celery and a glass of milk from the refrigerator and taken them into the living room. At that point she heard the sirens for the first time and realized it was around six in the morning.

Fire engines. Many of them.

She finished her milk and put down the glass on the onyx coffee table.

She sat in the darkness and listened to the wailing sounds of the city stirred rudely to life for an emergency. What had he done? But then, she was the only person in the world who knew that Max Escher had set fire to the Pentagon.

The thought stirred in her belly. She closed her eyes and saw his eyes and that lopsided grin.

She felt his hands on her, touching her, feeling along the outline of her brassiere and then touching her lower, along her back and thighs.

She opened her eyes and reached for the remote on the onyx coffee table. She clicked on the television and selected CNN.

"— to the fire in the Pentagon. Responses are now coming from engine companies in the District as well as the Virginia suburbs of Alexandria and Arlington. We have reports, unconfirmed reports so far, that there are six injured persons and that one of the injured was a woman who jumped from a third-floor window. We now go to Leslie Fisher, who is at the scene."

She shivered.

Was she cold?

Max had said he could touch her or he could break her neck. He had offered her the choice with a nonchalance that had frightened her.

Yes. And fascinated her. Michael Horan was violent and selfish at times and very witty and sometimes just a bore. What was this Max Escher, who could offer her a choice between being humiliated or being killed?

He was burning the Pentagon.

Her eyes were shining as she watched the pictures on the television screen.

He was big enough, then, for what she wanted. She endured the meetings with the other radicals, with the Greens, with the idealists and the merely hopeful, she endured the wild-eyed political musings, because it was all she had to work with. Her grandfather had said you have to work with the material at hand. Use someone like Michael Horan with all his flaws because he was the best thing available. And keep looking for someone like Max Escher, who was the weapon. She could pull the trigger now, she was sure of it. Max Escher would go off and that would be the mark she would leave on the world — not some pathetic attempt to make explosives in a house in Queens like her father, but a real mark, a landmark that changed history. The woman on the bus, Rosa Parks, or Roe v. Wade or . . . why not? Britta Andrews. And Max was the reliable weapon she had been looking for.

Like any weapon, he was dangerous. He

had an outlaw edge to him. She would control that. She could do that, control people, but not always get them to perform adequately.

"— the Yellow Line is shut down because of the fire in the Pentagon Metro station, and we go to —"

"Damn," Britta said to the screen. "Damn you, Escher, you did it, just like you said you'd do it, you really did it. All right, Mr. Max Escher, you punk bastard, you impressed me. You really did."

"What are you doing, Brit?"

She turned. He was naked in the doorway of the bedroom, his hair tousled, his belly thickened by age and excess, his shoulders and hairy chest beginning to slacken after years of indulgence. In that moment, she saw no attraction in him.

"Didn't you hear the fire engines?"

"They woke me up again, I thought I was dreaming them."

"Really, Michael, get a robe on."

He blinked at her and turned back to the bedroom. She wanted to savor this alone and turned back to the television screen. Live pictures of flames leaping from broken windows lit the screen.

But Michael came out of the bedroom again. He was wearing a blue terry-cloth robe.

"What is it?"

"The Pentagon. Someone set fire to the Pentagon." She glanced up at him.

He was frowning, scratching at the hairs of his chest.

"The Pentagon," he repeated in a dull, thick voice.

"I know who it was," she said. She smiled.

He sat down on the couch next to her and looked at her. "What do you mean you know who it was?"

"You wanted to know, darling. All my secrets. So I'm sharing them now," she said.

"He burned the Pentagon? Some kind of a bomb?"

"They haven't said that." She couldn't tell him everything but it was hard to keep it a secret. She wanted some credit just for knowing. "I'm sure it wasn't a bomb. That would be too crude."

"Who burned the Pentagon?"

"Someone." Teasing and smiling.

"Britta, stop this."

"You don't want to know his name, do you, Michael?"

"What does this have to do with Dove?"

She liked that. She hadn't brought up the Dove again after her first hint that night in Sam and Harry's, and he was making the connection now because he guessed the Dove was about violence. Just when she thought to give up on Michael, he would show this sparkling insight.

"Everything."

For a moment, they were silent, watching the news correspondents describe the scene. Then Michael reached for the remote and muted the sound. He looked at her and waited.

"You know what I've always thought," she said in a low voice. "I'm bored with meetings, compromises, preaching to the converted. I won't throw myself in front of a freight train, even if it's in a good cause. I'm not the martyr type. It suited my father, but my grandfather thought martyrs were useful fools for people to manipulate."

"Your grandfather? You quote your grand-father? One of the great robber barons of the century?" It genuinely surprised him. Until now, Michael thought Britta would have hated her grandfather.

"Not what he did but how he did it. He could truly use people for a purpose. Everyone wants to use people or wants to be used. That's the way it is." She was staring at the screen and he saw her in profile.

"This person. This person who set this fire in the Pentagon. What is he, Britta? Does he want to be used?"

"Yes," Britta said.

"To do what?"

"To do something for me."

"Something that involves the money from that bank. The money that Clair Dodsworth arranged for you."

"Yes." Then she looked at him, waited.

He shook his head.

"You don't want to know," she said.

"I know too much. You think this is a game, Britta? Someone set fire to the Pentagon and you know who it is."

"What are you going to do, Michael?"

"I don't know."

"I do. You're going to do what I want you to do."

There it was.

"No. You're too dangerous, Britta. You've turned too dangerous for me."

"I was always too dangerous. You weren't afraid. You let the press see me and touch me and you went and won your re-election despite it. Come on, Michael. I'm real. And dangerous too."

"I should just leave you."

She stared at him with her cold, blue eyes framed by that beautiful face and her short blond hair. Just leave. Just like that.

"I think you should, Michael."

"Britta."

"No, Michael. Don't touch me."

He held her arm.

"Let me go, Michael."

"Britta, you're getting into something deep. Clair and the money in the bank and whoever this . . . this pyromaniac is —"

"You're weak, Michael, I see that, I didn't see that before. Let my arm go."

He dropped his hand but held his earnest pose. "Britta, I didn't mean anything."

"You threaten me one minute, now you tell me you didn't mean it."

"I didn't threaten you, for God's sake."

"I told you you didn't want to know everything. Then I trusted you. I was wrong to trust you."

"You weren't wrong."

"Go home, Michael, we don't have anything to talk about. I'm sorry I thought you were stronger."

"I am," he said.

"No. Go away, go find another girl."

"There isn't another girl."

"Then go back to your ex. She's waiting for you. You can crawl back into her bed. She'll forgive you."

"Britta, don't be a bitch —"

"But I am, Michael." She looked at the fire on the screen. "I am a bitch." Rich bitch, little Miss Rich Bitch, he'd show her that he wasn't a punk.

"I want to stay," he said.

"I want you to go."

"Don't throw me out."

"You've thrown yourself out."

"It's six in the morning."

"Yes. You'll have to call Haley out of a sound sleep or get a cab. I don't care what you do. You can walk home."

"Britta, listen —"

But she wasn't listening to him. She was watching the fire on the screen. She was thinking, planning a step ahead for when she would call Michael back to her. Planning what she would tell Max Escher next.

Ten

Devereaux never wanted to tell her because it was too painful and because it would share the burden when he thought he should carry it alone. In the end he did tell her about Mona, but only the part about Mona the agent and how this Mona was lost in Lebanon on a secret mission that he had approved. He didn't tell her everything.

That had been weeks ago and Rita Macklin had never brought it up again. She had worked in her job as a journalist on the magazine and he had worked in his. She had made him suppers late at night after he took the last Metro home. Four days ago he had told her he would not be working late at night anymore.

This Sunday morning was full of the wail of sirens. They were up at gray dawn. Without speaking to each other, they had dressed in the semi-darkness of the apartment. When they were together, they had developed the habit of walking the streets of the empty city at this empty time. Now they were walking toward the cathedral. They seldom talked on morning walks. They shared the silence of each other and the empty city. But on this fog-shrouded morning the silence was shattered for long minutes by the sounds of distant sirens.

"I wonder what the sirens are for?" Rita said. She turned to look at him. Her face was bright with health. She wore her red hair short now. She wore a green sweat suit and swung her arms when they walked. Devereaux, stuck in the drab conformity of his existence in intelligence, dressed as casually as he could, which was very formal for a morning walk. He wore chinos and a black turtleneck and a gray windbreaker.

They walked on in silence, leaving her question behind them. The great cathedral was finished now, after a century of stonework, and its grounds were still gloomy with night in the gray morning light. There was fog everywhere in patches and the streets were utterly deserted. Wisconsin Avenue stretched before them, all the way to Bethesda, where she had first lived. He had walked all the way to her apartment more than once.

A jogger came around the corner ahead of them on Wisconsin Avenue and jogged slowly and steadily down the walk toward them. The jogger wore a red stocking cap pulled low on his forehead. He wore earphones and a yellow Walkman tape recorder was attached to a belt at his waist. Devereaux suddenly stopped and waited for the jogger to pass them.

"What is it?" she said.

"I don't know," Devereaux said.

"It's just a runner."

"I saw him yesterday."

"He lives around here."

"I saw him on L Street. I was watching a man on L Street and I saw a jogger in a red stocking cap at the corner of Connecticut. He stopped and he had a yellow radio. He looked at me."

"What's it about? Who were you watching?"

"It's still the same thing."

"You said you wouldn't be late anymore at night, I thought it was finished, whatever it was."

"It's more complicated now," Devereaux said. He began to walk again. But Rita Macklin held back.

"Is the business with Mona finally finished?" she asked him. Gently.

He walked on as though to leave this question behind. Then stopped and turned.

"No. It's not over."

"Are you close?"

"Closer."

"Where's the answer?"

"Part of it's here. In the District."

"Why don't you have to work until the last Metro train anymore?"

"Because the man I met at night is dead."

Rita looked at him. She had wanted to ask this for a long time. It was unasked because she was afraid of the answer, the real answer, and not the one he pretended to give her once. "Who was Mona?"

"An agent. I told you before."

"But who was she?"

"I don't understand that."

"Who was she, Dev?"

Her face was beautiful in her way. Her eyes were green and fresh and her smile, when she smiled, was so honest and open that it made sunshine for that moment.

"I worked with her. In East Germany. A long time ago."

"Did you love her?"

"I don't think so."

"Was she your lover?"

"No."

"Are you lying to me?"

"No."

"I don't believe you."

He stared at her.

"I put up with secrets. I put up with that. But not lies, Dev. Not now, not after everything."

He said nothing.

"I wouldn't care if you had her as your lover. If you even thought you loved her. It was a long time ago. Before you met me . . ."

"I went into black with Mona in 1986. After I knew you. I was gone six weeks."

"I remember. I didn't know where you were gone to but I'd just get that damned report from Section once a week, nonsense about the trip being extended. Just to let me know you weren't dead."

She stopped and bit her lip. She had a lovely slight overbite.

"You were lovers and now you feel guilty about her. That's what this is about, isn't it?" And she was angry all of a sudden.

"It's about more than Mona. It's about six dead agents sent in separately with no contact between them and never coming out of Lebanon. I approved the operation. I was senior adviser. I greened it and they died for it. It's more than Mona."

"No, it isn't. Was she a pretty woman?"

"She was pretty, I suppose. Not the way you are."

"What was she like?"

"I can't say that I know. I know she was

a good intelligence agent."

"And what else was she?"

"She saved my life in Leipzig. She got me out of a bad thing. I made a mistake and I should have been killed and she got me out."

"Otherwise, I would have called up for my weekly message and they would have sent a man to my door instead, is that it?" Rita said.

"I suppose they would have. We weren't married but they knew about you. I think they would have sent someone around to talk to you," Devereaux said.

"So this is for Mona?"

And she saw that rare thing in him. It wasn't tears. He never cried. He would retreat into the arctic cold of his face, of his gray eyes, retreat and tumble back down a steep hill inside him until she saw the lost, panicked, frightened thing in his eyes that replaced tears. Sometimes she had wished he could merely cry because then she could have comforted him.

"Devereaux," she said.

He shook his head at her.

She took his hand.

"For Mona," he said, explaining it all to her.

Eleven

Lt. Col. John S. (Jack) Cavett did not hear the pager on the nightstand until his wife shook him awake.

Well, not his wife anymore.

He made a sound, opened his eyes, reached for the pager. He pressed the button to stop the screeching beep and blinked at the number displayed on the LED screen. "What the hell do they want? It's Sunday. The war is over."

He threw his legs over the side of the bed and sat there a moment, elbows on thighs, staring at the floor. The floor just lay there, waiting for Jack to make the first move. He licked his lips until they weren't dry anymore.

"What is it now?" she said.

"How the hell do I know?" He scratched his hair and then his chest. He licked his lips some more.

"Don't talk to me like that, Jack. We're not married anymore and I don't have to take that."

"Sorry." He was still licking and scratching

himself awake. His back was to her. Liz Palmer Cavett. Make that Liz Palmer Cavett Fredericks. Or make that just Liz because she didn't really ever belong to anyone, not her parents, not Jack Cavett, certainly not to little old Bob Fredericks down in Chicago.

"You have to go?"

"I don't know what I have to do. I carry that fucking pager because it's SOP for DIA personnel when we're on a mission. And, as General Bobby Lee says, we are always on a mission. I forgot to tell you last night I was on a mission, didn't I?"

"I thought you were off on the weekends. We used to be off on weekends. I thought we were going to fuck all morning."

He smiled at her. "Maybe we are."

She ran her hand along his thigh. "You're still a good fuck, Jack. I have to say that. You're about an eight, I'd say. You're not that big but you use it well and that's pretty good."

"You've done enough comparison shopping," Jack Cavett said.

"I've had a good share," she said and laughed. She could do it to him pretty good, stick in a pin and take a hit when it came. She'd wanted to tie him up once when they were first married just for fun and just for fun he let her and then she made it scary. Liz could turn it scary even if you thought you knew her, even if you were in love with her. Liz was like a haunted house sometimes, rooms opening onto rooms that you didn't want to go into.

"Come here, Jack, I want you to do me," Liz said.

Her voice was pure sex, rough and scratchy like wool pulled across a baby's skin. That was just a physical quirk, though, without intent. Her voice turned rough when she was sixteen and her neck was broken in an auto accident. The accident had damaged her voice.

He wanted to do her. It was the reason they were in this room in the Washington Hotel on Sunday morning. Liz never lost her looks. She was forty-two going on twenty-two; her hair was brown and soft and full and her eyes were the color of blue diamonds. If she wanted you, you came running.

Instead, Jack got up, pulled up his boxer shorts, and walked to the credenza where the telephone sat. He picked up the receiver, punched eight to get an outside line, and then dialed the number displayed on the LED screen.

"You piss me off, Jack," Liz said.

"Just let me see what this is about. Some fuckup. Someone accidentally dialed me up when he was trying to page someone else. I'll jump on your bones in a minute, Liz."

"Maybe I won't be in the mood then."

In the mood. Sure, like it was a casual thing.

"Section Three Four, Sergeant Tompkins, sir."

"This is Colonel Cavett."

"Yes, sir, Colonel, sir. General Lee wants you, sir, on the ASAP basis, sir." Pause. The sergeant was thinking about telling a colonel to get his ass moving. "That's the way the general phrased it, sir."

"General Lee on duty today?"

"Yes, sir, he's calling everyone, sir."

"What's this about, Sergeant?"

"About the fire, sir."

"What about the fire?"

"The fire, sir, in the building. In the Pentagon, sir. It's on television."

"What's on television?"

"Building was sabotaged by terrorists, sir, around oh five hundred, bombs or something, there's been a fire and a red alert, sir."

"Slow it down, Sergeant. Someone set a fire in the Pentagon building, is that it?"

"Lots of fires, dozens of fires, sir, every level, sir."

"Is the building under attack?"

"No, sir."

"Then where the hell is Section? Are you in the building?"

"No, sir. We're in a trailer rigged up in the south parking lot, sir."

"Then why is he calling me?"

It was a question beyond a sergeant's knowledge and it was unfairly asked. They both knew it. Sergeant Tompkins tried, however: "Maybe because you're EOD liaison, sir. If there were bombs involved, sir."

"I'll be there on the double, Sergeant. Thanks."

"Yes, sir."

He held the phone in his hand and looked at the receiver. EOD. Bombs. Explosive Ordnance Disposal. That had been his specialty for ten years. He had gone into EOD because he thought there was an understanding it would lead to a slot where he had a chance at bird colonel before his retirement. When he left his last tour in Germany, they had stashed him in Section Three Four in the Defense Intelligence Agency headquarters in the Pentagon. While he was waiting for his early retirement, it was a good place to hide out the last few months. Everyone was being edged out of service ahead of time, it seemed. They didn't need all those old soldiers who hadn't made it to general by the time their years were in. Jack could have argued that he had a good record, good efficiency reports. He could have argued, but it came down to clout on the general staff and Jack Cavett didn't have any. As for the understanding he thought was implicit in choosing EOD, well, it was a one-way understanding. He had never been a friendly, schmoozing sort of career man who could lick his way up the ladder. All he had ever wanted to be was a soldier and being a soldier had been enough for him. He had twenty-three years in and he was going on forty-six and this was all it was ever going to be and all the further it was ever going to go. He was glad they had quartered him at Indianhead Naval Propellant Plant down south of the District. It was an EOD school and he felt comfortable to be around EOD people in the last days.

"So where is it that's more important than being with me right here?" Liz said, breaking his thoughts.

He replaced the receiver and turned to look at her lovely nakedness on the tangled sheets.

"There's a fire in the Pentagon."

"There was bound to be. What a rotten old building."

"A lot of fires. Arson. Terrorism of some kind."

"What do they think you are, a fireman?"

"They told me to come," he said.

"They think you're in quarters at Indianhead, don't they? It'll take you an hour to get to the Pentagon from there. So come on over here, Jack, and put out another fire."

"I've got to go," he said.

"Duty calls. Fuck the fire. Fuck the Pentagon. Fuck the army. I want you to fuck me."

"You did your best on the last," Jack said.

"Shut up, Jack. Just shut up and come over here and let me suck your cock."

Liz looked like a million and dressed like a fine lady and she could make a sailor on San Diego shore leave blush. She always had dressed well, even on a first lieutenant's pay. They would show up at some damned social evening, the old officers-and-wives thing, and he would be standing there with a weak scotch in hand and a bleak expression, waiting to escape, and he would hear her laugh in that throaty way with the general and then she would come over to him when she had socialized enough to suit her, and she would slip her arm in his and say something that was incredibly obscene. Just whisper it into his ear. Play out a scenario that would have been pornography if it had been written down. He would put down his drink and she would lead him back to quarters and then they would play it out. The one Liz — the bawd — was clothed all the while in the other — loving, army wife Liz, who did not have any lady friends.

Sure. Why the hell not? Fuck the army, as Liz said. She had drummed it into him in the last two really bad years of their marriage.

"Come here," she said.

The curtains were drawn tight against the gray-morning city, and this room was transformed into a dirty little secret that defied time and the world. He went to the bed and she opened her mouth for him and tasted him. He could look down at her face and she was looking up at him, lying on her side on the bed, while she did it to him.

Not too much. When she thought he was ready, she pulled him on top of her.

He fell on her in bed and entered her and she climaxed almost right away. Then it was slower, they both wanted it slower, it was like a lingering kiss between them. She nibbled on his earlobe, and when she began to go faster because she couldn't help it, when she was making little cries against him in that throaty voice, it was something other than love or a kiss. Perhaps it was a sharing of loneliness. She shuddered as he shuddered and that was all it was.

It had been love once, not just the sex. Love when they had the kid and then the kid died. Maybe it would have been all right if that hadn't happened. Tommy would have been about a senior in college now and that would have been all right. Jack Cavett knew people who raised kids who didn't love each other, and he knew people who didn't have kids who did, so maybe it wasn't the kid at all. But not them, not he and Liz. After Tommy died and they knew there weren't going to be any more kids, they still had sex. The love part just left quietly, like a guest at a wake signing the register and putting on his hat and going away without saying anything to anyone. They had sex for a long time after the thing about the kid and they fooled themselves into thinking the stranger hadn't left. And then she had other sex with others and she never fooled herself into thinking it was anything like love. She never called it that. But she and Jack fooled each other for a long time.

She was cheating on Bob Fredericks now but it wasn't cheating. It was just getting some sex, some variety. She could make those blue diamond eyes sing across a telephone line, and when she told Jack Cavett she was going to be staying in D.C. for the weekend and she wanted him to get his ass over to the hotel — well, he could see those eyes just by hearing her voice. He had to come running. Everyone was so careful about sex now but Liz was born reckless, like the time she was in that auto crash and came out of it OK. Better than OK, with a broken neck and sexy new voice. She lived, she really lived, and it amazed men. In a colorless, careful, politically and socially correct world, she was Technicolor, a loose cannon, anything you wanted to say about her was OK and was probably true.

"I wish you had kept it hard, I really want to do it again."

"I'm only human." He nearly smiled at her but that would have broken his heart.

"Only a mere man."

"The weaker vessel. God intended it that way. Otherwise, you couldn't stand us." He kissed her on the forehead and got up. "I have to shower and shave."

"You don't have a uniform."

"Bobby Lee won't mind."

"They'll know you weren't on base. At Indianhead, I mean."

"Maybe they already know. Maybe I don't care."

"Careful, Jack. You're falling out of love with the army."

"I'm not leaving the army. They left me."

"Like I left you."

"Like you left me."

"Don't you hate me, Jack?"

"No, Liz."

"Why?"

"Because it wasn't your fault."

"Whose was it? Yours?"

"It's nobody's fault what happens."

"You let me do what I wanted to do."

"I had to, Liz."

"Why?"

"Because I loved you. You never loved me the way I loved you, so I had to let you do what you wanted."

She bit her lip. She said nothing.

He went into the bathroom and turned on the shower and stepped into the tub. The water fell on him, and he thought of whether he still loved her. Well, what of it?

He shaved with an electric razor from his Dopp kit and stared at his face in the mirror. He always shaved with an electric, always had. He had hated the one part of basic when he had to shave with a razor. He didn't know why he hated the blade. In 'Nam, when he was in the jungle, he never shaved at all rather than use a razor. His beard had been red then. His blond hair was cut short, not GI cut but neat and short.

He dressed in the bedroom while Liz watched him from bed as she had done so many times. Like a lot of soldiers, he had no real feeling for mufti. His clothes were conservative and behind the times because they never wore out. He picked up his service tie — black wool — and started to make a knot.

"Nobody wears a tie on Sundays unless they're going to church, Jack."

"Well. I guess you're right, Liz." He put the tie carefully into the small weekend bag. He placed the Dopp kit on top of it. He wore a brown tweed sports coat he had bought in Scotland years ago. When was that? When they were stationed in Mildenhall in Suffolk. Thirteen years ago? They were still married then, even though the kid was dead and love had walked out of the funeral parlor. The tweed was made on Harris and it would never wear out. Guaranteed never to wear.

He turned to look at her. She was naked still and she nodded at him. "You'll pass inspection."

"When do you go back?"

"I had a booking for late this afternoon. Since we're not going to have fun this morning, maybe I'll just go back now and surprise Bob."

"Maybe Bob will surprise you."

"Jack, not Bob. You're an eight and he's a four if he tries hard. I made sure of that before we got married, there's only room for one sleep-around in a marriage. I ornament Bob. He wears me at his parties and testimonial dinners. I'm good to show off to the chairman of Northern Illinois Power and Poop. He frankly wouldn't mind if I screwed the chairman."

"He said that?"

"No, Jack, I said that. I get Bob hard twice a week, regular as clockwork, and he's in pig heaven. If I wear my 'fuck me' heels to dinner, Bob worries all night because he's going to have to manage an erection."

Jack smiled. She could say anything and did. In the old days together, she would draw verbal portraits of the other officers, of their wives, Jack's friends and enemies. She always got it right.

"Sometimes I wish we were still married," Jack said.

She frowned then and looked away. She pulled the sheets up over her breasts. "No. Don't wish that, Jack. Take things as they are. It's better."

"Nothing's better."

"I'm sorry they're forcing you out."

"I am too."

"I could get Bob to help you when you get out."

"No. I can cuckold him but then I can't turn around and ask his help."

"Bob wouldn't mind."

"I'd mind."

"What are you going to do then when you get out?"

"I ran into someone the other night. You

remember him. Max Escher. He said he was in town on business and we had dinner together. He says he does arson investigations for a security firm, International Management. Out of suburban Chicago. I told him my sad story and he told me his and we got drunk."

"Max Escher. I remember him all right. He was weird."

He looked at her. "How weird?"

"Weird. You know. You know how men look at some women and say they wouldn't fuck them on a bet because they were crazy? Could be a nice-looking woman but they just know. You don't mess with crazy people. Max Escher is one of the crazy people."

"So you didn't fuck him?"

"I wouldn't even have tried."

"Did he try?"

"Sure. He tried."

"Max said he might get me into this company, this line of work. I know about arson, we took the same course."

"Arson investigator."

"Sure. It's something. You've got to do something. You're lucky to get a job when you're forty-six."

"It would be nice to have you in Chicago. I miss you sometimes and I can't always arrange a trip. I can be sitting there looking out the window at the lake, sitting with a gin marty in the middle of the afternoon and think all of a sudden about Jack Cavett. I wish we had this morning."

"I'll see you again."

"Two weeks. I go to New York in two weeks to shop for Christmas."

"They've got shops in Chicago."

"I want New York. A dose of unreality. Two weeks, Jack? Weekend at the St. Regis?"

"I think so," he said. He was running after her again.

"Make sure," she said.

"I'll make sure."

"Kiss me."

He kissed her.

"See you, Jack."

He went to the door. He closed the door on her. He left the room so quietly, it was as though he had never been there.

Twelve

Hanley had watched the news about the Pentagon fire on Sunday afternoon and made calls to Section and worried about the fire though Section was not involved at all. Still, Hanley had an ominous feeling all Sunday and had almost called Devereaux, to share his ominous feeling.

On Monday he went to his offices in R Section at 8:00 A.M. His secretary gave Hanley the message: Mrs. Neumann, director of Section, wanted to see him at 9:00 A.M. He had an hour to wait and he used the hour to let his sense of disaster fester.

Mrs. Neumann had a corner office that commanded a view of the traffic-choked Fourteenth Street bridge over the Potomac. Mrs. Neumann, a large, raspy woman in her fifties who was one of the very few women to rise to high ranks inside the intelligence community, stared with bleak eyes at Hanley as he entered the room. She said, "Close the door."

He closed the door and stared at the visitor seated on the red leather chair to the right of Mrs. Neumann's oak desk. Clair Dodsworth returned the stare.

"This is Mr. Hanley, Mr. Dodsworth, our director of operations."

"I know of Mr. Hanley." The voice was dry, without inflection. His old hands were folded atop a cane that stood between his legs. It was a judicious pose.

Hanley did not sit down. He was not invited to take a chair. He stood by the window and waited.

"Mr. Dodsworth said he is being harassed by agents of Section. To the point where he was falsely imprisoned in a car on Friday."

"Was he?" Hanley said.

"Hanley, I want to know about this," Mrs. Neumann said.

Hanley looked blankly sincere. "So do I. I don't understand, Mr. Dodsworth. Of course, I know who you are. But our agents don't operate in this country. It's not in our charter at all."

"I'm aware of your charter. I advised President Kennedy when we drew up the charter of R Section." Silence. Again, Clair Dodsworth demonstrated his careful knack for displaying his casual power.

"So perhaps you're mistaken," Hanley said.

"One agent is a man named Devereaux. One of your senior advisers, I understand."

"Really?" Hanley waited.

"Really," Dodsworth said.

Silence.

Mrs. Neumann looked at Hanley. "I want to know about this."

"I'll make an inquiry —"

Dodsworth held up his hand. "This is absurd, Mr. Hanley. I'm an old man and not without my resources in this city. I was harassed by your agent and another man I can't identify, and I was forced into a car."

"What car?"

"A car with false license plates."

"False license plates," Hanley said, noting it with a nod.

"Your agent named Devereaux."

"Devereaux is on leave. He has been on leave for some weeks now."

"Where is he?" Mrs. Neumann said.

"I haven't been in touch with him," Hanley said.

He stared at Mrs. Neumann and Mrs. Neumann felt the full force of Hanley's lie. Of course it was a lie. Hanley was in touch with every agent.

"How did you come by this name, this Devereaux?" Hanley said to Dodsworth.

"I have resources."

137

"I see. Perhaps your resources are mistaken in this. I can't believe an agent of this Section would be so foolish as to cross someone as powerful . . . well, and to break rules of our charter. We won't stand for that at all," Hanley said. "I'll make a full investigation, Mrs. Neumann. It would help me considerably if Mr. Dodsworth could provide me with some access to his resources so that we can go over this."

Another moment of silence.

"Mr. Hanley. I have no wish to pursue this so long as you call it off, whatever it is you intend to do in harassing me. I can assure you, Mrs. Neumann, I don't take this lightly. My associate and friend, Mr. Carroll Claymore, was murdered. As you know. I have been at pains cooperating with the Washington police and to have this harassment, this unconstitutional and illegal assault on my person . . ."

He seemed at a loss for words but it was an effect. The lingering silence underscored what he intended to say and said it better than words.

"I understand," Mrs. Neumann said. "I can assure you, if there has been a breach of our charter here, people will be punished. We have no wish to do anything illegal."

The words lay there, flat and legal.

Clair Dodsworth turned and smiled at her then. It was not a pleasant smile. "Mrs. Neumann, illegal or not, I can't put up with this invasion of my rights and my privacy. If I have to apply to other . . . resources . . . I am capable of it. Does R Section want a thorough, outside audit of its intentions in regards to me and my person?"

"We have nothing to hide," Hanley said. He was assuming his flinty face, the one that lied so well. "If proper authorities wish to scrutinize our operations — well, there are certain legalities to be observed. Let's remember, we're dealing with very secret matters."

"Secrecy can be a blanket to cover illegality," Dodsworth said. "As the Central Intelligence Agency has discovered from time to time."

"We're very poor pickings compared with Langley."

Mrs. Neumann watched them pick and choose their weapons, and waited in silence, hands folded on top of her desk.

"And so am I," Dodsworth said. "My integrity is impugned for whatever reason. I am a loyal servant of my country and I have been in service for nearly five decades. I've served in the cabinet twice and I've sacrificed myself to duty. At the end of my days I don't want my integrity impugned by anyone, least of all by secret agents of a secret organization inside the bureaucracy."

"I want a thorough investigation," Mrs. Neumann said at last. "Will that satisfy you, Mr. Dodsworth?"

He gazed at her. There was no smile this time. "Let us say, Mrs. Neumann, that it had better satisfy me."

"All right, let's say that," she said.

Hanley watched the old man rise on creaky limbs. Dodsworth went to the desk and gave a slight bow to the woman behind it. "I trust this will be done with dispatch."

"As quickly as possible. Isn't that right, Mr. Hanley?"

"As quickly as possible," Hanley said.

Dodsworth turned, looked at him a withering moment, and then went to the door. He pulled it open. A security guard was waiting for him to escort him to the front lobby and remove his identification card that designated him a "Visitor." Mrs. Neumann might have gone to the front lobby with him but there was no need to pretend to hospitality. The threat had been made and she understood it. And so did Hanley.

They watched Dodsworth leave the antechamber with the security guard, and then Mrs. Neumann nodded at the door. Hanley crossed the green rug and closed it. He sat down in the red leather chair next to the desk.

"Tell me," Mrs. Neumann said.

Hanley began at the beginning. Part of it she knew. She knew Devereaux had approved the Lebanon probe, she knew about the last message of the agent called Mona. She knew that Devereaux was preparing a follow-up. She knew the investigation all centered on terrorist activities funded in the Mediterranean and elsewhere by a shadowy Arab bank called International Credit Clearinghouse. But that was all she knew. She would not have authorized Devereaux to meet with Carroll Claymore; or to blackmail him; or to spy upon a particular citizen named Clair Dodsworth. Or, finally, to harass him.

"Did you authorize the events of Friday?"

"No," Hanley said.

"Devereaux made a mistake."

"Why does he know of Devereaux? Why does he have the name? No one had the name," Hanley said. "Unless it comes from Lebanon. Unless one of the six agents we lost there in the spring revealed it."

"You know the rumors. About Devereaux and Mona?"

"Yes."

"He's made this into something private."

"We lost six agents in Lebanon on one operation. It should concern us."

"We've lost good men before," Mrs. Neumann said.

It was a very cold thing to say but it had to be said. Hanley might have said the same thing. He had said a similar thing to Devereaux, but he had bent in the force of Devereaux's obsession. They might all have to pay for the obsession.

"Devereaux is finished on this," she said. "There was a monumental act of terrorism twenty-four hours ago in the Pentagon. Could this be related, this five-million-dollar transfer of monies from a bank in Liechtenstein to District Savings Bank?"

Hanley looked at his hands for an answer. Then he shrugged.

"Defense Intelligence Agency," she said. "Turn it over to them."

"That'd betray the operation," Hanley said.

"It would save Section further embarrassment. Maybe a congressional audit. Clair Dodsworth could arrange that, that was no idle threat."

"DIA operates in and out of the United States," Hanley said.

"Now you're beginning to understand," she said. The sarcasm, wrapped in her raspy voice, was more a bludgeon than a rapier hit.

"I want Devereaux to turn this over to General Robert E. Lee at the Pentagon. This morning. About the transfers of monies, about Carroll Claymore. I'll talk to General Lee and explain the parameters. If he wants Devereaux to liaison with his office, then, fine, Devereaux is his problem, not ours. I just want this out of Section before I go home today." She paused. "You understand that, don't you?"

"I understand we can't take care of our own," Hanley said.

"Man, don't you see how deep this has gotten? Devereaux's mesmerized you. Mesmerized himself. It doesn't matter if he was Mona's lover or not, what matters is not his personal grudge but the good of Section."

Hanley might have delivered that speech. Perhaps it was true; perhaps the thought of six missing tacks on a flat map in his office and the force of Devereaux's words had led him to do the wrong thing for whatever right reason.

"What if General Lee isn't interested?"

"He's interested," she said.

"How do you know that?"

She stared at Hanley for a moment and then reached for a notepad. It was covered with words in her small, precise scrawl.

"He called me last night at ten. He told

143

me that Devereaux had crossed into DIA's investigation of certain terrorist networks and he would appreciate cooperation with us on the matter of funding from International Credit Clearinghouse. I told him about Lebanon, about our missing agents, but then he told me that he had been surveilling Devereaux the last two months and that Devereaux had met on several occasions with this Carroll Claymore. I couldn't tell him it was news to me. I couldn't tell him my director of operations had kept this from me. I just took it all down and said I would look into it and he said it was urgent because of the act of terrorism against the Pentagon, that he was trying to find the money that had to be behind any act of terror carried out by that many people. He said the FBI and DIA were in a race on this and he intended to win that race, even if he had to give Section a black eye. He said that to me. He said that to me at ten o'clock last night."

Hanley looked very wan in that moment.

Mrs. Neumann rasped at him: "I'm giving him Devereaux and everything we have. And he's giving us a lease on life. Do you understand me, man? I'm not giving him your head but I could if I wanted. I want to think you temporarily lost your judgment. You get hold of Devereaux right now. You tell him the new world order of things. You understand me, man?"

Perfectly.

Hanley rose and looked at her. He felt sick and frail.

"It has to be done," he said.

"All right." Softer now.

"I'll do it." In the same voice used over the years to acquiesce to a hundred different jobs that were wrong and dirty and had to be done.

Thirteen

Britta called Max Escher at the 800 number shortly after Michael Horan left her on Sunday morning. Horan had apologized and she had let him apologize, but she had been very calculating with him. She was freezing him out for a while, letting him think about her, about his need for her and how much greater it was than her need for him. She wanted him to understand that and in the certain way of very beautiful and very smart women, she knew that she would prevail.

There was only a recording device at the end of the line and she had used it, speaking into the phone while keeping her eyes on the television screen. The fire was great and out of control. She had said to the recording device, "You've impressed me, Mr. Escher." And replaced the receiver.

She waited all night Sunday in her apartment for him to return the call, but she knew the bastard wouldn't do it. Escher had a twisted streak, he was definitely the punk type.

On Monday morning she woke early and donned her stretch yellow jogging outfit and put on makeup and went out into the somber dawn. She ran for twenty minutes and two and a half miles.

When she returned, she stripped off her running clothes and dumped them in the hamper and took a long, tingling shower. She dressed and went to the kitchen to make decaffeinated coffee and rye toast.

The downstairs doorman called up while she sat in her kitchen, drinking black coffee and chewing dry rye toast.

"Got a Mr. Escher here, Miz Andrews."

"You can send him up, Henry."

She went to her bedroom and recoated her lips with lipstick. She took a pair of gold earrings out of a box in her bedroom and thought that she would not wear earrings in the morning, not for a punk like Max Escher. She fitted the earrings on her lobes. She went to the door when he knocked. Then hesitated, to make him wait for her. He knocked again. She touched her blond hair, tucked in the front of her blouse.

She opened the door.

"You were lucky to catch me," she said. "I was just on my way out."

Escher wore a tan raincoat today because it was raining, but the same checked shirt or

147

its cousin and the same sports coat he had worn in Lafayette Park on Saturday. No tie. He was clean shaven but the outline of his shadowed cheeks emphasized his rough good looks. His brown hair was spiky, cut short, brushed down hard. He looked at her with those same amused brown eyes that had haunted her Sunday in the company of Michael Horan. Fuck Michael. This one didn't talk about it or discuss the possibilities or weigh the options the way the politicians did. This one went over and burned down the goddamned military, one man. If the movements had had him during the Vietnam War, they would have stopped their stupid marches on the Mall, talking to the president, getting arrested. Just burn down the fucking Pentagon, that's all.

The jumble of thoughts made her excited. Her face was flushed and he noticed it and smiled at her in his peculiar, condescending way. She wasn't accustomed to being condescended to.

"Lucky ole me, catching you before you went out. I was out of town yesterday but I picked up your message. You got a nice place, I knew a nice girl would have a nice place. Here." He took off his raincoat and handed it to her. "Little wet, started to rain."

That was something else to annoy her. He

seemed to find it easy and amusing to annoy her. She threw the coat on a chair. He caught the anger in the gesture and smiled crookedly.

"Don't take no shit, right?" he said.

"That's elegant and accurate," Britta said.

"I'm just an old soldier," he said. He went to the windows and sat down in a large, green wing chair. He put his feet on the footstool.

"If you have wet shoes, don't use the footstool."

He studied that, his head cocked to one side.

"I don't take no shit either, Britta."

She let it go. She folded her arms across her chest.

He let her wait.

She walked to a straight chair across from him and sat down.

And he waited.

"Why burn down the Pentagon?"

"Why not? Put in twenty-two years, pricks said this down-sizing thing was causing problems and they made me a deal to get me to resign. Only there was no saying no to the deal. When they wanted you on the line in 'Nam, then Max Escher was good enough to get shot at or maybe get blowed up when the device had one booby trap he hadn't figured out. Put in your time and then they announce the end of the cold war. Guess who won? Not me. Probably Japan and Germany. Well, I didn't have any love for those geniuses. I think I told them that, don't you think, Britta?"

She just stared at him. Rain beaded the glass.

"Didn't I do it, kid?"

Smiling.

She said, "I'm not a 'kid.' This is about business."

"Yeah, yeah. But I'm not very polite."

"No. You're not. And I can't deal with a crazy man. Someone who's fighting his own personal battle."

"You heard about me from the Greens in Denmark, didn't you? What a nice little job I did for them? You contacted me, not the other way around. So you want me to burn something down or blow something up, am I right? So let's talk about it."

"You've heard of Dove?"

"I heard of it. In Denmark. Very booga-booga."

Waited.

She looked hard at him. She didn't want him to misunderstand her. "We want a fire. We don't want an act of terror or obvious sabotage. We don't want any comebacks."

"I don't want comebacks."

"You did a good job in Denmark."

"It was a good job. They still can't figure out what went wrong."

"How did you burn the Pentagon? They can't —"

"They'll figure it out but there won't be any way they can use it. You hear of snafu. Old army expression: Situation Normal, All Fucked Up. Except in movies they couldn't say 'fuck,' so they said 'all fouled up.' You in the service for twenty-two years, you learn that, you can use that to your advantage. I won't tell you exactly what I did till I can trust you. When you start telling me what you want."

The French mantel clock struck nine.

Escher glanced at his Rolex. "Clock is fast."

"Maybe your watch is slow."

"Not in my business. Time is money. OK, Brit — I think that's what I'm going to call you — I think I can assure you that I'm not a crazy man or whatever you think. Fair enough. I hit the Pentagon because it was my last duty station, worked in a section of intelligence for a little prick named General Bobby Lee. He made out the efficiency reports and he suggested upstairs that maybe my time in the army was past, even though I was only vested to twenty-two years. That's the way the army is today, they're letting good people go, throwing out the baby with the bathwater, all because they think this Russian thing is over. Well, Bobby Lee is going to have to

151

investigate how the big ole Pentagon got done in, and he isn't going to get the answer easy and he sure isn't going to get me. I planned on that thing, off and on, for more than a year. And it shows, a nice piece of work. You're impressed, you said so on the message recorder."

Yes. Impressed. It arose in her now like a shiver. Her eyes were shining and they were looking at him. "Can I get you something, Max? Get you some coffee?"

"Coffee is fine."

"You want cream?" She rose.

"I like it like my women, hot and black."

That made her frown. One moment he could make her shiver with his casual sense of power, the next he revealed what a punk he was. She had never met anyone like him, not even in college days. They were very earnest and certain in college.

When she came back with coffee on the silver tray, he was at the mantel, looking at the back of the French clock. She saw he had wide shoulders and a narrow waist and his buttocks were taut against the material of his slacks.

"You should get this clock cleaned," he said, closing the back. "Damned shame, nice piece of machinery."

"Thanks for your professional advice."

He turned, the slow and lazy grin that was more malevolent than pleasurable flitting wide across his face. His eyes had a kind of compelling madness to them. "I know about clocks, Brit. You know about clocks in what I do."

"And you weren't anywhere near the Pentagon yesterday morning," she said.

He smiled. "In fact, I was in Chicago on Rush Street, and I picked a hilarious fight with someone around three in the morning, which is four in the morning here, and since I was seven hundred miles away, I couldn't have been here."

She poured the coffee. He was back in the wing chair and he held the cup in both hands, feeling the warmth, sipping at it the way a soldier sips at coffee offered him standing guard in the rain, cautious and grateful at the same time, hiding the cup in both hands so that the duty officer wouldn't see it if he walked by.

"I want a fire that has no arson. No clues at all. No bombs, nothing like that."

Max Escher stared at the rain beading on the windows.

"I can do that," he said in a soft voice.

"Are you sure?"

"Lots of fires have no cause. Even with smart investigators for insurance companies

153

who know they were set."

"There's a small group of us who believe that the days of protest are over. There has to be action. War against the enemies of the planet."

"I didn't mind wartime. I minded being shot at but there were other things I didn't mind. It concentrates you."

"Environmental war."

"That's Dove, is that right? What is Dove?"

"People who think alike."

"But what's it stand for, has to stand for something."

"You heard about it in Denmark, they didn't tell you?"

"No."

"I won't tell you."

"Then you can kiss my ass, Brit, because I don't need to go off into anything half-cocked. If you don't know what you're getting into, you get left holding the bag."

She thought about it while she stared at his profile. He was sipping at the coffee without grace, both hands around the cup, cup to lip, slurping it.

"Directorate of Violent Environmentalism."

He laughed.

She waited. She didn't frown now. She waited.

He turned to look at her. "God. Names you people come up with. Greenpeace. Queer Nation."

"They're not us. Brothers but not from us."

"Just so the money is green."

"We have the money. On line. Instantly obtainable."

"I bet you have money."

"Not my money. Money we obtained. You have to know that."

"All right, I don't care where the money comes from. What do you want to burn?"

She leaned forward, elbows on knees. She searched his face. "Chernobyl."

He waited for something else.

Silence.

"Go to Russia?"

"No. Bring the lesson home," Britta said.

"What lesson?"

"Nuclear power is a constant disaster waiting to happen. Nuclear power is poisoning the world, the environment, our rivers and trees. And our bodies. There are a hundred nineteen nuclear reactors at work in the United States alone. And in Europe, my God, go through Britain sometimes, Manchester and Birmingham, and the reactors are everywhere. France. And —"

"I don't need a speech, Brit. I don't need a motive. I've got money for a motive."

"Don't you even see the rightness of it? My God, the way you struck at the warmongers yesterday —"

"I was a motherfucking warmonger, Brit, don't forget that. I was striking at a bunch of candy-ass brass who threw my sorry ass out of the only career I ever had. I don't have to sign on to any causes anymore, Brit. I done my causes time."

"I want you to understand us."

"You want me to see the rightness, then I see it. Whatever you want. But what do you want me to do?"

"Can you make a fire without any trace of the source of it? That it was set deliberately?"

"I told you that, you weren't listening. The trouble with rich people is they do all the talking and none of the listening. I told you that Saturday night. Everything is in the ignition. The ignition has to be totally consumed. The fuel of the fire is obtainable. I used it yesterday. Not so hard."

"What is it?"

"That's a trade secret. It worked in Denmark, it'll work on what you want."

"I want you to open your shirt, I want to see if you have a wire."

He grinned. "Why not just feel me up like I did to you Saturday night. It makes

156

for a more trusting —"

"This is business, Mr. Escher. This isn't about sex. You can buy your sex with your earnings on this."

"I'd rather have love," he said. Still smiling.

"Your shirt."

He took off his coat and opened his shirt. His chest was pale and strong and there were tufts of brown hair across his pectorals and the brown nipples. And she saw the tuck of skin beneath the rib cage on the right side and she looked at him in question.

"Sniper. Right at the end in Saigon. I didn't even know I was hit until later, went right through me. That got me a silver star, I believe, the medals mean less and less. You want to keep looking. You want me to take off my pants?"

"You're a fatuous bore," she said.

Escher just grinned and buttoned his shirt slowly and tucked it into his trousers again. He put on his coat and sat down. He picked up the coffee cup again with two hands.

She got up and turned to the window and looked down at the rain on the sad street. The rain made her thoughts sad. The sadness turned to pity in her. She always was strong, stronger than her dad, perhaps as strong as Grandfather. She did things without pity but she could not stop pity when it came to it.

Pity never decided her actions but she was human, she told herself. She was a general and people would now die but the cause was good. It was just like war and war was its own justification because it was a good war. The suffering would lead to a good end.

"They wanted to justify the bomb in the beginning. That's what it was all about." Her voice was dead and detached and she spoke to the window glass and beads of rain. "They dropped the bombs on Japan, and after the war they said this terrible thing was a weapon for peace. They said nuclear power was nuclear energy. Otherwise, people would have never let them build more bombs. We built bombs for fifty years to destroy the planet. Now we don't need them. And we don't need nuclear energy because that's all it was, a phony excuse to keep us in the nuclear business."

"That's a nice speech, I haven't heard that one. I've heard a lot of them — about whales and rain forests — but that's a nice one," he said.

"Do you really trust nuclear energy?"

"I don't think about it."

"The prime secret of World War Two was nuclear and now we trust it to a bunch of men in private power companies out to maximize profits at any cost," she said.

"You want to burn a nuclear power plant," Max Escher said.

Silence. The rain on the glass. The silence went on and on. They listened to the rain on the glass.

She turned. "Yes, Max. That's it. It takes around ten years to build a single new plant now with all the review process. And a lot of our reactors are old, very old, and they're coming up for license renewals. Burn one reactor —"

"That could kill a lot of people."

"I said this was a war," Britta said.

Soft rain. Tap, tap, tap against the glass. She felt sad for those dead people. She had really thought about them and about the sacrifice to come and she felt pity, but she could not let the pity change what had to be done.

"Burn it down someplace else. Like France or Britain or something," Max Escher said. "You want to burn one down here, you kill Americans."

"It wouldn't matter over there. The British might shut down their nuclear energy, or the French, but we wouldn't. We'd say it was like Chernobyl. We always say it can't happen here. We think only foreigners get bad luck."

"We had Three Mile Island and it didn't stop anything."

"Nobody died. People have to die. In hundreds and thousands," she said.

"Jesus," Escher said. He got up and started to walk around the room. The carpet was white and so were most of the fabrics. The wood was very light on the mantel and on the stretches of bare floor. Max looked at things and she turned to watch him.

"You can't do it."

He stopped, turned. "I didn't really figure you for that cold, Brit. I thought maybe I'd fuck around with you, do a little eco-disaster for you or your people like I can do. I didn't figure on a nuclear power plant. I suppose you got one in mind."

"Yes," she said. "I can get details of the plant. Dimensions, schematics, everything. You might say I've done the groundwork. All you have to do is do the burn."

"How'd you get schematics for a power plant?"

"I own it in a way. And besides, it's due up for renewal in two years. There are schematics in Washington. At the Nuclear Regulatory Commission, in Congress —"

"Senator Horan. You and Senator Horan. I'll bet he's on a nuclear subcommittee or something."

"Or something," she said.

He was grinning despite himself. "You are

one complicated lady, Brit. But don't go trusting a politician, not even if you go to bed with him. Politicians are used to fucking people."

"I'm not trusting Michael. He'll do it for me because he has to."

"Because you're blackmailing him?"

"I can do that if it comes to it. But it won't come to it. He'll help me because I ask him to."

"I don't know." He was frowning at his coffee. "I don't know."

"You don't want to do it." She did not smile at him. Her blue eyes were dull. She turned. "Then go away. I'll find someone else."

Just like that.

"Hey," he said. "I didn't say that. I said, I didn't figure on a nuclear power plant in this country."

"No one has," she said. "Not even the person putting up the money."

"Bullshit. Whoever it is, whoever they are, they know. Not down to the dotted *i* and crossed *t*, but they know. You're kidding yourself about that. Nobody puts up money on dreams."

"Fools do." And she was thinking of her dad and she didn't want to think about him. "I want to know if you can do this —"

"I know about power plants. Had a three-week course in nuclear safety when I was in EOD in the last year. They were trying to help me find a career choice."

"Were you impressed by nuclear safety?"

"Well, one thing I could figure out right off was how you could sabotage it," Max Escher said. "I could figure that out well enough."

He was bragging, strutting before her, demanding a fight if she disputed him. Britta saw all that.

"I told you I own a nuclear power plant. I own eighty thousand shares of Northern Illinois Power and Light. It was a gift from my grandfather, one of the things my dad didn't screw up. When you own that much of something, you take a proprietary interest in it," Britta said. "I don't like owning nuclear power plants. I'm going to sell my shares very soon. A controlled sell-off over two weeks. The shares are going to be worth less, I think."

That put it over the edge. They were talking about something real now. He stared at her and then went to the windows and looked down at Q Street in the rain. Rain is such a sad thing in Washington because it is mourning and memories and because it takes the magic out of the trees lined along the parkways and because it shuts down all the bright colors.

"I want two million dollars," he said in a soft voice. "I want part of it in front and the rest of it when I'm ready to blow. I don't want to wait on my money. I want to know when you want the job and then I have to look at it to see when I can do it. Two million dollars and expenses. There'll be a few expenses."

"I thought —"

He turned and his voice was hard. "I'm not fucking around with you, little rich lady. I want two million dollars and no comebacks, and if you make a comeback, or your drunken senator friend, I'll kill you. I'll do it just like I did the Pentagon and you'll be as dead as those people who died Sunday morning. I just want you to know that if you think you're hard, I'm harder."

She said nothing but she didn't make a move. "I'm as hard as anyone I know," she said. "We'll agree to two million dollars."

"You've got the money?"

"We've got the money."

"When do you want it?"

"By Christmas."

"Merry Christmas, America," he said.

"I want it burned, I want a radioactive cloud that covers the eastern half of the country, and it might sicken and kill thousands but that's what you have to do in war. People will die but the planet will be saved finally."

"Oh, yeah, saved," he said. "God help me from people out to save me."

"I don't want anything to do with you, Escher, I just want your skill without your bombast and braggadocio."

He frowned. "What are we burning?"

"It's sixty-four miles northwest of Chicago. In Rock County, south of Rockford, Illinois."

"What is it?"

"It's built on an old seminary site. It was called Eleven Holy Apostles Seminary. They shut down the seminary years ago and sold off pieces of it. Farmland, you know."

"Why would I want to know that?"

"A mission," she said. "You're doing good on holy ground."

"Don't tell me that stuff, tell me what it is."

"A nuclear energy plant, one of the biggest in the country. The Apostle nuclear reactor site. We're burning it down, Max, you and me. Burning the Apostle."

Fourteen

Devereaux carried a brown leather attaché case. He was led through the water-stained corridors of the building by a staff sergeant with the white armband of the MPs. The sergeant carried a sidepiece.

The Pentagon was back functioning in bits and pieces, here and there. The building smelled of stale smoke. The fire was struck out — the fires were struck out — by 1245 hours Sunday. Large sections were undamaged but they were connected by other sections full of blackened walls and wet floors.

The president had placed the armed forces on red alert for a time, but when he went on television the second time Sunday — at 2100 hours Eastern Time — the ready status had been reduced to yellow. Congressmen of both parties were cluttering CNN and C-Span with suggestions of sabotage and a call on renewed war against terrorism. The conventional-wisdom theory was that a trained team had assaulted the building during the small hours of Sunday. The president of Russia announced that the disaster at the Pentagon was not connected in any way with activities of the KGB. This last was unnecessary, but the president of Russia liked to appear as often as possible on the worldwide service of CNN.

Hanley had laid it out pretty hard for Devereaux and Hacker. Section was to back off and turn the investigation evidence over to Section Three Four of the DIA, which had requested it. Devereaux had been under surveillance by DIA for two months anyway and his cover was now blown by the stupid attempt to frighten Clair Dodsworth. Hanley had said all this and waited for Devereaux to respond in a cold, warlike manner.

Instead, Devereaux had shrugged and begun to gather the papers. He had not protested.

It was 1305 hours Monday.

"Right through here." The sergeant had unstrapped the holster containing the 9mm Beretta-built sidearm, which had replaced the Colt .45 automatic as the standard military pistol. He seemed ready to shoot someone. Everyone in the building seemed dazed or on edge. Devereaux had been made to walk through the metal detector at the entrance shoeless, beltless, and with his pockets emptied totally into a plastic tray.

The sergeant stopped at a security desk manned by a second lieutenant whose pistol was on the desktop in front of him. He stared at the civilian and read the pass and then picked up the telephone. He spoke into the receiver and placed it back on the hook.

"I'll take it from here, Sergeant."

"Yes, sir."

Devereaux noticed the second lieutenant holstered his pistol with a reluctant look on his face. He couldn't help it. He smiled at the look.

"Come with me, sir," the lieutenant said.

General Bobby Lee's office had been turned into charcoal. This temporary ops room had lime-green walls and too much noise. He had a table for a desk in the corner and the only privacy afforded was that the other tables were kept some distance away. Devereaux followed the lieutenant to the general.

Bobby Lee hadn't slept for thirty hours and looked it. His face was haggard but clean shaven. He wore his woolly pullover sweater, but this time the epaulets were trimmed with stars of rank. Nobody but a civilian was looking like a civilian today.

He stared at Devereaux and then nodded dismissal to the lieutenant.

"Siddown, Devereaux."

Devereaux took a straight chair. He balanced the attaché case on his lap.

"That's for me?"

"It seems so."

"I wanted to let you run with it, see how far you got, but this is a mess. I've got to get some answers. What was it that Carroll Claymore said to you? The last time?"

"Money was transferred into a line of credit in District Savings Bank. Five million."

"From whom?"

"From the ICC branch in Liechtenstein."

"But from whom?"

"Yes. That's the question."

"Was any of it used? Between your last meeting with Carroll Claymore and Sunday morning about oh five hundred hours?" General Lee said.

"I don't know."

"I got the Sisters snooping on my Territory, I don't like that one bit."

"The FBI won't come close to solving it. The FBI catches white-collar criminals and browbeats crooked politicians. The FBI wouldn't have a clue to the people behind this," Devereaux said.

"What's it about for you, Red?"

Bobby Lee leaned forward. He had crossed Red's path too many times in the hot war days for them not to know each other better than most and to understand each other.

Devereaux stared at him for a long time. "We had six go into Lebanon by various routes last spring. They were working apart from each other for security reasons. On ICC, on the money behind the line of credit for terrorists. None of them came out."

General Lee waited, still leaning forward to catch the low, flat voice. But Devereaux had stopped talking and the silence grew between them.

"I just lost a building," Bobby Lee finally said. He sat back in his chair. "Fifty-one casualties, including nine dead. One of my men looks like a piece of charcoal, you understand."

Devereaux said nothing.

"You know what security is here? Is at just about any base or fort I can show you? Civilians. Rent-a-cops. Goddamned military is nickel and diming itself to death. You walk into just about any installation we got in the world and some candy-ass, know-nothing, five-dollar-an-hour security guard is checking ID cards at the gate house because some genius around here figured it's cheaper to have him do it than have a soldier do it. I swear to God, we might as well contract out to the Puerto Rican gangs in New York to run our next war for us because they work cheaper."

Devereaux looked down at the attaché case

on his lap. Then he glanced at the general: "You think this fire is connected with the money transfer to District Savings?"

"It's what I got to think, I got to get moving on this, I've got to show something. They called me up for a briefing three times today. You've been crossing and crisscrossing our intelligence ops in the Mediterranean, asking the same kinds of questions we asked. I was willing to follow behind you, see where you got. I don't think any one of us has all the answers. But now I've got to get cracking on my own. This . . . this arson in the building is my ass, Devereaux."

"Tell them about ICC. They'll like ICC," Devereaux said.

Bobby Lee looked at his fingers. They were stubby and thick. "I can do that, that would give them something to gnaw on for a time."

"Just don't get specific, Bobby Lee," Devereaux said. "I get closer and closer in this and I want some room. If you get the credit for it, it's all right by me. By Mrs. Neumann."

"You got spooked over there at Section? I didn't expect cooperation right away from Mrs. Neumann. I didn't expect you to land on my doorstep."

Devereaux stared at the soldier. "Someone spooked us. They want me to cooperate with you because we were scared off this particular

170

path," Devereaux said.

"By who?"

"Dodsworth. Clair Dodsworth. Said we were harassing him."

Bobby Lee began to smile. It was a slight smile in a ferocious face and Devereaux did not react to it.

"Were you? Harassing him?"

"Yes."

"Why?"

"To see what he'd do."

"You harassed him enough to scare Mrs. Neumann."

"It seems so."

"Is that what you expected?"

"It was a possibility."

"So if I hadn't jumped in to rescue you, you'd be shit out of luck. I mean, she could just as soon told you to stop the operation."

"She could have done that," Devereaux said.

"And?"

Devereaux let it go in silence.

"You still think like you thought in Vietnam. You still don't give, do you? You're still the Lone Ranger, Red."

Devereaux said nothing again.

"You gonna be square with me?"

"I was told to give you everything," Devereaux said.

And Bobby Lee saw what it was. It was a question.

"All right, Red. As far as I can, you and I will trust each other in this. As far as I can. But I'm not going to hang for you."

"That's good enough for now." Devereaux opened the clasps on the attaché case, raised the lid, and removed a sheaf of papers. He closed the case and rested the papers on the lid with his hand covering the papers. "You know about the line of credit. From Liechtenstein, but I think directed from Beirut. If it comes from Lebanon, it's for terror. Something big enough to require five million dollars in credit. Maybe this, your fire in the Pentagon."

"We don't even have a cause on this," the general said. "This was an absolutely first-class arson job. Not a clue yet."

"Give that to your bosses. Tell them you're on the trail to the terrorists."

"That'll only work so long."

"Everything's temporary, Bobby Lee." Softly.

"You don't think it was the Pentagon fire, though." The general's guess was shrewd enough. Devereaux shook his head.

"Why not?"

"The five million line came in a week ago. They didn't set this up in a week, whoever they were. But it might have been set up using different loans with different banks at different times, all coming from International Credit Clearinghouse."

"So it's not Lebanon or ICC, then, involved in my fire? And you want me to give it to my bosses that I'm looking into ICC?"

"Because you are, Bobby Lee. You've been doing it in the Med, you've been doing it for two years and you don't get anyplace. But now Clair Dodsworth surfaced to accuse me — by name, Bobby Lee, by name — of harassing him. I like that, I really do."

And the general saw that Devereaux had flushed the prey, had forced movement in the thicket of underbrush, had directed the action instead of making the reaction. And he saw the cold, deadly thing that was in the gray eyes of the other man. The son of a bitch really did like it.

"You know about the Institute for World Development?" Devereaux said.

"Vaguely. Civilian group, sort of connected with the environment, right?"

"It's a phony. I think it's a phony. But it's got a five-million-dollar line of credit now from a Middle Eastern group interested in the export of terror to the West."

Bobby Lee suddenly stuck a Life Saver candy in his mouth. Devereaux never even saw where it came from. The general began to chew on the hard candy.

"I don't want to mess with civilians. Not in this country. Nothing to do with civilians or politics."

Devereaux said, "But I don't much care."

They both stared at each other, one of them chewing and cracking the candy. "All right. There's things you can do and things I can do."

"A woman named Britta Andrews is the patron of this institute. Her father was a radical in the sixties who blew himself up in an underground dynamite factory in Queens. Britta is very left. She's made trips abroad to the Greens in Western Europe. Early this year, there was a big fire in Copenhagen, a political fire —"

"I remember it," Bobby Lee said.

"She had been there four weeks earlier."

"And now the Pentagon fire —"

"If there's any connection. Have you ever heard of a group called the Dove?"

Bobby Lee stared again. He shook his head then.

"I know this. And now you know this," Devereaux said. He was putting brackets around the information he was going to give.

Bobby Lee waited.

"It doesn't exist except in rumors. When

our agent was investigating ICC at the beginning, before she went to Lebanon, she found this curious rumor repeated a couple of times. She heard the story in Paris the first time and then in Brussels. No proof of anything."

"What is it?"

"It's supposed to be a group of violent environmentalists dedicated to financing terrorism against their favorite targets. Dove is Directorate of Violent Environmentalism. It doesn't have any apparent leader, any apparent place it comes from, it's like a network of like-minded people. It was supposed to be behind the Copenhagen burn that destroyed all the records in the department of the environment."

"I didn't hear anything about this . . . Dove."

"No one did. Except it was a rumor and Mona said it was all part of the web connecting ICC with this and that all over the world. Arab money used against Western targets, neatly laundered through committed cells of people who are willing to blow things up and shoot things down."

"What the hell does the Dove — even if it exists, which you can't prove — what the hell does it have to do with my problem?"

"Why were you following me all those

weeks, Bobby Lee? I knew someone was following me and I couldn't quite make them, but someone was behind me all the time. The jogger yesterday morning —"

"We didn't have anyone on you yesterday morning."

"A jogger came around three times and he had a yellow tape recorder, a Sony, I think, and he held it a peculiar way, like a camera —"

"What the fuck do you think — I know what you look like, I didn't have anyone taking a picture of you," General Lee said.

They waited for a moment and thought about it. The room was big and filled with sound. Phones rang and voices were too loud. Except in this corner of the room.

"Then someone else was following me, Bobby Lee, all the time. Following you following me. Following Carroll Claymore. Someone who knew my name. More likely, a lot of someones. You can use me, now, Bobby Lee, you see that."

The general stared at the spy until he found the words. "You want it that bad, put yourself out there on a swing and see if anyone takes a shot?"

"That bad."

"It was this woman agent, wasn't it? The one who didn't come out of Lebanon?"

"It was her. That was part of it. I don't know what it is now because it gets bigger and dirtier when I think about it."

"You were friends?"

"We were friends."

Bobby Lee said, "You make this too fucking personal, I don't like that."

"You're military. You won't touch a civilian. I don't mind. As far as Mrs. Neumann is concerned, I've dumped everything into your lap and R Section is out of the business. Fine. I 'liaise' with you now, Bobby Lee. I touch the civilians. I sit on the swing and you watch the back door to see if anyone wants to take a shot at me."

"If we do it that way, I want someone close to you, someone who reports to me. No, no, you're gonna get a Tonto if you want to play Lone Ranger. I've got to give you a liaison. I need everybody I got here. I got to keep tabs on you." He stared at his fingers for an answer. "Got a guy named Jack Cavett on TDY with my section, a light colonel waiting to get out, putting in time. EOD man. He's been helping us identify some of the shit we pulled out of Iraq in the war. I was so crazy yesterday when this happened, I put the suspicion on him, I swear to God, because he was EOD and because he'd been in Special Forces, you know, but it was crazy, he was

177

over in a hotel in the District humping someone he won't say who. I'll use him, keep me in touch with you. I don't want this to get out of our hands."

"You can have all the credit, I told you, Bobby."

"This is running deep with you, Red. I've seen you do this, let it run deep and you do the craziest goddamned things — you cut off your own balls if you have to, just to get it done — I don't want anything crazy."

"A rich woman in town with a radical heritage who dates a big-shot Democratic senator, makes nice to half the fringe Green people in Europe and here. Her father would have loved to burn down the Pentagon. Except now, nobody cares, do they, Bobby Lee?"

"Fucking terrorists," the general said. "I'd impale them by the asshole on sticks covered with shit."

Devereaux said, "I want to follow the money trail, General." He used the rank for the first time. "Langley won't do it for you, Langley fucked up when the marines were wiped out in Beirut. FBI can't reach that far, you know that. And you've got a fire to explain away. You need me, Bobby Lee."

They waited again while they thought about it. Now Devereaux lifted his hand, picked up the sheaf of papers, and passed them across to the general, who looked through them, slowly, page by page, making up his mind about Red. This report and that, a copy of the message given Devereaux by Carroll Claymore that night on the Red Line platform beneath Union Station. The general looked at it, the transfer of funds into District Bank, thought about the videotapes he had watched, thought about the long journey they had both traveled by different paths to reach this point.

Robert E. Lee looked at Devereaux at last.

"I'll call Colonel Cavett. You can use him. He's the cover for you, Red, the one who makes it look like you're really working for me. Don't forget me, Red, my ass is in a sling on this."

"I won't forget you, Bobby Lee."

And the general believed him.

Fifteen

Escher followed the Rock River Road south from the tollway. Thickets of bare trees crowded on knolls along the river. The road twisted back and forth, following the course of the river. The river was dark and swift here and it looked mean against the autumn-brown landscape. The locals called the wind that morning an Alberta Clipper, blowing down a thousand miles unchecked from the snowy plains of the Canadian province. Here and there were houses on the knolls above the river, and bare yards were littered with pickup trucks and rusting wrecks and summer lawn chairs. For a long time, there was nothing but these midwestern tableaux of isolated frame houses and thick, unexpected forests that grew where the land was too steep or too rocky for farming.

He passed through the small riverfront town with its long main street full of shuttered stores. As in most small towns, an out-of-town mall had swallowed all the lifeblood from the business district. He counted one restaurant open and three bars, a small gas-and-grocery market, an old-fashioned drugstore with a family name on the sign and an ill-lit hardware store. At the south end of the town were two churches, separated by the river road. On the left was a square, brick building with "Swedish Evangelical" carved in stone over the entrance. On the right a wooden sign before a Midwestern Gothic stone church said there were masses at 7:00 P.M. Saturdays and at 8:00, 9:00 and 12:00 on Sundays. It was Eleven Holy Apostles Catholic Church. The town itself was called Apostle.

Escher turned left at the single traffic light and followed Seminary Road off the main street. He crossed an elderly iron bridge that spanned the dark river. The road rose up the hill on the other shore and curved gently south.

All this land had once belonged to the Eleven Holy Apostles College and Seminary, which went out of business in 1954 after celebrating its centenary. Some of the seminary land had been acquired by neighboring farmers, who expanded their working acreage. For a long time there was no other demand for the rest of the land, and the order of priests that owned it sought buyers who were not there.

Then, in 1966, Northern Illinois Power and Light Company bought five hundred acres three miles outside the town of Apostle. For eighteen months there were rumors about what the utility intended to do with the land but the company waited on its announcement. The announcement came in late 1967 and it made front-page news, even down in Chicago sixty-four miles to the southeast.

After many delays in construction, the nuclear power station was opened in 1975. The delays had been technical as well as political. Very few people ever knew that a leak in the coolant pipes at the core of the Red reactor had resulted in an unauthorized emission of radioactive steam in 1973 during a test run. The cover-up, if that was the right term, was essential at the time because the anti–nuclear-power people had been joined by the antiwar movement (it was still the Vietnam era) in attacking the "corporate dogs of greed who will sacrifice our futures for their profits."

Still, the Apostle reactors — so named after the seminary and the nearby town as a public relations ploy — were far enough away from the population mass called Greater Chicago to ensure that the protests about the plant received little public notice. Picketing the reactor site was only covered extensively in small-market Rockford, nineteen miles north.

The Apostle might not even have existed, it was so unnoticed. It was within one hundred miles of the 12 million people who lived in Milwaukee, Chicago, and Gary, and the hundreds of suburbs between that were scattered over three states. The reality of all those people living so near the Apostle was masked by the seeming isolation of the plant itself. Here was nothing but farmland, a few trees, scattered farmhouses, or shabby riverfront settlements of underemployed, untrained rural workers who could not find anything better to do than to exist.

Escher turned off Seminary Road into Brick Farm Road. He followed the road over another grassy knoll and around another thicket of bare trees that concealed a creek and then he saw it, just that suddenly.

Steam rose in clouds from the cooling tower at the end of a gigantic windowless building that housed the steam turbines for the two reactors. A network of power lines marched on steel legs from the cores out across the brown bare fields to the horizon.

Escher passed under a group of lines that spanned Brick Farm Road and felt the sudden tingle that comes from being so close to high-tension lines. The lines hummed constantly. The humming and the wind were the only sounds in nature.

Or perhaps it had not been passing under the power lines that made Escher tingle in that moment. Perhaps it was the sight of the Apostle itself, unlike anything in nature around it, billowing steam into the gray sky and sitting in splendid isolation surrounded by miles of chain-link fencing. There was not another thing — tree or building — within a half mile of the Apostle. No thought had been given to landscaping the grounds around the nuclear plant or disguising in any way its purpose and presence. It was plucking power out of the core of the universe and translating it into kilowatts of mundane electricity to run and light the world.

Escher pulled over on the soft, sandy shoulder of the narrow road and rolled down the side window of the rental car. He read the wooden sign posted on the fence:

No Trespassing.
Property of Northern Illinois Power
and Light Company.
Visitors enter through the main gate
at Sauer Road.
Trespassers will be arrested and
prosecuted under criminal statutes.

"Terrifying," Max Escher said to no one. He looked at the fence. It was ten feet high and it was not topped with razor wire. He knew it would not be electrified either. The fence was a joke. There were a lot of jokes, Max Escher thought, because he already knew so much about the Apostle.

He had prepared himself. He had read the brochures from Britta Andrews about the history of the nuclear plant and about the protests during its construction nearly two decades earlier. He had listened to her talk, listened to the idealism in her voice, watched the tightness in her jawline as she laid out the operation for him. He would have to breach the security of the Apostle. He would have to arrange the burning in such a way that it could not be covered up and it could not be explained away by Northern Illinois Power and Light. He would have to burn the Apostle and not let it seem an act of terror or sabotage but something that had gone wrong inside the plant. She had been very clear about this and he thought she was very clever to hire him and then instruct him in that particular way. A nuclear power plant that destroys itself would make the world tremble again over nuclear power, but this time it would not be a fire in distant Russia, like Chernobyl, but a fire at home, in the heart of the country.

He wanted one hundred thousand dollars

for expenses and setups on Wednesday. She didn't flinch when he said it. She said it would be done and he believed her. He really believed her because he believed this was a go operation, and it was a matter now of planning and details for the battle and he felt like a soldier again, immersed in minutiae while feeling the peculiar stomach-churning strength that always came to him before the time of danger.

Escher picked up the field glasses lying on the passenger seat. He looked across the field and studied the plant.

He saw the gate house about a quarter mile in from Sauer Road. Beyond the gate house was a parking lot filled with cars and pickup trucks. There was a second chain-link fence on the perimeter of the long turbine building and the two buildings that contained the reactor cores. The first reactor was called Red and the second was called Blue, and painted lines inside the turbine plant indicated which machinery was connected to which energy core. The two reactors were twins with duplicate sets of controls, generators, and cores. A four-story administration building was attached to the turbine building at the south end. The giant concrete bowl of steam called the cooling tower resembled an egg cup and it was at the north end.

He studied the layout for a long time, ignoring the cold wind that pinched his cheeks red. The wind promised rain or snow. No cars passed him on Brick Farm Road while he studied the plant and its buildings.

When he was satisfied, he put the binoculars back on the passenger seat. He took out a legal pad in a black vinyl folder and began to sketch in it. He wanted to compare his memory and his sketch to the photographs of the plant she had given him, which were back in his motel room on the toll road. It was one thing to study a problem and another to be inside it, to feel it as a diver can feel the way through murky waters and not be panicked or lose a sense of direction.

When he was finished, he closed the vinyl book and capped his fountain pen. He put the pen in his jacket pocket, rolled up the side window, and started up again. He drove down Brick Farm Road to an unnamed dirt back road that warned against trespassing. He drove down the dirt road. The soil was wet and the car left marks in the sand.

The dirt road went behind the plant, away from the gate house and the parking lot. Behind the turbine building were three trucks marked with the familiar gray symbol of Northern Illinois Power and Light.

Escher continued along, feeling the outline

of the plant as he drove, considering where it was weak and where it was strong. He had no doubt that he would get inside the Apostle. The problem was simply how.

At no point was the chain-link fence anything more than a joke simply outlining the extent of the private property. *Not even razor wire,* Escher thought. *A kid could climb that fence and be inside.*

The dirt road finally came out on Sauer Road, a mile from the main entrance to the Apostle.

This road was busier than Brick Farm Road, and when Escher pulled over again on the wet sand shoulder, he picked up the field glasses very quickly. He would not have the leisure of a long surveillance.

The field glasses — he'd bought them in Frankfurt nine years earlier — were very powerful. He always had a steady hand. It comes from the nature of the trade he had been in. If you had a nervous hand, you couldn't make it in EOD, let alone in demolition in Special Forces. He focused the glasses on the guard in the gate house, who had emerged from the shack to pass through a visiting car. The guard bent down and wrote something down and Escher studied the guard.

Escher smiled because he read the patch on

the sleeve of the guard. He had asked Britta Andrews and she had been puzzled and annoyed by the question because she didn't see the relevance of any answer. He had let the question go. He decided then he would find out first thing because it was so elemental a thing, and Britta had not seen it.

The white patch on the blue sleeve read "Barnes Security."

Escher put the field glasses down again. Barnes Security. It was locked in his mind.

He pushed the stick into drive and made a U-turn back north into Brick Farm Road and then to Seminary Road and then left down the hill to the old iron bridge over the river. In less than a half mile, he was back in Apostle, Illinois, population 712. A garage at the top of Center Street housed the two-man Apostle Police Department and the red and black engines of the Apostle Fire and Rescue Volunteer Department. The top of the brick garage was adorned with a single siren horn. One window, at the back of the building, was covered with bars, and Escher figured that was the jail.

Now he wanted to feel the town the way he had felt around the edges of the nuclear power station.

He glanced at his Rolex and decided the shift would change in another hour or so.

Shifts always change in a narrow time zone, no matter what the industry or plant. It was time enough for him to get a bite to eat and get inside the skin of the town.

Betty's Diner was clean and bright and the food was agreeable. He ordered the meat loaf special and it came on a single heavy plate. The meat loaf was covered with a brown sauce and on the same plate were mashed potatoes and string beans. He ate everything on the plate and two pieces of white bread besides, and this earned him a smile from the waitress who wore "Fran" on her nameplate.

The shift was changing when he entered the likeliest bar on the street. The other two bars were named Tommy's Tavern and My Brother's Place. This bar was called Nuke's, and Max Escher guessed it was as good a place as any to feel his way forward to the next step.

By 6:00 P.M. he and Bernie were friends.

Max Escher had intended to be very cautious, feeling along carefully the way you dismantle the ignition device on a mine when you can't just blow the damned thing up. But Bernie had come to him like a Christmas present, wrapped and ready to be opened. And there were still twenty-nine days to Christmas.

Bernie talked about pro football in that

loudmouthed way of someone who has studied all the statistics and watched all the games and never quite figured out what it was really about. They talked about the cost of health insurance as well. They talked about the Chicago Bulls basketball team, and Bernie did not know very much about that sport either. They even told jokes.

Bernie Lund had three or four jokes of the usual barroom kind and Max Escher matched him, joke for joke, so that Bernie Lund thought Max was a pretty good fellow. The bar filled up with lonely men; a few of them were alcoholics but most of them were just lonely. One man played the jukebox and one man sat and stared at the television set as though he was afraid to go home.

Bernie drank ten beers between 4:14 P.M. and 6:32 P.M. and four shots of Christian Brothers brandy. He weighed 175 pounds and was about six feet tall and he looked good in his Barnes Security blue uniform with his large blue eyes and straw-colored hair. He smoked Winston cigarettes and he was very conscious of brand names. He drank only Budweiser beer and only Christian Brothers brandy and smoked only Winston cigarettes, and he thought General Motors pretty well made the best cars on the road, and he was a Buick man, although he did not own one at the present time.

Escher watched him drink himself into a stupor and he measured the man as if he was watching him through field glasses.

Bernie had been married at seventeen. Then he had done a stretch in Rock County Jail up in Rockford for beating up his sixteen-year-old wife when she was pregnant. The girl kept the baby but she left him, and the last he heard, she had drifted downstate and taken up with a widowed farmer. He guessed the kid would be four by now and sometimes he missed the kid but not most of the time. When he talked about missing the kid, his eyes went wet and Max had patted him once on the shoulder on his way to the rest room. He had stayed in the rest room long enough for Bernie to compose himself.

Bernie said he had gotten his record expunged after his probation was over because it seemed it was the only way to get a halfway decent job. It had cost him five hundred dollars in bribe money to have it done and he had gotten the money — well, he didn't know Ted that well to tell him. He winked at Ted. Ted was Max Escher, good old Ted.

Bernie had tried to enlist in the marines after he cleaned up his record because the marines was the only branch of service — he made the marines part of his brand-name identity. That was why he had gone through the trouble of getting his record expunged in the first place but the marines had rejected him because of low test scores. It was a blow, as though Anheuser-Busch had refused to serve its beer to Bernie Lund.

One summer he had worked in farming but quit in the middle of the harvest, he hated it so. It was dull, hard, demanding work and the farmers were stupid and they looked on Bernie the way they looked on everything they owned, on horses and tractors or Mexican stoop laborers. Bernie had ceased to be a white man once he bent his back for the stupid farmers in their fields.

Max Escher sat and listened and fed a line or lie every now and then. He knew that kind of resentment, the kind that fueled Bernie's existence.

He had not expected it to be delivered so easily to him, all wrapped up and sitting on a bar stool in a saloon called Nuke's. He would have gotten it, tomorrow or the next day or next week, there were bound to be a lot of Bernies in jobs like plant security, a lot of Bernies discontentedly settled into loserhood at the beginning of their adult lives. But this was serendipity to have it so soon in the form of a twenty-two-year-old ex-con who guarded a nuclear power station for the Northern Illinois Power and Light Company, guarding a $3 billion facility for $9.13 an hour, less deductions.

Bernie turned out to live in a rented trailer in Rockland Estates, which was a field full of rented trailers connected to electric lines and septic fields. The park was in a thicket of scrub trees and a few elms on otherwise unusable land two miles west of Apostle, Illinois, on County Trunk BB.

He invited Max to join him and they would smoke some grass. They smoked grass at the kitchen table, where there were burn marks in the Formica. Bernie drank from his bottle of Christian Brothers brandy and they broke open the twelve-pack of Budweiser, which Bernie had brought home for a "nightcap."

The marijuana was not terribly toxic, Escher thought. It didn't have the qualities of the stuff he had smoked in 'Nam or even Germany, but Bernie was one of those guys who could fake himself into a marijuana high. Bernie thought he was really flying and Max Escher watched him all the while. Bernie said the guards got tested for dope twice a year. It was supposed to be random but you could find out easy when you were to be tested.

When Bernie finally passed out at the table, his head down and snoring, his arms folded in front of him, Max Escher sighed. He got up then and went through the trailer. He started with the pigsty that was Bernie's bedroom. Bernie had pornographic magazines under the bed. Escher picked them up, one by one, and noted which ones seemed to have more wear than others. The magazines were the usual thing. They portrayed women in a variety of submissive and salacious positions, except for the last one, which portrayed women in leather who carried whips and who were dominating small, thin, cowering, and quite naked men.

Max Escher thought about that.

Then he replaced the magazine and continued. In a dresser drawer was a photograph of a small-faced pregnant girl in a plain dress cut low over small breasts. There were also photographs — all Polaroid photographs with finger smudges on them — of the same girl in a variety of naked, sexual poses. She was not pregnant in these photos.

"Must've been the first girl to go down on you," Escher said, looking at the photos and thinking of the man sleeping at the kitchen table. He looked around the bedroom and saw it was the testament of a lonely young man. Exactly the kind of loser he expected to find somewhere among the ranks of the rental cops who stood guard over a $3 billion nuclear power plant.

He decided to slip one of the fingerprinted smudged Polaroids into his jacket pocket. Then he probed around some more, sifting through piles of laundry. The bedroom smelled stale with odors of cigarettes and dirty sheets. Everything in the place needed GIing. Escher was a professional soldier and he was trained into the army way of order and he abhorred the disorder of civilians all around him, especially the losers who have lost so much self-respect they have ended up living like animals.

He went back into the kitchen where Bernie snored away at the kitchen table.

"You are a sorry shit, Bernie," Escher said in his uninflected voice. He studied the soft face of the young man, the open mouth emitting snores like sighs. He thought about the women in the magazine who carried whips and lashed the cowering, naked men. He was trying to figure out the best way to use Bernie Lund.

And then he shrugged and went to the door of the trailer and opened it on the cold, bitter night. It had rained a little and the rain had turned to sleet and made frost on the moonless fields.

"Sorry shit, sorry dog-ass shit," Escher said to no one. "And you're just perfect for what I got in mind," he continued, closing the door of the trailer and feeling his way along in the darkness to his car.

Sixteen

Britta Andrews decided it was time to let Michael Horan in from the cold.

She chose a black wool dress for this purpose and gold earrings and a gold necklace that framed her pretty white throat.

Haley brought the car around to her apartment building on Q Street Northwest, and the senator waited for her for five minutes, standing in the foyer of the apartment building and exchanging small talk with the doorman. Haley sat behind the wheel of the big car, listening to a sports call-in program on the radio.

She also wore a small mink. Everything was understated.

She let herself be kissed once between the foyer and the car and then let herself be kissed again in the backseat. She was keeping it cool and Michael sensed this finally and pulled away from her. Haley started up the car and began the run down into the heart of Georgetown.

"I thought we were done being mad at each other," he said. He tried a smile. It was the private version of the public smile that endeared him to voters and media alike. It was an honest and sincere sort of smile that could acknowledge mistakes, admit errors, and shrug its message that the smiler was only human after all.

Britta was immune. She stared at Haley in the rearview mirror and saw that Haley kept glancing back at them. Whatever she had to say to Michael could not be heard by Haley, even if he was one of the invisible little people.

"I'm not angry with you, Michael," she said in her soft, sure voice. "I don't have time to be angry. You disappointed me is all."

"I don't want to disappoint you," he said. It was a good and contrite beginning.

"You think I'm just silly, don't you?" She turned to him, anger in her eyes. It was so unexpected that Michael flinched. What had he said now?

"I don't think you're silly, what are you mad about?"

"Dogs get mad, people get angry," she corrected him.

Haley drove on, pretending not to see or hear. Traffic was light this Monday night. The stores were all open because Christmas was twenty-nine days away. The sidewalks were lightly populated because no one walked after dark in the District unless they were safe or poor or crazy.

"I don't say anything about what we quarreled about," he said. "Not to anyone."

"I don't care what you say to anyone," she said.

"Nine people died in the Pentagon fire, Britta," he said in a very calm voice.

She stared at him in the darkness of the car. She knew the number, of course, it had been on television. But this wasn't television news, this was a man who shared a bed with her, a powerful man, and he was announcing the death toll and it was a sort of private accusation.

"I had nothing to do with that," she said. Then glanced quickly at the rearview mirror and saw Haley's eyes on her. Well, what would Haley do about anything? He was absolutely loyal to Michael; Michael had fed and clothed Haley for nearly fifteen years; Haley was a servant and a servant understands his doglike relationship with the master.

Still. She had blurted it out and she wanted the words back in case Haley heard her. And understood what she was talking about.

Michael Horan looked at her and shook his head slowly and slightly.

She said, "Do they have any idea who set the Pentagon fire?"

He just stared at her for another long moment and then blinked, as though coming out of a trance. He settled in the seat. He shook his head. "The latest suspect is a Libyan terrorist ring commissioned by Colonel Gadhafi. I don't think they have an idea, and when in doubt, blame the Libyans. Not that they're not usually behind a thing like this. What they can't understand is how there were so many fires set simultaneously."

"Can you imagine that happening in 1969? I mean, it would have blown the military mind completely. Can you imagine what they would have done?"

"They would've shut down half the college campuses in the country and put everyone with long hair in concentration camps."

"That would've been great," Britta said. "Too bad it came fifteen years too late."

"You really are a bomb thrower —" he said and interrupted himself. He needn't have bothered.

"No. That was my dad. I don't throw bombs, Michael."

"I'm sorry, Brit."

"It's all right." She patted the back of his hand. She was forgiving him.

The restaurant on M Street was French.

The walls were white, bare of ornament, the wooden floor was polished oak. The maître d' was middle-aged and the waiter wore earrings, long hair and had a small, pencil-thin mustache. He looked dreadful but reasonably clean.

Haley was in the car, listening to the Washington Bullets game on radio.

When they were left alone with their drinks and menus, Michael Horan said, "Are you sure of what you're doing, Brit?"

"I'm sure. Don't worry, Michael, you're not involved. As of Sunday, you stopped being involved in my life."

"I don't understand, you agreed to dinner with me."

Her eyes were very cruel because she was certain now that Michael Horan was hopelessly in love with her. She loved him back, of course, but love comes in different depths.

"I thought we should end as friends," Britta said.

"I don't want to be your friend. I don't want to end anything," Michael said.

"But I told you before you had to be nothing less than a friend. I needed you and you're afraid. I don't know what you're afraid of Michael. Unless you don't trust me and that makes me angry, thinking you wouldn't trust me. You wouldn't trust me because I'm a woman and women are just things and you can't trust them to serious matters, can you, Michael?"

He stretched out his hand and touched hers on the table. She didn't withdraw it but her eyes didn't leave his face.

"I trust you, Britta. I just want you to be careful, to be sure of what you're doing."

"I know what I'm doing."

"I talked to Clair today. I asked him . . . about the money. The credit line. He assumed I had spoken to you. He said I would have to talk to you further about it. I was angry. Clair Dodsworth makes a good commission in handling my portfolio —"

"This has nothing to do with your portfolio. I don't want you to interfere in my business, Michael." She removed her hand from his and picked up the stemmed glass of wine and tasted it. It was cold and smelled faintly of flowers.

"Damnit, Brit. I want you," he said.

Yes, he did want her. He wanted her very badly. He had scarcely touched his glass of Black Label, he was sitting there on the other side of the table and he was really pleading with her for another chance.

"I want to know something," she began.

"What?"

"I want something but I don't know that you can give it to me. If you've got enough gumption."

"What do you want?"

She stared at him a long moment as though considering and then suddenly shook her head and put down her glass. "Nothing, Michael. I almost weakened there. I do miss you. I mean, I will miss you, but it's better this way. You've got a career and I've got the things I have to do."

"I want to help you," Michael Horan said.

"Nothing," she said, shaking her head again.

"Brit, what do you want me to do?"

"Do you really want to help me?"

"I don't want to help you do anything . . . anything illegal."

"I'm not going to do anything illegal."

"You know who burned the Pentagon."

"So what? Are you going to tell on me, Michael?"

"No, I just —"

"You're a child, Michael. I know the people behind that fire set last spring in Copenhagen, the one that destroyed all the records in the environmental department. But I didn't have anything to do with it. I told you, a lot of us know about each other but we all have different methods. You don't think I'd do anything illegal, Michael."

She said it in a steady, sure voice and added a smile to complete the impression. And touched his hand on the table.

Michael said, "What do you want me to do, Britta?" It was the moment they both had been waiting for.

"I want some notes. Copies really. We're planning a paper at the institute on the safety of nuclear power and I want some of the evidence you've collected. In the subcommittee on nuclear plant safety. The hearings, the secret hearings . . ." She said it carefully and made it just vague enough.

Michael stared hard then. This was making the step. This was involving himself.

"Why, Brit?"

"A paper from the Institute for World Development. Publicize the lack of security and safety in nuclear power plants. You've got the information, Michael, the subcommittee has it."

"But it's secret. I can't leak it to you."

"Of course you can. It's done all the time."

"But it's against the rules."

"Not in a good cause."

"I —"

"It was a good cause to try to get Clarence Thomas, wasn't it? You voted against him, didn't you? And I'll bet you know who leaked the Anita Hill investigation."

"That was different," he said.

"None of it's different, Michael. Except me. Except that I'm asking you for this, that's the difference, isn't it, Michael?"

She was very good at it.

"But if I give the notes on our energy hearings to you, when the FBI investigates the leak, they'll link you to me."

"Poo on the FBI," Britta said. "Besides, the institute won't release the findings, we'll have a third party. Like Green World in Britain, some organization like that. The point is: are you willing to help me?"

He thought it over in the next few seconds. He looked at her and wanted her. He looked at his hands on the table and always wanted them covered by her hands. He thought about it and decided they were on the same side and that this was not an illegal thing, not illegal in *that* sense of the word. He saw that it might be a good thing, to let the world know how badly flawed many of the nuclear power reactors were. . . .

She saw he had given in and she waited for the words. The words came slowly and diffidently and she allowed him his dignity. He was doing it, the last link in the thing, the bit she would give to Escher when she armed him and sent him to destroy the

Apostle. The Apostle, she knew, was under review for past problems, and the flaws of the Apostle would be contained in the secret notes of the secret hearings. She could give the secrets to Escher.

They ate their dinner in silence, without any tension between them except the sense of anticipation building.

Michael took her to her apartment in the big car. Haley kept his eyes on the road as the car meandered up Wisconsin Avenue in the thinning late traffic. It was a cheerless, starless night and the orange anticrime lamps made weird shadows on the side streets.

Haley watched them in the backseat. He watched them through the rearview mirror. He kept his eyes on the road most of the time but he could see everything in little glances. He saw Michael put his hand on her knee and he saw that she kissed him. Haley saw Michael let his hand rise between her stockinged thighs. He wondered what that would feel like, just once, to push her back down and let his hand roam up her stockinged thighs and smell the perfume on her body and kiss her. The way Michael was kissing her now, full and deep, tasting her. He wondered about a lot of things as he drove or as he waited or as he dreamed in his room on the single

bed in the back of the house above Rock
Creek Park or as he listened to the radio late
at night and remembered songs he had sung
when he was a child.

Seventeen

Jack Cavett lit a cigarette and inhaled the smoke. Sometimes, at night, after a few drinks, he smoked a few cigarettes.

Devereaux sat next to him. This was a bar down the street from the Dupont Circle Plaza. It was bright and not loud and the barman was watching a basketball game on television. Jack Cavett had picked the bar.

They had tried to see how well they would work together. In the time it took Jack Cavett to drive from the Pentagon on the other side of the river into the District, they both thought it was going to be difficult.

"I'm not in intelligence," Jack Cavett said to Devereaux. He had said it once before but they weren't counting. Jack Cavett was drinking vodka and Devereaux was drinking beer and it wasn't an even match.

"I don't know what game you and General Lee are playing but I'm overmatched already and I don't like it. I'm resigning my commission at the end of the year, that's five weeks and counting and I don't need shit."

"You won't get any, Jack."

Devereaux had let him talk through dinner. Gen. Bobby Lee had insisted the two men get to know each other over dinner. Bobby Lee was very big on people revealing their innermost thoughts while ingesting the meat of dead animals.

"Maybe I'll tell you the game," Devereaux said. He said it in a flat voice without a salesman's edge to it, as though he didn't care what Jack Cavett thought.

Cavett shook his head. "I don't want to know, don't you get it? You and Bobby Lee are cooking up something and it doesn't involve me. I'm just marking time —"

"Special Forces and EOD. Why'd you go into Explosive Ordnance Disposal?"

Cavett blew out some smoke and took another sip of the chilled vodka. "Maybe the same reason I went airborne. Extra pay for a little extra work."

"OK."

"Look, Devereaux, I was in intelligence twice, both times working as Special Forces. We blew up an Iranian operation in London once. I didn't want to get involved like that again. I backed out. You must know that. Bobby Lee knows that. I don't like killing kids. Four kids, we didn't know there were kids involved, SAS never told us. That's intelligence. You know as much as you're supposed to know and no more. Well, fuck it. You and Bobby Lee play spook with each other and leave me out of it."

"Bobby Lee was a good man in 'Nam," Devereaux said.

"Is that right? Well, bless him." He toasted with his glass. "Must be why we won the war."

"Who do you think burned the Pentagon?"

Jack Cavett shook his head. "I don't know nothing. I get paid once a month and keep my mouth shut and brass shined."

In fact, he was wearing civilian clothes. Bobby Lee had insisted Jack change to civvies for work with Devereaux.

"You weren't in Indianhead when you were called Sunday morning."

"No. I was in the District. I had a date."

"With whom?"

"A gentleman never tells."

"Then maybe it's not true."

"What's not true?"

"Bobby Lee said you were in intelligence. You knew how to rig bombs. You were in EOD in England when the IRA set off those bombs, killed those horses —"

"I was dismantling a booby trap set in Lakenheath. Air force EOD team was in

London and I was in Lakenheath, except the booby trap I was taking apart wasn't coming from any goddamned Irish Republican Army. It was the antinuclear crowd, the violent fringe of it."

"Could you have burned the Pentagon?" Devereaux said.

Jack Cavett looked hard at him then. It was right down there on the bar between them. He turned to the barman at the far end and said, "Gimme another one."

The barman left his basketball game, came and poured, and took wet dollar bills on the counter. He went back to the game.

Jack Cavett raised his glass and toasted Devereaux. "Here's to war."

Devereaux waited.

"I could burn it down," Jack Cavett said. "Maybe even do a better job than was done. The Pentagon is a disaster waiting to happen. I've been there five months, I've heard the stories. Fires all the time. Electrical problems, heating problems, the building'd be condemned if the government didn't own it."

"How would you do it?"

"Do what?"

"Burn the Pentagon?"

"Why? You think I burned it? You want me to hang myself?"

"Who were you with in that hotel room?" Devereaux said.

"My wife. Liz. My ex-wife. She's married again so she might not appreciate vouching for me," Jack Cavett said.

"All right, Jack," Devereaux said.

"Look, I told you to fuck you and fuck Bobby Lee. I'm immune and I'm too short to be fucked around by anyone. My papers are in channels now."

"Money," Devereaux said, interrupting the colonel. "Money came into the country more than a week ago. Line of credit. I think it comes from a certain source to finance terrorism. Coincidentally, a week later, the Pentagon takes a burning. Bobby Lee and I have to be on the same page now." He used the cliché because he thought Jack Cavett was used to living in a world of clichés.

"So you're after the terrorists. I hope you catch them," Jack said.

"I'm after the money. Let Bobby Lee handle his own problems. I want to know where the money came from and who it's going to."

"I don't care," Jack Cavett said. "I'm the burned-out case, the officer on his way out. Shit, man, I'm history in the army. What do you think I care about any of this?"

"Because I don't need a liaison who's a stone around my neck," Devereaux said. The words were flat and hard. "If I have to motivate you, I'll motivate you. I'm not playing, Colonel."

"And I'm not afraid, civilian. Not of you or the general or any of your booga-booga spooks."

"We'll start on your wife. Your ex-wife. And her husband. We'll start with them. Then we'll put the FBI on you and on your wife and we'll have the IRS look you over, the last five years of returns."

"Fuck you, Devereaux," Jack Cavett said.

"All right, Jack, fuck me and fuck everyone but don't fuck up what I have to do. Want to do. I can't have someone on the brakes."

"All right," Jack Cavett said. He grinned but it was not meant to be pleasant. His eyes glittered in the lights of the bar and he was a little bit drunk and he knew it. "I went around in the morning and I was looking for points of origin. I talked to a couple of spec fours in communications, I looked at the room where one of the fires started. I'm not looking for anything in particular, I just talked to these kids. I asked them to describe the way the room looked before the fire. They thought the colonel was crazy and they started telling me. Table. Gray metal chairs. I drew a little picture. They would keep looking at the picture and keep adding things as they remembered them. I wasn't the only investigator but some of these arson investigators they brought in . . ." He shook his head. "I should get a job with Max after I resign, I could do the job better than some of them. They're looking for what set the fire. Shit. That not important."

Devereaux studied the face. Jack Cavett was lean and mean, exactly as he had been in OCS twenty-four years ago. He drank a little more now and he still smoked the damned cigarettes when he had a few drinks and he was about ten pounds heavier than he was in jump school but, hell, he was in good shape. Devereaux had noted all that but he had studied the face to see the lie or the hidden thing and he could not see a lie now or any hidden thing.

"What's important, Jack?"

Jack grinned again and it was the glassy smile of a man on the other side of being sober. He reached into the pocket of his leather jacket and pulled out a piece of yellow paper. He unfolded it. It was an ordinary second sheet, yellow and rough, and it contained a rough pencil drawing.

There was a desk and two chairs and a radio transmitter on a second table. There was a telephone on the desk, and on a third table there was an ordinary civilian radio and an automatic coffee maker.

Devereaux stared at the drawing for a moment and then looked at Jack.

"See it?"

Devereaux shook his head.

"See, you're looking for the wrong thing. You want to know who set the fire in the Pentagon but I just want to know how they did it."

"They. It was they, Jack?"

"I assume that. It was a lot of fires."

"I'm interested. I follow the money trail but maybe we can follow this," Devereaux said.

"Look. What does the room have that can be turned into an incendiary device? You've got the desk itself. You can put an incendiary in one of the drawers. It has to have a timer and a small amount of space. You could even put it behind the drawers. All right. You've got the radio transmitter but you eliminate that."

"Why?"

"Because it's not common. To the fires. You see what I mean?"

Devereaux shook his head again.

"Nineteen or twenty fires, we can't be sure which, but they went off like clockwork around oh five hundred hours Sunday. So what was the common element in the fires? Every fucking fire in the building was in a room with a table or desk. That's a common element. But not every room had a radio transmitter."

"And not every room had a regular radio?"

"I haven't finished that yet. I just had all morning before you and Bobby Lee gave me new shipping orders."

"The coffee makers," Devereaux said.

Now the grin was genuine. Cavett was caught up in his explanation. "I like the coffee makers. You know why? Every coffee maker has got a timer on it. So you can set it the night before and wake up and have fresh brewed coffee. I checked three other locations where the fires started and every one had a coffee maker. What if every location had a coffee maker?"

"Could you rig up a coffee maker to start a fire?"

"That's not hard. They start fires in homes without having any accelerant. The fuse on coffee makers is pretty simple, and if it's damaged or suppressed, the coffee maker just keeps heating up until it can melt through the plastic shell and set on fire whatever it's sitting on. This is not a new thing."

"And with accelerant —"

"Yeah," Cavett said. They let the silence speak.

Devereaux looked again at the drawing. "Give this to Bobby Lee."

"You give it to Bobby Lee. I don't want to be involved in this."

"Who's Max?"

"What?"

"Who's Max?"

"Max is Max Escher. We knew each other in service. He got out eighteen months ago. Before his time. Landed a job as a national arson investigator out of Chicago and he bumped into me a couple of weeks ago and we talked about life after the army."

"He was in EOD?"

"Whole thing. Airborne, Special Forces, then EOD."

Devereaux probed at it, wondered if it meant anything. And decided it didn't. "What's your wife's name?"

"My ex's name. Liz."

"Liz what?"

"You going to start down that road?"

"I want to know about you, Jack. You figure this out, how the arson could be started, and you don't want to tell anyone."

"I might tomorrow. I might have just told you, Devereaux. Cover yourself with glory, give your theory to Bobby Lee before the brass tears the general a new asshole. I don't care. The day the army announced it was leaving me, I left it. Fuck the army. I gave it twenty-four and two silver stars and a cigar box full of campaign ribbons and fuck it. I did my time and I just want to be left alone."

"I want the same thing," Devereaux said.

"What are you talking about?"

He stared at Jack and saw himself in the reflection. He understood the stupid sense of uselessness.

"I sent in some people on an operation. Nine months ago into Lebanon. It was about a money trail and they didn't come out. None of them. It was my fault and the very least thing is that they should have something to show for losing their lives."

It was Jack Cavett's turn to see himself in the reflection. He put out the cigarette and picked up the drink and tasted it. He put it down between them.

"Personal," Jack Cavett said.

Devereaux nodded but made no sound.

"All right, Devereaux."

Devereaux waited.

"I won't fuck you up," Jack Cavett said. "But I want you to give this to Bobby Lee, I don't want to start getting buried in this investigation. I don't care who burned the Pentagon, I'm just curious about how they did it."

Devereaux turned it over in his mind. And then picked up the yellow sheet of paper and refolded it and put it in the inside pocket of his sports coat. "All right, Jack, I'll give it to him and don't get in my way. When Bobby Lee wants to know what I'm doing, you ask me what to tell him."

"That's the way I want it."

"You won't be involved."

"Even more the way I want it."

And they both thought it would stay that way.

Eighteen

Devereaux and Rita Macklin made love to each other. When he was satisfied, she was not. It happened that way sometimes. She got up and went to the window naked and looked at the streets in the light of gray dawn. The streets were wet.

"It's raining," she said.

"Come on back to bed," he said.

"I think I'll take a run."

"In the rain."

"A little run," she said.

She dressed in the gloom of the bedroom and he watched her. She put on a white sweat suit and then slipped on a short waterproof jacket with a hood. She ran in every season.

"Take care," he said. They always said that to each other when they parted. It was just a thing they said.

He rose when she left and put on his robe and padded on bare feet into the living room and looked down at the street. She always started out down New Mexico Avenue as far as the park. He watched her emerge from the building and saw her begin to run.

And then he saw the jogger behind her. The same jogger he had first noticed when they took their Sunday morning walk up Wisconsin Avenue. The jogger had a yellow box on his waist and raised it to his eye. The yellow box might have been a tape recorder but it was really a camera and Devereaux was certain of this now. At that moment he felt a shadow of fear for Rita. He stared at her retreating figure and stared at the runner who followed and there was nothing he could do about it.

He went into the bathroom and took a long shower and then he dressed in clean, warm clothes. He wore a black turtleneck sweater and dark trousers. He took down a navy blue raincoat and hung it over the back of a kitchen chair and turned on the coffee maker. He brewed a pot of coffee and thought about Jack Cavett and his theory of arson.

He dialed a number in Maryland.

When Jack Cavett answered the phone, his voice was still thick with sleep.

"Jack, I have to go to Section this morning," the lie began. "I want to push back our meeting to this afternoon. Can we meet around four?"

"Just so I can tell Bobby Lee what you're doing."

"I'll think of something," Devereaux said.

"Then you're not really going to Section."

Silence.

"That's right, Jack. I'm not really going to Section."

Another silence between them. Devereaux had passed along Jack Cavett's theory about the coffee makers to Gen. Robert E. Lee and he had kept the general in the dark about the source of the theory. He had done this to win a measure of trust from Cavett. Now he needed to test how strong the trust was.

"All right. Sixteen hundred," Jack Cavett said at last.

Devereaux put down the phone. He poured himself a cup of coffee and drank it. It was hot and a little bitter.

He went to the window and watched for her. He saw the jogger emerge from the park and then he saw her coming around a corner. He noticed a large, thick man in a raincoat standing on the opposite side of the street in the doorway of a sleeping apartment building. There were no others on the street.

Bobby Lee had called off his watchers. Clair Dodsworth had gone to Mrs. Neumann and told her to stop harassing him. These men in the street below were watchers and that meant that they worked for Clair or they worked for the man Clair fronted for. There was no other explanation.

She opened the apartment door while he was rummaging in the closet off the living room. She stood there and closed the door and noticed he took the pistol out of the box on the top shelf. He removed a clip from the same box and slammed it home into the butt of the automatic pistol. He checked the action, sliding a cartridge into the firing chamber. He had not carried a weapon for nearly a year and she had hoped he would never carry a weapon again. He was out of the field now, he was a senior adviser: he worked on plans and he designed operations. Why did he have to carry a weapon again? Hanley didn't carry a weapon, Mrs. Neumann didn't carry a weapon —

She put her hand in her mouth to make certain she would not say anything.

The Beretta was black and he wore the weapon in a slim holster on his belt. The holster was fixed over his left buttock so that it did not show. It is worn this way by most professionals because it is more comfortable and less noticeable to others and because no one really believes in the quick-draw anymore.

"Why?" she said.

"Two men are following me. Following us. A jogger followed you into the park," he said.

"Are you sure he was following me?"

Devereaux said nothing. He went into the kitchen and poured a cup of coffee for her. She tasted it and held the cup with both hands. She was wet from exertion and from the cold rain. Her face glowed.

"You didn't run very long."

"Just around the park. It was too cold."

"I don't think I'll be very late," he said.

"I fly to Atlanta tomorrow morning. Early. We're doing a piece on CNN."

"All right. I'll be home early tonight."

They spoke around the pistol he had taken down from the box and put in a holster on his waist. But the pistol was there in their thoughts.

"Who do you think they are?" Rita said.

"I don't know."

"This is about the business with Mona," she said.

"I think so."

He stared at her.

"I never met her and I hate her," Rita said.

"She's dead, Rita."

"Good. I'm glad she's dead."

He stared at her for a moment in the bright silence of the kitchen. She put down the coffee cup. "No. Not that. Not dead. But she's become an obsession and she's taken you. Like a ghost. Now you're going out with that, that weapon, and it never will end, will it?"

"It'll end."

"When you're dead."

"It'll end."

She turned and bit her lip. She spoke with her back to him. "Wear a cap. It's a cold rain and it's not going to let up."

"All right," he said. He went back to the same hall closet and took down an Irish tweed hat. It was gray and it was the color of ice and of his eyes. She had bought it for him long ago and he had never worn it. He'd wear it now to tell her that it wasn't like that, the way she thought, about Mona. He took the raincoat and slipped it on.

"I hate this winter," she said.

"You had snow in Wisconsin when you were a girl," he said. "You want snow. Maybe we can go to Wisconsin this winter."

"I liked snow. The days were always bright and clear. I made snowmen and snow forts. I miss the snow, that's the thing I miss."

He bent and kissed her.

"I love you," she said.

He repeated it.

"Take care," she said.

"You take care," he said.

The rain was mean and cold. He walked to the Metro entrance, and he knew they were following him, even without looking around to spot them.

The early morning train was not crowded and one of the watchers made a clumsy move to run up to the next car so that he would not step into the same car with Devereaux. It was not very good, Devereaux thought.

He got off at Connecticut and climbed the stairs to the street. He walked in the heavy rain now to K Street and ducked into a Peoples drugstore. He bought a small notebook and a pen and slipped them into his raincoat pocket. He kept watching the round anti-theft mirrors in the store. He was deciding how he would separate them.

He left the store and walked back down Connecticut to the Metro station and down three flights to the entrance level. He was not in a hurry. He bought a ticket at the automatic machine and pushed through the turnstile.

The train came whooshing into the Red Line station, headed in the direction of Union Station.

The doors opened and discharged a soggy collection of passengers, who bundled off toward the escalators at the far end of the platform.

Riders on the train sat and stared blankly at the three men left on the platform. The riders didn't really see them. Devereaux turned to look at the two men and then stepped onto the train.

He waited a moment. Then he stepped off.

All the doors began to close.

One of them stepped off in time.

The train started up out of the station and Devereaux stared at the passing cars and riders. The other man, the jogger, was caught on the train, staring back at Devereaux on the platform. Devereaux thought they really weren't very good at all — they should never have been separated this easily.

For a moment Devereaux and the second man stared at each other across the length of the platform.

The second man wore a brown fedora with a wide brim, snapped down over the eyes. He was dark and his bulky overcoat concealed a large body.

Devereaux turned toward the escalators and began to ascend. He felt the prod of holster and pistol in his belt over his left buttock. The pistol was reminding him of the next thing.

He had no taste for this anymore. He had been in the field for too many years to have any taste left. The years of the cold war had chipped away at him and this was all that was left, a piece of cold marble with a hollow core. In those years, in those foreign places, it had been a war at least and he had been a soldier who endured it. But this wasn't war anymore. He was in a soft, routine job in an obscure bureaucracy in the District of Columbia, a city full of suspended reality where life was soft jobs and long lunches and languid flirtations and bourbon at four. Yet the weapon in the holster on his belt prodded against the small of his back and reminded him of the other reality.

He rode the escalator up and reached inside his raincoat and removed the weapon and punched off the safety. He slipped the pistol into his right raincoat pocket.

The man in the brown hat was behind him, some forty steps below him. Did he see the slight movement?

At the turnstile level the floors were wet. Men shook their umbrellas dry on the floors as they entered the station. Women with matted-down hair came into the station toting briefcases, and as soon as they were in the dry space, they touched their hair and then gave it up because it was hell to look good in a November rainstorm.

Devereaux asked the attendant for a map of the Metro and he noticed the swarthy man walk through the turnstiles to the ticket machines. He looked as though he might be buying a ticket. It wasn't very good and there was no need for this because he had been made, didn't he realize that? Devereaux had made him and there was no need to pretend otherwise.

Devereaux thought he could lose him, go back down the stairs and play the same game he had played to fool the jogger. But then it would just be put off until tomorrow when the same men would wait on New Mexico Avenue and watch the apartment and wait for him to leave it. Wait to follow Rita running in the park.

Devereaux realized he had no intention of losing this watcher. That's why he had taken the pistol down from the box in the closet. Why it was in his pocket now with his right hand wrapped around the grip and trigger guard. For Mona and the five others he had condemned to death.

He crossed the ticket level to the stairs. He jogged up the stairs. The rain fell in sheets now, much more than formal mourning, real grief. Lightning crazed the darkening sky and thunder rolled in waves down the broad avenues at the center of the city. Traffic formed a funeral cortege, headlamps on in daylight, everything slow and gloomy.

The watcher stood on the second landing by the McDonald's and he was staring straight at Devereaux.

Devereaux smiled then. It was thin and without any mirth or humanity at all. He crooked a finger to the man in the brown fedora. That was all.

He turned then and walked quickly along Connecticut, this time in the direction of Dupont Circle to the north. Up the block he crossed a street, and then turned into the lobby of the Mayflower Hotel.

He slowly walked through the long lobby to the elevators. The watcher was behind him, really coming after him now because the watching game was over for both of them. It was fine now, it was clear what this was, and it suited Devereaux.

He stood at the elevator bank and one of the doors slid open. A man and a woman got off. He stood aside and let them pass and then stepped onto the elevator. He stood in the back of the elevator, reached forward, and punched a floor button. Six. It was six but without any plan at all. He stared out the elevator door at the lobby and he wondered if the man in the brown fedora would step onto this cage with him. In a way that would have made it easier.

The door slid closed.

The elevator rose slowly and reached the sixth floor. The door slid open and he stepped into the corridor.

The morning corridor was busy. A maid was in one of the rooms cleaning and her laundry and cleaning cart was parked outside the open door of the room where she worked.

Devereaux had been a watcher many times and he thought the two men who followed him were not discreet enough. He thought they were stupid, in fact. If the target goes into an elevator, you don't follow him, you wait in the lobby. There are too many chances he can lose you if you follow him. He was sure the swarthy man would note the floor he got off at and follow him.

He waited. He heard the television set on in the room being cleaned. The cleaning maid was watching the "Oprah" show while she worked.

The elevator bell pinged.

The door slid open on six.

It was all right. Only the man in the brown fedora was in the elevator cage. Devereaux had thought about that too, about what he would have done if there had been other passengers in the cage.

But there weren't.

Devereaux stepped into the cage facing the swarthy man. Maybe the man saw it in his eyes. In that moment he looked like a man who didn't believe in what he saw.

Devereaux took out the pistol and pointed

it straight at the man's head.

They waited, frozen.

The doors slid shut.

Devereaux fired.

The swarthy man did not make any sound. The hole between his eyes was dirty and there wasn't even any blood at first. His eyes crossed comically as though trying to see the hole. Devereaux reached behind him and punched seven.

The dead man began to slide down the wall of the elevator cage.

The doors opened on the seventh floor. Devereaux stepped out of the cage and waited for the doors to close again. There were two cleaning carts propped in front of two open doors on this floor and more television sounds.

Devereaux crossed to a door labeled "Stairs." He pushed open the door and started down the concrete stairs to the lobby.

He opened the lobby door and began to walk back to the Connecticut Avenue entrance. He'd almost reached the door when he heard a woman scream in the lobby behind him. He turned and saw that a crowd was gathering at the elevator bank. He pushed through the doors to the street.

Hanley and Mrs. Neumann were beyond this now. If it had been personal about Mona, then this was personal too. They were watching him and that was a threat to him. And to Rita. Now he had returned the threat. They wouldn't truss him up like Carroll Claymore and strangle him on the lawn of Potomac Park.

A tall man in a gray tweed hat and dark raincoat strode up the street toward Dupont Circle. He carried a pistol in his pocket and it was warm against his palm. The rain was very hard now and the clouds swirled in so low that it seemed like fog above the buildings.

Devereaux thought they would have to move against him now and bring this into the open. This would not be a matter of special pleading or hidden influence to stop an investigation or vague bureaucratic threats. Not anymore. There was a dead man in an elevator in the Mayflower Hotel and he was carrying a message just as Carroll Claymore had carried a message in death.

Nineteen

Liz and Bob Fredericks lived in a three-bedroom condominium on the twentieth floor of the 400 East Randolph Building.

The concrete high-rise was perched on the shoreline of Lake Michigan at the north end of Grant Park near the yacht club and the Monroe Street harbor. Their apartment windows commanded a view of the harbor, lake, and park, as well as the skyline of the Loop, which stopped abruptly at Michigan Avenue. It was a good building as condominiums go, and very isolated from the rest of the city. She would often sit at the window with a drink in her hand in early afternoon, like now, and think about her life. She would not really be seeing the cityscape or the lake but she would be seeing little scenes from her life. Sometimes it was when she had been a child, sometimes it was when she and Jack Cavett were young and married, sometimes it was just her alone, a scene of her alone, disappointed at the way everything had turned out.

Like now.

Liz cried often in the early afternoons when she was alone and she was drinking.

By the time Bob came home, she was a different Liz. She could put on the different Liz the way she put on makeup. But this was the naked Liz crying, utterly naked in her soul, without any pretense or defense.

"Oh, Jack, it just turned out this way, didn't it?"

She would speak aloud sometimes to her memory. Sometimes she spoke to Tommy, who'd died. Tommy rode his bicycle down the street they lived on in the officer's section of post housing, and he rode it carelessly as kids do, and he was struck by the drunken master sergeant's car at the corner and that was all. At least Tommy would never be disappointed because he would never have to be any older. Little Tommy.

When she cried, she became angry with herself and with Jack Cavett, who'd let her go. Sometimes she just wanted to slap him, hurt him, wound him, kill him, kick him in the nuts to make him puke, make him cry out with pain and beg for mercy, and then kick him again in the teeth.

"I'm sorry, so sorry, Jack."

She reached then for the gin bottle and

poured a little more medicine into her glass and took a taste of it. They had both been disappointed in everything at the end and it had started with the death of the kid but it hadn't stopped there. The kid. They always called him "the kid" and it was meant to show their love for him. Shit happens. So they stopped laughing together at things. Even after the grief was gone, replaced by the dull leaden mourning that people always carry after someone close dies, even then they realized they could not laugh anymore. Slowly, drop by drop, day by day. They disappointed each other until all the disappointments added up to a final sadness that neither of them could bear in each other's company.

She sat for an hour and grieved and stared at the lake and the city and saw nothing but scenes from her memory. She often did this.

Today the telephone rang and intruded on her grief. She let it ring at first but the phone insisted and she got up, went to the phone stand, and picked up the receiver.

The doorman spoke a name.

She waited a second and shook her head. The name intruded on the haze she had created. She asked him to repeat the name but the next voice on the phone belonged to the visitor.

"Hi, Liz, just passing through town. Jack

told me you lived in Chicago now and I thought I'd say hello while I had a chance."

Waited.

She closed her eyes and saw the face that belonged to the voice.

"All right, Max," she said in her raspy voice. "Come on up."

She was wearing a wool sweater and baggy cotton slacks from summer. She patted her hair and carried the glass into the kitchen and put it in the sink. Then she retrieved the bottle of Gordon's on the window ledge and carried it into the kitchen as well and put it back into the refrigerator.

She heard him at the door and went to it.

She had never cared for Max Escher. He was creepy and he had wanted to sleep with her at a time in her life, in her marriage to Jack, when she wasn't very particular about whom she slept with. But not Max. She could not have slept with Max even if it had not been an act of betrayal of Jack.

She opened the door.

He still carried his cocky, crooked grin, the one that was challenging and mocking and just a little crazy. That was it. Just a little crazy.

"Box of candy. Hope you aren't dieting."

She took the box of candy and looked at it and then at him. "We diet till we die," she said. "Come in, Max."

"Not interrupting?"

"Not interrupting."

"I saw Jack."

She closed the door. "Is that right?"

"Couple of weeks ago. He's getting out of the army at the end of the year."

"I know."

"I told him I might line him up something."

"It's been six years," she said.

"Six years. Time flies," he said. He walked into the living room and looked out the windows. "Wow. Nice view." He always said things like "wow" without any embarrassment. "I like this view."

"It's a nice view," she said, standing somewhat behind him, watching him go to the windows, exclaim at the view, watching him look around the room, calculate the wealth of the room with his eyes.

"You work in the suburbs," she said. "Why'd you say you were passing through?"

He turned to her. The grin was gone. There was something else about the eyes, too.

"You talked to Jack since I saw him."

"Yes," she said. "On the phone." And then she thought it was stupid to lie about talking to Jack, what did it matter what Max Escher thought about anything?

"He called me the other day," she said, adding to the lie.

"You ever see him?"

"No. I never . . . He said he was trying to line something up and he mentioned you. You work for an investigation company or something."

"Yeah. Insurance investigations." He tried his grin again. It wasn't as good as before. "Army's leaving Jack same as it left me."

They waited. They were not friends, they had never been friends, and their connection was Jack and a common past.

"Get you a drink?"

"You got Wild Turkey?"

"No. We've got some Early Times. Bob doesn't drink bourbon. No one drinks bourbon anymore."

"I drink it," Max said. He said it in a peculiar way that was not pleasant. "But I'll drink some Early Times. Rocks. Splash of water."

He followed her into the kitchen. She pulled out the bottle and took down a glass from the cabinets. He was watching her in profile and she resented it. She poured the whiskey over ice and splashed a little tap water into the glass. She gave him the glass.

"You gonna have a drink?" he said.

"Just some Perrier." She opened the refrigerator door and he was behind her. She reached for a bottle of Perrier water.

He said, "Bob likes to keep his gin in the refrigerator? Saves on ice. Come to think of it, you kept the gin in the refrigerator, didn't you, Liz? That's your gin."

"I don't drink in the afternoons," she said.

"Sometimes you did."

"That was then, this is now."

She was angry and she didn't want him to see it. She turned away from him and took out a church key and popped the top of the bottle of water. She poured the water in a glass.

When she was ready, she turned back to him.

"Well, cheers," he said and clinked glasses. She tried out a smile.

"I said I was passing through, I'm passing through. Doing work on the West Coast the last few weeks, big arson up in Portland, Oregon, we're running it down."

"Is that right?" she said. Then she thought she should be nice to him. For Jack's sake, in case Max would give him a job.

"That's nice that you want to help Jack."

"I like Jack. I always liked Jack."

"It's nice what you're doing for him."

"I can do that for him. Would you like that, Liz?"

"I'd like to see Jack get a job."

"No. I mean, would you like to have Jack

241

living in Chicago? Close at hand, I mean?"

She stared at him. Maybe it was the afternoon gin, she didn't know what to say. His smile was still there but it kept changing its shade or its meaning.

"Sure. We're friends. We stay in touch."

She walked back into the living room. It was a larger room. She walked to the wall of windows and looked out at the gray day of the city. She looked at the lake, gray and green beneath the clouds. He was behind her and she was afraid he would touch her.

But he said, "Liz."

She turned to Max.

"I'll get Jack that job if you want me to."

She turned back to the window. She pressed her forehead against the window and felt the cold. The park below was brown, the trees pretended to be dead.

Then he touched her.

He touched her very lightly on her back. He let his hand linger a moment on her back.

She turned to him. Her eyes were wide.

"I can do that if you want," he said.

"Get Jack the job," she said.

"I want to know what you want. I want to do something you want to do," he said.

"I don't want anything," she said.

He smiled at her. He touched her arm now and he caressed it for a moment. She knew what this was and she thought she was petrified and would never move again.

"I didn't know you were married to Bob Fredericks, didn't even know you were in Chicago until Jack mentioned it to me. We had a few drinks together and talked about the old days. He's up in the Pentagon now, filling out the time until he resigns. His paperwork is moving through the pipeline, he might even get out before Christmas."

He kept caressing her arm above the elbow. She stood there and felt it and didn't feel it.

"Bob Fredericks seems like an old man. He's got white hair. Saw in the paper. What are you, some kind of a trophy for him?"

"Do I look like a trophy wife?"

She snapped out of it and pulled her arm away from him. But he just smiled at her.

"You look good to me, Liz."

"I'm forty-two years old," she said.

"You still look good. You always looked good. Some women never lose their looks."

She said nothing.

"Liz, you cheated on Jack but you never cheated with me. Why is that, Liz?"

She wanted to move away from him but she couldn't. She was afraid of making any move at all.

"Why is that, Liz?"

"What I did or do is none of your business."

"But I just wanted to know."

"Why don't you leave, Max, just leave. I think you said the wrong thing," Liz said.

And then he spoke in a flat voice that carried no inflection and gave equal weight to every word. "You fucked everything that moved on that post, just before you and Jack split up. You fucked the fucking supply sergeant. Jack knew you were fucking around but even Jack couldn't ever know how many guys you sucked off. You drank all afternoon and you always kept the gin in your refrigerator and you sucked off every cock on that post except mine."

She was very frightened now because he wasn't moving away from her and because this building was built like a brick shithouse and it was so soundproof she could scream and even someone next door wouldn't hear her and because Bob wouldn't be home for another six hours and because there was nothing she could do if it came down to it. She could fight him a little and call the cops afterward and she could go to a hospital and let them look inside her and scrape her. She —

He grabbed her hard and pushed his mouth on hers and she pushed her arms against his chest.

And then he let her go, just like that.

He frowned at her.

"Fuck you, Liz, and your rape fantasies. You could beg me to fuck you and maybe I would then, but I don't need it that bad. Not from you, not from any broad."

"Get out of here." Soft, empty voice.

"I'm going to get out of here, Liz, but I want you to know something. You want to help out Jack, you put out for me the way you didn't when you were married to him. It hurt me, Liz, you were such a slut with everyone and you wouldn't even let me touch you. I was hurt. That rankles me still, Liz, that's a real insult."

She did not speak.

"You think about Jack because he still thinks about you. It was terrible to see him. He talked about you and about the kid who got killed and I felt sorry for him, I really did. Never expect pity from a woman, let alone a whore like you, Liz. You don't even think you owe Jack something, do you? For humiliating him, making him wear the horns. God, women. Well, think about Jack, Liz, and I could arrange it for him, he would work right out of Chicago, you'd be able to leave your old man in the morning and drop in on him when you got the blues and you wanted to drink a little afternoon gin.

Your old man wouldn't know the difference, he really looks like an old man. So think about it, Liz, because I can do it for him if you want me to."

"Leave," she managed. Her voice trembled.

"Here's my number on a card in case you change your mind, Liz. You call and talk to the recording and leave a message for me. Tell me where and when and I'll try to be there. I can pretty well fix it for Jack to get a job. Everyone needs a job, he's not going to live on partial retirement."

"He can find a job. He doesn't need me."

"You think it's that easy, Liz, you haven't worked for years. He's forty-six years old looking for work the first time in more than twenty years? You'd be surprised how many people are out looking for a job, shit, there's people who'd work for food. I wouldn't tell Jack, don't worry, if that's what's worrying you, I wouldn't tell Jack or Bob or anyone else you happen to be currently fucking. I just want to be part of the club. I want to be initiated, you might say."

"Leave," she said again, almost like screaming but she felt drained of screams.

He grinned at her. "I'll leave, Liz, when you come over here and give me a kiss."

She stared at him.

"Come on, Liz," Max said.

She stood very still, hoping the horror would pass.

"Then I'll just come over and kiss you good-bye."

He went to her and held her a moment.

He kissed her and she felt his lips and she did not move, she felt his arm around her waist, she stood absolutely still and waited for it to pass.

Then he was finished.

Stepped back.

"My card," he said. He dropped it on a side table. "Give me a jingle, Liz."

She could only stare.

"I know you're going to call me, Liz, I just know it. You'd do anything for Jack, wouldn't you? Don't you feel guilty about leaving him? Besides, Liz, it's just fucking and I'm a good fuck, I really am, and you've fucked men, haven't you, Liz?"

He went to the door and opened it and looked back at her once and closed it. He was grinning all the time.

You've fucked men, haven't you?

She felt so cold.

And then she began to cry again.

Twenty

Britta Andrews read the Xerox copy. There were 234 pages of testimony on the Apostle nuclear power plant in Illinois. The special subcommittee on safe nuclear practices had heard the testimony in secret. The testimony had come from contractors, plant inspectors, members of the Nuclear Power Commission, the Federal Bureau of Investigation unit charged with nuclear safe practices. It was all so good because it was so secret.

He was sleeping in the bedroom. She had let him crawl back into her good graces and she had enjoyed it as well. Michael Horan wanted her very much and he became more considerate now in his lovemaking to her because she had once withdrawn herself from him. He knew she had wanted him slowly and he knew that he should linger when he licked her neck under her chin and then when he licked her nipples. He was a gentleman and it was perfect for her and she gave him pleasure.

And now she read the report spread out on the breakfast bar in the kitchen. It was so very good. The Apostle had had twenty-nine serious violations in the past eight years and it had been very close once to being shut down until the violations were cleaned up.

There was an investigation of a welder who smoked marijuana on the job in the plant and the dismissal of three security guards who were selling liquor on the premises.

She would show the report to Max, but after Max did what he had to do — after he burned the Apostle — the report would surface very quickly in the world's press and it would condemn nuclear energy even while the world reeled in horror at the Chernobyl created outside Chicago.

Of course, Michael couldn't know any of this yet. He was still sensitive about these things. He still was afraid of making a real decision. Like all politicians, he wanted to avoid decisions or anything that was painful. It had to be done, and in time he would have to know and he would then be part of it, part of her, really, and he would have to accept that.

Britta wore a satin white nightgown and drank a glass of skim milk and she was very beautiful. It was the middle of the night. She read the words of testimony and wanted Max to call her. She realized everything she was doing was momentous and that it would change the course of history and she was very calm.

Britta was amazed at how calm she was.

Twenty-one

Clair Dodsworth said, "I don't understand the wisdom of this meeting. At this time. The business has been resolved, hasn't it?"

The visitor was a good-looking young man of dark complexion whose eyes were the color of a cup of Turkish coffee. His eyes were liquid and they might be on fire. His voice by contrast was soft, modified by an English public school education and further refined in the mill of Oxford University.

"The business has not been resolved. It has taken a turning and we can't be concerned now about appearances or timing," the visitor said.

"Appearances are always our concern. Appearance is what attracted . . . you . . . to seek my services."

"An unfortunate thing has happened," said Abdul Khashogi. "A man I have employed from time to time was the man who was found shot to death in an elevator in the Mayflower Hotel."

"It was in the newspaper."

"Yes. But not the identity of the man. The police speculate this was a drug murder and let them so speculate. But it was not that, Clair. Not at all."

Clair Dodsworth said, "I don't want to be concerned with any violence. Any violence to anyone."

The visitor named Abdul Khashogi smiled. His smile was perfect in that brown face. His teeth were perfect. "Clair, there is violence in this world. And terror."

"I represent you. Your interests. In this city. In the government circles I —"

"You speak as a lawyer drawing a new contract."

Clair shook his head. "This is not a new contract, Mr. Khashogi. We have a contract, verbal and written, and I am noting it, not redrawing it."

Abdul Khashogi sat for a moment and stared at the older man. They had coffee on a table between them. They were in Clair's offices on L Street. The coffee was too weak for Abdul Khashogi's taste. He was the operating officer of International Credit Clearinghouse and he had flown all the way from Syria five days ago because he wanted to oversee matters that were beyond the competence of Clair Dodsworth. He was not the president of ICC, not listed on its board of directors in any country where it operated. He was, in a sense, the political officer of ICC just like the men the KGB once placed as "political officers" on every ship and in every unit of the armed forces of the Soviet Union.

"Clair." He let the name linger in the surrounding silence. "You are being paid very well by us. Five hundred thousand a year for your skills, your contacts, and for your sterling reputation. When you agreed to sell us these things, we, in turn, naturally sought to protect our investment in them. If you are disgraced, your reputation ruined, if your contacts shun you, then, well, the money we are paying to you would be money lost in a bad investment."

It was said in a voice brutally soft.

Clair flushed. His withered cheeks momentarily took on color at the outline of the cheekbones. "A man cannot sell his good name. He lends it to a good cause."

Abdul Khashogi said, "Your colleague, Mr. Claymore, was a very unfortunate man."

The color in Clair's cheeks drained.

"Carroll," he said.

"Carroll spied on you, Clair. He spied upon you on behalf of this agent of R Section. Why is this damned R Section so persistent in this?"

Clair said nothing.

"They knew of his penchant for children, for little boys. Pederasty is still a frowned-upon vice in this country. I shouldn't wonder that in a few years it will be a celebrated cause, but not at this moment. They used him."

"You should not have done that. I would have . . ." Clair Dodsworth faltered for a moment. "I would have taken care of this."

"We did not kill him. He killed himself. He betrayed you. I can assure you of that. When you spoke to me of this Institute for World Development, I was intrigued because you assured me that this woman, this Miss Andrews, was a capable force. My . . . associates . . . are tired of empty gestures and threats. I fear the Arab peoples cannot be taken seriously until we replace our love for empty gestures with quiet action. It speaks much more loudly. I am the operative, Clair, I convey the monies to people like Miss Andrews. To the people of the Dove."

"She wants to demonstrate the insecurity of . . . of a particular nuclear power station."

"And that will please my . . . associates. Who sit on their oil and see the price of it diminish day by day. If there is no more nuclear energy, then so much the better. It's a small investment, Clair. We were willing to chance it but not at the price of having this

. . . this agent of R Section probe to our very heart."

"She wants money to research —" Clair began.

Abdul held up his hand. He stared at Clair with amusement. Did Clair really believe this or was he merely postulating an argument before the fact?

"We watched Mr. Devereaux of R Section after you made your protestations to this woman, Mrs. Neumann. Why are there so many women involved in this, Clair? These are not womanly matters. Terror. Intelligence."

"She withdrew her agents. I named them. I named Devereaux. The name that was given to me."

"That was a mistake, Clair." Softly. "You reveal too much to them. So that when we watched Mr. Devereaux after, we didn't know that he knew. He must have known. He separated the watchers at the Metro station on Connecticut Avenue. A trick. Then he lured one of them to the Mayflower Hotel and assassinated him in an elevator."

"I'll protest this. I can make a contact at Langley. I can confront Mrs. Neumann."

The Arab shook his head. "You have nothing to protest."

Clair paused and thought about it. The

coffee turned tepid in his cup. He stared at the cup as though he could see how cold it had become.

"Mr. Devereaux," said Abdul Khashogi. "He has boxed you, Clair. You can hardly say you knew agents shadowed the man, can you? You didn't know about them. He is very bold and I must say I admire what he has done while I deplore it. What he has done cannot be acknowledged at all, even in protest."

Clair Dodsworth suddenly shrugged. He stood up and loomed over the visitor.

"I will resign. I don't need grief at my age. I've had a long career in this city and I won't risk it now for some tawdry business involving spies. You wanted Carroll and I to arrange a way for ICC to get into the banking business in this country without a lot of snooping from the banking authorities. I think we served you."

"You did well. We've shown our gratitude. You made us aware of the Dove."

"The Dove isn't an organization as such. It is . . . a network of like-minded people. I know only a little about it but I know that Britta Andrews is part of it. You got that from me."

Khashogi waited. He was not smiling now. He waited in the silence and Clair knew he was expected to say something and he couldn't think what it should be.

"What do you want, Abdul?"

"What will the Dove do with my money?"

"I told you. A plan to expose the failings of the nuclear power industry. There are secret files. Of testimony —"

"Pah. Not for five million dollars in credit."

"There are secret files of testimony," Clair persisted.

"And her friend? Senator Horan?"

"He has access to the files."

"And she bribes him?"

Clair felt uncomfortable with the last question. He made a face and went to the window and looked down the narrow length of L Street.

"I don't think that's involved," Clair said carefully.

"No. Neither do I. Then why has one hundred thousand dollars of this credit line been withdrawn by Miss Andrews?"

Clair turned, startled.

"You didn't know this?"

Clair shook his head.

"I'll tell you things now, Clair, because you have to know."

"I don't want to know."

"R Section sent six agents into Lebanon last spring. To find the sources of funding for the bank. For ICC."

"I didn't know any of this."

Abdul Khashogi held up his hand. "We discovered all the agents within three weeks. They were pathetic, really. One killed himself."

"The others."

"Are dead," Abdul Khashogi said. "That should have been the end of it. This R Section could not even acknowledge it had authorized an operation like that. We waited, to see if they would send others."

"And all the while, I was setting up ICC to control District Savings Bank and I was never told this." It was an accusation. And a defense.

"It didn't concern you. But obviously it does now. This agent, this Devereaux, he was senior adviser for operations. He authorized this penetration in Lebanon. He was betrayed to us by one of the agents, a woman. Obviously, then, this Devereaux has now connected you to the bank and this Devereaux feels you are the key to breaking into the secrecy of ICC."

"Why didn't you tell me any of this?" Clair's hands began to tremble. He could not will them to be still.

"It did not concern you then. It concerns you now. You must be in contact with Miss Andrews and determine precisely what she intends to use these funds for. The credit line, which she has already dipped into."

"I don't want to know," Clair said.

"But you must. Then Miss Andrews must use her connection with Senator Horan to counterthrust. Against this agent for R Section. Against R Section itself. Am I not informed that R Section, like the Central Intelligence Agency, is not authorized to operate in this country? Then why is Mr. Devereaux operating here? Should he not desist?"

"I have friends in Langley —"

"The last thing we need is to involve yet another intelligence agency." Abdul now sounded annoyed with the older man. "I want this Miss Andrews to inform you what she will do with the money extended to her, to this bogus Institute for World Development. To her and to her friends in the Dove. Such as you, my dear Clair."

"I am not part of the Dove, I am aware of —"

Abdul waved his hand impatiently. "No more denials, Clair. You move in all circles of power and the Dove represents one such circle. You sell your name and your influence, and your influence extends into every place. ICC wanted an American bank connection and you could provide it for us, you could cover us, become our American agent. And then you inquired what we intended to use the bank for and we made it very clear, I think, that there was a need to establish a real way to use our funds for profit and for political gains. You thought to tell us of Miss Andrews. Of course we knew of her, her work in Europe on behalf of the Greens. And then there was the fire in Denmark where she had so recently labored on behalf of the violent fringe of the Green movement. This intrigued me, Clair. Her father was a violent radical himself. In his time. I want to know now what she will use this money for. And I want her friend, Senator Horan, to stop this harassment of you, of the bank. Of my associates."

Clair stared at him for a long moment. When he spoke, his voice was soft. "Then why not take care of Devereaux yourself?"

"We may," Abdul Khashogi said. "But this extends beyond him, doesn't it? If R Section authorized six agents to penetrate the ICC in Lebanon, then it has authorized his illegal activities in this country. How many more are there? I want an investigation of R Section itself, Clair, to stop this."

He leaned forward then. "The bank is more important than any other consideration. I want Miss Andrews to reveal her intentions. To you. And to use her influence with her famous friend to stop R Section. You understand that now, don't you, Clair?"

Twenty-two

Max Escher came up behind her as she entered her apartment building on Q Street, and slipped his arm around her waist. Henry, the doorman, watched to see what she would do.

The action startled her.

Max grinned his cockeyed grin. Britta's instinct was to be angry with him but the grin stopped it and the doorman who watched them stopped it. She was not in the habit of providing entertainment for people like Henry the doorman. They went into the elevator.

"How are you?"

"I thought you were going to call me," she said.

"I was thinking about that and then I thought it was better to see you. I wasn't wrong about that. Fly out seven hundred miles to see you and you're worth every mile, kid."

"I've got something for you," she said.

"You got a kiss for me?"

"I've got secret testimony on what a wreck

the Apostle power plant is. A subcommittee of the Senate, a secret subcommittee."

He frowned then and let his hand slide off her waist. They rode to her apartment in the elevator in silence. She was puzzled by that. She looked at him curiously and then fished her keys out of the purse and unlocked her front door.

He followed her into the front room. Everything was neat, ordered. It was her way in life to be neat and orderly. She thought she could never marry anyone because that would be a messy corner of her life she would have to live around. If she wanted companions, she could always have companions. And there were servants, as many as she wanted to buy. Like Max now, who was a servant in a way, who acted like he was more. He sprawled his frame onto a precise white chair by the window.

She closed the door. "I don't like to be touched when I'm not asked," she said.

"Is that right?"

It was a punk's reply, she thought.

"I've got hundreds of pages of testimony," she said. "Really good stuff, you can use it in your research —"

"Oh, that's horseshit. I've got no time to read a bunch of transcripts. I've got the plant schematics —"

"Then how're you going to get into the plant?"

He stared at her for a moment. "You look so good, I could eat you up. The funny thing about me is that I get that way in operations. Always have. Get my adrenaline going or something, it affects my testosterone."

"I don't want to hear about it."

"I don't want to hear about your fucking testimony. What'd you do to him to get him to give you the papers? You go down on him?"

"You are crude, Mr. Escher, and I despise that," she said. Her voice was full of frost.

"What'd you do for him?"

"I didn't do anything for him. He did it for me."

Max Escher smiled at that. He looked out the window then, away from her, still smiling. "I bet he did. I bet you stamped your foot and he jumped. I just bet he did."

He turned back to her. "You're used to running men, aren't you, Britta?"

"I want you to read the testimony."

"I don't have to."

"Why?"

"I know the way in."

She held her breath.

"I know the way in and I know the way out. What do you think of that, Britta, that I already figured it out?"

"I don't believe you."

"I don't care if you do. I've got it set up. I have to arrange a couple of things. Get some soup for the fire. Get some other things. And I got to set up a guy. He's waiting to be set up but I got to work on him very carefully so that when it blows, he won't know he did it."

"What man?"

"Guy I met."

"Where? Here?"

"No, not here."

"Where then?"

"Look, Britta. You're paying for the burn. For the fact of the thing. Not for knowing every detail."

"I'm paying a lot of money."

"So far, you advanced a hundred thousand. That's not a lot of money. A lot of money is two million dollars."

"You expect me to hand it over like that?"

"Just like that. In hundred-dollar bills, not in sequence. Old bills. That might take a day or two but you can do it. Rich people can do anything if they want to."

"I don't want to."

He stared at her. She was still standing in the foyer, still wearing her fur coat, her keys still in hand.

"Then we got nothing to talk about," he said.

"I want some guarantees."

"And I don't want comebacks. The less you know, the less chance there is for a comeback."

"Are you a fool, Max? I'm totally involved."

"You're involved with all kinds of people. You know some people in Europe, you know people here. You know about the Dove network. You know a certain U.S. senator. See, you already know more than me. But I don't want you to know every damned detail."

"I'm the one who's paying," she said to him. It was a rich way of speaking.

"I'm the one who's doing," he said. "Two million dollars, Britta. Ought to fit in a big suitcase."

"And when will you do this?"

"Oh, a week or two at the most."

"I can't sell my stock in that time."

"The eighty thousand shares in Northern Illinois Power and Light? Shit, Britta, are you crazy? You want to sell all your shares a week before one of their nuclear plants burns down? Are you crazy? You want to call that much attention to yourself?"

She hadn't thought of it.

"Go for the long term. The stock'll drop but that's a sacrifice you have to make. For the cause. It'll come back. Might take a year or two or three but it'll come back. It's not as though they're not going to need electric power in Chicago even after we do a Chernobyl on it." He was grinning at her again.

"You might be right."

"Of course, I'm right."

Silence again. She took off her coat and noticed she still had her keys in her hand. She put the keys on the telephone stand. She hung the coat in her hall closet and turned to him again.

"You look good, kid," he said.

She did look good. She always did.

"I could eat you up," he said.

The voice made her tingle. Exactly like moving under high-tension lines.

She went to the kitchen and took a bottle of Perrier out of the refrigerator. She carried it to the counter, opened it, and poured it in a glass. She carried the glass into the living room. He was there, still sitting sprawled on the small white chair. He was too large for the chair.

"How are you going to burn the Apostle?" she said in a calm voice.

"The best way to burn something is to use what you'd call rocket fuel as the accelerant. I've developed my own primer, my own invention, you might say, it's all plastic. It was originally developed out of the technology for plastic guns. I was involved with that for awhile while I was in EOD. We were called in to lend expertise to a team constructing a model for airport security. Model was too expensive they finally decided. Assholes. Anyway, I've got a supplier for the rocket fuel. There. I told you something, Britta. Now you owe me two million dollars."

"I won't pay for something I don't even know is going to happen."

"It's going to happen."

She sipped her sparkling water.

"I burned the fucking Pentagon, didn't I?" She waited.

He sat up straight suddenly. "If you don't trust me to do this, then it won't be done. I don't want to come back to you after I burn the Apostle and ask you for the money. You might set me up. Your friend Senator Horan could have me taken care of. I don't really trust rich people. I sure the hell don't trust politicians."

"But I should trust you."

"No." He got up then, big and loose-limbed. He said, "I don't need it that bad, honey. I was getting carried away by it, it's an exciting thing, but I don't need it that bad. I can do little things. Four or five burns a year and let the cop arson investigators chase their shadows and let me laugh my way to the bank. I don't need something this big where every fucking federal agency in the world is going to be on my case. I don't need it that bad."

And he crossed the room to the foyer and stretched out his hand for the knob on the front door.

Suddenly — she never knew why she did it — she put her hand on his. She made him wait. She was very close to him now.

"I can get you the money. It'll take a little time to get the cash is all. I trust you, Max."

"All right," he said. But he still held the doorknob. And she still covered his hand with her own.

"I just wanted to know. For me."

"I think you could sell some of it. Some of the stock. But not all of it. Not even most of it," he said.

"Escher," she said.

She kissed him then because he was so close. Because the foyer was small and because they were crowded against each other. When she kissed him, he kissed her back.

He released the doorknob and slipped his hand around her waist easily, as he had done on the street. He pulled her to him and pressed her against him and she was still kissing him and they were reaching into each other's mouths with their tongues. They could not explain in words what was happening to them.

It had to do with the smallness of the foyer and the touch of hand on hand and it had to do with other things. Perhaps the thought of really doing it, of burning the Apostle.

She used her free hand to reach his crotch and she held him there, felt the growing muscle beneath the material of his trousers.

He kissed her. Every man kissed her in a different way. She could tell who the man was by the kiss. She slipped her free hand from his crotch around his buttocks and he did the same thing to her, felt her beneath the satin material or whatever it was she was wearing. They were touching each other, here and there, and her breasts pressed against the material of her shiny white blouse and then he reached his hand inside her blouse and felt her breasts. Then he took his hand from inside her blouse. He had very broad shoulders and his arms encircled her as though to make her small against him, to crush her breasts against his chest and she couldn't stop kissing him and then tasting him, licking his neck and clawing the shirt on his back.

They made it to the bedroom, stumbling down the hall, fell on the bed and tore at each other's clothing until their crotches were naked and they could make sex to each other still partially clothed.

Britta thought he would never come.

She gasped and came again and again, he rubbed away inside her and she could not describe the pleasure of it.

And when he climaxed, his body became rigid and she held him as fiercely as she could, forcing him deep into her, entwining his back with her legs and biting him, shoving her finger into his rectum to make it even more fierce.

And then, for a while, they just lay there, gasping and not speaking.

"It's going to burn, Britta. I know exactly how it's going to burn. It's going to burn through the cooling pipes to the core. D'ja know the cores are inspected visually every twenty-four-hour period — there's a walk-through with a nuclear engineer and a security guard — d'ja know that? Shit, I know the Apostle now like we had been friends."

He was talking to her but he was talking to himself in a whispery voice in the bedroom, letting the words float up like clouds to the ceiling. Just lying there in the bed, his shirt unbuttoned and his trousers in a heap with his underpants at the end of the bed and his penis lying against his inside thigh, weeping.

She listened to the words and saw it happening, saw the Apostle burning, saw the poisonous release of steam. She saw the pitiful wretches screaming, she saw all the death that would come in the painful weeks and months and years that followed, saw it and had pity, real pity in her heart, but saw it had to be done. It really had to be done.

He was still talking and she reached over his body and took his penis and held it for a moment and then she dipped her face to it and she took it in her mouth and she felt the muscle grow rigid in her mouth.

He stopped speaking. The words were in the room above them and they both saw the power in the flat words that hung like clouds.

She wanted to suck him forever and he pulled away from her lips and he opened her legs again and it was much better, what he wanted to do for her.

And when it was over the second time, they were exhausted and they slept. And when they woke up, it was without any words because they didn't need them.

He took a long shower and he rubbed her body with soap. He soaped her breasts and he kissed the nipples of her breasts in the shower. She giggled then and he grinned at her.

"You'll do it," Britta said.

"I told you," he said. "It's just easier than I thought it would be."

"And you have to tell me."

"And you can't tell anyone."

"I won't tell anyone."

"Then I can tell you," he said. He felt very happy with her. He soaped her between her legs and it felt good to her. She soaped him between his legs. He watched her hands on him.

The water fell on both of them from two shower heads. The steam rose in the bathroom. It felt good and free.

"Security," he said.

"Mmm," she said. She was making him hard again.

"It's security, always is. A billion-dollar facility and they hire junkies and ex-cons and every other kind of lowlife to do the security. Saw it when I was stationed down at Indianhead. That's the naval propellant plant, they call it, but it's the EOD school. Explosive Ordnance Disposal. And they do some testing there. So what kind of security they got? Civilians on the gate house. I looked at it, Britta, that feels so good, keep doing that, that feels good —"

"You looked at it," she said, rubbing him.

He closed his eyes on the shower. "Fucking rent-a-cops. You call that security? You think you can't get in and get out with a badge and an identification card and a uniform? Hell's bells, I can do it just like that, but I've got to set someone up first, got to do that."

"Do what?"

"Set up someone for the Pentagon."

"They don't know it's you."

"Sure, but they keep looking until they've got a real live body in hand. Set that up, go back to Illinois, set up the Apostle, set up my body out there. Everything is about setup."

"You really are something," she said.

"Yeah." He opened his eyes. "I never did it wet."

They did it wet.

Twenty-three

Jack Cavett picked up Devereaux at the corner of 14th and K streets at 1620 hours, a little late because of the traffic backed up on the bridge. Devereaux slid into the passenger seat and then removed the pistol and holster from his raincoat pocket without any comment.

"I want to use your glove compartment," he said.

"It's not locked."

Devereaux put the pistol and holster in the compartment and shut it. Cavett stared at the weapon and then at the glove compartment and then released the brake and started up the street. The traffic was dense but it was moving at least. Jack Cavett went with the flow. The two men did not speak for several minutes.

Then Cavett said, "I bought a coffee maker this morning for something to do. I found the model in a Peoples drugstore on sale. I took it back to the Pentagon and took it apart."

Devereaux stared through the windshield at

the gray afternoon descending to early evening. The morning rain had turned to an afternoon of edgy sullenness. Washington does not like the cold and it shows in the faces of the pedestrians on the street, in the impatience of the traffic, in a hundred small ways that suggest a massive municipal annoyance.

"General Lee came around finally to watch me take it apart. He asked me how it would have worked and I told him. You simply bridge the built-in fuse and create a different timer for a long-range detonation. General Lee said they'd found the remains of one of the coffee makers and he asked me how I knew which model to buy in the drugstore. I told him I asked one of the men I'd interviewed if he remembered the model."

Devereaux waited.

"Any of this interesting to you?"

"I don't understand how they could get all those coffee makers into all those offices," Devereaux said.

"The general said the same thing."

"Go ahead," Devereaux said. It was a grudging voice.

"I said it was the Sherlock Holmes theory. When you've eliminated every other possibility, the one that remains has to be the truth, regardless of how silly it looks. This had to be a recent setup and the general said he remembered the coffee maker had arrived at their office less than a week ago. So he went off to doodle it over and about an hour ago he asked me what I thought the accelerant was and I said it was probably solid-state rocket fuel mixed with a little gasoline and bits of Styrofoam for thickening. He gave me a funny look and went away. That's my day. General Lee doesn't like me."

"That's why he assigned you to me."

"No. He wants to give you a free hand without appearing to give you a free hand and I'm the only officer he has right now who doesn't know a damned thing about intelligence. So I'm a messenger. Anything you want to tell the general, you tell me, and I won't understand the significance of it."

Devereaux looked hard at Jack Cavett then. They were heading out southeast, down past Bolling Air Force Base, down into Maryland on Highway 210, the Indianhead highway.

"We going all the way to Indianhead?" Devereaux said.

"No. Just a place I know where we can get a sandwich and have a beer. And you can tell me why you're carrying a pistol."

"I can't do that, Jack."

Cavett nodded, watching the traffic. For another little while, they were silent.

"So what do I tell General Lee?"

"You tell him that two men are following me. Day and night. And that since he's not keeping me under surveillance, the men come from somewhere else. I think from the Middle East. You tell him that and tell him the agent from R Section wants to know what to do next."

"That's why you're armed."

"You don't have to tell the general anything about that."

"All right."

Devereaux stared at Cavett. When Cavett spoke, he kept his eyes on the road: "Someone inside. This is an inside job. Someone who knows military procedures. For procurement, distribution. Someone familiar with the quartermaster corps operations, something like that. Or civilian procurement for the Pentagon. Or GSA. You get a coffee maker and you keep it. That simple. It's called scrounging. Never look a gift horse in the mouth. Your outfit gets ten extra Jeeps, you keep the ten extra Jeeps. Or you trade the Jeeps for something else you want with another outfit."

"I was in 'Nam," Devereaux said. "I wasn't in the military but I understood how it worked."

"So the coffee makers were parts of a Trojan horse. Even made coffee. Until the timers went off and the coils overrode the fuse and heated up to the point where they ignited the accelerant. Simple. Five hundred hours on a quiet Sunday and the Pentagon started to burn down."

"Why don't you just tell Bobby Lee all this instead of making him work for it?"

"Because I'm not in intelligence. They borrowed me in my last days in uniform to look at leftover hardware we captured from the Iraqis. Study their bombs, various weapons, put in my expertise."

"You know a lot about what started the fire."

"I don't know anything," Jack said. "I'm a soldier and I keep my mouth shut."

"But you tell me," Devereaux said.

Cavett looked at him then. "And you showed me your weapon and then made it a secret between us and away from the general. You see, that's how it works. You trust me and I trust you. That way, in five weeks, I get my papers finished on time and I put on civvies. The general could get all involved in this problem he's got and he might put me on hold for months. Hell, he could extend me indefinitely."

"But you're a career man. Why —"

"Because I want to get out of the army now. I've lost it," Cavett said.

He pulled into a parking lot on the highway

in front of a white frame building festooned with beer signs and neon in the windows. It looked like a small, cheerful place. "You want to have a beer?" Cavett said.

Yes, Devereaux thought then. Cavett had lost it, and Devereaux understood what that was. When you've lost it, it's better to walk away than to pretend. Maybe Devereaux had lost it there when Mona pressed him on her plan to go to the heart of the problem, in Beirut, to root out the core of the ICC bank and find the terrorists at the top who supported all the little terrors at the bottom.

They went into the bar then after locking the car, and they sat for an hour and talked about the wars in Vietnam and in other places. They had not become friends but they had recognized the sense of loss that was common to both of them.

Twenty-four

Cavett had driven Devereaux to the Metro in southeast Washington and then committed the long drive back to Indianhead. He was in his quarters in the BOQ, polishing his shoes, when he got the call.

"Jack, it's me."

Liz. The broken-voiced Liz. In the middle of the evening when her husband might be home.

"What's wrong, Liz?" He knew it was something wrong.

"I tried and tried to reach you yesterday, called the Pentagon, they kept saying those lines weren't working —"

"What's wrong, Liz? Where's Bob?"

"I can't tell Bob, of all people."

"What's wrong, Liz?" He was trying to keep his voice calm. He knew she'd been drinking, he could hear the slur in her voice. And the edge of panic in her voice.

"Jack, it's Max Escher."

"Max Escher? What about Max Escher?"

"When we were in the hotel room. You said Max had bumped into you out of the blue and said he was working in Chicago for some security service or something."

Cavett waited. He realized he was holding a shoe in his left hand. He put the shoe down on the night table and waited.

"Jack. Are you there?"

"I'm here, Liz."

"Jack. I'm alone tonight. Bob had a big meeting with the board. He's staying out in Schaumburg tonight. Jack, I'm frightened."

"What happened?"

"Max Escher came here. He said he could get you a job after you left the army. He said . . . he said I would have to sleep with him."

Jack closed his eyes. He saw Liz in his mind. And then he saw her sitting with a bottle of gin in her hand and she was being crazy. "What are you telling me, Liz?"

"He said I fucked everyone except him. I told you I didn't like him, not when we knew him, he had a crazy look to him, I told you that, he tried to get me twice, I never told you that, he tried once when I was home alone and you were gone on TDY, that time we were in Mildenhall, he tried . . ." Her voice trailed off and Jack Cavett realized that Liz was crying.

"Are you drinking, Liz?"

"Yes, God, yes, I'm drinking. He touched me. He came up to the apartment and I let him in and then, I swear to God, I thought he was going to rape me."

"What'd he do?"

"He kissed me."

Who didn't kiss you, Liz? In the kitchen, on the beach, in the pool, playing golf, who didn't kiss you, Liz? But he shook his head even as he thought these things.

"Jack, I know what you think of me. Jack, I never slept with him, never. And he said he wanted me, it was like a trophy he wanted, and then he'd get you a job in his company. In Chicago."

He waited. Sometimes, he had no words.

"He gave me a number and I was to call him when I was . . . ready. Jack, I've hurt you and hurt you, we all of us hurt each other, but I can't do that. Not even for you."

"What was the number he gave you, Liz?" She repeated the number to him and he wrote it down.

And then she said, "I'm sorry, Jack. I don't want to involve you in this but I can't tell Bob — this is something from the part of life I never talk about. About the service."

"What do you mean, don't get involved?" He was warming up now. He felt the churning in his stomach and it was part of the frustrations of these last months on his last tour of duty, seeing all the disappointments of life crystallized into this. An old army buddy who wants to fuck his old army wife in exchange for a civilian job. "Don't get involved? You can't tell Bob Fredericks because he's only your husband and he mustn't know that you were a tramp in your previous life when you fucked everything that moved on post. Except, apparently, for this one little guy because you didn't like the look in his eye."

"Fuck you, Jack." No tears, no slurring of words. They knew how to fight with each other. They had learned that.

And just as suddenly, he gave it up. He didn't want to fight with her anymore.

Softly. "I'll call Max at this number, Liz. He won't bother you anymore. I promise you."

"I didn't sleep with him, Jack."

"I believe you, Liz."

"Do you really?"

"I really," he said.

"I love you, Jack," she said.

What could he say to her? They both knew in the end that love wasn't enough, it wasn't a strong enough thing.

"Don't worry, Liz. I'll call Max. I won't take the job in any case," he said.

"And then that's my fault —" She interrupted herself with silence.

"It doesn't matter, Liz. Old soldiers get jobs. I can teach, do something like that."

"I wish you were here now, Jack, I really do."

"But I can't be. Not now."

"I don't care about the army now," she said.

"I don't care either," he said.

There was another long silence and that was a form of communication too.

"Take it easy on yourself, Liz," Jack Cavett said.

"All right, Jack." The quiet of her voice broke his heart then and he had to end the connection. He sat on his bunk for a long time and stared at the phone and saw Liz in his mind and thought of all the things they should have said to each other over all the years.

He picked up the phone and punched in the 800 number that Liz had given him.

The number connected and he heard a beep activating a recording device.

"Jack Cavett, Max. I talked to Liz. I don't think you want to scare her and I know sure as hell you don't scare me. That's the message, Max."

He replaced the receiver and his hand was shaking. He thought about it and he wondered if it was strong enough and he almost called the 800 number again, to make a threat that was more . . . more what?

"Liz," he said once to no one. He realized he wanted to get dressed and go out and have enough drinks to dull his thoughts. And he realized he wouldn't do this. Instead, he picked up the shoe from the nightstand and slowly began to work the polish into the leather. He did this carefully and for a long time and the smell of polish and leather soothed him.

Twenty-five

Devereaux took the subway train to Union Station, changed to the Red Line, and got off at the station on Wisconsin Avenue. He held the pistol with the safety off in the pocket of his raincoat. It was nearly 9:00 P.M. and he was thinking about Jack Cavett and the quiet vehemence of his last remarks about the army, about how he hated it, about how he had even felt betrayed by the service for abandoning him. They had talked about 'Nam for the most part and their roles there and they had even talked about specific operations. Old war stories told by old soldiers, one a civilian intelligence officer and the other a military expert in Special Forces.

He thought about Jack mostly because he thought Jack had known an awful lot about the fires in the Pentagon.

He was sharing it with Devereaux but Devereaux wasn't really interested in the Pentagon fires unless it could be traced to ICC in Beirut. Maybe Jack Cavett was explaining how it was done out of pride. Maybe he would have to rethink Jack Cavett.

And part of his mind was thinking about the jogger.

The night had turned surprisingly warm and the stars had come out above the city. Devereaux was bareheaded, the Irish cap in the other pocket of his coat. He had called her and said he would be a little late and she would be waiting for him and he would put the cap back on when he got to the apartment building.

The car slid to the curb. He went to the door on the passenger side and opened it. Hacker was behind the wheel, staring at him. And Hanley was in the backseat.

Devereaux slipped into the car and pulled the door shut.

Hacker started up the silent, dark side street. He stared straight ahead.

Hanley said, "A man named Sharom Mohammed was found shot to death in an elevator in the Mayflower Hotel."

Devereaux said nothing. He also was looking through the windshield.

Hanley spoke to his back: "He was a registered agent with the Palestine Liberation Organization."

"Registered?"

"At the United Nations."

"Oh. A diplomat."

"A registered diplomat," Hanley said.

"He was out of his territory," Devereaux said.

"You don't know about this," Hanley said. It was not a question.

"No."

"You can't kill people in the District," Hanley said.

"Just drug dealers can. I think that discriminates against white people," Devereaux said. "Besides, I'm on liaison with General Lee in the Pentagon. The Section isn't involved anymore. We gave him what we had."

"General Lee said your liaison man, this Colonel Cavett, spent the day in the Pentagon but he didn't have an appointment to see you until four. Were you busy?"

"I was engaged," Devereaux said. "It was a private matter."

"What was it?"

"I was shopping for a birthday present."

"For whom?"

"For me."

"Your birthday is in March."

"I buy myself presents all the time."

"Tell me what this is about," Hanley said.

"Someone killed a Palestinian in the Mayflower Hotel. I was nowhere near the

289

Mayflower Hotel."

"Mrs. Neumann received a call this afternoon. From Senator Michael Horan of Pennsylvania. He wanted information on you."

"Why?"

"The very question Mrs. Neumann put." He paused. "He was vague at first and then a bit more resolute. He said that he had received information that R Section was in violation of its charter, was operating inside the country."

"Did he?"

"He said it was a private communication."

"From Clair Dodsworth. I suppose Clair Dodsworth knows a lot of senators. I wonder why it was Senator Horan."

"Because you made the link yourself. From Senator Horan to his friend, this Britta Andrews. And the Institute for World Development. There are nineteen names on the committee of the institute and four of the names have the Nobel Prize attached to them. These are not inconsequential people."

"I suppose not." Devereaux turned in his seat then to face Hanley. "What do you want, Hanley?"

"I want to know what you're doing that you're not supposed to be doing," Hanley said.

"For Mrs. Neumann."

"For me."

"And Hacker," Devereaux said.

"You're going to have to trust me," Hanley said.

"I haven't been to see Clair, I haven't watched him at all," Devereaux said.

"But he had second or third thoughts about you," Hanley said. "Would it have to do with the death of a Palestinian in the Mayflower Hotel?"

"Why don't you ask him?"

"Damn you. Mrs. Neumann is being left to twist alone in the wind on this. She protected you. She said she would need some sort of order from the senator's committee before she could reveal any private dossier on one of our active officers."

"Good for her. What did the senator say?"

"He fumed. Mrs. Neumann cannot be cowed so easily. She stood up to him."

"Good for her."

"And she called Clair Dodsworth to complain, to say that he went back on his word to leave Section alone. And Clair Dodsworth, she told me, seemed somewhat shaken. Mrs. Neumann can create that effect."

"She's very strong," Devereaux said. "She's been a good director."

"I don't want an evaluation of job performance, I want to know what this has to do with the death of the Palestinian."

"Yes. That's interesting, isn't it?"

"I could put a watch on you," Hanley said. "I could send you to our station house in Guam."

"I could resign," Devereaux said.

"Maybe that would be better."

"It won't end this. Not until it's ended," Devereaux said.

Then there was silence. The car slid along the glitter of M Street in Georgetown, miles from his apartment. He figured that Hacker would just keep driving around until Hanley told him to stop.

"All right," Hanley said.

Devereaux said, "It has to be this way."

"Mrs. Neumann wants to talk to you. In the morning."

"All right."

"She's going to ask you a lot of questions."

"All right."

Then Devereaux turned to him again. "You didn't tell her about the dead Palestinian."

Hanley said, "There'll be a story in the paper."

"Then she'll read about it. But you didn't tell her what connection you've made."

Again, it was not a question.

292

"No," Hanley admitted, slumping back in his seat at last. "No. I didn't tell her."

"That's good," Devereaux said. "It would have upset her."

Twenty-six

Max Escher used Britta's telephone to call his 800 number and retrieve his messages. It was about an hour or so after Jack Cavett made his call and left his warning. When Max listened to the sound of Jack's voice, his face became drawn. Some people, when they are angry, go red in the face; some, like Max, become very still and pale.

Max Escher looked across the room at Britta. Britta was sitting at the breakfast bar, drinking a glass of skim milk. She wore something like a nightgown, all white, shiny, with very thin shoulder straps.

She had taken a call from her senator and she had told him some lie about how she couldn't see him tonight. The night had turned warm. She and Max Escher had made love in the afternoon, and when he grew hungry, she sent out for Chinese food. They had eaten a lot of the food out of the containers.

There were no more messages. Max, still frowning, put down the telephone.

Britta looked across at him as though she expected him to confide in her. The trouble with women, Max thought, was they mixed up sex with all kinds of other things. That was one trouble with them. Like Britta, staring at him.

"I don't understand some women," he said now. He was thinking about Liz and thinking about Jack. Liz had called Jack and Jack had ruined any chance he had with that message. Worse than ruined his chances. Jack was a candy, he had let Liz walk all over him, let Liz cheat on him, and it was a little late to be pulling this tough-guy routine. He was a candy-ass like all the candy-asses Max had to put up with.

At least Britta wasn't. She had a fine ass and she was hard, really hard. Her eyes reminded him of his own eyes.

"What don't you understand?"

"You look good, I can't get over how good you look. I'm glad to be here."

"You've got to get out of here in the morning," she said. "Michael's upset about something, I can tell by the tone of his voice. He asked me if I'd shown the secret testimony to anyone. On the nuclear power plants. On the Apostle failings."

"You were right," Max said. "I read it over some when you were taking a nap. It's pretty much what I thought it was, maybe a little worse. They've had some real security screwups. They had a drug ring operating in 1987, they sure kept that down. One of the guards sold cocaine to a DEA agent in Elgin, Illinois, and he blew the whistle on the others. That's real insecure of them, employing people like that. They do random drug tests but everyone seems to know how to fix them."

She finished the glass of milk and blotted her lips with a cloth napkin. She didn't believe in paper towels. Besides, cloth was nicer. She looked at him across the room. "What don't you understand about some women?"

"Do I scare you, Britta?"

The question was sudden and it was meant to be sly. He waited for her.

She shook her golden head. "I thought you were a punk and then I thought you might just be crazy. But I know now. You're doing this because you know how, a professional. I can't convert you to my causes and that's all right. It's one less link between us. You don't scare me — is that what you want to know? Do you scare some women?"

"They say they're scared."

"Do you hurt them?"

"I've never hurt a woman," he said. He was thinking about Liz and Jack and trying to decide something. "What if some man said he was your friend, your old buddy, and then he turns on you just like that, starts making threats?"

"Does this involve me? Is this going to get in the way of something, Max? I don't want any private grudge to get in the way —"

"It has nothing to do with this thing," Max said. "I figure that my old friend is going to have to take the blame."

She hesitated. "For what?"

"For the Pentagon burn," Max said.

"Don't go getting sidetracked," Britta said.

"Listen, kid, I know how to handle myself. I can take care of business. You take care of your end." He was getting annoyed with her now. What was it about women that they always said the wrong thing?

"I gave you the target. Got you a hundred thousand dollars down. Now I'll take care of the rest."

"You're hard, I like that."

"Hard as I have to be."

"You know this'll go on and on, you know that? After the fire, the Apostle'll be leaking, they aren't going to know how to handle it — the one thing I know about bureaucrats, they don't know how to handle things. They'll be running around, so busy covering their asses they won't know what to do about the leaking. I wouldn't want to live in Chicago.

297

Live in those fancy places they got in the city." And he was thinking of Liz, maybe Liz not even realizing it at first and the company running around to cover it up and the government investigating everyone at the plant. Investigating Bernie Lund, who was probably asleep right now dreaming his drug dreams in his crummy trailer with the porno magazines under his bed. Liz might die of leukemia or bone cancer and all her pretty hair would fall out. That made him smile.

"You wouldn't even want to be in this country when it happens," he said.

"I won't be. We have an antinuclear conference in two weeks. In Gstaad."

"I was never there," he said.

"It's far away," she said.

"I pretty much figured out the package, how bad do you want it to be?" He was like that, changing directions in talk to follow rabbity thoughts. "I mean, we can only burn so much of it. I figure on just one reactor core, the Red core. There's two of them. The cooling pipes have to malfunction massively and too quickly for them to pull down the control rods."

"That's meltdown," she said.

He nodded. "Partial. I can't guarantee it'll melt down to China." He smiled like a car salesman. He was proud of what he could guarantee, though.

"But you can guarantee it'll happen."

"It's going to happen unless you say no and say it pretty fast," he said.

She just stared at him then.

That satisfied him. "They've got a paint shed on the bottom level of the generator building. Keep their paints there, wire cage. The painting crew gets lazy, leaves it open when they're using it. The first fire is there, that'll divert everyone." He was seeing it, seeing them running their disaster fire drill, everyone covering up from minute one, the painting crews and the tradesmen inside, welders, everyone. He grinned at her. "Do you want to do that again?"

She stared for a while. Then she held up her finger and crooked it at him and he got out of the chair and came to her. There weren't a lot of preliminaries this time because talking about it got them both hot for the other thing. He thought about Liz for a moment when they were doing it again and he thought about Liz under him but that thought passed and it was just this rich lady and this retired soldier and this place alone on a warm Washington evening.

Twenty-seven

Morning always brought meetings. It's in the Washington blood.

Clair Dodsworth wanted to meet with Britta Andrews to discuss the institute and she agreed to meet him in his office at eleven and she thought it would be about the money still in her account at the District Savings Bank.

Britta met with her broker at nine, opening bell on the Street, and said she wanted to dispose of all her shares of Northern Illinois Power and Light Company over the next ten days. She named a floor figure for the shares and the broker thought it could be done above that figure. Britta did not take advice from someone like Max Escher, who had wanted her to hold the stocks and suffer a loss. The very rich do not suffer losses. Someone who's never had much money wouldn't understand that.

Then she went to Michael's health club at ten and waited for him at the juice bar. She had a small glass of tomato juice while she waited for him. She wore a severe suit and a severe look on her face because Michael just didn't seem as important to her in the light of this morning as he had seemed before. She had taken charge and was just beginning to realize it, just beginning to come out from Michael's shadow of power. It was her arrangement with Max and Michael wasn't really in the picture, certainly not at the center of it anymore. And he had insisted on meeting him, with a certain amount of male arrogance in his voice. She thought she had broken Michael of that.

He came out of the corridor that led to the indoor courts with a racquet in hand and sweat on his broad forehead. His graying hair glistened with sweat and his eyes were bright. Like all senators, he was privileged to use the Senate gymnasium but he kept this second club membership because he golfed here as well. And he really couldn't invite Britta to his offices in the Longworth Building. Washington did have some rules about propriety.

He sat down across from her and ordered a large orange juice. When the counter clerk moved away, he stared at her for a long moment. "You haven't passed on that testimony."

"No," she said.

"Well, you'll have to give it back to me.

This was a bad idea. I was called by Clair Dodsworth yesterday. There's an agent named Devereaux in one of the intelligence sections who's causing some problems. Who's asking questions about dealings of Clair's bank."

"What's that got to do with me?"

"I called for a file on the agent and the director of R Section rebuffed me. Clair wanted the file and now I'm exposed by asking for it. I made a mistake. Maybe they're checking on leaks from my subcommittee."

"Oh, poo, Michael, an intelligence agency isn't going to investigate a senator. Sometimes you forget how powerful you are."

"Clair said the agent, this Devereaux, was working with DIA —"

"Spare me this alphabet soup stuff."

"Defense Intelligence. In the Pentagon. Where they had a fire on a recent Sunday morning," he said. "You know who caused that arson. What do you want to do, Britta? You want information on nuclear plant safety. My God, Britta, I'm talking about an intelligence officer investigating —"

She covered his sweat-stained sleeve with her left hand. "Take it easy." Her voice was very calm. "I could give you the testimony back or just destroy it for you. If you trust me to do it."

"I trust you. My God, I've trusted you so far that I'm worried now."

"You don't have to worry," Britta said.

"Clair . . . told me some things. He said the agent I mentioned had . . . harassed him recently. And that Carroll Claymore had been spying on him for the agent."

"Carroll's dead."

"Exactly," Michael said. His hand was trembling the way it did when he wanted a drink. It was 10:15 in the morning and his hand was at four in the afternoon.

She felt the tremble in his arm. "I don't know anything about Carroll Claymore. I think I met him once. Exactly once. I'll call my attorneys if I get harassed by any FBI pig. They tried it with my father and they tried it with me and I'm not afraid of those fascist pigs," she said. Her voice was very calm and it made his hand tremble even more.

"Britta, whatever you're getting yourself involved in —"

"We're involved in," she said. Bright and hard, gemstone eyes. "You and me, Michael. You wanted to know my secrets and I told you some of them."

"But what are you going to do with those secret tapes?"

"I told you. I wanted to get them out. Get

303

them in the press. Public radio, *New York Times* —"

"This is more, Brit. Don't lie to me. You know who it was that burned the Pentagon."

She stared deep into his eyes then and her eyes were glittering. "Yes. And you know I know. And now you're becoming tedious. Don't you want me anymore, Michael?"

"I love you," he said. He hadn't touched his orange juice. He looked at the glass as though he wondered how it had gotten there.

"Don't become panicked. It's very simple. I'll explain to you. I know this group in Germany, very much opposed to the American military presence in Europe, and I knew they'd hired a man . . . a team of men . . . to inflict sabotage in the Pentagon. I think it's wonderful. Don't you think it's wonderful? And I told you, I told you my secret."

He had to stand up. He stood up and leaned on the bar, leaned his head over his orange juice. He stared at the glass.

"This is terrible, Britta." His voice was low. "Do you know what it is you've just said? You're in a conspiracy —"

"We, Michael. I know and you know. We."

Silence. He picked up the glass and then put it down without drinking.

"Clair Dodsworth said he has to talk to you. About that line of credit —"

"I know. I'm going to see him if I can get you calmed down," Britta said.

"What's the money for, Brit?" His voice very dull. The question was not one he wanted answered.

"The propaganda machine we're setting up at the institute. We were going to start our campaign with the leaks you gave me. Now you're trying to back out of it."

"I'm not —"

"Yes, you are," she said.

"I'm not —"

"You're just a politician after all, aren't you? I mean, Michael, you looked different to me only a few days ago but it comes down to you're just another politician. Weak. No stomach for any hard choice."

"What do you want me to do?"

She thought about that. What could he do? Britta might have made him part of it, part of the scheme, but he obviously would panic. No, maybe she always had her doubts about him. Maybe it took someone like Max Escher to show her a real man who could carry through a commitment.

"I feel sorry for you, Michael," she said then.

"I'll do what you want me to do, I just have to know —"

"I'll go see Clair and make it all right and

I'll call you this afternoon and you won't have to lock yourself in the broom closet with a bottle of scotch. Is that all right, Michael?" Her voice cut through with contempt then and it briefly brought a blush to his cheeks. His eyes fired up.

"Don't patronize me —"

"Then be a man, for God's sake, and stop scaring yourself over shadows. Spooks. Spies. I'm not afraid of them, any of them, and they know it. You're a senator, Michael. For God's sake, act like one."

But then, she thought, maybe he was.

Twenty-eight

Devereaux and Rita Macklin woke up at dawn because she had an early flight to Atlanta. She wanted to be home that night and she thought she could do the CNN piece in a long day of interviews. She wasn't terribly interested in the story she had been assigned and it showed on her early-morning face. Perhaps neither of them wanted to face the things they would have to do that long day looming before them. They parted in the street in front of the apartment building and he kissed her briefly and they said "Take care" to each other and then she climbed into the cab. He had not wanted to ride to National Airport with her even though it was on the way to the Pentagon.

He didn't want to involve her anymore in this. She had asked him again about Mona while they sat together in the kitchen and ate a late, cold supper, and he had lied to her enough for her to understand the lies would just create other lies.

He walked to the Metro station and took the train again, first the Red Line to Union Station underground, and then he transferred to the reopened Yellow Line that jogged south through the District across the river to the Pentagon.

Gen. Robert E. Lee was still using a temporary office at the back of a huge undamaged room on the second level. He had scrounged folding screens — rather, the major who served as his gofer had — and it suggested privacy.

It took Devereaux about fifteen minutes. He told General Lee about Senator Horan's inquiry and about Hanley's conversation with him. Not the part about Hanley's guess that Devereaux was linked to the shooting of a Palestinian diplomat in the Mayflower Hotel, not that. The secret of surviving in a world of secrecy is to keep the secrets in compartments. Still, there was enough to make it interesting for an old secretmonger like Bobby Lee.

And then Devereaux talked to Bobby Lee in the way of a wary trader making a deal by offering something he didn't have to offer. He talked about the bitterness of Col. Jack Cavett and Jack Cavett's detailed ideas on how the Pentagon fires were started and fueled. He laid it out carefully, betraying Jack Cavett's ideas and all the good-old-boy conversation of the night before.

Bobby Lee tapped a yellow number-two pencil on his desk for a while after Devereaux finished.

"You don't like Colonel Cavett?" he finally said. He didn't look at Devereaux. They both looked at the pencil.

"I don't know that it matters."

"Why're you givin' me this?"

"Because you're interested in the fires. Because your bosses are. Because I want more time for the things I'm interested in."

"Michael Horan's on the Armed Services Committee."

"I know."

"You want me to stand up to him if he next comes poaching in my waters?" Not really a question but turned up in tone at the end to suggest one.

"What would you do? If he gets rebuffed by Mrs. Neumann, he comes over here next."

"Well, I got to say, you're a rotten son of a bitch, Red. I really got to say that." Flat voice, fine Virginia drawl, but with a soldier's hard edge to it.

"Jack Cavett's not my buddy."

"Neither am I."

"No. But you're what I've got to work with."

"You're suggesting Colonel Cavett knew something about those fires because he's got so many specific ideas about how they were set."

"I'm just telling you what I'm telling you."

"Suppose I tell this to Jack Cavett now? What's he going to tell me about you?"

"He'll tell you I'm a rotten son of a bitch."

"When you get what you want — when you get to the core of ICC — you gonna share it, Red?"

"I told you I would."

"I bet you tell all the girls all kinds of stories."

Devereaux said nothing.

"You're putting yourself way out there, Red." The general just looked at him with a cocked-head, quizzical sidelong glance that waited for an answer.

"Well, I tell you, I like what you just told me about Colonel Cavett because we developed some information on our own. Lab analysis didn't tell us shit about the accelerant but there was something we finally put together on the computers. Got the computers up and running yesterday afternoon and there was this FBI report of seven weeks ago of a quantity of rocket fuel taken from one of our civilian manufacturers in Washington state. This isn't the first time this sort of thing has happened. Whole pipeline of suppliers leaks like a sieve. But it's in the context, timewise."

Devereaux said, "I have to see Mrs. Neumann at nine."

"You gonna tell her the truth?"

"About what?"

"Damnit, Red, about Colonel Cavett and all."

"She wouldn't be interested."

"How do you keep it all separate in your head? How do you remember who you told what to and who your friends are?"

"I remember my enemies," Devereaux said.

"You want Colonel Cavett to keep dogging you for me?"

"It's whatever the general wants."

He shook his head. "I don't believe it, Red. I think you told me the truth, but your conclusion —"

"I didn't conclude anything."

"You implied a career officer with twenty-four years in service seriously decided to sabotage the Pentagon because he was pissed off at the army for dropping him?"

"I don't know about motives, Bobby Lee. I told you what I heard."

"And you heard it because he trusted you."

The general dropped the pencil softly on the desk pad.

"I wouldn't trust you," the general said.

"That'd be the best thing," Devereaux agreed.

Twenty-nine

Devereaux returned home at 7:30 P.M. She had said she'd catch the 5:00 P.M. flight to National from Hartsfield International but she might be a little late. So he wasn't alarmed that she wasn't there. He poured a glass of vodka and took a shower. He changed clothes. He looked in the refrigerator for something and found an opened package of Brie. He took the remains of yesterday's baguette and spread on the Brie cheese and ate it and drank his glass of vodka. He waited for her.

There were three men in all, two in the long limousine. They had pulled up at the arriving passengers' curb at National just as she started to walk to the cab line, and they were very good at it. One walked behind her and the limo rear door opened just as he shoved her in.

Rita Macklin hit the floor and laddered her stockings. Her purse fell from her hand and the light bag was wedged against the opposite door. The man who had shoved her inside slammed the door shut behind her and continued to walk away, down the crowded walk, through all those phalanxes of passengers who had seen and heard nothing or pretended to.

The car picked up speed. The windows were smoked. She brought her fist up and hit the second man in the crotch very hard and he made a dull, angry sound and then he sprayed Mace into her face. The sting of it forced her eyes shut and she began crying and she reached for his leg and hit him hard on the thigh and he reached down and pulled her hair back and she still could not see.

She felt her face was burning off the bone. She groped in the confusing darkness and realized she could not rise from the floor. She felt the car gaining speed. She reached out and the man grabbed her arm and twisted it back behind her.

The tears fell on her cheeks from the stinging gas. She had been Maced before, covering demonstrations; she knew the effect would pass but the panic rising had nothing to do with the physical effect but with the sense of her powerlessness.

The second man pulled her up painfully, her arm twisted behind her, and he was wrapping something around her wrists. She blinked again against the tears and could vaguely make him out in the darkness of the car. The lights of the airport were scarcely visible beyond the smoked windows. He said something then and slapped tape across her mouth. It was duct tape and she tasted the adhesive and now she couldn't resist.

He said something to the driver in a foreign tongue.

Then he spoke to her in clear, calm English: "Devereaux does not prize you, Miss Macklin."

She blinked but she was still tearing. She was sitting next to him on the leather seat cushions, her skirt above her knees, her legs splayed on the floor because she couldn't move to rearrange them.

"He has a lover named Rachel Horowitz. Or he did. Do you know her? But she was called Mona in the service of R Section. I'm sure you've heard of Mona."

She shook her head against the sound of his voice.

"If this man loved you, he would not expose you to any danger as he does now. He does it for love of this Mona. He was her lover when he was living with you. What do you think of a man like that? Not only to have a lover while he had you, but then to expose you to this danger? Mona is a political agent and he would rather have you face danger than not to do her bidding. What do you think of that?"

In all this the tone of voice never changed. She couldn't speak because the tape was across her mouth. She blinked her eyes again. The Mace still stung and there was a terrible smell but she could almost see the man next to her.

"He was told not to pursue this matter for his own sake and for the safety of you. He was told this but he said it didn't matter, that you did not matter that much to him."

She listened now. She blinked her eyes again. She listened to the terrible voice with a sense that this was true.

"We aren't interested in your . . . harm, Miss Macklin." The speaker had paused then, as though searching for the right word. There was almost no accent to the voice but the words selected were odd. Very formal and oddly put.

"Do you see that we could harm you? That you wouldn't be safe? We could kill you this easily." And he snapped his finger then.

Yes. She could see him. Thin and dark, wearing a dark zippered jacket and a green shirt beneath. His hair was thick and oily in the dim light of the car. She tried to see where they were going but they were beyond the airport, slicing into the Beltway, heading north into Virginia. The homebound traffic around them was thinning and she was alone in the world.

Mona, she thought. *Rachel Horowitz.*

She thought of Devereaux in the morning, his face set against some task he did not want to do. She thought of his kiss, which was short and absent. "Take care," he had said.

Her face was covered with tears.

The car rode the Beltway around into Maryland. They were in Bethesda now, on Bradley Boulevard, not far from the place she had once lived in alone. Before Devereaux, a thousand years ago.

"You should leave this man. This man is death to you, Miss Macklin, believe me when I say this. He is dead himself and he is death to you."

She looked for landmarks but she felt so disoriented that they might have taken her to a foreign country. She sat very still. The car was sweet scented with the smells of both men and she realized they were wearing a musky sort of perfume or lotion.

And then the car stopped. It was a warm night again and still. The man on the seat next to her picked up her valise from the floor and her purse. Her lipstick and wallet had spilled out of the purse. He replaced these things in the purse. And then he smiled at her.

"He is dead," the man said. "And you, will you be dead as well? He betrayed you."

He removed the tape slowly and it stung her lips. She gasped for breath and had not realized she needed to breathe so badly.

He took out a long, slim knife and opened it. He was still smiling at her. Then he pulled her arms roughly and forced her to bend at the waist to her knees and she felt the blade between her wrists. He was cutting the tape around her wrists.

She pulled her hands away and rubbed her wrists and looked at this dangerous, soft-spoken man.

"Will you leave him now, Miss Macklin?"

She stared at him.

He waited.

She nodded her head then.

He smiled at her. "That would be the best thing. Perhaps he would tell you the truth if you left him. How he was Mona's lover in the years when you shared your bed with him. He's insane, I think. And very danger-ous. To himself. And to you, pretty lady."

"What do you want?" she said.

He shook his head.

"Can I go?"

He stared at her, smiling in the darkness.

"If you leave him, then you can go. In safety and peace," the man said.

She took her purse in her left hand. "Go now," she said.

"Yes. Now."

And he said nothing further, even as she opened the latch of the door with trembling hand.

Thirty

The wooden galley building across the street from the brick enlisted men's bay burst into flames shortly after 11:00 P.M. It was the Naval Propellant Plant at Indianhead, Maryland, twenty-nine miles south of the District.

The place was empty. The fire spread across the floor quickly, as though being poured on the floor. It reached the front entrance before any alarm was sounded. By the time the first fire engine arrived, the fire was boiling beneath the roof waiting to burst through. The fire fed on the oxygen trapped inside the building and as it depleted the oxygen, it created enormous pressure at every point in the structure, and when the first, inexperienced fireman crashed open the front doors, the flames exploded like a bomb and flung him back nearly fifty feet until he crashed against the fire truck itself.

It was a terrible conflagration and the men and women in the enlisted quarters were awakened by the sounds of sirens that reached up and down the quiet, tree-lined streets of the base. The men and women were gathered from every branch of service because the propellant plant was also the all-services home of the Explosive Ordnance Disposal school.

Colonel Cavett was awakened by the sirens. The sirens came out of some dream. He thought of Liz and then he remembered they had last awakened together in a Washington hotel room to the sound of sirens.

He pulled on his green class-A shirt and black tie and slipped on his service hat with the silver insignia of a light colonel.

He walked down the street to the galley, past the commissary and recreation building, seeing lights on in every house now on the street.

Most were dressed in civvies, some of the enlisted men were drunk because they had spent the evening in the bars in Indianhead. He moved among the crowd watching the firefighters, listened to the jokes. "Someone was going to pay for that SOS this morning," a sailor said. Shit on a shingle. Jack Cavett knew hardly anyone. He was puzzled as he stood and watched the flames. Fires are usually smoky until they reach the point of boiling pressure — the need for fresh oxygen — when they burst through roofs and walls and begin to eat the sky to feed the flames. This fire was so far along . . .

He had interviewed twice in one day, first with General Lee and then with a Captain Carmody. Both of them wanted his expertise on what might have caused the Pentagon fires and he had dished it out slowly, carefully, not wanting to give away too much but not wanting to lie. He had offered several possibilities, and through it all he had realized Devereaux somehow betrayed him. General Lee even hinted that he could be extended in service, his paperwork already in the pipeline held up until this Pentagon arson was resolved. He had tried to reach Devereaux all that day but Devereaux had suddenly disappeared from the radar screen. He had felt lonely again, disappointed in Devereaux as he was disappointed these days by most people, and he had felt deeply resentful.

This fire was set, he thought. He stood and watched it and he felt it. This fire was set.

Another arson.

Pentagon.

Indianhead.

He shivered in the warm night and felt the heat of the flames that colored everything.

Thirty-one

Rita Macklin walked all the way to Wisconsin Avenue before she could find a cab to take her home. She didn't call Devereaux. She didn't want to talk to him unless she could see him. There was a small bruise on her left wrist and her stockings were ruined. She had put on her jogging shoes and put the heels into her valise so that she could walk more easily.

He was waiting for her, reading one of those yellow reports he brought home from R Section from time to time. He stared at her in the doorway. Then she shut the door and dropped her purse on the table and put her valise on the floor. She crossed the room and stood at the kitchen entrance off the foyer and looked at him. The clock on the kitchen wall read 9:05.

"Her name was Rachel Horowitz," she said. Her voice was dull, on the edge of exhaustion. "You were her lover, weren't you?"

Devereaux said nothing.

"I don't even want a lie," she said.

"What happened?"

"What the hell do you think happened?"

He stood up. He wore chinos and a loose gray sweater. The gray matched his eyes and it was the color of the ice between them in the room.

"I was kidnapped. At the airport. In a limo. They took me to Bethesda and dropped me. They told me about Mona. Her name was Rachel Horowitz, wasn't it?"

"Yes."

"Then you were her lover."

"No."

"Jesus Christ, don't lie to me."

He took a step toward her because she looked terrible and she was shaking.

"Don't come near me, don't come near me. If you told me the truth, that was one thing. But you lied. You always lie. You live a lie, everything in your life is a lie because it has to be. Secrets and lies and spies and shit, I'm sick of it."

"Rita." He did touch her and it was a signal for her to collapse. She had to hold on to him, just to get her legs back. And then she pushed him away. Her eyes were wet and red. "I'm going to the bathroom." She turned away from him.

He listened to her in the shower. He made

her a glass of scotch whiskey the way she liked it. He poured himself a second glass of vodka. He waited for her in the semidarkness of the living room. The drinks were on the glass coffee table.

She came out in a terry robe bundled over her flannel gown. She wore the flannel gown when she was very cold or very afraid or just because she wanted to feel safe. The flannel gown, she once said, made her feel as safe as if she had been in her parents' house as a little girl in Eau Claire.

She picked up the drink, held it with both hands, and sipped it. She put it down. Her eyes were red and she had rubbed off all her makeup and she looked a little better but her face was still pale.

"What happened?"

She told him then. She had a good memory and she could even imitate the voice of the second man.

"I wasn't Mona's lover. Not then, not ever," he said to her.

"Why's it so important to lie about?"

"If you want me to lie, I'll tell you I was her lover. Would that make it better?" He was angry and she thought that was a very odd thing for him to be.

"Why did you take the gun yesterday morning?"

"Because I saw men following you. When you went running. They're pressing me because I'm getting close. Now they've threatened you."

"I don't know what to believe. You never tell me."

"Not before. I keep it separate."

"What'd you do this morning? You looked terrible. You were going to the Pentagon but you wouldn't ride with me to the airport. I keep thinking I'm losing you."

He stared at her for a long time. "You haven't. You won't. Unless you leave me," he said.

"Tell me about Mona."

"I can tell you that," he said.

"And what can't you tell me?"

"There are . . . complications. I had to use someone this morning who told me . . . confidences. I suppose I was thinking about that." He paused then, uncertain. He was never uncertain, she thought. She saw this vulnerable uncertainty in his manner and she thought it was terrible to see.

"It doesn't matter about the betrayal. What matters is Mona. I'll tell you about Mona, all the truth."

"Tell me," she said.

"I knew Mona. Rachel. Rachel Horowitz. Very bright. I knew her because we worked on operations. I told you that. She saved my life once when I did a stupid thing in Germany. In the East. We had to live together as man and wife for six weeks in a village outside of Leipzig. Her German was the best, I was so-so, so we went everywhere together and she managed the language. We lived as husband and wife but we didn't. I mean, make love. We slept in the same bed. A double bed with a sagging spring. We just went to sleep and we didn't make love."

"Why?"

Devereaux smiled. It was a wan smile. "You've gotten so sophisticated, Rita. You think we should have?"

"You were together, thrown together alone in a place, under tension, for a long time . . ."

"Being under stress doesn't make romance easier."

"What's really true?"

He shook his head. He tasted the vodka. "She was a lesbian. She told me one night, she was drunk, we were alone and the window we were waiting to have opened — well, the opportunity was going fast and it was gnawing on us and Mona drank too much and she told me. All about it."

"Then so what?"

"I didn't want to know, Rita."

Rita shook her head.

"That made her a risk, Rita. We couldn't use her. And she told me and she knew the next morning and she couldn't face up to it, that I would tell Hanley and she'd be separated out —"

"You people make so much of —"

"Rita." His voice was hard. "It's the way it was. Is. The rules. If she broke one rule, she'd be as likely to break another. Don't ask me to justify it. It's the way it was. Shit." He took a drink then, a long one, and he thought of Carroll Claymore and the little blackmail he had arranged to get the stuff on Clair Dodsworth to lead to the ICC managers to . . . an endless chain of deceptions and blackmails. And lies. Rita was right about all the lies.

"But you didn't tell on her," Rita said.

He shook his head.

"Why?"

He stared at the woman he lived with and couldn't think of the words.

"Because you fell in love with her," she said.

"Yes."

"You'd lie for her."

"I could justify it to myself."

"You fell in love with her and you never slept with her."

"I never slept with her."

"And you stopped loving me."

"No."

"Or I was your hetero lover and she was your lesbian lover."

"No. You fall in love with people, I suppose. I suppose I never had any experience with it until I met you. Then I was in love and that was that. Maybe it was your fault, Rita."

"My fault."

"You taught me to love."

She folded her arms across her chest and stared at him. "And now she's dead. And now you're willing to put me in harm's way for her."

"No. Not that. Not that." He shook his head and dropped his arms.

Rita put down her glass and came to sit next to him on the couch. She stared at him with her red-rimmed eyes. She kissed him then. When she was finished, she said, "What do we do?"

"I quit it," he said. His hands lay on his lap. He stared at them. "It'll take a couple of days. I shifted some of this to the Pentagon. To Bobby Lee. I'll shift everything, everything I have. I'll get out of it and R Section will be out of it. Mrs. Neumann won't get any more phone calls. They'll watch me but I won't do anything and then they'll stop watching me. Watching you. Maybe Bobby Lee will do the job."

"How will they know you quit?"

"They'll know. I'll leave all the clues and they'll know. I did it for Mona, Rita, but not to harm you. Never that."

"I know."

"I love you."

"I know," she said again.

"But they told you to leave me. You'll have to leave me, Rita. For a while."

"I won't do that."

"You have to."

"But where would I go?" she said.

He already knew.

Thirty-two

Devereaux saw Hacker's signal from the living room window. Hacker flashed the headlamps three times.

It was 1:00 A.M. They had not slept. He had made her a little food. They had not mentioned Mona again.

Rita Macklin was dressed in jeans and sweater and carried a small bag. Her hair was brushed back severely from her pale features. Her eyes were still bloodshot from the Mace.

It was colder now. There were no stars.

Rita got in the backseat of the black Ford Escort with smoked windows and black-painted bumpers. Devereaux got in next to Hacker in the front. He laid the pistol on his lap.

"Someone's going to follow us?" Hacker said.

"I suppose so."

"Well, we'll cover ourselves."

"We don't have to do it that way,"

Devereaux said. "Drive this thing and lose them."

Hacker grunted and then began a series of maneuvers through the safe streets of Georgetown. He was good at it and they saw the first car right away and then the second car. Like most good surveillances, they were following the black Escort in sequences, first one car and then the second taking the lead, shifting positions, cutting off into side streets only to reappear at other side streets.

"If we just go to the safe house, the baby-sitters will take them out," Hacker said.

"You don't understand, Hacker. Everything changed tonight. I don't want to harass them anymore."

"Your woman," Hacker said. As if Rita were not sitting in the backseat.

"Other things," Devereaux said.

Hacker grunted again. "All right," he said. He picked up the radio. He gave a number and said he was pursuing two men in a green Chevrolet, license number such and such, on Wisconsin Avenue in Georgetown. Drug dealers, Hacker said.

The first car — the green Chevrolet — was pulled over minutes later by three black-and-whites with flashing roof lights. Hacker smiled in the rearview mirror.

"How did you manage that?" Devereaux said.

"We've tapped the District Police," Hacker said.

"And the other car?"

"I can take care of one car," Hacker said. "One car doesn't have a chance."

The Escort fled down an alley into a mews and then back onto the street. The second car was a black Toyota and it was having its troubles because the driver was probably hesitating over what to do about the police stopping the green car.

That's the way Hacker explained it.

The safe house was called "the house in Virginia" inside Section. It was in Great Falls National Park on the Virginia–Maryland border above Arlington. Hacker took the Beltway north into Virginia on the same route the kidnappers had used earlier in the night.

When he pulled off at Virginia 738, the Old Georgetown Pike and swung east to the entrance, he was pretty sure no one was following them.

The house was not marked on any map or visitor's guide because it officially wasn't there. In fact, it was a one-story log-cabin –style home with two full-time baby-sitters at all times. The baby-sitters looked like football linemen and carried Uzi machine guns with forty-round clips.

The headlamps were turned off now as the car approached the house along a narrow dirt lane.

"How can you see?" Rita said to Hacker.

He grunted and pointed to a green screen on the dash. "Sensors alongside the road guide us in. They know we're coming. More important, they know if anyone is following."

Devereaux stared into the blackness as they plunged along, bumping over the dips in the roadway.

"I didn't think we were going to quit this," Hacker said. He looked at the screen, not at Devereaux.

"I'm out. Hanley can do what he likes."

"You said we can't quit."

Devereaux did not speak.

"Your friend is safe. However long it takes, she's safe."

"She can't live in the Virginia house the rest of her life," Devereaux said. Rita wasn't there for either man.

"We can protect her," Hacker said.

"Drop it."

"I don't want to quit," Hacker said. "I don't have a wife. I can do it, pick it up."

Devereaux said nothing. Rita reached across the back of the front seats and touched him on the shoulder. He placed his hand on top of hers.

The baby-sitters were watching television and drinking coffee and eating buttered toast. They offered to give her some toast and she took it and ate but she didn't drink the coffee. The first baby-sitter watched a green monitor screen in the other room for a few minutes. When he came back, he said no one was following but they both carried their Uzis when they moved around the kitchen and watched her eat buttered toast.

She took another shower in the bathroom off the guest bedroom. She took Seconal for the third time in her life because she was so desperately tired and she knew she couldn't sleep. He sat with her on the edge of the bed and held her hand until she was sleeping.

When he went into the kitchen, the baby-sitters were at the table, making ham sandwiches. The night shift made them hungry all the time. There were two other baby-sitters for the day shift and they were sleeping in the baby-sitters' bedroom. The baby-sitters worked seven days on, seven days off, rotating two crews and a third, relief crew brought in from a similar house in Louisiana. The ghostly voices of an old movie came from the television set in the next room.

Hacker just sat and stared at him. In the fluorescent light of the kitchen, they both looked bloodless.

"What are you going to do?"

"Call Bobby Lee."

"And then what?"

"Put him in the picture. It's what Hanley wanted. Mrs. Neumann wanted."

"And then what?"

"I'm getting out of it is what."

"And then what?" Hacker said again.

"Then nothing. Nothing that concerns you."

"Then you go after Clair Dodsworth, just you and him. That's the way you're going to do it."

"No," Devereaux said.

"Don't fiddle-fuck me, Devereaux."

"No. Rita's my weak spot. If they can do that, they can do the other thing. They must be getting very nervous about something."

"So you wait a month or two months and you set it up. You just whack the old man, that doesn't get us closer to the bank, to what Mona wanted."

"No, that would be pretty stupid all right. Just wet down one old man."

"But you're gonna do it." It was no question.

Devereaux said, "I'm calling Bobby Lee

now, you take me to the Pentagon."

"Sure. I'm up for the night."

"And then you make sure she's got what she wants."

"I thought you were doing this for Mona. You sent Mona into Leb. You greened the operation," Hacker said.

"You don't get it, Hacker, sometimes you don't win. I'm giving it up. I just quit. Let Bobby Lee have it."

"Fucking DIA'll fuck it up, they don't care."

"They want the money trail too."

"They don't care. They don't care about the six we lost in Lebanon. Now you don't care."

"All right, Hacker, that's enough."

"It's not enough, I'd like to ram it down your throat."

The baby-sitter at the door said, "You guys gonna fight? Take it outside, we have to account for damage in here."

"We're not gonna fight. What am I gonna do, kick him with my wooden leg?"

Five minutes later, Devereaux came away from the telephone and stared at Hacker for a moment.

Hacker put down his cup of coffee. "You talked to the general?"

"I talked to him." He was staring at Hacker

without seeing him. "They arrested Colonel Cavett an hour ago. There was another fire, at Indianhead. They're talking to him about the Pentagon fire."

"Did he do it?"

Devereaux just stared at Hacker, thinking about something else. About how he made Cavett dirty for Bobby Lee to keep the general off his back for a few more days. Just a little betrayal to throw the general a bone.

"What are you gonna do?"

But now he couldn't say at all and the other men in the room stared at the agent and they saw the indecision that had marked him like a stain and they looked away from him then because it is a bad thing to see in another's face.

Thirty-three

Escher rented a car at eleven hundred hours at the Seattle–Tacoma airport and drove north to Seattle. The day was typical of the northwest coast with clouds and sun playing chase across Puget Sound and into the green, wooded mountains. Mount Rainier sparkled along its snowy slopes when the sun thought to shine on it. It rains almost every day in Seattle but it is usually not long, not hard, and it comes as a refreshment after hours of sun. It never stops anything from going on. Even the prostitutes from the east side who work the Alaska Way and First Street and Public Market carry umbrellas.

He drove along with one hand on the steering wheel and thought about things. He thought it was odd that Britta Andrews wasn't afraid of him at all. He thought she was a hard little bitch — hell, she was going to finance burning down a nuclear reactor. Was that hard or was that hard? He was as hard as she was; he could do the burn and not think twice about it.

Then he thought about Liz Cavett, who was not nearly as beautiful as Britta — and who was she to be such a bitch? To turn him down and then compound it and call in her ex–old man to threaten him? Not as if she wasn't going down on everything in trousers, where did she get off telling Jack Cavett that Max scared her? He wanted to rape her, he would have thrown her down with one hand and done it, but that wasn't what he wanted, he wanted her to want it as much as he did, and get off her high horse. Well, fuck her. And fuck Jack Cavett too. Let him explain setting fire to the galley at Indianhead, candy-ass cuckold son of a bitch. Max had put out the hand of friendship to him and he had spit on it, so fuck him.

The man named Roberts he was dealing with in Seattle could get nearly any kind of arson device, but Escher used him exclusively for what he called rocket fuel. It was good stuff, Roberts handled only good stuff. It was solid state, stolen out of manufacturing plants all over Oregon, Washington, Idaho. The burn capital of the country was in the Northwest, every fire investigator and arson dick knew that. Aerospace up here. Rocket fuel sent up the rockets and burned down the factories, and Roberts brokered the stuff as good as he had ever seen.

Roberts was out of Tacoma, closer to the Boeing plants, but he always made his deals in Seattle. Like Roberts always said, "You don't shit where you sleep." Roberts was a lot like Bernie Lund in Apostle, Max thought. They both had their pat sayings and little pieces of jargon they took as gospel. Couple of useful losers if you asked Max.

Roberts looked like a nerd sitting in the lobby bar of the Olympia Hotel. Glasses, shirt buttoned up to the collar, no tie. *Haircut must have set him back two bucks,* Max thought, entering the bar. The man was sitting at a small, round table and he was being served by one of the statuesque waitresses, who looked as though they were picked for the job by Louis XVI to look exactly like Marie when Marie was dressed up.

"Hey," Escher said.

"Hey, man," Roberts said.

Escher sat down.

"How's it going?" Escher said.

"It goes. How you doin'?"

"Everyone I can."

"Those you like, twice, huh?" Smiled a nerdy smile. "Well, I got it."

"What a coincidence. That's why I'm here."

"Where you been, Max?"

"Here and there."

"That right?"

"Right as rain," Escher said.

"You been in Washin'ton lately?"

"Naw, man, you know I'd look you up if I was up here."

"No, man. I mean the other Washin'ton."

"Other Washington."

"Want a drink?" the woman said. Max looked at her. Nice figure, big woman, not little like Britta. Liz was bigger than Britta. He gave her a smile and she gave it back. Max made an order. She went away.

"That was some burn. Burning the Pentagon." Roberts was staring at him through those nerdy horned-rims. Even had white tape on one earpiece. Guy had to be worth $300,000 a year and he dressed like shit, Max thought.

"Yeah. Some burn," Max said.

"Someone sure had a hard-on on the military. That's what I think," Roberts said.

"One of you draft dodgers," Max said. Keeping it light.

"Wasn't no draft when I got old enough."

"Well, suppose some guys have hard-ons, that don't mean they go burning things down. People get laid off, they don't burn down the factory."

"Sometimes they do."

"Well, that's an interesting theory."

"I know you had a hard-on."

"Is that right? You know all about me, Roberts?"

"Well, you said you did."

"I say a lot of things."

"Not that many," Roberts said. He just sat looking at Escher through those thick glasses, he looked like a bird.

"I watched the news. When I got up. Arrested some colonel. This morning on the news," Roberts said.

"Is that right?"

"That's right. Dude you mentioned once to me."

"Is that right?"

"Didn't you mention this guy who was in the army with you named Cavett? Like the guy on TV, the talk guy, named Dick Cavett. I remembered the name because I remembered Cavett, you don't know too many people named Cavett."

"You heard that name? On TV?"

"Naw. They didn't say a name. Everything is a secret up there. In D.C. But I made my calls. My little sources, you might say, people I deal with, and I got it unofficial that this guy they're holding was named Cavett. You talked to me about a Cavett. Said his wife was fucking everyone when she was married to him, you told me how she liked you to do her doggy-style."

"Oh." Escher just sat there.

So they had already pinned it on Jack.

He began to smile at Roberts and Roberts didn't understand the smile. Pinned it on Jack, it was all Liz's fault, maybe he'd take care of Liz now himself.

Roberts was staring at the grin.

Escher blinked. "You lookin' at something?"

"The last deal we made, I knew you were planning somethin' big. That was big, Max."

"Maybe you're jumping to the wrong conclusion."

"No, man. Biggest thing in the last three months, last three years, is the Pentagon burn, nothing like it."

"Is that right?"

Roberts said, "That's why I was asking you about being in Washin'ton. In the other Washin'ton, I mean, not state."

"I know what you mean, for Christ's sake, you don't have to repeat it. You got the stuff I want or what am I doing here?"

Roberts said, "The package. It's out in the car. In the lot."

"That's more like it." The woman brought the drink and Max dropped ten on her plate like it was a big deal. He waved off the change. He never could get civilian prices straight. Maybe he should have asked Britta for more money, maybe the rich bitch thought $2 million was getting off light.

He tasted the drink.

"This is the best shit I've handled in a long time," Roberts said.

"You always sell good shit."

"Thanks, Max, but I really had to grease this one. There were a couple of guys in this one, in a new wing of the ordnance plant. I couldn't go to the sources anymore, had to go to the weapons assembly plant."

"Is that right?" Tasting the drink and looking right at the nerd.

"See, I got what you want. But I want twenty-five thousand."

Oh. That was it. Escher put down the drink on the little table between them and leaned forward. His voice was soft as a purr. "Deal is fifteen. Always is."

"I didn't know you were burning down the Pentagon before," Roberts said.

"Is that what I was doing?"

"See, I never heard of Cavett and Cavett would have dealt with me or someone I know. Only so many brokers for this stuff. He would want the good stuff. I knew that was rocket soup used in the Pentagon just the way they described the burn. So it wasn't Cavett, was it?"

"Is that right?" Escher said. Saying inane things like that was just a way of thinking. He was thinking over the next three or four things already.

"Well, Max?"

"You know I don't like to be held up. I think a deal is a deal. We shake hands on our deals, like gentlemen."

"I could have hit you for more, I kept the price down because we've done business in the past."

"But this is like putting a gun to my head."

"Then don't do the deal. Whatever you want to burn down, you find another broker. Hell, use aluminum chloride, you can get that shit out of farm supply stores."

"I want rocket candy."

"Then maybe you should just do business with me and pay and not get snotty about it."

One of the reasons he never did like Roberts was he knew that Roberts dodged the draft, went to Canada, and waited it out working in the chemistry department at McGill University in Montreal. Hiding with the frogs. And now pretended he had been too young when the draft ended, not only a coward but not even man enough to admit it.

Max smiled in a lazy way and put down his drink. "I guess you got me, pardner."

"I guess I do."

"I brought in fifteen, I'll have to get some more money out of my trunk."

"You do that."

"I parked in the lot down the street."

"I'm down the street too."

"Then let's go do it. Here. Here's the fifteen and you can keep the wallet to carry it in." He flipped through the dollars. Fifteen hundred $100 bills. It never failed to make an impression. He wiped the leather with a wet paper napkin.

"I got billfolds," Roberts said. But he tucked it into the pocket of his corduroy jacket.

Cocky little bastard. "You get me the ten, I'll get you the package."

"Might as well," Max said. "Right in broad daylight. Then I can get a turnout flight outta here."

"Back to Washin'ton. The other Washin'ton."

"Look, man, don't keep on me about that, OK?"

Roberts looked at him. "Sure. Whatever you say."

Max thought that Roberts was feeling full of himself and would have to tell someone someplace about sticking it to Max Escher and one thing might lead to another and you never knew. A stitch in time saves nine and this was too big to blow over a little nerd like Roberts.

They crossed the street and went down the block. It began to rain, the soft light rain of Seattle, which is as beautiful as rain in the movies. Most of the time it just wets down everything and everyone and no one pays attention to it.

The parking garage had six levels, two below ground and four above. They were both on the roof level, the last to be filled.

Escher figured it out while they rode the elevator to the roof level. He had bought some shit in D.C., which, outside of South America, is the shit capital of the world. Six nickel bags of the white stuff securely packaged in Federal Express air bill plastic envelopes, the packaging desired by all the more sophisticated users and dealers because the bags used for air bills never break and they're free. It's one of the reasons Federal Express supply boxes around the country are always short of the pouches.

The way to do it was to open one of the pouches and give it to Roberts and save the other five for Bernie Lund and whoever else had to be brought in on it in Chicago.

They walked to his car. It had stopped raining in the time it took them to reach the roof. He opened the trunk and revealed a small overnight bag. The big suitcase of money was going to be waiting for him in D.C. when Britta coughed it up. In two days. The big score in two days. Two million, two days. This was the change still left from the $100,000 advance.

Escher took out the bag and closed the trunk. He unzipped the bag and Roberts grinned but looked around him as though some "Miami Vice" helicopter was about to hover into view. Max glanced down at him once. Asshole saw life through watching television, which showed you what an asshole he was.

He counted out the money in $100 bills. One hundred $100 bills. He hesitated. He looked at Roberts. "You wanna do some shit?"

Roberts stared at him. Those flat brown eyes had told Escher the first time he met Roberts. The coke heads all get those flat eyes, like cats gone myopic.

"Why, you got shit?"

"I got shit like you wouldn't believe."

"I didn't know you did shit."

"I do shit."

"Walk over to my car. I got the grey Lexus. Over there."

"That's a new car for you."

"I traded in the Caddy. I got the top Lexus."

Yeah. You would. Escher pocketed the bills and put the bag back in the trunk, then walked over to Roberts's car.

They got into the front seat of the Lexus. It started to sprinkle again. Drops beaded the windshield.

He took out one of the Fedex pouches. "This is not street shit," Max said. But it was, probably cut nine ways from Sunday.

"Mm," said Roberts. "First thing, my money."

Max handed over the roll of bills. The little shit counted them and stuffed them in his pocket. "OK, we got a deal. The rocket candy is that brown bundle on the backseat."

"Same as before," Max said.

"You'll like the stuff."

"You'll like this stuff," Max said. "You got sticks."

Roberts took out two plastic straw stirrers from the glove compartment. They were wrapped by McDonald's. "Take the legal pad, down on the console, we do it there," Roberts said, taking charge. He opened a straw, threw the paper on the floor of the car, tried to tear open the sealed pouch.

"Take all day," Max said, taking the pouch

and opening a corner with his pocket knife. He sprinkled a little on the pad.

"Ladies first," Max said.

Roberts didn't even frown. He didn't even ask Max to make a line, he took dope like a big slob, just sucked it up.

Max broke his neck while he was bent over the legal pad, half of the hit already in his nose. He didn't make a sound.

The blow was part karate, part army manual, all Special Forces, worked up to with a thousand squeezes of a hard rubber ball every day in training. They called themselves "the guys with rubber balls." It had been a good time.

"Greedy little shit," Escher said to Roberts, who was still bent over the cocaine on the legal pad. He pushed Roberts up into a sitting position behind the wheel then and turned on the ignition. He took the billfold and the loose money out of Roberts's pockets and put them in his own. Then he reached in the backseat and picked up the brown bundle. It was a foot cubed. He opened the passenger door and walked back to his car and put the brown bundle in the overnight bag. He closed the trunk and went around to the driver's side and got in. He started the motor and went across the roof and slid into the empty stall next to Roberts's Lexus.

Max got out of the car. He opened the driver's door of the Lexus and carefully pressed Roberts's dead hands on the steering wheel. Then he sprinkled more of the white stuff on the seat and then threw the rest of the bag on the floor. The last thing was to put Roberts's foot on the accelerator pedal. Then he pushed the gear on the console into D, reached down with his hand, and gave the accelerator a goose.

The car bolted ahead toward the concrete retaining wall twenty-five feet away.

Escher got back into his car and started for the down ramp. He heard the crash. He drove carefully downstairs and paid his ticket and pulled into the street.

The Lexus was hanging over the edge of the parking garage. Max Escher turned in his rental car about the time the first policemen on the scene told the detective there was nose candy all over the inside of the wrecked car.

Thirty-four

The meltdown at the Three Mile Island plant had scared the other nuclear operators more than Chernobyl. Chernobyl was a one-in-a-million thing, a Russian thing. The Russians built nuclear plants on their own principles. Comparing Chernobyl with anything in the West was like equating the Cyrillic alphabet with the one in the West.

The Three Mile Island blow had scared everyone from the Nuclear Regulatory Commission on down to the private plant operators who had billions invested in the process. It had also scared ordinary people when they thought about it.

Since Three Mile Island, nuclear power plants went to a green-board concept in their reactor control rooms. In a green-board room every function of the plant is monitored by color codes in the control room. When the function is correct, the board is lighted green. When something is wrong, the red light flashes, and in theory the control room operators can isolate the malfunction and move to fix it.

In the movies nuclear power plants resemble the flight deck of the starship *Enterprise,* with vast television monitors in a darkened room isolating each section of the plant. In fact, they are bright, humdrum places without television monitors. They have many gauges, both analog and digital, as well as all those green and red lights clustered around switches controlling and monitoring each function.

What happened at Three Mile Island, among other things, was that every Tom, Dick, and Harry crowded into the control room at the critical moments in the meltdown and no one could get anything done because everyone was in the way. That would not happen now. A separate ops facility for disaster-control personnel was set up to leave the actual control room uncluttered.

In the event of a disaster.

That is the way it was on the last day of November inside the nuclear power facility at the Apostle in northern Illinois. It was a textbook operation, employing nearly a thousand men and women in a variety of jobs, from control room director to people like Bernie Lund, a security guard who assisted a nuclear engineer each day in the on-site visual inspection of the Red reactor core.

Bernie Lund was higher than a mushroom cloud on 'ludes this Thursday morning, but it did not affect the safety or security of the plant. It was his day off. And his next random drug test was weeks away.

Emmett McCarthy, a retired Rockford police lieutenant, was in charge of plant security at the Apostle. He was an employee of Barnes Security Services, which had the $5.1 million yearly contract from Northern Illinois Power and Light Company to guard the facility.

McCarthy was not a fool.

He realized his security force was not ideal. It doubtless contained ex–gang bangers, dopeheads, drunks, ex-cons, sex fiends, and the mentally feeble, but you worked with what you had.

He tried to explain this to Ingersoll, but sometimes it was like Ingersoll came from another planet instead of just Washington, D.C.

Ingersoll was the inspector from the Nuclear Regulatory Commission assigned to the Apostle. Each nuclear plant in the country had an NRC officer assigned to it to ensure plant security and safety. They generally worked five days a week, from nine to five, and they considered themselves the ombudsmen of the plants they inspected. Ingersoll was a get-along guy, but every now and then, he liked to needle McCarthy.

He needled McCarthy today, the last day of November, about a woman named Selma Harris who had been arrested by Chicago police in a drug raid two days earlier. Selma Harris had been employed as a security officer in the entry room to the generator building.

"This isn't the first time this has happened," Ingersoll said for the second time. They were walking among the turbines in the generator room, McCarthy glancing this way and that, looking at the welders on the Blue turbine. The Blue reactor was shut down at the moment, waiting for fresh fuel rods of uranium. It was a good time to do repairs. Red reactor was up and the vibrations of its turbines in the generators made the building tingle with the sense of energy.

McCarthy said, "You work with what you get. I see football stars making millions get caught in drug tests. We test here as best we can. You can't have a test every day on every employee. And these people aren't million-aires, Ingersoll, they make twenty-four, twenty-five thousand a year. They don't give a shit."

"But it's your responsibility."

"I take responsibility. I take my responsibility to the plant, to the brass at Barnes Security, I take it to everyone." He wanted to add he wasn't going to take it from Ingersoll.

Ingersoll shook his head. "Maybe we need a whole new procedure in our drug-abuse tests."

Ingersoll was big on ordering up whole new procedures. He could do it, make the recommendations, but Ingersoll was a smart enough bureaucrat to understand that making waves wasn't exactly what the board of Northern Illinois Power had in mind. NIPL — the seldom used stock market acronym for the power company — had its own influence in Washington, and Ingersoll might end up guarding a nuclear plant in Buffalo. *Wait till he spends a winter in Buffalo,* McCarthy thought, and smiled at the thought.

"I don't think anyone wants that around here. I don't mind it. Let's see, we've got a hundred seventy-one security personnel, we could test them — what? — daily? weekly? monthly? Urine and blood tests or just blood tests? Test them when? Before duty or after duty?"

"You just want to put up obstacles —"

McCarthy held up his hand. They were standing in the middle of the generator building on the upper level, right between the quiet west side, where welders worked on the down Blue generator, and the humming, surging east side, where Red reactor was still running and feeding the turbines that drove the generators, which made the power. Workers crawled among both beasts, which sat nose to nose like immense steam locomotives of another era, one alive and vibrating, the other brute down and waiting.

"I've got no objections to anything you want to do. You tell the administration and the administration tells me. I just don't want the needle for this, Ingersoll. We test them twice yearly."

"You're responsible —"

"No. You're responsible. You people authorize this thing, it's built, it's still gotta be run by someone. By people. And then you fail to get the best people and you want to blame some flunky like me." He shook his cop's face. "It don't happen, believe me."

Ingersoll stared at him a moment and then took a step back. Literally. He stood on the dead side of the room now, where the blue lines were painted on the floors to define paths in and around the Blue reactor operation. "I think I want to recommend a monthly test on a staggered basis, divided into groups that we change randomly," Ingersoll said.

McCarthy shrugged. "It suits me. What's it gonna cost?"

"Why do you care?"

"I don't care. I'm a cop, I never owned stock. What d'ya think NIPL is gonna care?"

"They'll pass the cost on."

"Whatever you say."

"I want an honest evaluation —"

"No, you don't. You want me to sign on. I don't wanna sign on."

"Why?"

"Because it won't work. You'll weed out a few and that part works, but what if we start finding it hard to recruit a work force? Then you gotta up wages, and now you're talking more than the cost of the tests."

"You talk like a union man," Ingersoll said. He was trying to sneer.

"I'm not in no unions, I'm telling you facts of life," McCarthy said, and now he was blushing and Ingersoll thought maybe it was a good time to drop it. McCarthy had his hands behind his back and was rocking back on his heels like a cop. Definitely a good time.

The safe, cleansed steam rose from the cooling tower and blew invisibly across the Illinois countryside. It was the hour after midnight. The stars were out in the clear sky.

The vapor mixed in the wind and blew across dead cornfields and the little towns that huddle along the Rock and Fox rivers and the Des Plaines River suburbs and along the Illinois River, which descends in a gentle grade down to the Mississippi. The northwesterly wind blew down across the Apostle plant and toward the glittering cityscape, where the skies were reddish orange from city lights and the stars could not be seen.

Thirty-five

It was unusual for the bank, any bank, to deliver money of withdrawal to the customer at the customer's residence. But then, $2 million in hundred-dollar bills is an unusual withdrawal. And not reported to any federal agency.

And the man who brought the money to Britta Andrews was also different. She had expected a security guard or two, not a young man in a neat blue suit, white shirt, flowered tie and with the face of the desert. His eyes were bright and black and his teeth were very white in that brown face.

"I have wanted to meet you." He spoke with an English accent. She liked that. She gave him a smile.

He put the case down on the coffee table. He bent and opened it. Twenty thousand $100 bills can be an impressive thing to see.

Her eyes opened wide. She was rich but her money was not real to her, it was just there. So many shares of stock, so many coupons to be clipped, so much balance in banks and mutual funds. Money was never as real as the sight of lots of real money.

"I suppose I should count it before I sign anything," she said. She stretched out her hand and touched the money. She touched it lightly and then with more authority and he watched her touch the stacks of money.

"I can assure you it's all there," he said.

"Can you?"

"Besides, you don't have to sign anything."

"I don't? You always must sign," she said.

"My name is Khashogi," he began, and sat down.

That was a little rude, she thought. And then looked at the money again and then sat down opposite him.

"I represent the International Credit Clearinghouse," he said.

"Oh," she said. She looked at the money in the suitcase and then at the neat young man.

He closed the lid of the case. He smiled at her. He said, "What do you intend?"

"I told Clair what we intended."

"Is that all? To make propaganda against the nuclear power industry? Through your . . . institute?" He smiled at her. "I don't think so, Miss Andrews. Otherwise, I would be disappointed."

"Disappointed in what?"

"In the Dove," Khashogi said.

"I don't know what you mean."

"We became aware of the Dove last spring when we questioned certain agents who . . . fell into our hands."

Britta said nothing. She frowned and rubbed her hands against her arms as though she felt a chill. She stared at the bright black eyes.

"Let me be frank so that I can impel frankness from you. My . . . people, the ones I represent in this, are interested in action and not in words. We feel assured by certain interests in Europe that you were an agent of action, not words. As was your famous father. And we were aware of your inquiries last summer in certain circles, principally in Bonn and Copenhagen, that you were seeking a certain type of person to work on an operation for you." Each clump of words was separated from the others by little hesitations in speech. The mannerism made the words seem very important.

She stared at him.

He made an open gesture with his hands. "Let me be frank."

"I hate it when people say that. It always means they're going to lie."

He shook his head. "Then I won't say it.

We desire action, Miss Andrews, action. Not words."

"What action?"

"Why do you need this money in cash? Delivered in this way?"

"Perhaps for action."

"I see."

He waited as though she had something more to say. But the silence lingered and he clapped his hands once then and got up.

"Well, then I won't take more time."

"Sit down," she said.

He sat, hands on knees.

"I'm going to destroy nuclear power in this country," she said. Yes. Her eyes were bright and blue and very cold, staring at the desert face and matching the hardness in the black eyes. "Is that what you want to know?"

She had wanted to say it. Just that way. Not to Clair, who was old and sly, and not to Michael, who was weakening, and not to Max Escher, who would dispute it in his punk's way and say that he was doing it, not her. Just one person had to know and it was this man. Khashogi himself. He would know and take it back to the Middle East with him and they would see, all of them. She had to tell someone it was she, she was the heroine in this.

"How are you going to do this?"

"Not with words," she said.

He waited again for her to say more but she just sat there like some queen of ancient Egypt, waiting for his admiration.

And he gave it, slowly and without reluctance. He gave her a smile and she saw the respect in it.

He got up then and bowed a little to her from the waist. She accepted the gesture, not by lowering her eyes but by staring directly at him.

"And no one knows of this?" he said.

"No one."

"Except the agent you are going to use."

"Even he doesn't understand. He's merely the weapon I have to use."

"An expensive weapon."

"Not for something like this," she said.

Again, he bowed to her. "I understand, Miss Andrews, I understand you and I admire you."

She didn't even acknowledge that.

"Let me congratulate you. Proleptically."

"I accept it."

And he left her then without another word, withdrawing slowly and quietly, leaving her sitting on the white chair by the window in front of the suitcase of money, staring at nothing at all but the immensity of what she was going to do.

Thirty-six

The Pentagon, like a wounded beast, was slowly coming back to life, licking its wounds. There was still water in the subbasement, where mains had burst, and there was a stink in the building from the septic waters. It was cold in some parts and too warm in others. The beast endured and breathed deeply and waited for the wounds to heal.

Devereaux passed through the metal detectors and followed his escort back through the labyrinth of the building to Section Three Four quarters on the second level. The general was waiting for him.

At first, Devereaux sat before the general's desk and said nothing. He searched the other's face as though he could decide what to say by what he found there. But there was nothing. Gen. Robert E. Lee looked blank, hard, like unformed iron not yet molded to a steel structure.

"You think Jack Cavett is crazy," Devereaux finally said.

"That's a legal defense. That can come in time when he talks to the Judge Advocate General. I don't decide if people are crazy."

"He hates the army bad enough to sabotage the Pentagon, and then to make sure you know it, he sabotages a mess hall on his own base."

"Galley is what the navy calls it. Galley. Yes, sometimes a firebug isn't happy until he's caught. They do what they do and they want to brag about it."

"He didn't do it."

"Is that right? I had an initial suspicion about him. He doesn't like being told to leave the service. He told you that. You told me all the things he told you. About how the fires were set, what was used as accelerant. Sure, I think he wanted to brag to someone who was outside it. Like you, dumb civilian like you. And you told me. You thought it was important enough to come and tell me what he was bragging about."

"He didn't brag about anything."

"But he told you shit, Red, he told it to you the way it was, and when that wasn't enough, he set fire to his own goddamned base."

"I shouldn't have told you."

General Lee smiled then. "Maybe not but you did and it got my job made a lot easier."

They sat and stared at each other. Blank face to blank face, poker players without cards, keeping the hands in their heads.

"I wanted to bait you, give myself time to work things out about ICC," Devereaux said.

"I know what you were doing, I'm not an idiot, Red. But it was good stuff you were giving me, really good stuff, you couldn't bait me without good stuff."

"It doesn't matter," Devereaux finally said. "I'm turning everything over to you, even the stuff held back. You go your own way with it. Section is out of this now."

"Are you setting me up again, Red?"

"No."

"Then why are you pulling your oars?"

"Two men abducted a friend of mine last night. The woman I live with. They scared her and drove her around and dumped her in Bethesda. Middle East types. They said I was a dead man and that she should leave me."

"So you finally got them to take a shot at you and it wasn't at you, it was at some civilian."

"Some civilian."

Bobby Lee said, "I'm sorry about that. Is she all right, your lady?"

"For now. They want me off this."

"So you want me to turn the rock over for you? It seems to me that's giving up the war because you get a few casualties."

"We've had six. Seven counting Carroll. Now, maybe, I'm responsible for eight with Colonel Cavett. That's too many for me, Bobby Lee."

"Not too many if you can nail these bastards."

Devereaux shook his head.

"All right," General Lee said. "You want to debrief to Major Gardner, he's in this, he'll know the references."

"I can do that," Devereaux said.

"I'll call him —"

"I want to see Colonel Cavett."

"Why?"

Devereaux said nothing.

"Oh, yeah, I see." He gave a brief smile that was like regret. He hated to see someone lose it, someone he had known in the old days. He turned away from the agent from R Section and picked up a phone. "Yeah. Sergeant, I've got a civilian here to be escorted to where we're talking to Colonel Cavett. You tell them to let him see him." He replaced the receiver. "You want to talk to Major Gardner then afterward?"

"I'll come back here."

"Naw," General Lee said, looking at papers

on his desk. He didn't have time for farewell interviews. He didn't really want to see Devereaux again. When your time's up, walk away from it. "I'll send him along to you to where we're talking to the colonel. You can find an empty debrief room around there. In all this mess. I've got to brief the brass at eleven hundred hours."

Devereaux understood.

Cavett was being sweated in a windowless room in the interior of the huge building. There were two of them, both full colonels, and there were two MPs outside the door. The sergeant let Devereaux wait outside while he delivered his instructions to the two colonels.

The colonels gave Devereaux the look when they brushed by him. Jack Cavett gave him a different look when he entered the room.

"Are you the next team? You going to run it in relays like you spooks used to do in 'Nam? I'm tired but I'm telling the truth," Cavett said.

Devereaux sat down on a wooden chair next to the wooden table. He looked at Jack in the same searching way he had studied General Lee's face.

"Jack, who wants to set you up for this?"

Jack Cavett smiled then. It was not pleasant. "You're the good cop, right? You're my friend."

"I wasn't your friend when I told Bobby Lee your theories of the Pentagon arson. No, I wasn't your friend at all but I didn't think this would happen. Who wants to set you up for this, Jack?"

"I can't imagine."

"The fire. In Indianhead. The same —"

"I don't know that. Maybe one of the defective coffee makers got sent to Indianhead. Maybe I did do it and don't remember it. You forget things when you get old."

"Are you forgetting anything?"

"No."

"You want me to call someone? Your wife?"

"My ex-wife? Christ, don't do me any more favors, stay as far away from me as you can. All I know, you set the fire in Indianhead. I don't trust you spooks, I never did, not in 'Nam, not now. You play games not only with the other side, you play with us. Well, you messed me up, spook, and I'll stand it but don't involve anyone else."

"What do you know about ICC?"

"I know what you told me. What the general told me. I don't know anything."

"ICC finances terrorism. We were after

them. They killed six agents. Killed a man here in the District. Tried to stop us."

"I don't give a shit," Cavett said. "This makes it easier in a way. JAG and a court-martial, they'll have nothing but circumstances and even the Universal Code of Military Justice frowns on just circumstances. Bobby Lee has me and he earns himself a breather but I'll stand it."

"How does it make it easier?"

"Leaving the service. My resignation. They can't do a damned thing to me and I think I'm beginning to show them I know it. They can't crack me because there's nothing to crack."

Devereaux sat in silence. Whatever he wanted to say didn't have words. He got up then. "I'll be in touch with you, Jack."

"Don't be in touch with me," Jack Cavett said.

The door opened then and a major was standing there. It was time to go, time to withdraw, time to pass it over to DIA and stop the fruitless, hopeless quest for whatever kind of justice or revenge he had wanted to gain.

Thirty-seven

Some said in an unkind way that the raspy-voiced director of R Section was built like a tank. Mrs. Neumann did have the ability to drive through problems like a tank. The inquiry from Senator Michael Horan festered into a problem for her and then into an obstacle. She called Michael Horan's office on the afternoon when Devereaux had requested a meeting with her at two. Devereaux had spent the morning at the Pentagon. She wanted to be forewarned and that's why she had called the senator. When she reached the senator, she tried to be polite and even friendly.

"I want to talk to you about your request the other day, Senator. For our file on one of our senior advisers."

"It doesn't matter now," he said. His voice sounded harassed. "It doesn't matter now."

"Why?"

"It was a request, you denied it, and the matter meantime is resolved."

"What matter was it?" Mrs. Neumann said.

"It wasn't important," he said then.

"All right, Senator," she said slowly. "Then everything is resolved?"

"It's satisfactory." He lifted his voice. "I appreciate your returning the call. I suppose you wanted to cooperate but it isn't necessary."

"Yes," she said then. "We wanted to cooperate."

Devereaux was not to meet with her at two. It was nearly four before she sent for him. He spent the two hours in an office they had given him. He had gone over photographs. Six of the photographs were of field officers, slain comrades in arms. They were color photographs, not very flattering. He lingered over the photograph of Rachel Horowitz, the agent called Mona, for a long time. And then the photograph of the slain Carroll Claymore. They had mocked Section with that murder and then they had panicked. Why use a senator? Why be so obvious? Why kidnap Rita Macklin off the street? The pressure was intense.

It must be something about to happen, he thought then. Something that connected all these people, living and dead, to something he was getting close to.

He put the photographs in a file folder and put the file folder in a box labeled "Eyes Only" and closed the box and locked it. He took it back to the Records and Research Section. He went back to the office and sat and waited.

She had Hacker and Hanley in the office when he arrived at a minute after four. Washington traffic piled up on Fourteenth Street outside her window. The day was warm and blowsy bright, it was like spring. The first of December.

"General Lee telephoned me at noon to thank me for your cooperation and to release you back to Section," Mrs. Neumann began.

Devereaux sat down across from her and looked at Hanley and Hacker.

"Mr. Hacker arranged to store Miss Macklin in the house in Virginia at a late hour last night," she said.

"I was going to tell you."

"He told me everything. I think he told me everything."

"I was going to tell you."

"I called Senator Horan this afternoon. He doesn't want your file anymore. It was almost friendly, talking with him." Her great rasping voice punched out the words while her mild eyes studied the face of the man. "He said the matter was resolved."

Devereaux waited.

"Hacker said you want nothing to do with the ICC matter anymore."

"It's what you wanted," Devereaux said.

"I was mistaken."

Hanley looked as startled as a rabbit caught in headlamps.

"Why?"

"Do you know that when he called me, I supposed it was about ICC. Or Clair Dodsworth. Something about this Institute for World Development that seemed to interest you greatly in the beginning."

"A five-million-dollar line of credit to the institute arranged in District Savings Bank. From a European satellite bank controlled by ICC," Devereaux recited. And then stopped. Waited.

"Two million dollars was transferred from the bank at closing yesterday."

"To what bank?"

"I misspoke," she said. "Withdrawn."

"By whom?"

"Miss Andrews, I presume."

"And?"

"And Senator Horan is no longer interested in you because you've turned this matter over to General Lee. As I instructed, I remember that, don't interrupt me. You continued on it without authorization."

Hanley stared at him.

"Perhaps I did," Devereaux said.

"They wanted you to stop what you were doing."

Devereaux waited again. The silence in the room muffled the noise of traffic below. Every nuance of the silence was being studied by the four people in the room.

"I feel," she began. Then stopped and ran her hand across her forehead. "I feel a sense of dread. In this country, in this capital, two Middle Eastern gentlemen abduct a woman who knows nothing, and send a crude threat to you. And you respond."

"I helped to kill seven people," Devereaux said. "She would be eight. I can't fight the Section and the power in this city. ICC has bought into Washington and I can't fight that."

"What are they going to do?"

He waited for her yet again. It wasn't a rhetorical question. She searched their faces and didn't find an answer.

"They're paying off the contractors who burned the Pentagon," she said.

Devereaux saw it then. The Socratic method but with flat statements to be disputed, not questions.

"No," he answered her. "They wouldn't want the general to be pursuing that."

"The general has his Judas goat."

"For the moment. Cavett didn't have anything to do with it."

"Devereaux," she said. She leaned forward, hands entwined on her desktop, commanding the room. "Cavett told you things. He hinted at things. An internal security matter, something that could be done from the inside. Using the very military pipeline right into the Pentagon."

Hanley was frowning. They weren't really interested in the Pentagon, were they?

"I kept you waiting for two hours while I ran a new search on Miss Andrews."

"I ran a search on her when Carroll Claymore —"

"Don't interrupt me." She picked up papers. "Miss Andrews attends an antinuclear conference of Green parties in Gstaad in the middle of the month. We're watching it. Miss Andrews also made inquiry last summer in Copenhagen — this is from our Danish station — about a certain kind of man. A man who could be involved in demolition."

"Did our stationmaster get a name?"

"No. The inquiry only. We've got an informant on a very low level in one of the Green groups. The more active sort of Green group, more aligned with . . . violence."

"Well," Hanley began. And Mrs. Neumann

took time to glare him to silence before she resumed with Devereaux.

"There's no coincidence here," she said.

He turned the statement over and looked at it. He nodded finally.

She clapped her hands once. "Good. Then what do we do now?"

"I don't do anything," Devereaux said.

"Miss Macklin? I understand. But that shows their desperation to keep you at bay for . . . for what? A few days? A week or two? They can't believe we'd stop."

"You wanted that."

"I never wanted it. I wanted you to have some cover to operate under. I sent you to General Lee. I read personnel files, too, Devereaux. You knew him in the war days. You could have cover in the Pentagon after the fire. Maybe the fire was connected to ICC, maybe not, but you could work more effectively if I didn't have you underfoot. And the less I knew, the more I could deny."

Devereaux stared at the remarkable woman and slowly shook his head. It wasn't denial. Something like admiration.

"So what do we do? I think we have to do something."

"Britta Andrews," Devereaux said. "We've rattled the wrong cages. Clair Dodsworth sicced Senator Horan on Section. The wrong cage, wrong action. Dodsworth has been at this too long to be frightened by us. He blustered at you. You reacted and he was satisfied. But then Senator Horan calls you. The relationship between Dodsworth and Horan is clear but we never pursued their relation to Andrews."

"Miss Andrews received the money. A lot of money. Do you think we underestimated her?"

Hanley had to break in. "She's a civilian. In this country. She was investigated after her father's death, she grew up in her father's tradition. She was in radical organizations, everything. But she's rich. Very rich. She doesn't need money from ICC —"

"Except for an act of terror," Devereaux finished.

"And she sleeps with the senator," Mrs. Neumann said. "Armed Services Committee. Labor Committee. Banking Committee. Nuclear Subcommittee Investigating Plant Safety at Nuclear Stations." She was reading from a list.

"Armed services. The Pentagon," Hacker spoke for the first time.

Devereaux said nothing for a long moment. "Give it to General Lee, he can handle the ball."

"I did," Mrs. Neumann said. "When he called to thank me for your cooperation."

"And?"

"He doesn't want it. Not with a twenty-foot pole."

"Why do we?"

"Because of what you said, Devereaux. We're very, very close and they're acting in a very desperate way," Mrs. Neumann said.

Thirty-eight

"I didn't expect you," Britta said.

"I had to see you," Senator Horan said.

They stood at the door, which was partially open.

"Can I come in?" he said.

"Michael —"

But he pushed the door and she yielded. The door opened wide. She put her hands behind her back and stared at him. He walked past her to the living room.

He stood in the middle of the room and stared at the closed suitcase on the onyx coffee table. He turned and looked at her.

"What's that?"

She closed the door to the hall. She came into the room. She stared at him without speaking.

"I said, what's that?" he said.

She said nothing.

"What the hell is going on, Brit?"

"What'd you want?"

"I wanted to see you. I need a reason

to see you now?"

"So you've seen me."

He went to her and grabbed her by the shoulders with both hands and forced a kiss on her. Her head snapped back and he pressed her lips with his mouth and she didn't fight it. She took it. When he was finished, he pulled his head back and looked at her. She just stared at him.

"You fucking bitch," he said.

She stood there with his hands on her shoulders.

He took a step back from her and dropped his hands. "Why don't you tell me what's going on," he said.

"What do you mean, 'what's going on'?"

"Clair called me a few days ago, he wanted me to get a file on some intelligence agent. I made the request and then, today, he tells me it isn't necessary anymore. 'The matter's been taken care of' is what he said. I said what's going on and he said it wasn't that important and then he said, 'Did you get back your copies of the secret testimony on nuclear power?' What the hell does he know about that, Britta?"

"He knows," she said.

His face was red. "I know he knows, I wanna know why he knows."

"Because I told him," Britta said. "I said

I'd get the testimony from you and we could use it all later. After we did what we had to do."

His face was still red but there was no anger in his eyes now. He didn't make a move for a moment and she didn't make a sound.

"Did you destroy the papers I gave you?"

She said, "No. But don't worry, I threw them away in the garbage."

"The garbage? People go through garbage —"

"What are you saying? Some homeless man is going to come across secret testimony? And do what with it? You really are getting paranoid, Michael."

He took a step now and grabbed her shoulders again. "You don't seem to understand, Britta. Clair wanted a dossier on an intelligence agent and then he told me the matter's taken care of, like I was an errand boy for him. What was taken care of? And then he tells me about secret testimony he shouldn't know anything about."

"I want you to take your hands off me." She waited. He finally dropped his hands. "I want you to understand a few things, Senator. You let yourself fall in love with me and you knew how dangerous I was. Well, you wanted to know everything, and I told you once you were in, you couldn't back out."

"What are you going to do with this . . . this man you think set fire to the Pentagon?"

That brought a sly smile to her face. She said, "He did set fire to it."

"The car radio said they've arrested someone."

"No. That's the wrong person. Max set fire to it."

"Max? Is that his name?"

"Open the suitcase, Michael. You wanted to know everything, then you can know everything now. Go ahead."

He stared at the case on the coffee table. He made no move.

She took a step and pushed him in the chest. "Go ahead, Michael, open the suitcase."

"Look, Britta, you shouldn't have *treated* that testimony I got you like . . . It's secret, for Christ's sake!"

"There aren't any secrets, Michael. Not when it's important enough. Especially in this town. You know it, I know it, Clair knows it —"

"Clair's bank arranged your line of credit, Clair wants me to investigate an intelligence agent and then he says it doesn't matter and then —"

"Open the case, Michael."

He stared at her as if she had become a stranger. Then, with a sudden gesture, he bent over and unsnapped two latches and lifted the lid of the suitcase. He stared at the contents for a very long moment. It might have been forever if she hadn't suddenly laughed behind him. It was a mocking laugh and he didn't turn to confront her or go red in the face again. He just held the lid of the suitcase and stared at the stacks of hundred-dollar bills that were fitted in rows and wrapped with paper bands.

"Christ," he said.

"It's a lot of money, Michael."

"What are you going to do, Brit? Tell me what you're going to do," he said in a defeated voice. He still held the suitcase lid and stared at the money.

"I'm going to spend some borrowed money," she said. She was smiling and her voice carried the aftermath of mirth.

"To start a fire," he said.

"To start a fire," she said.

He stared at the money and then suddenly dropped the lid. His hands had lost their sense of touch. He stood with his hands held apart, like a priest making a blessing, staring at nothing.

"You're going to burn a nuclear power plant," he said. "You're going to fight nuclear power." His voice was dead. He could not make a move. It was like the dream in which

386

he couldn't run away and the bogeyman was coming through the door and the room was dark. He couldn't move. "You're going to fight it by burning down a nuclear power plant."

She didn't say anything but she was smiling behind his back.

And then he turned to her, blinking his eyes. "Is that it?"

"Yes, Michael. You wanted to know everything and now you know."

He groaned then and there were tears in his eyes. He groaned a second time. It was quite terrible and she couldn't smile anymore. She took a step to him and grasped his hands, which were cold.

"Michael. Michael," she said in her low, urgent voice.

"Oh, Jesus, stop, Brit. You have to stop."

"It can't be stopped, Michael."

"Brit, Brit, you'll kill people."

"We'll save the world, Michael. We are going to save the world."

He shook his head then, back and forth, back and forth. "No, no, no. This is monstrous, horrible, this cannot be. . . ." He wasn't seeing her, feeling her hands on his, he wasn't anything. "Don't do this, Brit, I don't want any part of it."

"You're part, darling," she said. Her voice

387

was low and she held his hands still but she was cold now. "You wanted to be part and you're part. You gave me testimonies and I'll use them. The institute can use them. And the other part, the Dove, well, you're part of that now too, darling. Clair's part and you're part, and we all of us, we're together in this, darling."

"This is insane," he said, blinking again as though to really see her for the first time, his eyes opening wide.

"It's an act of war," she said. "War against the polluters and profiteers."

"I won't —" He interrupted himself with a gurgling sort of sound. He shook his head. "I'll go to the FBI. I can't be part of this."

"You're part of it, dear. You can't go to the fascists." So calm. "Don't you see that? Clair told me about this intelligence agent because Mr. Khashogi wanted him to tell me. To tell me that even an agent of the government could be threatened." She smiled brightly and still held his hands in hers. "They kidnapped his girlfriend and they frightened him. They can do anything, they really can. Clair said they could kill anyone who interfered." She came close to him so that she could smell his whiskey breath. "They could kill you, darling."

He just stared at her. He couldn't move

and couldn't speak. His eyes were the only animated part of him, widening in horror.

"They could do anything. I can do anything."

And he saw it was true.

"Kiss me now," she said.

He kissed her because she compelled it. The kiss had no taste to him, inspired no passion. He thought he would never be in passion again, he felt so cold and old and dead.

"Where, Britta?"

"Of course, darling," she said. She kissed him again, lingering like a vampire, sucking all the life from him. It made her tingle, the sense of fear she had inspired in him.

And then she pulled back. She smiled again. "The Apostle. A very bad plant, you've heard it in the testimony. Sloppy procedures. Really, darling, it could cause problems at any time."

"But you'll pick the time." Each word tolled. He just stared at her and saw nothing but death. Tasted ashes on his tongue.

"I'll pick the time. And place. Imagine, Chicago. The first controlled nuclear reaction during the World War was in Chicago, under the stands of the University of Chicago football stadium. Imagine if they hadn't controlled it, Michael, it would have destroyed Chicago then and there. The irony,

Michael, think of it."

He could only stare and taste the ashes.

"Besides, it's Chicago, it isn't as though we need Chicago. It isn't here, Michael, it isn't New York. Or Boston. It's only Chicago, Michael," she said, trying to comfort him in his state of shock.

Thirty-nine

Max told Bernie Lund he had some good shit.

"Where you been?" Bernie wanted to know.

"Been here and there, doin' this and that," Max said. "Bernie want some good shit or what?"

"What kinda shit?" Bernie wanted to know. He let Max buy him a beer in Nuke's. Let him buy him two beers. Max was all right but Bernie didn't want to let Max take his friendship for granted. Bernie had his pride. What shit was Max talking about?

Turns out it was very good Colombian. That's what Max said. Bernie didn't know good shit from bad. He just knew the stuff made him able to leap tall buildings in a single bound. Made his rented trailer a palace. Gave him a hard-on that wouldn't quit. Made him the King of the Road.

Max followed him home and they had a girl with them. Her name was Carlette, she'd do Dobermans for the real thing. She had these coked out eyes that look like black dimes with

a lot of white around the colored parts. Carlette wore jeans and a sweater and nothing
else and it didn't take her long to take care
of the jeans and sweater. They were all laughing, it was so hilarious, doing lines on the
kitchen table.

Shit, one thing led to another. They had
whiskey and beer and lines. Carlette took both
of them on right there in the kitchen. Bernie
wanted to go to the bedroom but she said
the bedroom looked like a dog kennel and
smelled about the same.

Neither of them really noticed that Max
wasn't doing any lines. He was laughing and
drinking and he was going at the shit but he
wasn't really doing anything. And he wasn't
drunk. And he only let Carlette use her mouth
on him, and wouldn't let Carlette do what she
wanted to do. And he was sitting there, looking at them like he might be watching mon-
keys in the zoo.

The next morning, Carlette made her own
way home, on foot, down Countryside Lane
to the farmhouse she shared with her stroke-
ridden father and her grown daughter and her
grown daughter's daughter — Carlette was all
of thirty-nine. That's when Max got down
to business with Bernie Lund.

Bernie thought they were just starting

again where they had left off. He had a line first thing and then a couple of beers to settle his stomach and Max was saying he wouldn't ever be able to work in a nuclear plant like Bernie because he was scared of radiation.

Bernie said there wasn't nothing to be scared of.

"That so?" said Max. Still, Max said, he thought he'd be scared.

Bernie wasn't scared of nothing or no one.

But what if there was that thing, the thing Max said he saw in a movie about meltdown.

Well, Bernie laughed, they'd all be going to heaven then. Heaven or hell, didn't make no difference, one place or the other.

Max watched him, threw in a word every now and then to keep it going. And Bernie kept on, never seeing how close Max was watching him. He kept on bragging on himself, on what his duties were in the plant, how macho his job was really. All because of a run-in he had had with a spic broad named Rosita Pina.

"What about her?" Max said.

Sergeant Rosita Pina, this greaser with a bubble butt, bitch was down on him, hated anyone who was Anglo. This line of talk set Bernie off for several minutes, explaining to Max how tough it was to be a white male in the world with all these colored broads demanding guarantees and all. Max let it run its head and then turned the thoughts back to the dirty job that Bernie had to do every day.

"What job was that?" Max asked.

Bernie gave him a slow country smile.

It was a fine country morning in the trailer park. The sun was shining on brown winter fields.

Did Max know about a nuclear power plant? About the core of the reactor?

Max had some knowledge. General knowledge. But Bernie educated him anyway in that maddeningly smug way of the ignorant.

He told Max about the core of the reactor where the chain reaction took place. About uranium pellets assembled in these tall rods all bundled together to make the reaction.

Max let him go on. Max was patient with Bernie and he thought it was all leading up to something better than he would have expected.

Bernie told him about chain reaction. About neutrons contained in the uranium 235 pellets and the uranium stacked in these zircoloy tubes — Bernie even spelled "zircoloy" for Max, just to show him — and about the core creating this great heat that was the origin of the universe.

"Of creation," Bernie said in an awed voice to awe Max and to awe himself.

Max shook his head to show he was awed.

And all the water pipes to cool the reactors were around the sealed core as well as the steam piping leading out from the core, all of this complex piping and tubes in the containment building around the core. The containment building was the last chamber between the reaction core and the generating plant. Had to have a special pass card to get in there. And Bernie did. Had the card. Went in every day after suiting up in a big yellow suit.

"And what?" Max said. He held his breath.

"Look around," Bernie answered. "Just look around, eyeball it with a nuclear safety engineer, make sure everything is running straight . . ."

But they had all those gauges and dials in the control room . . . Max left the thought unfinished.

Bernie grinned. He said the plant rule was a security guard and a nuclear engineer put on the yellow protective suits every day and go into the containment building and actually look around, see if there was any water leaking on the floor, see if there was anything that might jeopardize the security of the core itself.

Bernie had interrupted his narrative to do a line on the kitchen table. He used a straw and when he looked up at Max, he was grinning at Max. He was so damned happy.

"This is good shit," he said to Max. He meant the street-cut cocaine.

Max smiled then. "Good shit," he agreed. Not the cocaine.

Bernie rambled on into another monologue about his days as a security guard inside the Apostle and Max just stared at him as though he was listening. He had figured on a series of fires, like the Pentagon burn, enough to give Britta a bang for her buck. Fire in the paint shed labeled in the schematics, fires in the generator building where they would have to shut down the turbines and disrupt power.

But Bernie had access to the containment building, the fucking heart of the power plant where the core was, where the actual nuclear reaction took place second by second, control rods rising and lowering into the pile itself, absorbing neutrons or not absorbing them, letting the atomic miracle make power and then harnessing the power which was turned to steam to drive the turbines and translating it all into surges of electricity. Damn. Bernie Lund had the open sesame to all that every day he was on duty.

But wasn't Bernie worried about radioactivity?

And Bernie said it was pretty safe, that the yellow suits were worn to keep radioactive dust off the inspectors as they made their daily rounds. Said it like that, like it wasn't nothing to Bernie.

Max smiled at Bernie as though he liked him. Max had the power now to do a real job, a meltdown kind of job, where he could get at the pipes in the containment building and then punch a hole in the concrete walls with his rocket fuel and let the radioactive steam build while the nuclear core began its long run to overheating. An atomic explosion — and all because of some mope who lived in a rental trailer and had served time in jail for beating up his pregnant teenage wife and who only got laid by a pig like Carlette because his buddy had brought along a bag of coke.

It was funny the way things worked out, Max thought.

And then he thought something else: *Thank you, Señorita Pina.*

Forty

Britta brought him the money the following morning. She handed him the suitcase in the huge, sterile lobby of Dulles International and he gave her a little kiss. They might have been a hubbie and his wife saying hello or good-bye.

But Max took the suitcase into the first rest room they came to. He went into a stall, locked it and opened the case on a toilet seat. He just looked at the money for a long moment, exactly as Senator Horan had done. He closed the case and unlocked the stall and came out of the rest room.

"I got a piece of luck, I thought it was going to take longer to set up, involve a few more people," he said to her. "But you don't need to know the details."

"I want to know everything," she said. Her eyes were shining just as they had been the other day.

Max shook his head. "The more things you don't know, the better it's gonna be."

"Max, it's all working," she said. Her face

was animated, he saw how excited she was. She was a tough woman, he liked that.

"Like clockwork."

They strolled hand in hand to a coffee nook in the main terminal and sat down at a plastic table. He went to the counter and got them two coffees in Styrofoam cups. They both drank the coffee black, and the chair that held the suitcase was between them.

"They even have the wrong man picked out for the Pentagon fire," she said.

"It was in the papers. No name yet but I know who it is," Max said. "Took care of that detail."

"You did it, Max," she said. He smiled at the compliment intended. "You really can do anything, Max."

"We can do anything," he said, and he squeezed her hand on the tabletop.

It was that kind of a morning — edgy, but everything was going right.

Three days later, Max Escher watched Liz cross the skating rink in Grant Park. The rink was not frozen; sunlight slanted through leafless branches. She walked west toward the facade of the Loop, which stops abruptly at the edge of the park. It was warm for December in Chicago. The small, clear Italian lights were festooned on winter-bare trees along Michigan Avenue. There were all the signs of Christmas in the shop windows.

Max thought Liz even walked as though she was better than other people.

Probably didn't even know her ex was under arrest for being a firebug. He would have liked to tell her, tell her it was her fault because she had called Jack up and told Jack to threaten Max Escher. For what? Because she was some fucking virgin schoolgirl? Shit, she'd go down on dogs and she was pretending she couldn't be touched by Max Escher.

Max watched her from the window of his new rental car, a Caddy. Max felt like a Caddy owner. Max had spent the night with Bernie again and they had done lines. Or Max had pretended to because Max didn't want to get crazy or euphoric or anything, he wanted to see this through.

Bernie was such a chump. He thought he and Max were going to be partners, set up a drugstore inside the nuclear plant. There were lots of places to stash the shit, Bernie said. He was carrying in a little and this made Max nervous and he hoped Bernie didn't get caught or fired. But you had to take risks, even with a retard like Bernie.

Showed off his security badge, bragged about working in the Apostle, how it wasn't

such an easy job, it had a lot of responsi-
bilities . . .

Max had just listened. Nodded when he had
to. Let Bernie be the big man.

He had explained everything about the
plant. Max wanted to know how safe it
would be to operate a drugstore in there. He
had Bernie make drawings even. Bernie lo-
cated the paint sheds in the drawings, the
materials room, where the workers washed up
after shift. And he talked about security.
About the security cards that provided access
to all the locked sections of the plant. How
Bernie, who had to wear the yellow radiation
suit with the helmet and mask, had top access,
right to the outside of the nuclear core itself.
The dumb shit had even explained nuclear
power to Max.

The NRC guy, guy named Ingersoll, wanted
the nuclear inspection engineer in the core
building to take a security guard with him.
Ingersoll believed in accountability, one guy
watching another guy. Besides, the way this
Ingersoll guy said it, the engineer looked
for safety of equipment and the trained eye
of the security guard looked for other kinds
of potential violations. Security violations.
Bernie had said this with such a straight face
that Max had nearly laughed.

Max Escher saw Liz turn at the sidewalk

on the east side of Michigan Avenue and head north, up the hump of the street toward the river.

Going shopping on Michigan Avenue. He shook his head, smiling. Stupid bitch was going to die, Max said to himself.

He followed along, sometimes getting behind a bus just to slow things down. Liz walked in that haughty way, striding along without a care in the world. She crossed the Chicago River on the Michigan Avenue Bridge. She passed in front of the Equitable Building and NBC Tower and the Chicago Tribune Tower. She crossed another street and turned into the lobby of the Intercontinental Hotel.

Nooner, Max said to himself. *Taking a nooner.* He smiled and shook his head and thought about it.

Suddenly, he pressed down hard on the accelerator and the big car leaped ahead, cutting off a cab, screeching to a stop at the entrance. The cabdriver rolled down his window to say something and Max gave him the finger. The doorman said he would take care of the car for Max because Max duked the doorman a Jackson.

Little bitch had a nooner going for her. It was one thing to pretend you were reformed, starting a new life, and couldn't give an old friend of your ex-husband a courtesy fuck, but to then turn around and be going at it. He really hated the bitch.

Max looked in the bar but it was empty. The girl behind the bar told him the restaurant was on the second floor. He took the stairs to the Boulevard Room. And then he saw her sitting at a table with a man with white hair.

The bald maître d' asked him if he wanted a seat. He shook his head. He'd put a little fear in her, he thought. He went over to the table. He stood there just looking at her until Liz glanced up.

"Hello," Max said then.

Liz lost color. He thought she flinched. She stared and Max thought, *She doesn't like this.* He grinned because he was making her look bad.

"This is my husband," she said. Her voice was calm, coming from deep in her throat. "Bob. Bob, this is a man who knew Jack and me in the service days."

Bob was a large-faced man with hard little eyes. "Hello," he said. He wasn't being friendly.

Max recovered. Looked at him for the first time. He stuck out his hand. "Max. Max Escher. I was in town and I thought it was Liz I saw on the street just now, you know how you're walking along and the last person you expect to see, well, you see them. I don't mean to interrupt, I thought I'd say hello."

"Hello," Bob said again.

"Too bad about Jack," Max said.

Liz put down her fork and looked at him. "What about Jack?" Liz said.

Max stared at her. What the hell had he just said? There was no name to the Pentagon arrest, that was stupid, just stupid.

"I mean, the army. Having to leave the army."

"It's just as well," Liz said. "He didn't much like it anymore."

"I know how he must be feeling," Max said, shoveling out the words.

"I'll bet you know," she said.

"Happened to me. Early out," Max said to Bob. He was grinning. He didn't feel the grin, though.

"You want to sit down?" Bob Fredericks said. Max thought he didn't mean it.

Max looked at Liz. She wasn't saying anything. "Well, got to run along," he said.

"Nice to meet you," Bob said, not extending his hand again, not letting anything in his little hard eyes say anything was nice about seeing him.

Max just stood and stared at Liz for a second. Just a second. Bitch didn't understand, he thought then. Just let it sail past her. It was all right. He'd take care of Liz later. Maybe give her a second chance. Bitch'd like to be alive, wouldn't she? That'd be worth something, Max saving her life before the thing went up. He'd have to think about it.

"See you," he was saying.

He'd think about it.

Forty-one

Devereaux drove to the house in Virginia and parked the car at the unseen lot a hundred yards south of the log cabin. He walked the rest of the way. He knew the baby-sitters saw him already on the television monitors. It was the dying part of the autumn afternoon. The darkness at the edge of the day was like velvet.

He brought a suitcase. She wanted some clothes and books and disks for the laptop computer. She spent the morning writing and making telephone calls. The baby-sitters usually watched television. The television was never turned off, even in the middle of the night.

They felt like grown children forced by circumstance to live with their parents. The baby-sitters were large, anonymous men and they didn't intrude, but Rita said it was like living with elephants. She was starting to rag at him because she had spent two days in the safe house and she felt like a prisoner.

He carried the suitcase up to the porch. The

front door opened and one of the baby-sitters was there with an Uzi held in both hands.

Devereaux passed through the door and turned right into the kitchen. She was sitting at the kitchen table, the laptop opened in front of her. She looked up at him and didn't smile. He carried the suitcase through the kitchen into the bedroom and placed it on the bed. He went back to the kitchen and sat down across from her. The muffled sounds of afternoon television came from the living room. The light was fading very quickly outside and the trees were losing their shadows. Night came upon them like spilled ink. She shut off the computer and closed it and got up and went to the sink. She poured herself a glass of water. She turned and looked at him and said nothing.

He stared at her. He felt he was waiting for something.

"This isn't going to end, is it?"

He shook his head. "Everything ends."

"What am I supposed to do? Stay here for a week? A month? Go into the Witness Protection Program? Dye my hair?"

"Rita."

She waited for him to say something more than her name.

"Rita, we can find some other place —"

"I can't find any place," she said. "If they

407

can use me to threaten you, they'll do it. Or kill me. As an example of what they can do. I've thought about it, Dev. This is never getting any easier. On us, I mean. Every year. You became senior adviser, I was happy. You were out of it, finally. Senior adviser. You go to work in the morning, you come home in the afternoon. Vacations. Nine to five. You read reports and make reports." She put down the empty glass.

"Mrs. Neumann wants to finish this," he said.

"Mrs. Neumann goes home at night. Watches television with her husband. Plays gin rummy, whatever she does. Do you know that fucking television has been on twenty-four hours a day since I got here? Do you know what that's like? I think they could use it to torture prisoners. Do you know grown men watch soap operas?"

Devereaux smiled then.

Damnit. She wasn't going to smile.

She shook her head.

He got up from the table. He came around the table and took her by the waist.

She said, "How do kids come back to live with their parents?"

"It creates romance. Like necking in a car."

"Did you ever do that?"

"I didn't have a car," Devereaux said.

"What did you do?"

"Use doorways. Gangways."

"Very romantic," she said.

"The romance is in the sneaking around."

They didn't say anything for a moment. He held her waist. Her waist felt good beneath his hand. He realized he never tired of touching her. She was the only real thing. If he could touch her, then it was all right. If she was a memory or a voice on the phone or if she went away on some job, then everything was a shadow of some real world not present.

He held her waist and looked at her. And then, quite suddenly, she hugged him and buried her face in his shoulder.

"Oh, Dev. I want to go home."

He held her.

"I just want to go home. I don't care. This safe house stuff is for spies. I'm no spy."

He held her still.

"Home?"

He looked at her. He kissed her on the lips.

"Home," she said again.

He pushed her back a little, looked at her face again, felt her waist beneath his hands.

"Wait. A few more days. I've got a few men now. We've started to —"

"I don't care —"

"Hacker is supervising the —"

"I don't care," she said, putting her hand on his lips. "I want to sleep in my own bed and make breakfast in my own kitchen. I want my life. Without any ghosts."

"It's just a place we rented for a couple of years," he said.

"It's home."

"Rita," he said.

"I don't care about how dangerous it is. You took the gun out of the closet that day. I'll keep the gun."

"You can go out here, you can run in the mornings here," he began.

"I want to go home," she said. Just that way, in just that voice. And he knew he had to do it, that this had come between them, just one more thing. And he thought Rita was still thinking about Mona and what Mona had meant to him.

"Pack," he said. "I'll tell them. Send a car to watch the apartment."

Maybe he wanted to go home too.

Forty-two

Col. Jack Cavett was confined to quarters in Fort Belvoir the first day, but then an attorney with the Judge Advocate General's corps had the order altered to "confined to post." The JAG lawyer had argued that Colonel Cavett had not been formally named, charges had not been specifically prepared, and that the board of inquiry set up to investigate the Pentagon burning had yet to produce a single bit of evidence specifically linking Jack Cavett to the fires.

Which is why Jack Cavett was not in when Liz called the first time.

She had been trying to reach him for two days. She had called Indianhead and they had told her to call the Pentagon. She had been shunted from one office to another in the Pentagon. Sometimes she would be given an extension to call that did not exist. Sometimes the phone would ring endlessly, untouched by human hand.

He went out in early evening to walk

around the post. It was dressed for Christmas. Inevitably, the tree that decorated the front gate carried the universal military message on its branches: Peace on Earth. Like most lonely people, Jack endured Christmases. Since Liz left him, he stayed at the edge of the celebrations. He would look at the party but he wouldn't dare take part in it.

The air was damp with expectations of a storm rolling across the Maryland and Virginia mountains down toward the Chesapeake Bay and the basins that drained from the Potomac River. He wore a light poplin jacket and civvies. He had nowhere to go, he had seen the movies at the post theater, he didn't know anyone at Belvoir. He could go to the officer's club but maybe some of them would know who he was. He dropped in at the PX instead and drank a couple of beers with two specialist fours who were in transport. They talked about football and that made it better for Jack. He liked talking to enlisted.

He went back to quarters at ten. They were sounding "Taps" throughout the post on the public address system. He had listened to the plaintive sounds of the song for nearly a quarter of a century on dozens of posts and bases throughout the world and it had never sounded so sad to him as it had these last few days. Maybe he loved the army after all.

The telephone rang. He went to the night-stand and picked up the receiver. He didn't speak.

"Jack? Is that you? I've been trying to call you for two days, I keep getting shuttled from one damned office to another."

"What's wrong, Liz?"

He knew that voice. He knew the distress that made its sexy huskiness turn down into something like panic.

"It was two days ago. I was meeting Bob for lunch. In the hotel, in the Boulevard Room —"

"Slow down, Liz, slow down."

"For Christ's sake, Jack, just shut up and let me tell you."

It was late at night. Maybe Liz had been drinking all day. Maybe not.

Liz said, "He came up to us. He was just standing there at the table."

Jack sat down on the side of his bunk, cradling the receiver in his left hand. He closed his eyes and saw her at the other end of the line.

"He was standing there," he repeated.

"Max. Max was standing there."

He kept his eyes closed.

"Max," he repeated.

"Max. Standing there and I couldn't believe

it. I told Bob he was someone we knew in the army and he must have thought it was something else. He was creepy. He was looking at me like he thought it was something else. Jesus, Jack, why's it taken me two days to find you?"

"I'm sorry, Liz. I should have called you."

"Bob is out of town tonight. They had a problem with the nuclear plant inspector in Galena. At the Dunedin nuclear plant, some damned thing. I'm just sitting here and I keep thinking Max is going to appear suddenly."

"What did Max want?"

"He was lying. He said he was surprised to see me on the street, like he was just passing through and saw an old friend. After he left, Bob got on about it — how did I know him? when did I see him the last time? all that shit. I told Bob off and we had a helluva fight." She paused.

"Jack."

He waited.

"Jack, what kind of trouble are you in?"

He waited some more.

"Jack, you're in trouble, aren't you?"

"Who told you that?"

"Max," she said.

He opened his eyes.

"Max said he was sorry for you. I said to him what did he mean and he said he was sorry about you separating from service. But that isn't what he meant. He was lying and I knew it. Now I really know it. Don't lie to me, Jack."

When the kid was killed riding his bike, the ambulance took him to the post hospital first and Jack was there first and then Liz. Jack went up to talk to the doctors and they told him. When he came back to her, Liz stared right through him and she said, "Don't lie to me, Jack."

He shook his head to get rid of the thought.

"Jack?"

"It's all right, Liz. There was a fire at Indianhead. They need a scapegoat. It won't get very far but it takes pressure off the brass. With the Pentagon fire and all. I'm confined to post," he said.

"Bastards," she said. "What do you need, Jack? You need anything?"

Jack couldn't speak. They had both used up too many words over the years, not realizing that the words are never replenished.

"Are you and Bob all right now?"

"I don't care," she said.

"Liz."

"Bob wanted to know how he had just happened to follow me into the hotel and I said I don't know and I really didn't, and Bob gave me this look, the little shit, I got

415

nasty then and Bob said he didn't care who I had to screw on the side but he was goddamned if one of my tricks was going to feel he had the right to make fun of him, of Bob. I told Bob I never went to bed with Max Escher, that he was a creep, and Bob said . . ."

She began to cry. He could hear her crying and he wanted to touch her and pat her shoulder and hold her.

". . . and Bob said how do I remember I never went to bed with him, how could I remember all of them."

"Liz," he said, patting her shoulder with words. It was all he could do.

His eyes were wet because she was crying.

Oh, Jesus. How we do manage to fuck everything up, don't we?

She was blowing her nose then and he guessed she was wiping her eyes. He could see her so clearly it broke his heart.

"I told him to stay away from you and he came back to you," Jack said. "I forgot the number. Give me the number again and I'll call him back —"

"Jack, don't you see it? He mentioned your name both times. He said he'd get you a job if I . . . did him and then he said in front of Bob he felt sorry for you. And you tell me now that you're under arrest. How did

416

he know you were under arrest?"

Jack waited. He wouldn't have thought of that. Not in a million years. He held the phone and stared at Liz and she stared right back at him.

"Jack, he means to hurt you," Liz said.

Same kind of a fire. That's what General Lee had said. Same fire. Fire in the Pentagon, fire at Indianhead. Pin the tail on the goat.

"Jack, I want you," Liz said. "I'll leave Bob, I want you, I really need you, I'm not a whore, Jack, I was never a whore, I was just —"

"Shh, Liz," he said. He shushed her again. "It's all right, Liz."

"It's not all right. It hasn't been all right for a long time," she said.

He had never heard her sound so lonely. Not even when the kid was killed. At least he had been there when the kid was killed. He had put his arms around her and they had both shared tears. They had cried it all out until there was nothing left, not even love.

After he replaced the receiver, he sat on the edge of his bunk and stared at the phone because he could see Liz still. When her image began to fade, he got up then and went into the bathroom. He looked at his sorry dog-ass face in the mirror. He washed his face then and toweled it and felt better. He went back into the other room and sat down on the edge of the bunk and picked up the receiver again. He waited for a line.

But he wasn't calling the general.

Forty-three

Devereaux took Rita home. It was nearly 6:00 P.M. when they arrived at the apartment, and two watchers waited in a gray car across from the entrance to the building. They nodded at him as he carried her suitcases across the street.

She went from room to room in the apartment and turned on the lights. She was smiling now. He took the bags to the bedroom and placed them on the cedar chest.

She went into the bathroom and took a shower, and when she came out, he was in the kitchen making coffee. He never drank coffee at night.

She was wearing a blue robe and came up behind him. She was warm from the shower. She slipped her arm around his waist. She kissed him. He turned and smiled at her.

"You going to stay up all night?"

"Yes," he said. He turned and looked at her. "Hacker. He called while you were in

419

the shower. Something's going on. He sent a car for me."

"You're going to leave me alone?"

"There're two watchers in the gray car across the street. There's another man in the serviceway behind the building. This is all right as long as you don't leave the building."

"All for Mona," she said then. She dropped her hands and turned away from him. He stood in the middle of the kitchen and looked at her.

"Was she dark?"

"Dark hair. Brownish black, I think. She was going gray too, the last time I saw her."

"She's really dead."

"She's dead," Devereaux said.

"I shouldn't feel this way. About her," Rita said.

"No. You shouldn't. I love you," Devereaux said.

"And you said you loved her."

"It isn't the same thing."

"I'll be all right," she said, turning, trying a smile. The smile was phony and they both knew it.

R Section at night is still full of people but the languor that overcomes the lobbies at the Department of Agriculture affects the perception of Section. It seems like a

420

secret party going on in a darkened apartment building, animated and yet without any sound track.

Devereaux crossed the lobby and signed in and rode the special elevator to Section. Off the elevator, he passed through another security gauntlet and then walked down a well-lit hall to the back of corridor 2. Corridor 2 led to the surveillance room. Hacker had said to meet him there.

The surveillance room was windowless and drab, dominated by an elderly conference table and ten chairs. At the far end of the room was a television monitor, tape machine, and other recording devices. The surveillance room was the place where they monitored surveillance films or listened to eavesdroppings from bugs and tapes.

But Hacker did not have any tapes.

He sat on the opposite side of the conference table. A large white plastic bag sat on a chair next to him. He had exactly a single page of notes written on a legal pad in front of him.

"Sit down," Hacker said.

Devereaux pulled up a chair opposite.

Hacker said, "Like Mrs. Neumann is always saying about computers. Garbage in, garbage out."

Devereaux said nothing. He rested his

frame in the chair, arms draped over the arms of the wooden frame.

Hacker smiled. It was a secretive smile.

"Two hours ago, Mr. Hacker of the Securities and Exchange Commission had a nice chat with Miss Andrews's broker. He's a man named Cavendish. He said Miss Andrews has been selling her stock in Northern Illinois Power and Light for no known reason. It's trading at eighty-one and seven-eighths, which is good but off the year's high of one oh three. It's expected to rebound substantially based on fourth-quarter earnings, but that's next year. From an analytical point of view, the sale doesn't make sense," Hacker said.

"How much money is that?"

"About six point four million dollars. Over the last ten days," Hacker said.

"Maybe she needs the money to secure her loan. Her line of credit at District Savings Bank," Devereaux said.

"Maybe so. It's just one of the interesting things about her. She had a visit from the senator in the afternoon. He didn't stay long. His driver is a man named Haley, Henry Haley, been with the senator since the beginning."

"You're full of odd facts."

"Espionage is just Trivial Pursuit at a

different level," Hacker said. He was feeling smug and it showed. Devereaux stared at him and waited for the show to go on.

"Garbage in, garbage out," Hacker said.

Devereaux waited.

"Here."

Hacker picked up the white plastic bag. "Miss Andrews is an environmentalist but she still uses plastic kitchen bags."

"Hacker. Her garbage?"

"Exactly," Hacker said.

Devereaux slowly shook his head.

Hacker grinned. "Never overlook the obvious things." He opened the bag. And he dumped the contents on the desktop. "Eggshells. A milk carton with a photograph of a missing child on it. A bread wrapper. Twelve bottles of Perrier, empty. Couple of pieces of junk mail with her name on the envelopes. I had to go through a whole dumpster before I found her garbage. Twelve bottles of Perrier water. Now, I really think a conscientious environmentalist would object to no-deposit bottles. . . ."

But Devereaux was staring at the paper in a file folder smeared with food stains. He reached to the center of the pile of garbage and extracted the manila folder. Hacker smiled. Because he had wanted to create the effect.

Devereaux flipped through the pages. The pages were bound twice at the top by staples. The staples had been inserted in a clumsy way, as a last-minute thought. Each page, top and bottom, was stamped "Secret."

Devereaux began to read.

Hacker had stopped speaking. Hacker sat and watched him read.

Devereaux read through the testimony transcript for fifteen minutes and Hacker waited in silence. There was a nuclear facility in North Carolina where radioactive water had been released into a river months after a multibillion-dollar cleanup of the plant's code violations.

There was a second nuclear plant where radioactive steam had been released in amounts far larger than acknowledged by the power authority. That was in upstate New York in a valley on the Erie Canal.

And there was a report on the Apostle, a nuclear facility in Illinois west and north of Chicago.

He stopped reading and put the papers down.

He looked at Hacker.

"Yes," Hacker said.

"I see the connections but I don't see the action," Devereaux said. "Whatever it is, it links Senator Horan and Britta Andrews."

"And Clair Dodsworth, who arranges financing with ICC in the Middle East."

"For whatever the financing is for." Silence again, waiting for the other to speak.

"We have to tap her phone. All of them," Devereaux said. "Clair Dodsworth. Senator Horan."

"We won't get an order for it. Not to tap a senator's phone."

"We can try," Devereaux said. "In the name of national security."

"Mrs. Neumann won't go along with that."

"We show her these transcripts." Devereaux shook his head again. "I can't believe she threw them out in the garbage."

"It happens all the time," Hacker said. Which was true enough. Devereaux had once done nothing but direct an assessment of a month's worth of garbage from the Chilean Embassy in Moscow and the only problem was in beating the KGB to the same task.

There was a knock at the door.

"What is it?" Hacker shouted.

"Telephone for Mr. Devereaux," the voice shouted back through the thick oak. "Patched through from eight hundred."

Devereaux and Hacker looked at each other for a moment. Devereaux got up then and went to the door. He said over his shoulder,

"Keep it together but separate out the transcripts."

He opened the door and followed the security officer to the telephone in the middle of the transmissions room. The phone was off the hook and the hold button was depressed.

Devereaux sat on the edge of the desk and picked up the receiver.

Jack Cavett said, "Is that you?"

"Me."

"My wife called me tonight."

He waited.

"I want to talk to you about it," Jack Cavett said.

And Devereaux listened.

Forty-four

Max Escher left the Apostle at 4:30 P.M. when his shift was over.

Actually, it had been Bernie's shift. He had worked it for Bernie. He had been Bernie, in fact.

Bernie was so totally fucked up from the candy that he was passed out in his bed in the trailer. He sprawled in the middle of a pile of money on the mattress. Max had given him that money. Max had said it was the start of their drug distribution business. Max had said he was going to take care of Bernie and Bernie believed him.

It was Saturday.

Max Escher had carried in a Thermos and lunch tin and passed them through the metal detector before he himself stepped through. He retrieved his keys and change in the plastic tray on the other side. Saturday was a sleepy time, just like the sleepy time a few weeks ago when he had gone into the Pentagon and ripped off a sheaf of purchasing orders from QC and had them made up to be sent through the pipeline. The pipeline was sacred and mysterious to everyone in the army. The pipeline might send a squad to war or withdraw a squad from danger. The pipeline dispensed orders and material and men, and sometimes, through a snafu, the pipeline might suddenly dispense twenty-eight civilian coffee makers with timers to select departments scattered throughout the Pentagon. The pipeline gave and took away and very few ever questioned it.

Saturday was a good sleepy time. It was cold outside the Apostle buildings and the wind keened on the brown prairie. Inside, it was generally warm, though there were cold and hot spots throughout the big plant.

The hardest part would be getting past the entrance hall security desk. That was the only time he really had to be B. Lund, sign in as B. Lund, get past the roster guard. The roster guard looked at him, then looked at the signature: *B. Lund.* "B. Lund" on the nameplate, the security card said "B. Lund." Close. Close enough. He wore a good wig and he had changed the color of his eyes with contact lenses.

Good enough if the roster clerk didn't know Bernie Lund, didn't go drinking with him.

"OK," the clerk said, looking up at Max. "You wanna open that Thermos bottle?"

"What for?"

"Checking," the clerk said.

"Checkin' what?"

"Booze. Some of them been bringing in booze when they say it's coffee."

Max shook his head. Some people had gall. He opened the Thermos. The clerk sniffed. The coffee smell was unmistakable. The clerk screwed on the cap. "Thanks man," he said.

Max smiled at him.

He went to the first security door and inserted the plastic card hanging from a chain around his neck. The card flipped the lock mechanism and signaled access with a green light. He pushed open the heavy door and let it fall behind him. The door locked with a click and signaled with a red light to the next man. One man at a time through one door at a time, each ingress and egress recorded in the central security office.

Max repeated the procedure twice more. The next doors led to a stairwell and then to the second floor of the generator building.

He had the schematics in his head along with Bernie's directions. The changing room for men was to the right, prior to entering the actual turbine rooms. Bernie's locker was

178 and Max waited until the area around the locker was empty on the theory that locker neighbors know each other.

When he opened Bernie's locker, he removed the other two Thermos bottles contained in it. Bernie had smuggled them in in previous days and Max had told him it was dope, hidden in the cavity between the glass inner liner and the metal outer liner.

He looked around him. There were a couple of other men in the room but they were not paying attention to him. Max took down the two Thermos bottles and put them under his arm. He shoved the locker shut with his knee. He carried a metal lunch box and two visible Thermos bottles. He edged along a changing bench toward the lavatory stalls. He opened the door on the farthest stall and went inside and closed it behind him.

The stall was half-dark. An efficiency expert had suggested low lighting for the men's room stalls to discourage reading by slackers who used the privacy of the lavatory to kill time. Northern Illinois Power and Light had been delighted with the findings of the expert.

But Max had his heavy-duty guard's flashlight.

He turned on the light and set the flashlight down on the tank pipe that extended through the ceramic on the wall. He wrapped the flashlight into place with duct tape around pipe and light panel.

The light played on the back of the toilet seat lid, which was in the down position. Max knelt on one knee and began work.

He unscrewed the cup of the first Thermos and put it on the seat. He unscrewed the glass liner and carefully poured the soup into the cup. The "soup" was grayish, containing flecks of Styrofoam floating in a heavy porridge-like sea of white rocket fuel crystals and high-test gasoline. It smelled dangerous and Max delighted in the smell of it a moment.

He stirred the mixture with his forefinger and some of it clung to his skin. He wiped his finger off with a piece of toilet tissue and shoved the tissue into the cup. He was nearly ready.

He opened the second and third Thermos bottles and did the same thing. A line of sweat began to break across his forehead and his eyes shone.

He looked into the opened lunch pail and selected the first item, a package of Hostess Twinkies. He unsealed the package easily because he had first unsealed it the night before. The yellow Twinkies cakes had been hollowed out and the cream core replaced by plastique.

This would be for the paint shed, Max thought.

He took out the bottle of V8 Juice and opened it. He put the three cups containing the rocket mix on the floor next to the toilet and then put the Twinkies on the floor and then the lunch box. His hands did not shake at all but he could feel the excitement build in him in the same old way it always had before an operation. He became very calm and very excited at the same time and the emotions were not in conflict in him in those moments, they seemed to complement each other.

He lifted the toilet seat back and emptied the V8 Juice into the toilet, letting the liquid fall across his open hand. As the bottle emptied, four buttons were caught in his hand. Each was the size of a quarter and contained both a timer and an ignition.

He closed the lid again and replaced the items on it. Beyond the closed stall door, he heard the voices of other men entering and leaving the lavatory.

He picked up the first timer and took a woman's hair tweezer off his key ring.

He squinted to see it better in the dim light of the flashlight.

He slowly moved the dial of the button the size of a quarter until the two minute engraved marks lined up. Ignition set.

A separate, inner circle was the timer. The clock could be set for up to thirty-six hours.

He thought of 3:00 P.M. Sunday, about thirty hours away. Because the timer was so small and the dial was imprecise, he could only make an approximation of the time. There were larger and more accurate timers and he had used them for other jobs, but here it was a matter of size and stealth.

He set all four timers and ignitions.

He stood up straight and his knee popped. Now it was a little tricky. He had to hope that no one would use this stall for a few minutes.

He opened the door and looked down the row of stalls.

The wall where they kept the various automatic dispenser machines was two hundred feet east in the anteroom to the lunchroom.

He wiped at the sweat on his upper lip. He closed the stall door behind him and stepped along the row to the changing room and then to the anteroom. He pushed six quarters into the soda machine, one after the other and struck the buttons. He got one Diet Coke, one Coke Classic and one 7-Up. He carried the three cold cans back into the lavatory.

The stall was still unoccupied except for the

cups of rocket "soup" and the other strange devices waiting on the lid of the toilet seat back.

Max knelt again and took all the items off the lid and lifted it. He opened all three cans of soda and poured their contents into the toilet and flushed.

Now he began to fill each can with the semi-solid soup mix of Styrofoam, gasoline, and rocket fuel. Then he imbedded each can with the quarter-size ignition and timer. He wrapped each can in duct tape until the markings were invisible and the can was sealed. The gray of the duct tape matched the gray motif used in the plant on painted walls and even on the turbine superstructures.

The package of Twinkies was Max's little joke. He shoved the ignition and timer into the plastique and then put the yellow cakes back into their package and rewrapped it. He would carry the Twinkies with him as a snack as he toured his duty area. As he placed the package in the paint shed near the oil paint cans.

The last item in the lunch box was a nameplate with white letters on a black background that said "C. Ericson." His new identity. He removed the B. Lund nameplate and fixed the new one on.

Now it was time to clean it all up.

He rinsed out the Thermos cups in the water in the toilet bowl and resealed the Thermos bottles. He laid one bottle in the lunch box and nestled in the three disguised soda cans. He slipped the package of Twinkies in his pocket. He left the empty V8 Juice bottle on the tile floor. He turned off the flashlight, removed the duct tape, and slipped it into his belt. He threw the remains of the duct tape into the toilet bowl and flushed. The bowl began to back up and he flushed again and the bowl's water rose over the lid.

"Damn," he said.

He opened the stall door and walked out gingerly, lifting his feet over the water spreading across the floor. He saw a man in dungarees and hard hat standing at a urinal, staring at the wall in front of him. He moved past him, carrying the two Thermoses and the lunch box into the changing room.

In the changing room, he put the lunch box and Thermoses back into Bernie's locker and took out Bernie's safety helmet and fitted it on. It was a tight fit so he loosened the headgear straps and tried again.

Now he was C. Ericson, one of nearly two hundred security guards in a large nuclear energy plant. And now all he had to do was kill time.

From everything Bernie said in his bragging

about the important job he had to do in the Apostle, Max reckoned he would do his walk-around of the containment building with the nuclear engineer about 3:00 P.M. It was always about that time of the shift.

Max enjoyed himself in the morning and the tension he had felt putting his devices together in the lavatory stall mellowed into a good sort of feeling. He felt like a spy. Like an invisible man.

He went past the paint shed — which was really a steel-fenced cage — twice and twice it was locked.

The third time was just before lunch at 11:30 A.M.

Two workmen in painters' white overalls were in the shed.

Max strolled in, his Twinkies in hand, and went over to them. Bernie hadn't known where they kept the oil paints. Oil paint burned like hell but not latex. He looked over the men and the paint on shelves and he said something about security, about a previous crew of painters leaving the shed gate open because it was easier than locking and unlocking the gate every time paint was needed. The painters heard him out and said nothing until he turned his back on them. Then one of them said something about someone being an asshole.

Max smiled at that and dropped the package of Twinkies behind a row of gray oil-based paints on a shelf near the entrance. The package was completely hidden. He passed through the gate and headed for the lunch-room.

He walked through the generator main floor and paused a moment to gaze on the turbines. The twin turbines — nose to nose — were the size of three or four old steam locomotives. Like the old locomotives, they reeked of power and naked strength, coiled beneath rounded steel shells. The Red reactor turbine was up and running, thundering and shaking the supports of the steel floor and transmitting the utter sense of thrust, motion, movement — all the while fixed to its bolted moorings on the floor.

Max felt the power in that moment.

The power of the turbines was his own.

It electrified him as it electrified the power lines that snaked across the open farm fields.

He felt it in his legs and arms and hands.

There was nothing in life like this, like this immense power plant all driven by the cryptic core in the containment building where the secret of the universe was split open second by second, forcing a controlled creation of the universe to serve profit and electricity and appliances so omnipresent they were never thought of. Max had never really thought of it. Not thought about the power at the source of all those things and then the power that was greater. The power of Max to destroy this great power.

It was in him and he knew it.

Britta had known it too. Wanted to be part of the power of it.

He drifted through the rest of the day, keeping to himself, strolling from level to level. The only thing that had changed was lunch. He had gone back to his locker, taken down the lunch box and chosen another stall in the lavatory to make the final transfer.

He hid the three cans on his uniform.

Two of the cans fit in the holster sling he wore around his waist, beneath his shirt. It resembled a slight paunch to others. It was foam with hollow compartments he had made for the cans. He had sewn the canvas sling himself. It was his own invention.

The third fitted in his jockstrap. The duct tape felt slick next to the skin of his muscle as he pulled the jockstrap up and the can fitted down beneath his testicles into the space between the cheeks of his buttocks. For all of that, it would be as easy to retrieve as the other cans, Max thought.

Bernie had given him the procedure. Bernie

had talked about changing into the yellow suit in the changing room. You could put it over your uniform except that you wanted to remove your pistol belt and flashlight. Bernie said he would go to the changing room early and get dressed, even removing his shirt. He had dwelt on this curiously and Max finally realized he was not comfortable appearing unclothed in front of other men. It had amused Max because it had given him the idea for hanging the cans of lethal soda on his person.

He put on the yellow anti-radioactivity suit at 2:24 P.M.

He slipped the pants of the suit over his uniform pants. He opened his button and fly then and extracted the cans.

He was dressed completely when Ray Dobson entered the changing room.

Ray Dobson was the nuclear safety engineer. He had thinning brown hair and sharp eyebrows.

He looked hard at Max for a moment.

"They replace Bernie?" Ray Dobson said then.

"I guess so. I dunno. I'm the new man. I didn't particularly want this job."

"Well, don't worry about it. This isn't dangerous."

"If it isn't dangerous, why do we have to wear these suits?"

"Protection. Core releases neutrons, some of them escape, get into dust." He talked in this clipped flat midwestern way as he pulled on his own protective gear. "Just a precaution, play it safe. If there is a radioactive leak, we just get the hell out of there. If you see a pipe leaking, you call me. See? If it's going into the core, it's just some water but if it's coming out, well, then, it's something else. Might be water, steam, well, you just sing out to me."

"How do I know what pipes go in and what are carrying stuff out?" Max said.

"Don't worry about it. Number one, you won't find any leaks. Number two, you just call me."

But Max really knew already which of the pipes carried steam, not from the core where the water was heated initially but in the condenser. He already knew a lot more than this asshole would give him credit for.

The containment building was a massive concrete block built to withstand any force of nature. From without. It was assumed, from calculations during construction, it could withstand any force of nature contained inside, but that was to be proven. It had not been proven at Three Mile Island and it had not been proven at Chernobyl.

Max moved away from the nuclear engineer

once they were inside the structure. The core sat with elegant innocence by itself in the center of the web of pipes and lines feeding in and out of it.

Queen bee, Max said to himself and slipped the first can out of his large, lumpy yellow suit. The room was loud with the hum of power and machinery and Ray Dobson was looking over a pipe on the east side of the room when Max slipped the first bomb beneath a steam pipe.

A radioactive steam pipe.

They were inside the containment building for ten minutes.

It took Max three more of those ten minutes to place the second and third devices. When the bombs reached 3,500 degrees Fahrenheit in twenty-four hours or so, they would rupture pipes instantly and melt down through the metal floor into the concrete, then punch through it. Max had no idea how much damage he would be able to inflict but he thought a partial meltdown would happen. He was so sure of it, in fact, that he intended to be long gone from the Chicago area before 3:00 P.M. Sunday.

He and Ray showered their suits down in the decontamination chamber outside the containment area at 3:35 P.M. In the hour that occupied the rest of his shift — the one he was subbing for Bernie on — Max took it easy. Groups of workers would move back and forth across the floor of the plant, here and there, it was like being on an army post in the middle of the afternoon where some men might be on a mission and others just taking a stroll. The turbines thundered their message of power and Max felt it all and it felt good to him, to have so much more power than even these huge, dumb machines. It was all like being in the engine room of an immense ship, all noise without any perspective of the sea.

When Max went off shift, he drove back to Bernie's trailer. He made a face at the stench in the place and removed his security uniform and changed to civilian clothes. He looked in on Bernie, who was snoring away the afternoon on a pile of money on a dirty mattress.

S'long, Bernie.

He saluted the comatose form on the mattress, a mocking military salute, hand at forty-five-degree angle to the perpendicular, fingers together touching the outside corner of the eyebrow. Snap. Salute.

Max smiled and turned back to the Cadillac parked outside. Carlette was there, admiring the car. She wore tight jeans and a loose brown sweater and lipstick. She wobbled her way across the lawn in her high-heel boots. She had been drinking a lot already. She looked at Max and said, "I come by to see if you and Bernie was here."

He frowned. He said, "Bernie's sleeping."

"Well, you're the party anyway," she said. She had a whiskey voice, the kind that got screechier later in the night but started out rougher than necessary in the afternoon. She walked over to him, flirting her way across the muddy grass. It was dark, and here and there in the thickets were lights from occupied trailers. Max heard the babble of television sets around him.

"I was wonderin', maybe we could go for a ride. I like your car."

Now this was exactly the kind of shit you had to put up with dealing with stupid people. Bernie fell in love in a bar and so now there was Carlette around to maybe describe Max and his car and . . . shit.

"Maybe we could," he said.

"Go up to Rockford maybe."

"They got anything in Rockford?"

"Got some nice clubs. Lounges. We could hear some music," she said.

He looked at her in the darkness and his eyes might have been glittering.

"Sure," he said.

★ ★ ★

443

He strangled Carlette on a county road called XX. He dumped her dead white body in a culvert by a farm field. They'd find her in a day or two or three. Someone would be driving along and see that white bloated body in the brown grass rushes. It was dead winter. She wore her brown sweater and jeans. She might be a dead dog hidden in the thick rushes of the culvert. Max didn't think about it again as he drove into Chicago in the dead of an early-December evening, all the sky glowing orange from the lights of the city painted against the darkness. He thought about Liz instead, thought about Liz in his bed. He thought about it a lot and it excited him because the killing of Carlette had turned him on. Sometimes it happened that way.

Forty-five

It was midnight Saturday when General Lee finally agreed to see Mrs. Neumann in R Section. And agreed to bring along the quasi prisoner Col. Jack Cavett.

It was nearly 0130 hours before Gen. Robert E. Lee was persuaded of Mrs. Neumann's arguments.

Devereaux, Hacker, Hanley, Mrs. Neumann, Jack Cavett, and the general were crowded in her corner office, where she commanded the desk and the chair that came with it. Everyone else was in a more vulnerable position, even Bobby Lee, who wanted a desk to hide behind.

"I don't see why we don't just arrest some people, go to the FBI," he kept saying, looking at Cavett with a mixture of contempt and suspicion.

"Because there's nothing to go to them with," Devereaux said again. "Jack says his wife was harassed by someone named Max Escher. It takes a long leap to go from that to setting a fire in the Pentagon. And at Indianhead. You jumped in, made your arrest, and now you've got to live with it."

Bobby Lee stared at him. "I still think I got the right man —"

Mrs. Neumann held up her hand. There were only two lamps lit in the office and it made everyone look a lot better than they felt.

"General." Her voice, still raspy, was softened by the hour. "We have to proceed cautiously. We imply there's a connection, we can't prove it. All we can prove is that some secret congressional testimony found its way into Miss Andrews's garbage. There's no connection yet between that and Senator Horan leaking the secret testimony. We're just speculating, and if we're wrong, we'll be worse off than if we did nothing."

"Then let's do nothing."

"We have to find Max Escher," Cavett said to the general. "He's the connection to everything. If we can find him, he'll connect everyone else."

"Where do you find him, even begin to look?"

"He's after my wife. After Liz," Cavett said. He looked sidelong at Devereaux. The men in the room were staring holes in him as if they knew all about Liz.

"He gave her a number. I've been trying to call her but she's either out or sleeping, she sleeps like a log," he said.

"Send someone from Chicago over to wake her up," the general said.

"General." Devereaux leaned forward, into the light of the lamp on Mrs. Neumann's desk. "We can't do anything officially until we have Max Escher and can tie these things together. We can't even search Britta's garbage dumpster. And we want ICC. Your outfit wants them as much as we do —"

"We'd like to clear up some things. In the Med," General Lee admitted.

"Then do it this way," Devereaux said.

"This way, there's no comeback to us. If Devereaux fails," Mrs. Neumann said.

The general looked at her. "What if I lose my only suspect?"

"We all take risks but we try to keep them down," Mrs. Neumann said.

He didn't like it but he signed off on it by two in the morning. It was one in the morning in Chicago and there was still no answer at the residence of Robert Fredericks.

General Lee provided transport. It was a military version of the B727 without windows and painted in desert camouflage.

The flight to O'Hare International took one hour and twenty-three minutes against light headwinds. The plane crossed the dark vastness of Lake Michigan and then the orange-lit grid of the city lights began, spreading out almost to the horizon as seen at thirty-one thousand feet.

The NRC inspector for the Apostle met them in the military hangar a half-mile from the civilian terminals. It was 3:30 A.M. Chicago time.

The wind was cold and dry, and when they spoke to each other, the steam from their mouths rose in quick bursts. Jack Cavett stood, hands in pockets, shivering in his poplin windbreaker.

Ingersoll was rubbing his gloved hands. He said, "This is the most extraordinary thing. We've made calls, I called Captain McCarthy myself, he's in charge of security. But where do we get extra bodies at this time of morning? And Sunday morning at that?"

"You need more security," Devereaux said. "General Lee wants to lend military support but there's a chain of command he has to buck. Maybe all the way to the president. We just don't have the time."

"This is so tricky. I mean, in the political area," Ingersoll said.

Cavett stared at him then. "Everyone's

worried about the politics. What if a terror team attacks?"

"Is that likely, really likely?"

"I don't know," Devereaux said. "We're speculating, based on some loose information."

"I wasn't even told the nature of the information."

"That's right," Devereaux said.

"Inside," Cavett said then. He had been thinking about it during the cold flight to Chicago. "If this is the man we think it is, he'll work it inside, make it look inside —"

Ingersoll held up his hand. "We've got complete security at the Apostle. You don't even know it is the Apostle that's the target. General Lee told me that, said you had a dozen nuclear plants it —"

"The man we want to see was in Chicago a couple of days ago. He works out of suburban Chicago. Or did. The company we thought he worked for told us tonight he quit six months ago," Devereaux said. "I don't really have time to argue with you, Ingersoll."

"I have to have accountability. We're not a bunch of free agents, you know."

"Look, man. What if this is true?" It was Cavett. He grabbed Ingersoll by the lapel. "What if it's true, you're just going to insist on reports and forms when your plant could burn down?"

"It's impossible. What do you mean, burn down? That's absurd. We have every precaution, there's a chain of command for emergencies we test on a regular basis."

Devereaux shook his head. "C'mon, Jack. We don't have time for this guy."

Ingersoll touched Devereaux's sleeve. "Who are you people? I don't want to be out of the loop on this. Let's start on the same page." He had every bureaucrat's cliché under control.

"We told you," Devereaux said. His voice was quiet in the wind, low and heavy. "We warned you. If you don't do anything, it's on you, Ingersoll."

"But I'm here," he began. "I mean, it's in the middle of the night. Saturday night, I don't know what to do."

But they left him then without suggesting anything.

The general had arranged for a GSA Dodge minivan as well. Devereaux drove from the airport along the Kennedy Expressway toward the towers at the center of the city. It was so cold now. Jack held his ungloved hands next to one of the heater ducts. "Goddamn. You live in Washington, you forget how cold it gets in the rest of the country," Jack said.

Devereaux glanced at the speedometer. They were doing seventy and he let it slack down a little to sixty-five. The speed limit was fifty-five. The tires hummed. Traffic was sparse, dark cars fleeing under orange lamps festooned along the pavement. The elevated tracks sat in the median between the north- and south-bound lanes and the platforms were all empty. The Loop seemed to lean up over them as they approached.

"I don't like Liz being out. She said Bob was out of town, she was scared, she wouldn't have gone out," Jack said.

Devereaux said nothing because he was thinking the same thing. There was no point in bringing it up. He had called Rita and awakened her and said he was leaving the city and that she shouldn't go out. If she needed anything, she should call Hanley at the special number. She hadn't said anything when he said "Take care."

"You don't think Escher could have . . . could have gotten to her?"

Yes, Devereaux thought. He thought exactly that.

They drove through the deserted streets of the old section of the Loop, under the arching elevated tracks. They drove east on Washington Street to Michigan Avenue. Then

Devereaux turned north to Randolph and then east again.

The bulky 400 East Randolph Building was isolated at the lakefront east of Grant Park above the Monroe Harbor yacht basin. Devereaux pulled up into the driveway and parked the car. The two men got out and walked to the building.

The doorman looked at them. Devereaux opened a card wallet and showed identification that said he was a special agent for the Federal Bureau of Investigation. The doorman rang the apartment for a long time. He said no one was home. Devereaux looked at Cavett. He saw how pale Cavett had become in just the last few seconds. Devereaux said they would have to look around.

The doorman didn't like that at all. He said nobody could just go and look around. The doorman asked what it was all about. Devereaux said it was drugs.

Cavett frowned.

The doorman wanted to call police. Devereaux said, "I am the police." That was true, the doorman thought. He called the garage man to watch the door while the doorman took the gentlemen to the apartment of attorney Bob Fredericks.

Jack Cavett stood pale and silent throughout. He said nothing. He kept thinking of what they would find in the apartment. The elevator whooshed them to the twentieth floor in the still, sleeping building.

The doorman fumbled with the master key and then pushed the door open. He let them walk in first. He didn't know what they were looking for but they were paid for it, not him. He stood in the door and watched them.

A fluorescent light was on in the kitchen and that was all.

Jack Cavett said, "Liz." Then he said it again, more loudly.

Devereaux walked to the rooms on the right and moved from the dim light into darkness. He pushed a switch and flooded the interior hall with light.

"Liz," Jack said again.

But the apartment was empty.

"What do we do?"

Devereaux looked at the doorman. "How long are you on duty?"

"Until seven," he said.

"I want you to call us when Mrs. Fredericks comes in. I'll give you a card."

The card contained an 800 number. No matter where he was, the call could be patched through to him.

"What are we going to do?" They were back in the gray government minivan.

Devereaux said, "There's nothing we can

do. Until we hear from your wife."

"If I could only remember that number —"

"It wouldn't do any good. Your wife has to call." He stared at Jack in the darkness of the parked minivan. "Will she?"

"Liz has all the guts in the world. But Max scared her."

"Max scares me," Devereaux said and started the car down the driveway.

Forty-six

They took a room on the fifth floor of the Hyatt Hotel on the south side of the Chicago River. Devereaux could not lie down. He went to the upholstered chair by the window and sat in it and looked out at the sparkling empty night city. He looked down at the river. It was nearly four-thirty in the morning in Chicago, five-thirty in Washington. Jack went to the bathroom and then came out in skivvies and climbed into bed.

"You goin' to sleep?" he said to Devereaux.

Devereaux shook his head.

Jack lay in bed, hands behind his head, staring at the ceiling.

Neither of them said anything.

The night passed, minute by minute. It was nearly five in Chicago. It was December and the northern darkness was on the city, framing each brief day with longer and longer periods of night.

Devereaux stared at the city beyond the windows and thought about Mona. It had all begun with Mona so long ago. He wondered if she had died well, but you couldn't determine that for yourself all the time. He wondered if there had been a lot of pain. He owed Mona his life so he had to pay the debt. He had to pay it twice. Once for himself, once for letting her get into harm's way. But not Rita. That was asking too much. Mona would never have asked for that.

The telephone rang at 6:15.

Neither man had slept, though both had dozed into states between consciousness and sleep. The ringing phone might have come from a dream. And then Jack reached out his hand for the phone.

"This is Liz Fredericks," she began.

"Liz. Are you all right?"

"Jack? The doorman said an FBI man called and —"

"Liz, where were you? You said Bob was out of town."

"I was afraid, Jack." She said it softly, but the voice was ragged the way it always was and was made worse by drinking. He knew she had been drinking. "I took a cab. I went to Rush Street, I —"

He closed his eyes and saw her. He could see her in a bar, sitting there alone for about two seconds before someone offered her a drink and a shoulder to cry on if she wanted that or anything else she wanted. Tell her some lies and listen to her laugh in that strange way of hers, slipping their hands around her, touching her.

"It wasn't that, Jack," she said. "I just didn't want to be alone. Bob called after I called you, he said he was staying in a motel for the night. I didn't want to be in this apartment with that . . . man out there."

"Sure," he said.

"Fuck you, Jack, I mean it."

Devereaux took the receiver away from Jack Cavett. Cavett just sat there, letting it go.

"My name is Devereaux," he began. "Are you all right?"

"I'm all right. I had a few drinks and then the place closed at five and I took a cab home. Who does Jack think he is, does he think he's my keeper? I'll fuck around with anyone I want."

Devereaux said, "We want to talk to you. It's about Max Escher."

"Fuck you, I don't know who you are either, do I?"

"I'm the man who wants Max Escher," Devereaux said. And that seemed to bring her down a little. "We have to talk right away, Mrs. Fredericks. Can we come over now?"

★ ★ ★

457

It was a different doorman. He called to the apartment on the twentieth floor and she said they could come up.

Liz was wearing a dress and a string of pearls. She had a drink on the kitchen counter. She was in stockings but shoeless. She looked at the two of them and led them into the kitchen. "You wanna drink?"

Devereaux said nothing.

"I don't want anything," Cavett said. "We thought something'd happened to you. We called you back all night."

"How would I know that?"

It was a private fight and Devereaux wanted to step out of the room but there might not be any time. The money had been drawn from the District Savings Bank, the senator had been called off the Devereaux trail by Clair, everything pointed to something happening very, very soon. And he was tired. And he was thinking of Rita Macklin, who was thinking about Mona. Everything was entangled in personal stuff and he had started it. With Mona.

He held up his hand and they both looked at him. He didn't say a word but they stopped talking.

"We think Max Escher is going to set a fire," he said.

"What's that got to do with me?"

"He wants you," Devereaux said. "We want him."

"Shit," she said then. She picked up the drink and started to taste it and put it down. The night had been rough on her. Her hands were trembling. "What do you want?"

"Call him," Devereaux said.

"I can't do that. I can't talk to him."

"Call the number," he said.

Cavett said, "You can't make her."

"Mrs. Fredericks." Devereaux went over to her. "Maybe Escher set fire to the Pentagon. Maybe he set another fire to blame Jack. Whatever it is, it's tied in to organized terrorism. I don't really have time to explain it all but it's all real."

"I don't have to do anything, do I, Jack?" She looked at him, hurt and expecting to be hurt again.

He just stared at her.

"But I'm afraid," she said then. She stared at him and Devereaux saw it was the best and only argument. He couldn't tell her not to be afraid.

It was Jack instead.

"You can't be afraid of him, I won't let you be afraid of him," Jack said.

She turned. She was looking for a fight. "Is that right? What are you going to do, Jack?"

"I won't let him hurt you," he said.

The wind blew against the window wall and they all heard it in the stillness.

"What are you going to do? Make me marry you again?" she said. "I couldn't go through that again, Jack. When you do a thing badly, quit."

Bob Fredericks had been there for a while. He was standing in the foyer off the kitchen and he was staring at them. How long had he been listening? They looked at him.

Bob looked like a lawyer who made $500,000 a year and didn't overwork himself for it. He had white hair but a good, strong face. He sat on three boards of directors besides the board at Northern Illinois Power and Light. It was the way to make money in business without working hard, just sitting on the board of corporations and voting to do whatever the CEO or the chairman wanted done.

When she saw him, she went to him and gave him a cheek kiss. He didn't kiss her back. He stared at his wife and then at the two others in the small kitchen. She turned to the two of them and stood by her husband.

Gray dawn light from the lake moved over the city, carefully unpeeling down narrow streets, separating the shadows in the alleys and gangways. It is a morning city, gray light on gray stones down gray streets, washing away the colors.

Bob Fredericks said, "What are you doing here, Jack?"

Jack looked at Liz. He couldn't even describe what it was, to see Liz standing by this other man. The man she belonged to.

"A man named Escher is in Chicago," Devereaux said. "We think he intends to torch one of your power plants. The Apostle."

"I just came from the Dunedin plant in Galena. We had problems. They shut down the reactor," Bob Fredericks said. "They wanted advice." He looked as tired as they were. "I couldn't sleep. I left the motel at three A.M."

"What kind of problems?"

"Leak in the containment building," he said. "Who the hell are you?"

Devereaux told him the truth.

"I want to see some identification," he said. "I never heard of R Section. What the hell is it?"

"I'm tired of showing cards," Devereaux said.

The hard-eyed lawyer started to speak, but Devereaux overrode him: "I want you to call Ingersoll at the Apostle and find out how much he's beefed up security."

"It's Sunday."

"I can get an order to shut down the Apos-

461

tle," Devereaux said. He said it evenly. He had no idea of what he could do or not do.

"I'll call the police," Bob Fredericks said then. "Alert the chain of command. Rock County Police, Rockford city police, we've got an emergency scenario set up."

"What are you going to do? Tell everyone to evacuate?" Devereaux said.

The rest of them stared at him.

"There's no evacuation plan," Bob said.

"No, of course not. Ten million people live within a hundred miles of the Apostle. You'd be killing people just by telling them to get out."

They thought about it. They thought of the highways filled with endless unmoving lines of cars. Of panic in a hundred little towns. Of riots and looting along the pleasant suburban streets. Of fires and a thousand other disasters that would come if the population was panicked.

"Call Ingersoll first," Devereaux said.

Bob Fredericks stared at him. At Jack. At Liz, who stood by him. He went to the desk in the front room and rolled his Rolodex. He called a number and waited a long time. "I want to talk to your father," he said.

Waited.

Devereaux glanced at his watch: 0715 hours.

"Mr. Ingersoll? This is Bob Fredericks. Yes, yes, I think we met at the Glen Oaks last year, at the outing. I'm . . . yes. I'm talking to them now. Put me in the picture, Harry."

Silence. Liz stared at Jack and he stared back at her.

Bob caught this and frowned while he listened to the NRC man on the phone. Liz was flawed goods in his mind but that had been all right as long as no one knew about the flaws except him. It kept her under control, it kept the whole situation under control. She was lucky to end up a trophy wife at the age of forty-two, she understood that.

"Well, it's in your hands then. I'm sure you and Captain McCarthy'll do the right thing," he said. "All right. All right. All right. OK. OK. Thanks, Harry."

Hung up.

Looked at Devereaux. "He's called in twenty extra men."

"You should start to shut down the plant."

"We can't do that just on — what? on your say-so? There's got to be local responsibility, we can't close down a nuclear power plant every time the government hears about a security threat, we'd never be open."

They let it hang there.

"Now, what I want to know is what you

463

men are doing in my apartment with my wife?"

"We want Liz to make a call," Jack Cavett said. Staring at Liz.

"What do you mean, how's Liz involved in this?"

Liz looked at Jack. Jack shook his head ever so slightly.

"I asked you a question, Colonel," Bob said.

"A man named Escher burned down the Pentagon. He's going to torch your nuclear plant," Devereaux said.

"What do we have to do with the Pentagon, there's a piece of logic missing here."

"He was the man who followed your wife into that hotel," Devereaux said.

"How the devil do you know about that? Liz?"

And Liz glanced at him and saw how hard his eyes had become. The tarnished trophy wife.

"Did you call Jack, Liz? Did you tell him that?"

"I told him. I was frightened. It was the second time, Bob, he came here days ago and he frightened me."

"Why didn't you tell me this? Why'd you go running off to your ex-husband? He is your ex-husband, Liz, or do you forget that?"

"No, Bob. I don't forget that," she said.

The gray morning light was drawn by Seurat, point to point to point, rendering depth and feeling and texture to the landscape of city and sky and water.

"Bob. I didn't do anything. Max came to me and he threatened me. He would have threatened me again if you hadn't been there. In the hotel that afternoon."

"Threaten you about what?"

"He wants me to . . ." She let it go.

Bob stared. His hands clenched. "He wants you to sleep with him? Why? Was he one of your army lovers, Liz? Before you decided to be respectable and drink gin in the kitchen at six in the morning?"

"I went out all night and got drunk," she said to him. "I was afraid to be alone, so I went looking for company. What do you think of that, Bob?"

"I think being a slut agrees with you."

Jack got up and stepped across the kitchen toward Bob. Devereaux reached in and grabbed his arm. Jack waited because Devereaux's touch was like iron encased in flesh. Bob's hard eyes were on him but they weren't showing any fear.

"Maybe it does," Liz said then. She looked at Devereaux. "I remember the number, that's the damned thing. I remember it."

"Tell him you want to see him."

"Where?"

"Anyplace he wants. When he wants."

"Why would he believe me?"

"I don't know," Devereaux said.

"You can't use her —" Bob began.

"Shut up, Bob. Shut up, Jack. Shut up."

"You want to see him as soon as possible," Devereaux said.

She punched in the numbers on the phone on the kitchen wall. The three men stood behind her. The gray morning light was filling the whole apartment, darting from room to room, showing where the shadows were hiding.

"This is Liz, Max."

She hesitated.

"If you're there, pick up on your machine." She waited a moment.

"This is Liz. I thought it over. I want to see you. Soon. Today if I can."

She replaced the receiver and stared at it and then she began to tremble a little. No one could move to touch her because she had to be apart from them.

Devereaux saw there was no comfort unless they lied to her.

"I really want to know about this," Bob Fredericks began. His voice was a monotone now, gray as the morning light. "I don't need

466

to be pushed around, Liz. Not by you. Or your ex-husband. Or this other man. I don't need this grief. Nobody does. I gave you a nice place, clothes, I gave you what you wanted, Liz, and I don't need to be treated like this."

Liz said, "I'm sorry, Bob. I didn't mean to do anything to anyone."

They waited in the front room. She made coffee and they drank it but she continued to drink gin. The gray light turned to fog and then the fog rolled out and the sun rose above the lake horizon. It was warmer and bright. They could look out at the lake and city and clearly see people on the walks in the park and playing football on the grass.

0930 hours.

The telephone rang.

Devereaux made a signal, got up from the chair by the window. "I'll go with you."

The phone rang a second time.

"Third ring," Devereaux said to her standing next to him. The phone rang.

She picked it up. He listened next to her.

"It's Max, Liz."

She trembled and Devereaux put his arm around her shoulders. He held her while she trembled.

"Where are you, Max? You downstairs? You can come up."

"I'd like to, Liz. Like to come. You know what I mean?"

She waited.

"But it can't be. What changed your mind, Liz?"

"You came on too strong at first," she said.

"Is that right?"

"That's right," she said.

"You fuck that old man you were with in the hotel?"

"Yes," she said. So softly he could barely hear her.

"That really your husband?" Saying it playfully.

"Yes."

"Man, I know I could do better than that. Better than Jack, in fact. I'm better than Jack."

She closed her eyes.

"Is that right, Liz?"

"I don't know, Max."

"You could know."

"How could I know?"

"You could come down to see me."

"You're not in Chicago now?"

"Last place on earth you want to be. You'd be smart to catch the first available out of there, Liz, very smart. Aside from just seeing me. You wanna see me?"

She opened her eyes and stared into Devereaux's face. He gave her no signal but he held her.

"Yes," she said in that deep, throaty voice. "I really do."

"You turn me on, Liz. You always did. I called you up twice last night, I really did, but you weren't home. You missed lucking out last night."

"Max, where are you?"

"Where's your old man?"

"He's out of town. On business."

"Oh. Well, why don't you follow his example."

"Why, Max?"

"Because you don't have a lot of time, let me put it that way," Max said. "You be out of there by two. Yeah. By two this afternoon. Not much time left, Liz."

"Not much time." She repeated it, flat word on flat word.

"You listen to Max, honey. You wanna be in New Orleans. I'm staying in the Windsor Court Hotel this morning. You take the very first plane you can out of Chicago for New Orleans. Trust me."

She looked at Devereaux.

He nodded.

"I really . . ." She was still trembling.

"You really want it," Max Escher said. "Go ahead and say it."

She trembled and didn't speak.

"That's all right, kid. You can tell me when you get here. But hurry, honey, I really got to emphasize that."

He broke the connection.

She dropped the phone on the carpet. Devereaux held her a moment longer and then said, "You did good, Liz."

Jack and Bob were on their feet, coming toward her. Devereaux bent down and picked up the receiver and put it back on the hook.

Jack reached for her and held her and she was held and didn't feel it. She didn't feel anything.

Bob Fredericks said, "You want to let go of my wife?"

Jack held her.

Bob Fredericks hit him then with the flat of his hand and Devereaux stepped between them.

"We don't need this," Devereaux said. He looked at Jack. "If he's out of town now, he's done it. Whatever he had to do."

"I don't believe this, not any of this," Bob Fredericks said. "I want to talk to someone in charge, I don't want to talk to you."

Devereaux said, "I really don't think there's any time to fuck around with you, Mr.

Fredericks. You call Ingersoll and tell him to meet us at the plant, you tell him that. The thing is in the plant, whatever he set, it's in the plant."

"I can't go off half-cocked calling an emergency. Based on what? On my wife's flirtation with someone she knew in the service?"

"Max Escher was trained in Special Forces, in demolition and bomb disposal," Devereaux said. "You believe that?"

"I don't know." He was looking at his wife, at the man who held her. "I can't get involved at this level, I've got considerations. My wife involved with an arsonist? You can't do that to me."

"You have to call Ingersoll."

"I'm calling the CEO, that's who I'm calling. I've got to get a reading on this. We've just fought off the papers in Dunedin, we can't have another —"

"You're going to have another —"

"The media. There's containment needed, we have to set up some strategy," he said.

Devereaux said, "It's ten in the morning. Max Escher told her to be on a plane out of here by two. At the latest. Four hours."

"We can't have a panic. I agree with you on that. Whatever it is, our security is trained to take care of it."

"Start closing it down, Bob."

"I can't do that without authorization," he said. "I have to notify the operations chief."

"Call him, then."

Bob stared at him for a moment. He didn't like to be ordered around. But he went back to the Rolodex on his desk and flipped it.

He punched in the number and waited. He said, "It's a bad time of the year. Bad time of the week, Sunday morning. I think he has a vacation place in Wisconsin. Oh. And the company's got a box for the Bears games. Home game today."

Devereaux didn't speak. He went to the window wall and looked out on the city. It was so bright and the sky was clear to the horizon.

"I've got to cover myself," Bob Fredericks said.

Devereaux decided. "We've got to go out there, Jack. You've got to find it. Or them. Or whatever is out there. You thought like Max without knowing it was Max. You guessed the coffee makers in the Pentagon. You guessed about the accelerant. You've got to guess, Jack."

Cavett released Liz. He was unshaven, as was Devereaux, and their clothes were soiled by a day and night of wear.

"Get Liz out of here, Bob. Get out yourself after you contact someone. Start shutting down the Apostle."

"What could he do? Set a bomb, the building can withstand —"

"Bob. Someone paid him two million dollars to do something, and whatever it is, it's worth two million dollars. What do you think it is?" Devereaux said.

Bob stared at him while Devereaux reached for the phone on the foyer table and punched in a series of numbers.

"I want you to talk to Bob Fredericks. We've got a line on Escher but whatever he was going to do, he did. Yes. Yes. The Apostle. Bobby Lee, you've got to get someone to shut down the Apostle. No, I'm not sure. Yes, yes. Damn." He slammed down the receiver. "He said he's in a bind with his superiors, letting you go, cooperating with R Section." Devereaux was talking to Cavett. "He said it's a civilian plant, the key is the NRA man here, he has to give the say-so on site."

"Harry Ingersoll," Bob Fredericks said.

Again, Devereaux picked up the phone. He looked at Bob Fredericks. Fredericks recited a string of numbers, beginning with an area code in McHenry County.

"Let me speak to your father."

Waited.

"Ingersoll. This is Devereaux. You've got

to shut down the Apostle." He waited again. "I don't have authorization, you're the fucking authorization. All right. We'll be there as soon as we can. All right."

He replaced the receiver.

"He wants to inspect with us, decide then. Nobody wants to make a decision."

"Aren't you letting yourself panic?" It was Fredericks. "We haven't heard a word about this and now, on Sunday morning, you're in my apartment, you accuse my wife of consorting with some kind of arsonist, you want to shut down one of the country's safest, most efficient nuclear power facilities. I mean, what's your authority exactly? I think we need someone to sign off on this."

Jack ignored him. Took a step toward Liz. "Get out of here. Get out of this city," he said.

"What can happen, Jack?"

He just stood there.

In a moment of silence they all tried to answer her question.

Forty-seven

Hacker sat in the back of the van parked on Q Street. He was drinking coffee from a Styrofoam cup and the remains of a chocolate donut rested on a newspaper folded to the sports section. The van bristled with electronic apparatus. No one had authorized its use in the early hours of Sunday and so Hacker had made a predawn requisition.

There were three targets of opportunity. He had picked the woman. The directional power antennas not only surveyed her apartment but acted as a tap on her phone line.

The outside of the truck said it belonged to Chesapeake and Potomac Power Company.

He listened to her and the senator make love shortly after dawn. He smiled in his thoughtful way, listening to the sounds of the mattress and springs, listening to their cries. Hacker thought the sounds of lovemaking rendered the act silly. When she began to cry in orgasm, the senator picked it up, as though they were dogs engaged in a barking contest.

Exactly like dogs, Hacker thought.

At 1130 hours Eastern Time, the telephone rang in the apartment. In the surveillance van the tape began unreeling. Hacker picked up the earphones and strapped them on. He fiddled with a knob to adjust the sensitivity of the listening devices. There were no bugs in her apartment but the whole of her window walls acted as a reflective antenna for every sound inside.

Britta: "Hello?"

Voice: "It's me."

Britta: "Max."

Max: "Don't wear my name out."

Britta: "Where are you?"

Max: "Windsor Court Hotel. In New Orleans."

Britta: "What're you doing there?"

Max: "Being out of Chicago. It isn't gonna be the healthiest place to be in a couple of hours."

Pause.

The voice-actuated tape paused.

Max: "Hello? You there?"

Britta: "Today? It happens today?"

Max: "It happens in a couple of hours."

Britta: "I can't believe it. I mean, I can believe it. But it's really happening. Now. Today."

Max: "Wanted to tell you."

Britta: "I want to see you, Max."

Max: "I'll be seeing you. Not now but down the road. When we see what happens."

Britta: "Max —"

The connection was broken. Hacker looked at his watch and then noted the time on a legal pad. He pushed a button and punched in a telephone number on a keyboard. He waited three rings.

He began to speak to Hanley.

Forty-eight

There was an orange parking ticket pasted on the windshield of the Dodge van when they climbed in. The ticket blew off as they pulled away.

It was 10:22 A.M.

A minute later, they were caught in a traffic jam on Lake Shore Drive. The Bears were kicking off at 11:30 at Soldier Field and thousands of cars contained Bears fans who wanted to arrive early to start drinking in the parking lots around the stadium.

Devereaux sounded the horn and pulled onto the frozen grass of Grant Park. He shot across the grass and the van bottomed twice.

They hit the street at Wacker, still punching the horn.

The van roared back across the Sunday-empty Loop toward the expressway junction.

The Kennedy Expressway was tight because of bridge repairs in the right lanes and they lost ten minutes before they reached the junction with the road to O'Hare Airport. The day was all gold, clear and cold. The wind was a soft breeze coming down from the northwest.

They pushed through the built-in roadblocks at the tollbooths and they both kept glancing at their watches. Max wanted Liz to be out of Chicago by 2:00 P.M. It was 10:46.

The van reached seventy-five miles an hour and it was the fastest they could go. Traffic was thickening all along the way as the highway crossed through the chain of northwest suburbs.

11:01.

11:15.

They picked up a state police car at State Route 47 and the cop pursued them for three miles before Devereaux saw the flashing lights in the rearview mirror.

11:31.

He jumped out of the van and went to the police car. The policeman got out quickly. Devereaux was holding up his FBI card case that showed his color photograph and his badge.

"What's going on?" the cop said, still standing behind his opened driver's-side door. Devereaux noticed the caution and stopped on the shoulder gravel.

"Emergency at the Apostle reactor," he shouted above the traffic.

479

"What do you want me to do? I'll give you an escort."

"Get us to this Route 20 exit, that far —"

"I can call headquarters, set up an alert."

"That's the last thing we want," Devereaux said. "We don't want any panic."

The state police car, sirens and lights and all, got their speed up to eighty-five miles an hour the rest of the way.

Forty-nine

Capt. Emmett McCarthy, in charge of Barnes Security at the Apostle nuclear power facility, thought Ingersoll had gone goofy. Ingersoll had called him in the middle of the night early Sunday and told him gibberish about an agency in Washington having information on a terrorist attack at the plant. McCarthy had responded as best he could, telephoning some of his reliable senior people to report for duty at the plant. But now he was here and where were the FBI and the cops, where was anybody at all, including Ingersoll?

Ingersoll had just called the plant again and said he was on his way to inspect it. He didn't tell McCarthy a damned thing of what to expect. McCarthy had put out a special guard unit on the fence periphery and issued them radios.

But it was such a peaceful morning.

The sun was shining strong. The stalks rotting in the black fields fluttered in the light northwest wind. The river beyond the plant was surging in a sluggish way, feeling in its river bones the beginning of the winter freeze. He wanted to be home, watching the football game on TV, drinking a can of beer.

What was he supposed to be looking for?

11:51 A.M.

Ingersoll awoke in the ambulance. The first thing he saw was the ceiling and an unfamiliar face leaning over him. He heard the sirens. He thought he might be dreaming that he was in an ambulance.

He started to get up.

The face said, "Just lie easy. You've been in an accident."

"I have?"

"You're gonna be all right."

There was a second paramedic and he stuck a needle into his arm. Ingersoll blinked and thought he didn't feel any pain.

"I've got to go to the plant. Meet these men. Men from Washington."

They stared at him.

He started again, trying to make them understand something.

Why were they staring at him as if he didn't speak English?

He stopped to hear the sound of his own voice. Then he closed his eyes. It was all right. He could wake up in a few minutes, he'd make them understand then.

Devereaux didn't stop at the gate house but drove straight into the parking lot south of the entrance. He stopped the van fifty feet from the building entrance. Both men climbed out and walked quickly across the asphalt to the door of the plant.

From the glass inset in the outer steel door, McCarthy watched them coming. He had been alerted by the gate house. He pulled the strap off the butt of his pistol in the holster but that was all. He waited as the men came through the steel doorway.

"We're supposed to meet Ingersoll here. Is he here?"

"Not yet."

McCarthy looked at the FBI card, compared the photograph with Devereaux's face. He handed back the card. He looked at Cavett and Cavett handed over his service identity card.

"We think there's a bomb in the plant. Or some kind of incendiary device," Cavett began.

McCarthy held up his hand. "We can just wait for Mr. Ingersoll —"

"We don't have time," Devereaux said.

"Is that right? Mr. Ingersoll said to go on alert. That was before first light and we're on alert. Which is why I'm here myself. I don't know who you guys are."

"We showed you —" Cavett began.

"That's paper. Cards. Like I said, I don't know who you guys are."

"We're supposed to meet Ingersoll here. Call him, see what's holding him up."

"You guys just stand over there. No, right there. OK." McCarthy crossed to the desk at the entry that led to the locked doors that opened on the corridor to the administration building. Behind the administration building were the doors to each floor of the generator building.

The room was defined by lime-green walls and a concrete floor. There were two airport-style metal detectors that barricaded the rest of the room from the place where Devereaux and Cavett waited.

McCarthy punched in a number and waited.

"Hello. This is Captain McCarthy at the plant. Is your father home? He did. Oh. Oh. I see. Which hospital? Oh. I'm sorry, dear. I'm sure."

He broke the connection. Looked at the two men.

"Ingersoll was in a car crash on the tollway. They've taken him to Rock County Hospital."

"Jesus," Cavett said.

Devereaux said, "Look, Captain. There just isn't any time. We think this thing is set to go off at two P.M."

"Oh. I see. Now you got an exact time and all?"

Two other guards on the other side of the barricade were looking at the two outsiders.

"Let me give you a number in Washington."

"Who do I say you are again? Who's going to answer the phone, J. Edgar Hoover?" McCarthy was watching them. His hand was on his belt but not on his pistol. The rest of the guards in the room were taking an interest.

"My name is Devereaux. Let me give you the number, for Christ's sake."

McCarthy looked at the gathering crowd of security guards. "Your card said your name is Flynn. You forget who you are?"

Devereaux stepped across to the desk and drew the Beretta in the same motion. He pushed the muzzle under McCarthy's chin and put his free arm around his chest. He shielded his body from the guards with McCarthy's bulk in front of him.

"We need access."

An alarm bell sounded from the bulletproof security cage on the other side of the room. The bell banged throughout the plant.

One of the young guards on the opposite side of the barricade drew his pistol and pointed it in the general direction of Mc-

Carthy and Devereaux.

McCarthy spoke in a calm voice. "Now, don't get silly. You shoot and they'll shoot both of you. You can't get in the plant. Whatever you were going to do, you can't do it now."

"I want you to dial the number I give you."

"Washington number."

"Eight hundred number. We use eight hundred numbers."

"And some man will answer the phone and he'll confirm to me that you're a good guy. You must think I'm as stupid as I look."

"Sit down. Easy. Dial the number."

McCarthy dialed the number and waited while it went through some sort of switching equipment. The voice on the line was clear. "Hanley."

"Who are you exactly?"

"Who are you? Exactly?"

"My name is Emmett McCarthy. Chief of security for Apostle nuclear facility."

"Jesus, man." Pause. "Is he there?"

"Who?"

"Devereaux."

"You want to describe him?"

"Gray eyes. Black and gray hair. About six foot two."

"All right." McCarthy passed the phone to Devereaux. Devereaux had shifted the muzzle to the back of McCarthy's wide head.

The bells kept ringing through the plant.

"We don't have any time —"

"Under two hours," Hanley said. "Hacker tapped a line. We got Max Escher telling Miss Andrews it happens in two hours."

"Tell this guy. He won't let us in the plant and the NRC inspector was hurt in an accident on his way here."

McCarthy took the phone again.

"My name is Hanley. I'm chief of operations for R Section and this is a matter of national security."

"That's what you say. Two guys come in here and one of them has a phony FBI ID and then he puts a gun to my head. I want authorization and it doesn't come from someone on a phone saying he really is who he says he is."

"All right." Another pause. "Will you call the Pentagon if I give you a number there?"

"Look, I'm not playing this phone game. No one gets inside the plant until I've got authorization."

Hanley sounded very calm. "All right. Wait a moment while I make another call."

McCarthy looked at Devereaux. "He wants me to wait. He says he's making another call."

Devereaux glanced down at his watch: 12:08.

Three more minutes passed.

12:11.

"Hello?"

"I'm here," McCarthy answered.

"Your authorization will be there in twenty minutes."

"Is that right?"

"We're sending a helicopter contingent of marines from Glenview Naval Air Station. They'll land in the parking lot. I suppose you'll accept their authority."

"Sure," McCarthy said. "Santa Claus will be landing with eight reindeer. You people set this up as some kind of emergency scenario — well, I think we've passed the test."

"This is no test."

"We get tested all the time but this scenario is the best I can remember. Eight hundred numbers. Phony FBI cards. And now what? Well, did we pass the test or what? Is Ingersoll really hurt or was that part of it?" McCarthy put his hand over the receiver and looked at Devereaux. "Are we passing the test?"

Devereaux blinked. He took the phone from McCarthy and spoke to Hanley: "It's me."

"General Lee came on board twenty minutes ago when I fed him Hacker's tap. We reckon it around two P.M. Chicago time."

"That's our information," Devereaux said.

"It doesn't give much time."

"Are you going to put the area on alert?"

"We can't do that." His voice was low, with a note of sadness. Or regret. "Whatever happens, we can't order an evacuation. Ten million people. My God, we'd have thousands of casualties just ordering the evacuation."

"You can order a shutdown at least."

"We're trying to reach the chief operating officer of Northern Illinois Power now," Hanley said. "Apparently, they had some sort of contaminant leak at another of their nuclear plants earlier."

Devereaux put down the phone then. There was nothing to say and the electric clock on the lime-green wall marched off the minutes.

Devereaux said, "I need you, Jack. I need to know what I'm looking for. I wouldn't ask you to stick around."

"It's what I'm paid for." He said it in a flat voice without any irony.

Devereaux looked at McCarthy. "Tell the boy to put his pistol away. No one's going to do anything until the helicopter comes."

"I don't think so," McCarthy said. "You're not going to put away your weapon, are you?"

Devereaux shook his head.

"Then it's a Mexican standoff."

"I wouldn't shoot accidentally," Devereaux said.

"Well, maybe that's a little bit of our edge. You never know what we're going to do."

And everyone in the room just stood there and waited.

The beat of the chopper came overhead at 12:40 and McCarthy registered a look of surprise.

Devereaux shoved the pistol in his back hard. "Stand up now."

McCarthy rose slowly.

"We back outside," Devereaux said.

"All right."

"Go ahead, Jack."

Jack opened the door. The guards in the room watched their captain back slowly through the door to the parking lot. A gust of cold air swept into the closed room and everyone realized how warm it had gotten in the last twenty minutes.

And through the open door they saw the dust-colored helicopter dip and bow, the wheels extended down fore and aft like fingers of a blind man. The *chop-chop-chop* of the M1 assault helicopter slowed as the wheels touched the asphalt.

Marines in combat dress, carrying assault rifles, hit the asphalt beneath the rotor blades and McCarthy's eyes began to bug out.

"You still think it's a test?" Devereaux said.

A young captain ran up to the three civilians standing by the open door to the complex. His face was lean, his eyes were bright. "Sir. Which one of you is Mr. Devereaux?"

"Me."

"Orders to escort you and Colonel Cavett into the plant, sir."

"Tell him."

"Orders, sir, from the Pentagon." He said it just like that and he held his rifle just like that.

"All right," McCarthy said. "I don't think it's a test anymore."

He led them into the anteroom. "All right, men. This is not a test. These men are going to inspect the plant and I want you to pass the word along. Let's not get anybody killed."

"That was the point from the start," Jack Cavett said.

The clock on the lime-green wall read 12:51.

Four more marines from the copter entered the anteroom. The rest deployed in a line alongside the building.

The marine captain looked at Devereaux. "What do you want, sir?"

"We're looking for a bomb. Or an incendiary device. It might look like a bomb and it might look like something else," Devereaux said.

Cavett said, "Have your men go in twos through the plant. We've got about an hour. If they see anything out of the ordinary, just report it, don't try to examine it. It might be rigged."

"Aye, aye, sir." The marine saluted the colonel and went outside.

"And your men," Devereaux said to McCarthy.

"You men heard them. Go in twos through the plant, every inch of it, you're looking for something that doesn't look as though it should be there. You and you, Benjamin and Judge, I want you to go into the screen room especially first and give it a good eyeball and report back to me."

"I ain't looking for no bomb," one of the guards said. "Fuck it. I ain't being paid to look for no bomb."

"I'm putting you on report —"

"I don't give a shit about no report, I quit. I ain't looking for no bomb."

Devereaux turned to one of the marines. "Put that man under arrest."

The marine brought his rifle up and the security guard stared at it. They all stared at it.

"Get him outside," Devereaux said.

The marine captain re-entered the room.

Devereaux said, "Nobody leaves. We

can't have any panic."

"Aye-aye sir." He began to post his men at the door.

McCarthy shook his head. "I don't want any of you to disgrace me. Yourselves. Get going, Benjamin. Screen room. The rest of you deploy on every level, start in from the bottom."

The minutes crept by.

The clock read 2:01.

Devereaux and Cavett were in the generator building. Cavett was being careful, slowly crawling up the ladders leading to the top reaches of the generators. He would pause here and there, looking into this cranny and that.

At 2:03 a marine found the lunch box hanging on a peg in a toilet stall with a broken toilet seat.

Cavett was sent to examine it in case it might be a bomb.

He was very careful and his face was beaded with a fine sheen of sweat. He opened the box and he half expected it to pop, explode, something.

It was just a lunch box with the remains of a mangled chicken salad sandwich.

2:13 P.M.

McCarthy found Devereaux and Cavett in

the men's rest room examining the opened lunch box.

He was wearing his blustering face again. "You said two o'clock, it's two-fifteen near."

Devereaux looked at him. His face was the color of ashes. "Shut up, McCarthy," he said.

At that moment the alarms sounded again.

They were all frozen by the sound. There were bells and sirens.

The men began to run back to the security anteroom. The floors were sopping with condensation from one of the coolant pipes. The water left puddles under the generators here and there and made the metal floor slippery.

Into the anteroom.

"Fire in the paint shed," one of the guards shouted. Other guards were running with fire extinguishers down the metal steps to the storage cages.

The alarm bells sounded automatically in the fire houses within ten miles of the plant.

Devereaux and Cavett raced down metal stairs to the cages in the bottom of the generator building.

The paint cage was roaring with flames. The smell of fire and paint chemicals was overwhelming. One of the guards fell. Devereaux and Cavett exchanged looks.

"Exactly like the Pentagon," Devereaux said.

Across the countryside there were the sounds of sirens. A dozen fire companies on dozens of trucks were racing down the narrow asphalt roads toward the Apostle.

The ponderous machinery of evacuation fine-tuned for years by Northern Illinois Power and Light lurched slowly into motion.

There were 19,503 people within ten miles of the Apostle nuclear reactor plant. Sirens now screamed from schoolhouses, fire stations, and town halls. The sirens puzzled residents at first. Eventually, news reports based on public relations announcements said there was a fire in the Apostle reactor and that there was no danger to the general population and that it was suggested that people stay indoors with windows and doors kept shut in the event of any accidental leakage of radiation.

The roads in Rock County began to fill noticeably almost right away. The cars fled north and west and even east, into the path of the wind. Traffic from shopping centers around the city of Rockford added to the mix. Some people thought the plant was exploding, some thought it was already leaking radiation. Some spoke of Chernobyl.

Slowly, panic set in.

2:31 P.M.

The white-hot fire was still contained in the paint shed. The first fire companies were on the scene, racing into the building with foam canisters and hose. The flames seemed to feed on water sprayed at them because the fire was so hot.

In the control room the director began the process of closing down the active Red core. The process would take seven or so hours. Slowly, the control rods would be lowered into the reactor's heart, slowing the process, bringing down the temperature of the water that ran through the core, which drove the turbines.

Every one of the 119 nuclear plants in the country had some sort of emergency evacuation plan and each was different and each was untested. When Three Mile Island had been evacuated, the governor had announced there was a danger only to pregnant women. Instead, 40 percent of the population around the reactor managed to clog the roads within hours.

The sirens wailed on. The wind blew down across the Apostle, picking up speed across the empty fields to the first picket of suburbs sprawled across McHenry and Kane and DuPage counties toward Cook County.

On this Sunday afternoon the Bears were beating the Cowboys in the fourth quarter by one touchdown and old Soldier Field was full and the decision was made not to tell anyone that there had been an accident at the Apostle because of the panic it would cause.

Cavett's face was streaked with dirt mingled with sweat. He and Devereaux and McCarthy were on the lowest level and there was water and smoke everywhere. The firemen tramped through the water on the floors and shouted to each other.

The fire in the paint room was slowly dying. It was a stubborn fire and every moment it seemed in danger of flaring up again but the smoke and water signaled the death of the flames.

Cavett said, "More than one."

"What more than one?"

"He set nineteen fires in the Pentagon."

McCarthy said, "We're still searching the plant."

"Who searches the cores? The reactor cores?"

"No one's gone in there, that's the one place he couldn't start a fire. You have to be an engineer to get in there. When it's totally shut down. We check them every day," McCarthy said.

"What do you mean, 'check'?"

"We've got monitors in the cores, electronic monitors to sense temperature changes."

"But you said 'check,' " Cavett said.

"A safety engineer. And one of the security staff check the cores every day. In person. They log in and out. Not in the core, you understand, in the containment building around the core."

"Who checked it yesterday?"

McCarthy stared at him a moment. "I'd have it in the log." They tramped back through the water to the security monitor room in the plant's anteroom. McCarthy knocked on the door. An armed guard, gun drawn, opened it. His face was white with fear.

"We want the log for yesterday."

The log was a diary book. McCarthy thumbed the pages. "Engineer was Dobson, security guard was Lund, Bernie Lund."

"What time did they go in and go out?" Cavett said.

"They went in at two twenty-six. Came out at three thirty-two," McCarthy said.

The three men looked at their watches. "Twenty-four hours ago," Cavett said.

McCarthy turned to the guard in the monitor room. "Are they on duty today?"

The guard checked more sheets. The warning sirens had been shut down inside the plant and the word had been flashed to headquarters in Chicago that the fire was contained. Still, sirens sounded from schoolhouses and fire departments and town halls, and the roads were now brimming with traffic moving away from the Apostle.

"Dobson's pass shows he's in the containment room for Red reactor. He's probably suiting up."

"And Lund?"

"Lund is missing. He was supposed to be on duty and he's not. He didn't report in sick."

The two security men stared at each other.

Cavett said, "I've got to see this Dobson."

They all understood. They didn't want to believe it but they all understood. It would take them five minutes to get to the other end of the plant and the containment room.

They ran across the second level where smoke was seeping up from the paint-shed fire. Their feet echoed their panic. The gigantic turbines were slowing but the process was hours short of being completed.

They flung open the door of the changing room on McCarthy's card.

Dobson had the yellow suit on but not the helmet. He turned to them.

He didn't say a thing.

2:59.

"Did you see anything yesterday inside?"

Dobson made a face. "I would've said. Why?"

"The security guard you were with. Lund. He's missing."

"I wasn't with Lund. I was with a new guy, forget his name."

McCarthy said, "Lund was signed in on the log."

"I don't give a damn about that, I wasn't with Lund."

Cavett said, "That's it. We've got to go in."

"What's it?" Dobson said.

"He's set the other bomb inside."

The word *bomb* just sat there for a moment between them.

Dobson grabbed his helmet. "I'll find it," he said and lifted the helmet on his shoulders.

"Open the fucking door," Cavett shouted.

"You don't have a suit —"

"We don't have time," Cavett shouted. He shoved McCarthy away and stripped him of his pistol at the same time. "Get back, Devereaux, I know what I'm looking for. Dobson. You with me?"

"I'll show you where we went," Dobson said calmly, his voice muffled beneath the mask. He stepped to the door and inserted the security card and pulled open the door. "Quick," he said.

The two men entered the containment

building. The door slammed shut behind them. A signal went to the monitor room that two men had entered on one security-pass insert. A red light flashed on in the control room but there were red lights all over the green-light panel now and it wasn't noticed at first.

The core was bathed in light.

The spacewalker and the civilian started across the catwalk.

The room was warm with the heat transmitted by the water pipes that penetrated every part of the room. The thick walls made the room feel like a tomb.

The two men moved slowly along the catwalk. Dobson had a flashlight as well. He probed the light here and there into corners.

Slowly, they made their way along the metal walkway.

It was 3:03 P.M.

Liz stood at the window wall and looked down at the city. The sun was starting its quick descent behind the Loop towers and there were long shadows across the lawns of Grant Park. The homebound crowd from the football game clogged the artery of Lake Shore Drive. It was all so silent from this vantage point, so far removed from everything, that a false serenity seemed to have taken over the world.

In the control room one of the engineers reported to the control officer: "There's something wrong in Red containment area. We've got an unauthorized admission on the panel."

They tried the switch again and the switch still signaled red.

The control officer just stared at the panel. "What do we do?" the engineer asked.

"We've got to seal it off."

"There are men in there."

"Give me that flashlight," Cavett said.

Dobson handed it to him.

"There," he said, flashing it down toward the rods. They both saw it, a small gray cylinder. Dobson started to reach for it.

"Back off," Cavett said.

He reached into the space between two steam pipes where the cylinder lay. He felt it gingerly. He lifted it, half expecting a booby trap but it came free.

He turned it over slowly in his hand. He tried to remember what he was seeing.

Ten years ago.

Blackpool in England and bombs were discovered in the hotel where the prime minister and her staff were staying. IRA bombs. Canisters set with a booby trap.

Canisters.

502

He began to pull off the duct tape. It didn't matter if he did it slowly, he thought. Max wouldn't expect the cans to be found and certainly not by an EOD man.

"Shit," Dobson said through his helmet.

In the control room, the second engineer picked up an internal line and spoke to security. He slammed down the receiver.

"Security says Captain McCarthy authorized the illegal entry into the containment building. What kind of a fucked up —"

"Then override the red signal, Charlie, and let's start getting this board back to green."

"On whose authority? I need authorization for this."

"Shit, Charlie," said the second man, who knew what he was dealing with.

"I don't like this," Dobson said.

But Cavett was staring at the soup in the exposed can. He knew exactly what it was. "You bastard," he muttered and stuck his hand into the grayish mix and fished around with his fingers.

He pulled out the quarter-size ignition and timer.

"Igniter," he said to Dobson. "The trigger."

He threw it on the metal floor just as it flared.

They stood and stared at the little fire of the ignition for a moment and then stared at the can.

"What is that stuff?" Dobson said.

"Rocket soup."

"What's that?"

"About enough to start a fire big enough to shut this reactor down. But there's more. There's got to be. And we're out of time."

"Who's in charge?"

"Mr. Olson —"

"But he won't authorize overriding the control panel?"

"Not until we get a security clearance here and we can't reach Captain McCarthy. I'm not taking the responsibility for unsealing the containment building."

The wrangling went on in the control room and the lights burned red on the panels. Someone had entered Red reactor containment building without authorization and no one in the room could undo that.

They found the second canister five minutes later and Cavett again stripped off the duct tape covering the top of the can. He fished in it again for the quarter device. His fingers were cut and the heady mix of fuel and gasoline filled the open wounds.

"Here."

He threw the second quarter on the metal deck. But this one did not flare. It sat on the deck as though mocking the two men.

"Keep looking —"

"How much time do we have?" Dobson shouted.

"I don't know, I don't know. How long were you in here? Ten minutes? How many cans could he carry?"

And they went back to the pipes, large and small, that crept in and out of the shuttered walls of the core of the reactor.

Olson listened to both men and then made a decision. He decided to call someone outside the plant. Besides, there was no urgency to unsealing the doors leading to the containment room. Whoever had sneaked inside the room could not get out until he had talked to someone in charge of security, even outside the plant.

They saw it flare, burning up through the duct tape atop the can and Cavett raced across the catwalk and reached for it.

It burned at his hand and he cried out and then tore his shirt off with one swipe down the front. He wrapped his shirt around the can and screamed at Dobson.

"Get the fucking door open!"

"It's going off!"

"It takes a moment to reach the temperature! Get the fucking door!"

Dobson ran to the door and inserted his card and pushed but the door remained locked. He looked through the thick, wire glass in the door and could only see the second door and no sign of McCarthy or anyone.

"All right, Charlie," Olson said, putting down the telephone. "McCarthy had escorted two men to the containment room. They had authorization but no entry cards, so let's manually override the panel and see what happens."

It wasn't as good as a written order but Charlie decided to do the brave thing. He pushed the trip lever to override door security to the containment building.

The door swung open and Dobson held it as Jack Cavett ran through, the smoking device in his hand.

He dropped the can outside the containment building and he saw that his hands were burned, that black flesh was dotted with white blisters and some of them were burst and he saw the white bones and blood and sinews. He saw these things for one moment and then fell unconscious before he could feel any pain at all.

The can burst into flames at that moment, sending shards of molten metal into the room, striking McCarthy on the legs and burning holes into Dobson's yellow radiation suit. Only Devereaux was not hit.

He ran to the security phone and picked it up and waited.

Then he told whoever answered that an incendiary bomb was burning its way through the metal flooring around the Red turbine in the generator building.

The sirens wailed until nightfall and then into the clear evening. The fire in the generator building was terrible, even worse than the fire in the paint shed. It seemed unquenchable. The liquid rocket fuel spread across a wide area of metal floor and ate through the metal and transferred heat from metal to metal. Pipes began to burst from the heat and there was water all over the flooring. And the process of shutting down the reactor continued its pace, degree by degree, control rods dropping into the pile inside the reactor core, absorbing the energized neutrons shooting out from the zircoloy-clad rods containing the uranium 235. Like a great beast, the plant shuddered as it tried to die.

The fight against the single fire went into the middle of the night, by which time the reactor core was cooled down sufficiently to be safe. The turbines were shut down and the electrical grid sucked energy from other fields in other states.

The cover-up was as good as it could be because, though many were involved at the plant and in the military, only a few had any idea of what was really going on. Or what the danger could have been.

The public relations officer in Chicago reported to the news media that a small fire in the paint shed inside the Apostle reactor had led to a shutdown on the reactor for safety reasons. He said the fire had been contained. This was all true in part and wholly a lie.

Fifty

On Sunday night the housekeeper and the chauffeur were not in the house in Rock Creek Park. They had the evening off. It was the favorite time of the week for Clair Dodsworth. He enjoyed the solitude of his own house without the solicitation of his help. He made tea for himself and brought out a plate of sweet cookies.

It was 9:00 P.M.

The news on television was vague about some vague disaster in an Illinois nuclear power plant called the Apostle. The news was linked with the equally vague news that a second plant in Illinois, called Dunedin, had had "an accident."

He watched the news and then turned off the television set and sat in the half darkness of his library. He had been rereading *Huckleberry Finn,* a book he had first visited seventy years before. The book put him back to that time in his life when he had been a child in southern Illinois, in the same part of the country where Twain had placed *Huckleberry Finn*. He was losing himself in the story and he didn't notice the two men until they stood in the entry of the library itself.

One man wore a jogging suit and the other, dressed in black, was Mr. Khashogi of International Credit Clearinghouse.

Clair put down the book and waited.

Khashogi entered the room. The second man stood at the doorway.

Khashogi looked at Clair in his leather chair. His eyes were dark pools. They glittered in the dim light of the reading lamp.

"Mr. Khashogi," Clair Dodsworth said. He spoke in a soft, civilized voice. He said nothing else.

"Miss Andrews and Senator Horan have been detained. About two hours ago. It was all done in secrecy. Not police, not even FBI."

"I see," Clair Dodsworth said. His hand dropped on the open book as though holding his place in it. "The fire at the Apostle went as it was planned."

"It didn't work, though. That was a lot of money for something that didn't work," Khashogi said. "A lot of time. Planning. A lot of money. And now this unfortunate trail."

"To ICC."

"Yes." They both spoke in appropriately somber voices.

"ICC will not be protected, I think. By Miss Andrews. She knew where the money came from."

"Yes."

"And Senator Horan?"

"I think he didn't want to ask too many questions."

"But now he'll be asked questions. Many of them."

"I suppose so. He has an immunity to an extent. But not from criminal prosecution."

"And you, Clair." Softly. "Do you have an immunity?"

Clair looked at the book on his lap. Jim and Huckleberry were making their escape on the Mississippi. It was a fine story, bathed in noble impulses. The greatest story of the country. Noble impulses.

"No, I don't believe so. Not in connection with the fire. But, as you said, part of the paper trail."

"What will you do, Clair?"

The men stared at each other. They understood one another, didn't they?

"What will you do is more to the point, isn't it, Mr. Khashogi?"

The dark man sighed then. It was a little sound in the vast silence of the house and this library room full of shelves of books.

"Alas," Mr. Khashogi said.

"Alas, indeed."

He brought the pistol out of his pocket and fired a single shot. The silencer muffled the sound to a slight *whoomp*.

Clair slumped back against the chair. The room smelled of cordite.

Mr. Khashogi stepped forward and fired a second bullet into the old man's temple. Again, it was almost silent.

He nodded to the man at the door. They turned and walked from the room, down the hall to the foyer, and into the street. Washington was dark and the thin streetlamps could scarcely dent the darkness. Each home was shrouded in shrubs and silence. It was colder now and there would be frost in the morning.

Hacker and the second agent were in the shrubs. They each carried automatic pistols and Hacker spoke first.

"It's over, Khashogi."

His voice was rough, without any strain of politeness or civility.

Fifty-one

They accused each other in separate rooms on Sunday night and into Monday morning.

The senator from Pennsylvania accused Britta of forcing him to let her see the secret testimony of the Nuclear Safe Practices Subcommittee.

He said that Britta had tricked him and that he had had nothing to do with the fire at the Apostle. There were two agencies involved in talking to him: R Section and the Defense Intelligence Agency. Even the FBI was not involved. Especially the FBI.

None of the men who questioned him had identities or wore uniforms.

They worked on him all night in a room in a house in a black ghetto in southeast Washington. He had no idea where he was because they had brought him to the house blindfolded. He was not allowed to urinate and he finally urinated on himself. They didn't strike him, they just asked him the questions over and over.

* * *

Britta Andrews was much tougher. She even denied the evidence of the secretly recorded telephone conversation. She denied knowing Max Escher. She denied everything.

This went on until midnight when they played her some of the tape they had made of Senator Horan's betrayal of her.

She listened to the tapes without saying anything for fifteen minutes.

Her lover accused her of wanting to burn down the nuclear power plant.

And there were records of her sudden sale of eighty thousand shares of stock in Northern Illinois Power and Light Company.

And so, carefully at first, she began to blame Senator Horan. She also began to blame Clair Dodsworth. She said they should ask Clair Dodsworth about the Dove, not her. She said she wanted to see her lawyer.

They pointed out to her that she had been brought blindfolded to the house in southeast Washington and that they had no intention of resorting to legalisms at this point.

That began to frighten her.

Mr. Khashogi and the jogger were taken blindfolded in a van to a house near Front Royal, Virginia. They had no idea where they were.

514

The men who questioned them were not as nonviolent as the men who questioned the senator and Miss Andrews.

One of the men said they'd do to Khashogi what Khashogi had done to the agents in Lebanon. Khashogi was stronger than either the senator or Miss Andrews and he refused to speak, though they questioned him all night long and into the gray, foggy mountain morning. He was not permitted to eat or drink or to urinate but he had remarkable self-discipline.

The cover-up of what happened at the Apostle was fairly complete. R Section was a small part of it and so was the DIA under General Lee, but for the most part it was well handled by the public relations staff and special emergency committee of Northern Illinois Power and Light. The cover-up explained nothing and some people demanded a federal investigation of the fire in the Apostle and the reported — but unconfirmed — leak of radiation from the Dunedin plant in the western part of the state.

Over the days, the worst-case scenario shifted to Dunedin. It was farther from Chicago and the media centers and the leakage was relatively small. There were the usual statements that it amounted to no more radiation than an X ray. This was a lie. The Dunedin leakage sickened people and plants and animals but the sickness was at a very low level and it would take a very long time before anyone noticed it. This was no Chernobyl.

The thing that might have been Chernobyl was covered in secrets in the coming days. There were no links between the agent who had gone to Chicago and the fires in the Pentagon. Everyone agreed on the secrets even while keeping secret diaries of the truth in case one of them decided to leave the game.

Col. Jack Cavett was part of the cover-up as well, whether or not he wanted it. He was promoted to full colonel and given another silver star for heroism but they had to finally amputate both his hands below the wrist. The operation at Walter Reed Hospital was as skillful as it could be but the prosthetic devices to replace his hands are still very crude. He became depressed in the weeks of his convalescence and he thought he might kill himself. He said this to no one but still, one afternoon in December, Liz came to see him. He showed Liz his metal hooks and Liz cried with him. They cried for each other and the mess of things, the way things turn out. And then she told him she was going to live with him for the rest of their lives.

In the end, Jack Cavett began to learn to use the devices that replaced his hands and he did not kill himself.

Every detail of the cover-up was complete. Even the detail of Bernie Lund, the missing security guard. He was simply arrested for possession of cocaine in his rental trailer by Apostle township police. And while held in jail, a farmer discovered the body of missing Carlette Disherman in a culvert and they decided Bernie had killed her as well.

It was New Year's Day when Jack Cavett was well enough to leave the hospital. For three weeks, he went through the rituals of rehabilitation, learning to use the clumsy new hands they gave him. He lost weight because he did not eat and he shunned the company of others. Only he could not shun Liz. She stayed with him and gave him love. Bob Fredericks was divorcing her and she would get the condo in Sarasota, Florida. Sometimes, Jack responded to her like someone asleep, suddenly awakened against his will. Slowly, Liz let her love seep into him. They went to Florida in late January and General Lee provided military transport.

Finally, Britta and Senator Horan cooperated in their separate ways and they were allowed to become part of the complex cover-up as well. They were explained certain things. Their silence ensured their survival; if they spoke of anything, they would not survive. It was not a question of issuing threats but of explaining the new reality. They were both guilty of criminal conspiracy and they would be allowed to get away with it if they cooperated.

Miss Andrews betrayed the Dove as she knew it. She knew it in Copenhagen and Berlin and in certain cells that operated in the south of France. She knew many names. The names were studied in certain agencies and photographs were made and the names were given to secret agencies in those countries. In some cases, arrests were made; in others, men were watched.

The last problem was Khashogi, who would not break down without torture. It seemed an insoluble problem. They kept Khashogi and the other man in the house outside Front Royal for three weeks, trying to decide what could be done. The men were guilty of the murder of Clair Dodsworth and probably Carroll Claymore and of so much more. But what could be done with such men? They knew too much about the corruption of a United States senator and his wealthy mistress.

And then they thought of it. Hacker, Hanley, Mrs. Neumann. But most of all, Devereaux. He had thought of it.

The ICC branch in Liechtenstein was closed on a Monday in January and all the records were seized. The same thing happened the following day in London, Paris, Berlin, Bonn, and Rome. In every case the credit for the information permitting the seizures went to Abdul Khashogi, who had asked for asylum in the United States.

No public mention was made of this. This was disinformation in its subtlest form, for the network that could not be destroyed. Unless it destroyed itself.

A council of sheiks who financed the ICC banks met in Riyadh one gloomy desert afternoon and decided to withdraw their support from the bank. To let the bank founder on its own. They wanted to pull back because Khashogi was busy betraying them.

The scandal began. ICC banks began to close everywhere in the world and the funds for terrorism began to dry up.

They held on to Khashogi until the end of January, while the ICC scandal rolled back and forth across the financial world.

Senator Horan resigned from Congress. It was part of the agreement.

Miss Andrews became a recluse that winter,

far from her friends in the radical violence movement. When she failed to show up at Gstaad for the conference before Christmas, there were grim suspicions voiced about her commitment to the causes.

In fact, the only loose edge to the cover-up was Escher. Of all of them, he had done the worst damage and could be least charged in it. The Pentagon fire and the Indianhead fire and burning the Apostle — all connected him to such official malfeasance and misconduct that half the heads in the Pentagon might roll if he were charged. It was a hateful compromise but security of the system was more important than a man named Max Escher.

Britta Andrews and Michael Horan.

They had only each other and it was not enough.

They dropped out of sight, shielded by their mutual wealth and by the understanding they had with the secret government. They were not prisoners in the sense of serving out their lives in a penitentiary. In any case, Britta would not have been penitent. She thought she was right and she thought her failure to burn the Apostle was really a failure of Michael's.

She wanted Michael to die. She thought all day long about killing him. At night, when he was asleep in the bed they shared, she thought about killing him. He would certainly drink himself to death in time but she didn't want to wait.

What she never thought about was Escher. Escher had been a weapon and he had been well used and he had escaped with $2 million. What she could never believe was that Escher might blame her for his failure at the Apostle. Might blame both of them. Might stalk them to her retreat in western Maryland, in the mountains beyond Hancock, might study them together as a biologist studies a slide of water containing microbes.

Might, in the middle of a January night, set their house on fire and wait and watch the flames and see that no one escaped the fire.

Fifty-two

Of course, you could not trust Max Escher.

No one thought to say that inside the informal cover-up committee.

No one thought to say that he was a thin-tempered man of petty hates and jealousies. That he had the means to burn down anything in the world.

Liz knew this.

Jack knew this.

They knew and could do nothing.

And Devereaux.

Devereaux knew.

Rita Macklin and Devereaux spent two weeks in February at Clearwater Beach, in Florida, about an hour north of Sarasota. It was the place they had first met ten years before. They got sun on most days although it also rained. The public beach was filled days and nights with revelers.

They reclaimed their share of mutual happiness. They made love in their rooms at the rental condominium and took rental boats into the Gulf of Mexico. The waters were warm and shallow and sea birds circled all day long.

One sunny afternoon, he got the call.

Liz said, "He called me this morning." Her throaty voice sounded down. "He said he blames me."

"What else?"

"He said he's got a proposition."

"The same proposition."

"The same. Except now it's to save Jack's life."

"Is Jack all right?"

"Some days better than other days."

"It takes time," Devereaux said.

"Is he going to have time?"

"What does Max propose?"

"That I meet him. In a public place at first."

"What place?"

"The shopping center down by the Gulf."

"I know. When?"

She told him.

"All right," he said.

"Do I go there?"

"No. You stay in. With Jack."

"He's eating now. He lost thirty pounds."

"He'll be all right."

"What are you going to do?"

"What I have to."

They broke the connection.

When Rita came back from the beach, he was dressed. He had a small bag packed. She frowned at him. But they kissed each other. The kissing had been good enough to bring them back.

"Where're you going?"

"I have to go down to Sarasota. For the night."

"Why?"

"Jack. And Liz. They're being threatened. Liz is."

"Why don't you call the police?"

"We can't do that. I told you. Everything that happened never happened."

"To protect nuclear power."

"To protect a lot of people. The Pentagon, for starters."

"Why're you part of it?"

"Because it was done this way or it couldn't be done. R Section was illegal, so was DIA, Northern Illinois, there were so many piles of dirt, we'd all have our own."

"I told you. The truth always gets out."

"You just think it does."

"And then it's really over?"

"Then it's really over."

"ICC." Paused. "Mona."

"It's over. ICC is self-destructing. Everything is over. Yes. And Mona."

"I'm sorry," she said.

"I'm sorry for everyone," he said. He kissed her again.

Max Escher sat on a wall by the sea and watched the gulls circle, and listened to their calls. He thought about Liz, tracking her down, finding out about the condo in Sarasota, and then getting a number. Really, it was a lot of work for a piece of ass but it was the principle of the thing too.

He sat and waited. The evening came on quickly and was warm. The sunlight lingered on clouds at the horizon but the city was turned to night. The white houses and tall pink condos were lit up for the evening to come.

Talk to her and make her understand some things.

He watched the man with grayish hair walk along the sidewalk that passed next to the beach. There were others on the walk but he watched this one. The man was on the tall side but not too tall and he walked as though he were going someplace. Maybe someone who'd been in service. Walked that way.

In all that had happened, Max Escher had never laid eyes on Devereaux before.